TRUST
NO ONE

MICHAEL HEARNS

BEATI BELLICOSI

ISBN: 978-1-7344075-0-1 Paperback
ISBN: 978-1-7344075-1-8 Electronic Book Text
ISBN: 978-1-7344075-2-5 Hardback

Library of Congress Cataloging-in-Publication Data
Names: Hearns, Michael, author
Title: Trust No One/Michael Hearns
Description: First edition. Miami: Beati Bellicosi (2020)
Identifiers: LCCN ISBN

First Edition: February 2020

Editor Julie Hutchings
Literary Editor Gail Gregg
Cover Design and Conceptualization by Dillon Hearns
Cover Art Beati Bellicosi
Author Photo by Tim McDonald

For Additional information and speaking engagements visit Michael Hearns on the worldwide web:
http://www.MichaelHearns.com
Beati Bellicosi Publishing a division of Beati Bellicosi multimedia
Copyright 2020 by Beati Bellicosi
Printed in the U.S.A

Acknowledgments

I would like to mention with my appreciation to Cliff Foyster, Peter Nazarkewich, Jonathon Hester, and Mike Sastre, for their encouragement, and advice as this book was being written. I would like to thank Gail Gregg and Julie Hutchings for their professional keen eye in the editing process. I would like to especially thank my son Dillon Hearns who endured a tsunami of uncertain times with me as we forged into the new beginnings of our lives. I most especially want to thank Ricki Witt Braswell who extolled encouragement, spirit, and support throughout the book writing process and whose amazing generous heart provided the muse and love that sustained this entire process. I also want to thank you the reader. Although you probably had no idea you would be recognized but still here you are reading this short section of the book. I applaud your enthusiasm for reading and I implore you to keep reading. The book gets better I can assure you.

To Ricki and Dillon. I love you both

Chapter One

YOU NEVER, EVER get used to it.

When the telephone rings in the middle of the night and assaults you from a deep sleep. The initial ring always elevates me off the bed while simultaneously filling my head with dread:

Who could be calling at such an hour?

I had made my disdain for such a vile intrusion very clear to the department. When they needed to reach me during the hours of the night that normal people are in bed asleep, they were to attempt to contact me on my pager first. That seemed like a good idea until I realized the absurdity of fumbling in a dark bedroom, trying to corral a continually shrieking pager that was repeatedly evading my half-asleep lunges for it.

These nocturnal interruptions weren't uncommon to an undercover police detective in the Vice Intelligence and Narcotic (VIN) unit. After eight years in VIN, I'd developed a concept to thwart the ringing telephone and shrill smoke alarm-patterned pitch of the pager. I'd set the pager to silent vibration mode each night before going to sleep. Putting the pager in an ashtray full of pennies on my nightstand guaranteed me of two things: constant location and no loud reveille. Now when the department paged me it was just a murmur of copper pennies jostling each other as the pager danced upon them in the night.

That was the sound that woke me at 2:11 A.M.

Still very much asleep, I heard the vibrating pennies and awkwardly grasped at the pager as it burrowed further into the pennies. I looked at the number displayed on the pager and saw it was the direct line to dispatch at the Coral Gables Police Department. And "911," call immediately.

From the doorway, I looked back at the empty bed. Being a creature of habit, I still slept only on one side of the bed. It was just a reminder of where my ex-wife Gina would have been. In times past, my assured confidence at not having awakened her was always shattered as I'd see her reach for a pillow and draw it tightly over her head. But since the divorce, it was just another reminder of the unwelcome changes my life was undertaking. I shuffled out to the Florida room to the telephone which was next to a large tropical print bamboo couch. In the early 1960's people here in South Florida converted their garages to additional living spaces and called them Florida rooms. Although not the case here, nonetheless the moniker held as I sat down on the couch and dialed the station.

"Coral Gables Police Operator Houghton," I heard a familiar voice say.

"Angela, this is Cade Taylor, did someone there page me?"

"Who?"

At that moment I wondered who actually woke whom up.

"Taylor. Cade Taylor. Did you page me?"

"Oh, hi Cade. Let me see who paged you."

Away from the earpiece but still audible, I could hear her yell to the open spaces around her, *"Did someone beep Taylor?"*

"Hold on while I find out."

Shortly, a male voice came on the line. "Sergeant Rainer."

"Scott, this is Cade Taylor, did you page me?"

"Cade, you still work here?"

Out of the 160-person Coral Gables Police Department, that was a continual comment from at least 140 of them due to the fact that for the last five years I'd been detached to a DEA task force, focused primarily on large cocaine trafficking and money laundering cases. I was rarely in our station. Within that time there had been such a surge in hiring and attrition that there were some Coral Gables police officers who had never seen me.

"Scott, I've never worked there. I'm just employed there."

"Funny. Some guy from the county called about ten minutes ago, a Detective Lloyd Trentlocke. He wants you to meet him ASAP at the end of parking lot two by the point at Matheson."

"Any reference?"

"All he said was that he was on a cell phone. I know we have three units out there assisting Miami Dade per Major Brunson."

"He called Brunson too?"

Major Theodore "Ted" Brunson was in charge of the Coral Gables Criminal Investigation Division (CID). The mere fact that he was notified at this late hour for something in Miami Dade's jurisdiction foretold this may be a very long night. I thanked Scott and said I'd be on my way—but momentarily I stared at the cradled telephone and ran events of the last twenty-four hours through my head. Nothing came to mind as important and urgent.

Dressing quickly into sneakers, jeans and a T-shirt, I grabbed a Hartford Whalers baseball cap and put it on to contain my shoulder-length hair, grabbing my badge, gun, and cell phone as I headed out the door.

The beaded water on my undercover Ford Explorer, as well as the puddles out front were an obvious indicator that it had rained. Spring rains would soon be coming to South Florida, and here in late February it was starting early. The night air was calm, and large white clouds were slowly moving across the Miami night sky. As calm as the night was the puddles splashing against the undercarriage were a prelude to how fast I was racing through the darkness. I lived in a section of Miami known as South Dade. It is almost equal in distance each way to the Courthouse on Flagler Street in Downtown Miami to the north, and south to the Caribbean Club bar just within the fringe of Key Largo. Both places are equally adept dispensing their own versions of justice.

The homes are older and established in my neighborhood. The area is part of unincorporated Miami Dade County, which means no streetlights and no sidewalks. Briefly taking notice of the rustling palm tree fronds back dropped by the clouds and stars a familiar comment ran through my head.

"Miami. Eden's evil twin."

Lloyd Trentlocke, the Miami Dade Police Detective who had ruined my sleep, was an old police academy classmate. I hadn't seen him since our academy graduation fifteen years ago. I wasn't sure what he was doing with Miami Dade now and I was very curious as to what he wanted from me at this time of the morning and more precisely why couldn't it wait until daylight. Thinking quickly, I turned on my cell phone and dialed the Miami Dade Police Department. I got a much more alert operator than Angela had been. I asked for Detective Lloyd Trentlocke. After some searching she transferred me to his voicemail, which is what I'd been hoping for.

"This is Lloyd Trentlocke of the Miami Dade Homicide Unit. I can't take your call right now. At the tone please leave a message and I'll return your call as soon as I can. Thank you."

Homicide.

Well that explains the urgency somewhat and it also makes sense as to why Major Brunson was called and why we had units assisting Miami Dade. But it still didn't explain why my disheveled self was now driving east in the middle of the night towards Old Cutler Road. Crossing Highway U.S 1, I would soon be nearing Old Cutler Road. I was supposed to meet Trentlocke at Matheson Hammock Park and Marina.

Matheson was named after an early pioneer family who donated the 630 acre parcel along the bay for park use and preservation. The thriving island community of Key Biscayne was donated as well. The island is visible across the bay to the east. Both generous parcels were as close as we Miamians could compare to an F. Scott

Fitzgerald East Egg and West Egg existence. Matheson sits directly on Biscayne Bay and has a tidal pool beach and a very large marina. Aside from the expansive frontage along Biscayne Bay it was a wild and natural habitat for many South Florida species of animals. It is known for the vast acreage of Mangrove swamp; their gnarled raised roots balancing the ecosystem of the bay like a grade school hallway monitor. Matheson was also known for the place where glamour photographer Bunny Yeager often took very risqué photos in the 1950's of pin up model Betty Paige. What a testimony to notoriety:

Tree roots and boobs!

Turning onto Old Cutler Road I would soon be at the park entrance. Old Cutler traverses along the bay shore like a scoliosis wracked spinal column. Its meandering tree-canopied asphalt road winds past affluent homes. Each residence is hidden in the night darkness by thick tropical foliage and original coral rock walls. Approaching the entrance to Matheson, I soon saw the reflective striping of both Miami Dade as well as Coral Gables police cars. I knew that parking lot two was still nearly a mile past the entrance. I gritted my teeth, worrying more and more about the situation I was heading towards with these officers posted so far away.

Catching a glimpse of my unshaven and rumpled self in the rear view mirror, I quickly thought it would be better to put the blue light on the dashboard rather than explain my arrival to both officers from both agencies. The blue light cast a surreal glint off of the patrol cars and puddles along the road. With nary a sense of concern or interest both officers were quickly behind me with nothing more than a wave and a nod. The dark tints of the Explorer obscured me from their nonchalance. The pock-marked asphalt had a noticeable couple of inches of water actually flowing slowly from the northern tendrils of the park.

Low flood plane.

High tide.

One of the by-products of paving over nature even if it is an access road.

The blue light roved over the tree line, and splayed across the forming macabre assembly of vehicles. The patrol cars were juxtaposed against the unmarked Ford Tauruses and Chevrolet Luminas. They seemed to be the requisite county issued car to their investigators. Off to the side was a typical crime scene van with its rear doors open. A few guys were opening and retrieving items from the shelves and cases in the van. Further down the way was a very non-descript white Ford Astro Van with tinted rear windows. The driver was hoping to get some sleep as he noticeably was attempting to shield his eyes from the portable lights that were being set up by the crime scene technicians. He was obviously from the Medical Examiner's office and he'd be the last person summoned in this endeavor to transport the body—or for that matter, bodies—from the park.

I still wasn't fully aware of why I was here.

I parked outside of the crime scene tape and made my way across the gritty parking lot towards the cordoned-off area. The yellow tape was anchored on one side to a palm tree and then stretched a good ways to a posted sign nearer to the water's edge. The sign had a bright yellow square with the picture of a crocodile on it. I only saw the Spanish part of the sign and it said:

"*Aviso cocodriles presentes. Especie protegida por la ley federal.* "

The rest of the sign said the same thing in English. It was a warning about crocodiles in the area and that they were a federally protected species. The saltwater crocs had slowly but steadily been making their way up this far north from Key Largo where environmentalists had reintroduced them into the wild in the late 1970s. With no known predators and an ample food supply they were now thriving and growing to be as big as Nissans. *Only in Miami,* I thought, *do we string crime scene tape to a crocodile warning sign.* From the sign the tape changed course and redirected itself back across the landscape to a Miami Dade police car where it was anchored snugly around the passenger mirror. This configuration assured the tape would stay in place, as well as the officer whose car it was affixed to. I approached the officer standing along the tape. "I'm with the Gables, I'm here to see Trentlocke."

The young Miami Dade officer saddled with the midnight shift due to low seniority showed his still freshly-retained academy training.

"Sir, I need your name and unit before I can let you go in."

"Cade Taylor. T-A-Y-L-O-R. I'm Vice Narcotics from the Gables. You know where Trentlocke is?"

The officer dutifully wrote my information on a small black pad.

"I don't know any Trentlocke, all I know is that homicide is by the water with the body."

"Is there more than one?" I asked.

"I don't know sir, I'm only aware of one," he said as he lifted the yellow tape.

I guess he forgot that he was also supposed to notify the lead investigator before he admits anyone into the scene. Ducking fluidly under the wavering yellow tape I scanned the perimeter for Trentlocke. I stayed exactly in the same spot and didn't want to traverse any further. The crime scene had been designated, but it wasn't my crime scene. One second you can be standing on the fringe and the next second you're in the epicenter of a newly-discovered additional scene. From where I stood, I could see downtown Miami and its architectural splendor illuminated, beckoning like a multi-hued beacon. Glass and concrete were melded together and placed adjacent to each other not so much out of a grand plan but more so out of available vacant parcels of land to build upon. Within my view was the island of Key Biscayne jutting off to the right across the Powell Bridge; it too lit like a shimmering oasis. In the foreground of this modern vista my eyes focused on the activity of a cluster of men standing near the water's edge, their neckties lazily buffeted by the bay breezes. There were three of them all in identical white shirts and bad Father's Day gift neckties. Of the three, the only one I recognized was Trentlocke. From where I stood the years had been fairly decent to him yet as he drew nearer I could see his brow had furrowed more and a tinge of gray crept across his temples. The other two stayed back by the water's edge.

At their feet was the faintly discernible body of a person.

Trentlocke was now rapidly coming closer and with each step he seemed to recognize me more and more. My long hair and goatee were not enough to make him not remember me. He looked up at me and noticed my Whalers hat.

"We got a hockey team now, you don't have to hang with those perennial cellar dwellers." An obvious slight to Hartford's dismal hockey team.

"You know me always rooting for the underdog; I'm just pissed because they may be moving to Columbus or some other po-dunk town."

"Yeah, I almost forgot what a Mecca for culture Hartford is," he said sarcastically.

We shook hands and chatted briefly never once discussing the obvious, which was why I was here. Trentlocke began to tell me that there was one body "that they know of so far. " He stayed rooted in place before me, his back to the water's edge, and continued to provide me with very vague aspects of the scene, all the while scanning my face for any expression or emotion. He was probing my eyes to see where they focused as he talked.

Although we were old academy classmates, he had an objective that I wasn't entirely clear about but I could sense it involved me very directly. Like most well-trained interviewers, Lloyd allowed his body to convey his meanings. While conversing with me he walked towards the others around the body. This was meant to get me to walk towards the body with him.

He casually put his hand on my shoulder and as we began to move, his hand glided down my back before he put his hand in his pocket.

Checking to see if I have my gun on me.

I didn't allow him to know that I had taken notice of this warm and fuzzy act between two old friends who hadn't seen each other in over a decade, and probably would not have ever crossed paths again except for the fact that there was a dead guy looming closer to us in the water. The other two homicide detectives moved away from the body as I neared. Trentlocke made no attempt at introductions and they both weren't interested in making friends. Always good to see the continuity of the county's arrogance and incivility still functioning. They faded from view, but they hovered twenty yards behind me.

Just in case I made a run for it.

"You know, you guys are right out of central casting."

"What do you mean?" retorted Trentlocke.

"Nothing Lloyd, now why the hell am I here on your homicide scene? You got my people calling me up at two in the morning and you and the Farckle Brothers over there have been looking at me like a barracuda watching a swimming Canadian. So just what the hell is going on here?"

Pointing as he squatted near the body Trentlocke said, "Why don't you look real good at our new friend here and you tell me?"

Not knowing if I was mad at the gang of three or with myself for showing part of my hand to these guys, I also knelt by the body and took in the view. White male. He had on dress slacks and one dress shoe. The shoeless foot was wearing a dark sheer sock. His other shoe was five to ten feet away. His pant legs—at least the backs of his pant legs—were dry. His right arm was tucked up under his body, his left arm limply rode the small swells that lapped at the shoreline. His torso and head were face-first in the water. His face was unseen by the sea grass and foaming water lapping against him. His dark hair wavered in the water and there was a possible contusion or small scrape on the back of his neck. He was stuck on the small jagged coral rocks that comprised the shoreline. Like miniature Velcro barbs they held him in place as the water rocked against his lifeless body.

"A little over an hour ago a boater heading out to Bimini called it in. He didn't stop. We're trying to track him down. His view was from the channel, but he thought it might have been a manatee in distress. Our road unit responded. The park gate was open."

I looked over at Trentlocke and he was now donning a pair of latex gloves.

"We've already photographed this side of him, took all the measurements. Notice we cut his back pockets off and in the left one you'll see what has us intrigued."

Trentlocke pulled the pant pocket back like a peeled grape. He reached under the flap and pulled out a business card. With very little fanfare and no hint of drama he put it to my face so I could read it. I immediately recognized the card.

It was mine.

Chapter Two

THE CARD WAS frayed slightly on the ends from the obvious onset of saltwater erosion on the parched paper. The ink was still clearly legible although the embossed ink stamp of my police badge upon the card had a fuzzy tinge to it. My mind reeled: Who could possibly have my card? Was it friend or foe? My momentary fugue was snapped back to reality upon my conscious realization that Lloyd and his cohorts were studying my body language and facial reactions from three disparate angles. I needed to buy time, and buy it fast.

"My business card. So?"

Bordering on juvenile flippancy with a slant of defiance the question to a question response elicited the smattering of time I needed to assess this confounding situation.

"So?" asked an increasingly agitated Trentlocke. "So what exactly is your connection to this guy?"

"I don't know from here," I said, nodding to the body. "What about the rest of him?"

Trentlocke motioned to the other Miami Dade detectives to come closer. Both of them sauntered over and knelt down, turning the body over so that the corpse would lay face up.

Laying their gloved hands on one side of the body and steadying the wavering, water-tossed corpse, they reached across the shoulder blade and pulled the torso upwards and towards them, leaving the left thigh and hip to juncture upon the coral and act as a pivot as the body rolled onto its back. The right arm did not flop out as many a Broadway actress would attest but actually stayed pressed against his body as it flipped onto its back. The salty brine had sloughed the color from his pale and puffy face. He was becoming marginally recognizable.

I looked at his face and started a mental checklist and memory retrieval spin as I studied his features. The recognition came slowly at first then rushed through with more clarity built upon familiarity.

"Gustavo Peralta," I said.

"Who is Gustavo Peralta?" said Trentlocke.

"He was a mid-level exchanger for the cartel. A fairly decent player, trusted enough to sit in or broker introductory deals."

Peralta lazily bobbed in the shallow surf as I continued to look at his lifeless eyes. Little shell fragments and sea sand grit were interspaced along his pants. The zipper to the fly of is pants was slightly undone most likely from the weight and rocking of his body on the coral. I could feel the penetrating stares of the gathered detectives and knew enough that if I said a few things I would keep their mind on my comments and not on their brewing assumptions.

"He was known as 'Costano'. It basically means coastal or person from the coast. I never got around to asking him, but by his features most likely Barranquilla in Atlantico."

One of the portly detectives chimed in and said, "How do you spell that?"

Inwardly happy they were now focused on what I was saying and not their previous convictions, I just looked back over my shoulder. I spied the detective jotting down my words on a Burger King napkin. I'm sure the napkin had earlier done double duty as a ketchup repository and possible booger vault.

"B-a-r-r-a-n-q-u-i-l-la." I spoke directionally towards him. It was obvious that he'd missed it so I gave it to him in the requisite cop-speak. "Bravo, Alpha, Romeo, Romeo, Alpha, November, Quebec, Uniform, India, Lima, Lima, Alpha."

"So how do you know him, and why does he have your business card?" asked Trentlocke.

Now it was circling back to dicey dialogue and to say too much would put me in a situation of being quasi-interrogated. I told the long story of how Peralta had come into my world and how that world functions and operates. Even though we had been in the same police academy class Trentlocke's career was obviously on the traditional path of law enforcement with the obligatory stops along the way in Burglary, Robbery, and now Homicide. I was part of a multi-jurisdictional task force of undercover detectives posing as money launderers and cocaine financiers, none of which is ever taught in a police academy. I needed to tell him enough to make it a legitimate connection without endangering anybody else. Whoever it was that killed Peralta could just as easily be looking to kill me or someone else.

It might not be a cute coincidence that my business card was in his pocket after all.

"Llyod, he was one of our confidential informants and the Gables is the agency of record for the task force. I documented him as a C.I and he probably got my card then. It was probably at least a year ago."

Now it got a little testy.

"You mean to tell me this guy has your crisp, clean business card in his pants from a *year* ago, and just happens to end up dead in swimming distance of your city? I'm supposed to believe that? What kind of bullshit you trying to pull here?" The ire was rising in Trentlocke's voice.

If I didn't play this right, soon Pudgy and Dumpy would also get in tune with the inconceivability of this happenstance and I'd be spending a good portion of my morning at Miami Dade Police Headquarters sitting in well-worn office chairs with a union representative who knows nothing about the law but is probably a decent first baseman on the union softball team. Hence his soft position as union representative.

Rising from my squatting position in an effort to make my words as big as my height I said; "All I know is the guy is a C.I.; We documented him. I'll need to see what exactly we've used him for and then we go from there. He is just one in the stable. I'll have to head into the Gables and go through the files before I know anything."

"You mean you documented him," said Trentlocke.

Careful not to fully reveal Peralta's link to me, I said quickly, "Whatever he was, he worked with the task force. I'll need to get more info before I can do much more."

Years of being a detective had taught me to skirt the truth with wording. Rather than say I couldn't 'say anything more' I chose the words 'do anymore.' It wasn't a lie and kept me from saying anything I shouldn't. Transition the conversation to me *doing* something rather than saying something I couldn't take back or recover from.

I walked over to the detective I had mentally nicknamed Pudgy. Without asking and before he could offer resistance, I put my hand on his shoulder and lifted my left leg showing the bottom of my shoe to Trentlocke. I lifted my right leg to do the same. Both were done rather quickly but the message was sent: any evidence underfoot picked up accidentally was being presented and I was leaving.

"Llyod, call me if you need anything, and let me know what the M.E. says. I should be through the C.I. files by noon"

I started to walk away from the gang of three and inwardly was waiting for the "hold on not so fast..." but it never came. I just kept walking, eyes straight ahead, knowing that any facial expression I made could be seen by the uniform officers and M.E. personnel. I walked the same direction out as I did in, and upon approaching the young Miami Dade officer who let me in under the wavering crime scene tape, I casually but with a measure of authority told him to note the time I left the scene. I didn't want Trentlocke or anyone else saying that I stayed on the scene and was argumentative or uncooperative. I wanted it to be relatively clear that I wasn't there long enough to of caused such things.

Besides I had bigger concerns than that.

I got to the Explorer and climbed in. I immediately started up the engine, the radio tuned to FM WWLV (Love 94) kicked in and Bruce Springsteen's "Racing in the Streets" had just started. No doubt at this late hour and with such a lengthy song the lone radio station DJ probably was taking a bathroom break. My mind was also "racing in the streets" but I needed to pull away from the peninsula of asphalt and ease away with no fanfare or excessive speed.

Controlled.

Ambivalent.

But I needed to put some distance between the crime scene and myself lest they try and call me back. Speaking of calling back, I looked at my cell phone. No incoming calls. Good.

The Coral Gables part of this equation was nocturnally absent. I immediately turned off my phone so that Trentlocke couldn't call me and ask me to come back about any ruse or "one more thing to clear up."

Once away from the eyesight and earshot of the crime scene I drove a lot faster than I did on the way in, salty splashes of water rumbling under the undercarriage. I created my own "No wake" violations on the Matheson Hammock service road. In the approaching far distance I could see the Miami Dade and Coral Gables police cars with their flashing red and blue lights. I slowed considerably. Upon drawing nearer I put on the blue light on the dashboard and plugged the chord into the cigarette lighter. My own windshield facing out spewed blue lights flashing, my vision protected by a faux leather sleeve on the backside of the light.

There is a method to this madness. Driving in with the blue light on alerts the crime scene people that I'm intended and inbound. By waiting until I get closer to the staged units, putting the light on silently communicates that I'm leaving and please part the way. When you drive up with the light on the whole way the attending officers sometimes think you want to talk to them and it delays your exit. I had no desire to talk and answer any questions about how much longer is it going to be? Will there be relief units? What's going on? Any and all of those rudimentary questions I didn't want to entertain and my timely deployment of the dashboard light worked like a charm.

The uniformed officers barely acknowledged me and once again in the rearview mirror I got a quick glimpse of my disheveled self, tucked underneath the Hartford Whalers baseball cap. I was free and clear of the Matheson Hammock entrance.

I drove south on Old Cutler Road and turned into a vacant field just off of Old Cutler and Sierra Circle. The field had trees and Florida holly bushes but enough space for a few cars to covertly park at night and not be seen. For years it had been a great spot for the Coral Gables south end midnight officers to catch a wink or two. Now with most of them currently assigned to the Matheson Hammock entrance, I was confident I could pull in unseen and collect my thoughts. Just as I started to park the car Bruce was ominously singing on the radio.

"...Tonight my baby and me, we're gonna ride to the sea
And wash these sins off our hands."

Chapter Three

TRUE TO FORM, no one was there. I eased into the slight coral rock rise, quickly lowered the windows and shut the engine. I needed a moment to collect myself and put these recent events into a form of thought that I could follow. My mind was doing mental gymnastics.

Peralta had been more than a task force informant—he was solely *my* informant.

I'd seen him two days ago at lunch. We were at Casa Juancho in Little Havana. He abhorred the familiar and common Cuban restaurants of western Miami Dade, and liked, as he said, to *"Comer bien entre los malos."*

Eat well among the bad guys.

He thought the cuisine of high-end Spanish food in the heart of Little Havana was an homage to his disparaging opinion of the neighboring bodegas and cafes. He garnered great delight in loudly proclaiming his disgustedly hatred for the Cuban exile community. He thought they and their political base were interfering with the progress and commerce of himself and his Colombian ruffians. On more than one occasion someone would try to shush his loud argumentative opinions and biased views.

I personally think it was all a blustering show of inflated arrogance.

Gustavo would always finish his verbal tirade and contentious speak with the same expression: *"Dame pan y dame tonto."*

"Dame pan y dame tonto," translated means "Give me bread and call me stupid." When you step aside of the actual literal translation it is more in the lines of, "I get what I want and no one can stop me," or "I don't care what people say, I get what I want."

There are people who are willing to do anything to get to the top of the pile. Gustavo Peralta was a money mercenary. If there was money to be made, he'd do what he had to do to get it. He had no allegiance or loyalty to anyone or anything. He'd sell the task force or me just as easy as he'd sell one of his trusted Colombian brethren.

It is the dialogue of an overly ambitious and ruthless personality of which Gustavo had an abundance of. His temperance and unsteady edginess weren't only his calling card, but in his DNA footprint. He'd come to the attention of the task force when he and three of his Colombian cohorts were running a Medicaid scam through an unregistered nursing home in Hialeah. When the Office of Inspector General went to investigate one of the Colombians tipped off the investigators that he could flip a few money-laundering cases for leniency. Truthfully speaking, all four of these Colombians were carbon copies of each other with Gustavo Peralta the most cunning of the four.

No one wanted the aggravation of possibly managing these four despicables so it fell onto me to document and manage or as we say in the business, "handle" these four. I quickly nicknamed them "The Four Horsemen" as in "The Four Horsemen of the Apocalypse."

Now one of the Horsemen was dead and he had my business card in his pocket when he died.

The stillness of the night was briefly punctuated by a faint screech made by a slow-moving white ibis flying overhead. Being so close to the bay it was most likely heading out to see if the high tide had pushed a small mullet or baby mangrove snapper into a crater or pothole, thus leaving the tasty fish vulnerable for prey. I was still trying to wrap my head around the whole situation that was now in front of me. The quiet of the night and soft salty breezes helped me to try and re-imagine things. Like a chef pouring over an intricate recipe, I systemically started cataloguing the recent events.

One of the horsemen was dead. Gustavo, the most ruthless of the four. Where were the other three? Did they have any part of this? When and how did Gustavo get my business card? What was he doing in Matheson Hammock and how did he get there?

It was a sundry of variables and trying to make sense of it at this late hour was not going to be easy. Also deep in the back of my mind I knew that the morning light would bring a slew of activity within my agency. I should prepare for myself for whatever lies ahead.

If I was to have any chance at being the least part effective tomorrow, I needed to get some sleep. What was I thinking? Tomorrow is today. If I headed home I'd have to get up earlier than I'd like just to beat the traffic into the Gables. Plus going home would just exacerbate the fact that Gina was gone and she would never be coming back.

The noises in a house made by people are often neglected background sounds. Heel strikes on a ceramic tile, the clanking of a coffee maker being set up, the timed intervals between a toilet flushing and the sink being turned on to wash hands, even the soft breathing of a sleeping wife. When those sounds are no longer there, the ominous silence of a house can be deafening. It can make the walls seem as though they are towering and falling at the same time. The lack of noise starts with the visual senses. Pulling into a driveway that once had two cars and now only has one, the lack of size six sandals near the front door, the mail stamped "Return to Sender." The cacophony of sounds within the realm of silence that these visuals can create is louder than a full minivan of toddlers at a Burger King drive-thru.

I contemplated the empty house and morning traffic and then weighed it against the option of going into the VIN office and sleeping on the couch. Although my rest would be uninterrupted within the quiet and unoccupied third floor of the police department, I again would be awakened up very early by the arrival of personnel and others at 7am. Plus, I'd have to explain why I was in the office sleeping, and since many did not know Gina and I were no longer together, I did not want to preemptively confirm an un-started rumor as true. That gossip will start on its own is inevitable. I could go to the Undercover Office and try and sleep on that donated faux leather coach we put in the staged front office. The U.C. office was designed to look like a working food brokerage firm with a plush front waiting office that housed not only the couch but also an eclectic array of silk potted plants and neatly placed *American Grocer* magazines on chrome and wood lacquered end tables. The U.C. office had a four-office layout: The outer front office was where we would meet with "clients." And then two inner offices, one supposedly the firm's principal office and another one with two desks and archaic, inoperable computers. God forbid any of these Colombian dopers ever tried to turn on a computer or had any idea about the food brokerage business. The last room that ran the length of the hallway and appeared to be one long continuous closet with slider doors was actually deeper than it looked. It was designated as a dual-purpose room. Primarily it was where we staged the SWAT team or any take-down team comprised of VIN detectives. It has a deep ceiling and floor acoustic baffle tiles and Kevlar inserts along the entire inner walls. A monitor in the corner shows a live video feed of the other three offices and allows the SWAT team leader to make a decision to move independently of the takedown signal if he sees danger unfolding. The same would hold true for the VIN detectives, although less encumbered with full tactical gear. The other purpose the room served was as a last-resort safe room for the undercover operative in case bullets start flying.

As I made the decision to go to the U.C. to get some sleep I quickly realized that the elaborate alarm system tied to the visual surveillance cameras in the parking lot and inside would literally have my every waking and sleeping moment on tape. Not an appealing sight especially, in lieu of Gustavo's death. I don't need additional questions of why I was in the U.C. office at 4am.

I needed sleep. It seems the more restless and sleep deprived I am the more tingly the synapses of my brain works. I actually think better sometimes when my mind is focused on just keeping the functionality of self going, rather than trying to be the operation of self. The connectivity of mental acuity connectivity...connectedness...*connections*!

Connections.

What connections did I have?

Then it struck me.

Ruthless!!

Just north of this darkened field off of Sierra Circle, further up on Old Cutler Road, was the highly-sought wealthy enclave of Gables Estates. It was a gated community originally created by the famed developer Arthur Vining Davis. As a younger officer I had worked off-duty in uniform, patrolling exclusively the community's streets. It was a perk of the affluent to have a Coral Gables officer patrolling their streets in addition to stationary and roving private security.

I started the Explorer and put on only the parking lights as I eased out of the Sierra Circle field. I didn't want my headlights to shine into a sleeping resident's bedroom window accidentally. Once I felt my tires touching the porous asphalt of the street, I turned my headlights on fully and eased onto Old Cutler Road, heading north back towards Matheson Hammock. As I headed to Gables Estates I saw a Coral Gables patrol car heading south, no doubt en route to Sierra Circle, his nocturnal routine interrupted rudely by Gustavo going and getting himself murdered.

"*...dame tonto.*"

All I could think of was one thing.

Ruthless!!

It was an incredibly short drive to Gables Estates and along the way I noticed that the exterior perimeter of Gustavo's murder scene was broken down and the police were gone. I eased through the gated drive with nary a cursory wave at the private security guard and headed east on Arvida Parkway, past the walls and hedges that each slumbering millionaire had erected around their mansions to keep other millionaires away. During my time patrolling within Gables Estates I'd become familiar with many of the residents and friendly with a few. One of which was Chadwick Benjamin Slausen. He joked that he owned the Columbia Broadcast System TV network, more aptly known as CBS. Nearly everyone knew it wasn't true, but in reality there was very little he did not own or could not purchase. He was a semi-philanthropic self-made billionaire who dabbled in everything from automotive parts for the southeast's biggest auto parts dealers, and scrap recycling centers in Texas and Oklahoma. His appraised $26 million mansion placed dead center in the middle of identical mansions on Arvida Parkway boasted the largest sea wall frontage on the widest part of the Arvida channel. The channel led out to Biscayne Bay, a mere two minutes away from cast off to full throttle from his imported teak ninety-foot dock. He was rarely ever at this house, often hop-scotching the globe from one of his many houses. Being that his house was dead center in the middle of the row of houses, his service entry on the east side was an ideal place to park the patrol car and be visible to speeders, and still not have to continuously patrol the never-changing community. Chadwick Benjamin Slausen encouraged it. He often dispatched his caretaker Octavio Nunez to bring aromatic and highly potent cafecito to the officers.

It was through these times that I became familiar with Octavio. Octavio and Slausen had a little arrangement. There were always spare keys and an empty Heineken beer bottle kept in the bait well of his yacht. When Slausen might be on his yacht entertaining a young, newly-acquainted nubile dancer or flight attendant that he may have just met winging in from Rio or Barbuda or some other exotic locale, he would put a note in an empty Heineken bottle and leave it on the transom of his yacht. Octavio had told me that the note nearly always said to wake Slausen with "an emergency" early in the morning and to spirit the young girl du jour away before Slausen's wife awoke and possibly discover his extramarital flings.

At some point Slausen's wife must have caught on to his wayward ways. They were now divorced. I only met his ex-wife once. Her name was Ruth.

Now I was pulling up to the palatial grounds of the darkened estate and could see the new sleek yacht he'd gotten after the divorce—appropriately named "Ruthless."

I parked just to the side of the service entrance knowing that Octavio would be coming to work at the house and entering through the gate. I put the blue light on the dashboard of the Explorer, highly visible so that he wouldn't freak out. I thought about putting a note along with it but I was concerned the roving private security patrol would see it and wake me too early or roust me inquiring "if there's anything I need."

I had faith Octavio would see the blue light, then search the grounds looking until he saw the Heineken bottle on the yacht. I hastily scratched out a brief note asking Octavio to wake me by 8:40am and headed out of the Explorer towards the east side of the property. For good measure I also set an alarm on my cell phone.

The front main gates of the house were sturdy iron vertical bars with ornate oxidized bronze welded pieces affixed in an artistic rendition of a jumping marlin along a sun-kissed sea. The gates were attached to ten-foot-high coral rock columns, most likely made by a well-known local Coconut Grove stonemason. A five-foot coral rock wall spread both east and west of the columns fronting the entire property line. The grout lines and etched markings on the coral stones were indicative of the same stonemason's handiwork. The lush tropical landscaping was professionally lit, with landscape lighting casting shadow and light in an inviting way. When I got to the eastern edge of the property, at the neighbor's property line. Similar to Slausen, this house too had a barrier wall, but made of stucco. I assumed correctly that each neighbor did not want the other's "inferior" wall attaching itself to their own and there was probably a gap of a foot or two between the neighbor walls. Most everyone separated their shared property lines with dense hedges eschewing the horrid chain link fencing of previous generations. Had my assumption been off I would have had to backtrack towards the main gate and look for a good place to climb the wall. Fortunately, I was correct and slipped through the gap, brushing through the well-maintained podocarpus hedge. I was now inside the wall and on the grounds of the estate.

Others would have preferred to sight-see, take in the opulence of the home and the grand views of Biscayne Bay. My only goal was to quiet the voices in my head and sleep as soon, and as much, as I could before having to contend with the events of tonight.

I hurriedly made my way to the yacht; the bilge pump softly murmuring and the steady, soft trickle of pumped water cascading into the bay. I stepped on the massive eighty-foot Hatteras, the vessel barely pitching under my weight. I opened the bait well, and in an orange Home Depot bucket were the spare keys and three empty Heineken bottles nestled atop some chammies. I guess ol' Chadwick couldn't risk just having only one in the bait well. I grabbed one of the bottles, partially wedged my note for Octavio in the neck and put the bottle on the transom. The spare keys had a Styrofoam key chain in case anybody ever dropped them overboard. The keys penetrated the well-maintained lock easily.

I stepped inside the yacht's stateroom and immediately saw a sectional brown couch that formed an L-shaped pattern around a marble high-top table. The rest of the yacht didn't concern me. I grabbed two folded beach towels and used them as blankets. Two of the three throw pillows with their monogrammed large font "S" would do nicely. With my shoes off and my hat on the marble table, I was ready for sleep in just a few scant minutes.

Anyone who has never slept on a boat or felt they could not sleep on a boat has not experienced the gentle float and rocking that lulls even the most overworked or stressed mind to sleep. I started to replay the night back through my head, expecting a circus of the mind to start again but drifted off to sleep somewhere near talking to the uniformed officer at the crime scene tape.

Chapter Four

MOST PEOPLE HAVE a difficult time sleeping in an unfamiliar place. That was never a real issue with me. I had slept on enough couches and in enough spare bedrooms in my high school and college days that to me there's a sense of familiarity in unfamiliarity. Through my years in VIN I'd learned to eat when I can and sleep when I can.

Because each day I went off to work I never knew when—or even if—the day would end.

The hours were unimaginably long. It's what we call "Doper Time." You're living the existence of a drug dealer, all the while being a law enforcement officer. There are no alarm clocks or "Gee, I wish I could but I have to be in the office tomorrow" excuses.

Eating dinner at 10pm in a normally closing restaurant that stays open just so the wait staff can get a $500 cash tip from the Colombians you're with is very common. It is just as common as drinking scorching shots of Colombian fire water called *"Aguardiente"* with men who, while licking the glistening alcohol from their lips, regale you with true exploits of their rise to prominence in the Miami cocaine trade. So sleeping in Chadwick's nautically-themed stateroom was not an issue with me. Understand, I said *sleeping*.

Waking up is a whole other story.

Early in my career I would awake in a semi-paranoid state of instant tactical assessment. Too many cocaine deals and close calls with the afterlife. Like the country song says, "Everybody wants to go to Heaven, they just don't want to go today." I was rolling off beds, reaching for weapons, my eyes wide with fear and apprehension. I was definitely singed by the lifestyle. It was unsettling and it unsettled Gina, and made me wonder if some time on the couch for some dormant PTSD police involved shootings was in order. Mostly through snoozing in cars on surveillance and long-protracted cases, I found myself all over South Florida in unfamiliar neighborhoods and places. Rather than startling awake, I adapted my waking to slowly opening my eyes and with a practiced, intentional calmness taught myself to look around slowly and try to remember where I was and why I was there. Sometimes it took ten to fifteen seconds of just looking around before I figured it out.

I'm not sure if it was the subtle clanking of Octavio's keys on the Heineken bottle or his Cuban accent calling my name that awoke me.

"Cadey, Cadey, Cadey."

Octavio was a few years older than me and in what is often common in Latin cultures he referred to my barely discernible youthfulness by calling me "Cadey."

I opened the door to see Octavio outside, one foot on the transom and the other on the dock, the Heineken bottle in his hand.

"*Oye Consorte*, you scared the heck out of me. I came in. I saw the Ford, the blue light, I didn't know it was you. I thought there might be a K-9 here. I didn't know if I should go in and maybe leave the gate open but then—"

It wasn't early but it was definitely not the right time, early or late, to hear the rapid fire staccato Cuban infused story of how he was surprised about me being there.

I held up my hand in a non-dismissive but mea culpa way and said, "Octavio, yeah, I know. Sorry. It was one of those nights and

I just had to crash. Thank you for waking me up, I'll be going in a second. What time is it anyway?"

"Your note said 8:40 but I know how you are so it's 8:30."

Without seeking an explanation to that comment I just said, "Thank you, Octavio. Let me just get my shoes on—"Before I could finish, he continued his original train of thought.

"Damn *Cabron,* you scared me with the bottle. I though Mr. Slausen was here hiding from the cops."

The comment about Slausen might indeed need an explanation but I knew it would have to wait.

I looked at him, the eastern sunlight glinting off his Maui Jim sunglasses and dancing through his salt and pepper hair. His mustache was neatly trimmed, his ever-constant white shirt rolled at the sleeves and tucked into his khaki pants. For a second I just looked at him and he started laughing. I shrugged.

"Asshole. *Quiero* cafe?" he said.

It's a way of communicating that most people in Miami abide by. A combination of English and Spanish, creating a further fusion of words that we affectionately refer to as "Spanglish."

In answering him if I wanted coffee I also asked if he'd be kind enough to make a whole cup of the highly potent cafecito. We in Miami drink it at stand-up cafe windows all over the city from small ceramic cups or plastic thimble-size shots.

"Yes, can you make it a colada, please?" I asked, hoping he'd make enough to provide six or seven thimble-sized shots. "I got to get to the office."

With a look a of feigned agitation he simply said, *"Cono,"* which means 'damn' in Spanish, and walked away.

I scurried back inside, got my shoes on and found the first bathroom or "head" as they like to say on a ship. I washed my face and wet down my hair, my reflection in the mirror still on a continual daily trajectory to haggard.

I grabbed my hat from the table and essentially repeated the same actions as six hours earlier as I headed to my SUV. Octavio met me at the vehicle and kindly handed me a Styrofoam cup with a lid and eight white plastic ribbed thimble-sized cups. I shook his hand and thanked him and left with an obligatory "bro hug."

Within moments I was motoring out of Gables Estates, towards my office about six miles north, almost a straight shot from Old Cutler to where it connects to Lejeune Road.

As I neared the police station I was as always struck by the sheer lunacy and inept architectural design of the building. It was designed sometime in the early seventies and had a glass atrium on the westside that roasted all of its inhabitants in the brutal South Florida afternoon sun. The result of this short-sided design gaffe was the necessity of having an air conditioning system that was so frigid you could hang meat in the building. Every civilian employee wore a pilfered winter jacket from a road patrol officer and they were constantly being mistaken as officers by the visiting public. The dispatch division had already fried two computer networks in the past two years simply because of personnel plugging space heaters into orange designated hi-tech electrical outlets. The four-story building had been designed for a heliport until the poured concrete roof was deemed too weak to hold a helicopter.

I maneuvered my vehicle around the two ladder fire trucks parked out on the street because the adjoining fire department couldn't park them in their own parking bay, due to the weight of the trucks possibly caving through to the often flooded basement below. I drove up the parking ramps to the third floor apron area where the detective division parked. The apron was noticeably fuller with vehicles than on most days. Unusual.

I parked as far as I could from the open-air apron closer to the east overhang, backing into a spot to avoid my license plate being seen by the surrounding larger office buildings.

In the undercover world you can never be too sure who sees what and where.

I grabbed the colada and slipped in under the overhang to

minimize my exposure to prying eyes. Once under the shade of the overhang I surveyed the cars on the apron: three unfamiliar cars with blue lights on their dashboards. A clear and often implemented tactic to let parking enforcement know these are cop cars and should be provided a "professional courtesy" if they're in violation of a parking infraction.

This was an early hour to get outside agency visitors. I just knew whatever it was, this was not going to be a normal morning.

I continued my walk to the side door under the apron that led to the east staircase. I swiped my credentials against the affixed card reader which granted me not only access but let anyone monitoring the bank of access cameras know that I was onsite. From the staircase door I could step right onto the third floor and turn a corner and be at the VIN office. It was a bit of a misnomer having the VIN office in the station, as those of us deep undercover actually were rarely ever there. It was just a place to gather mail and to do administrative things like sign SOPs and other department-related documents. It was three offices within one. Gary Fowler, our in-house financial administrator took up one. I always called him "Big G' and it had nothing to do with his size or girth but simply a nickname I heard a guy once call his buddy in an elevator in Chicago.

Our secretary, Ileana Portillo, was a Cuban American twice divorced, single mother of two, who worked in the center office, and it was she that visitors always saw first. The larger office off of Ileana's was for the unit lieutenant. The lieutenant was Ken Poulsen. Poulsen was what I inwardly referred to as a 2A ascender . He was promoted to the rank of sergeant due to attrition and promoted to the rank of lieutenant due to abdication when the previous lieutenant left the agency to pursue a non-law enforcement position with Discover Card. Attrition and abdication were the only things that furthered his career. Poulsen carried himself with a smug, inflated opinion of himself. He had an elitist attitude and was quick to abuse the power his rank afforded him by seeking personal favors, gratuitous false praise, and constant homage from the underlings who wanted to be in the VIN Unit.

Ileana looked up at me from her desk. Both Gary and the lieutenant were absent.

"Speak of the Devil and he appears," she said by way of greeting in her Cuban accent.

"Hey where are Big G and the L.T.?"

"When *ju* ask like that it sounds like *a* gay porn title," she said, barely looking up at me over her reading glasses as she continued to type away at some unknown document on her computer. "Actually they are where *ju* are supposed to be in *Broonsone's* office," she said.

She could never pronounce Brunson's last name.

I figured there would be some sort of meeting or discussion about Peralta but didn't have any idea when. By coming into the office without being summoned I was trying to get in front of it and not be behind it.

"I'm supposed to be where? Down at Brunson's?"

"*Aye Por Dios* Cade don't *ju* ever answer *ju* pager? Poulsen has been having *my* page *ju* all morning since 7:15."

My mind quickly envisioned lots of copper pennies all askew on my nightstand.

"What about my cell, did you think to call my cell?"

"I'm just the messenger here Cade, he said to keep trying *jur* pager and that was it."

I wordlessly turned and headed out the door and down the hall towards Brunson's office.

Major Brunson was probably the last of a dying breed. His father was an American G.I. who'd been stationed during World War II at the Richmond Airfield Blimp base in the scrub pine and palmetto section of southwestern Miami Dade County. His mother was a local girl from Miami whose parents had owned a five and dime store in Downtown Miami. He was born and raised in Miami where his parents settled in the northeast corridor neighborhood known as Lemon City. By his early teens as Lemon City became more integrated, his family moved blocks north on Biscayne Boulevard to the village of Miami Shores. He still lived there to this day. Brunson was a fair man but a man of uncompromising ideals. He had the inflection in his voice that was neither a pure southern accent nor an accent that can fully be defined. More like a subdued slower cadence of the cartoon character Fog Horn Leg Horn. He pronounced Miami "Mia-A-Muh" and was prone to profanity in such a haphazard way that it caused many a quizzical look when he went into one of his tirades. He was a quick-tempered man, prone to kicking the standard department-issued army green metal wastebasket in his office. He was fastidious about his perceived image, and usually feeling guilty about an outburst he'd try to swap out his dented waste basket with someone else's on the odd chance the Mayor or City Manager should visit his office. He wore black western-style boots always under his suit and uniform pants and he had a strong inclination to sample hot sauces, of which there was usually one or two on his desk. They always had eye-catching names like "Heart Breaking Dawn's Cauterizer" or "Screaming Sphincter Cayenne Pepper Sauce."

Niceties aside, my gut told me this was going to be a screaming sphincter kind of morning and I wasn't referring to the hot sauce.

When I reached the major's door I could see the usually neat "Law Officer" magazines sloppily about the coffee table. There were obviously people here early this morning and they had been waiting.

I stepped into the outer office and had my eyes met by the taciturn stare of Charlene Muscanera, the CID secretary who, although a civilian, had a fingertip on the pulse of everything that cycled through Major Brunson's division. I could hear murmured voices from deep inside Brunson's large office, which came replete with an also very large conference table. Charlene was entrusted as the gatekeeper of all things CID, and although VIN operated fairly autonomously from CID, in the organizational chart the unit falls under the domain of CID, therefore making Major Brunson the supervising commander of all of us. I had to answer to Lieutenant Poulsen, and he in turn answered to Major Brunson.

In her full gatekeeper capacity Charlene finally broke her piercing gaze and said in a hushed tone. "You're late. I can go in with you to try and soften it, but the major is none too pleased."

"How can I be late? I didn't even know to be here!"

I should have taken the same tact that Charlene did and whispered, because no sooner had I said it then from the major's office I heard Brunson's booming voice call out, "Charlene! Is that Taylor?"

Charlene had moments when she was polished and perfunctory. This time rather than yell back through the door she quickly picked up the phone and dialed the major's four-digit extension. There wasn't much of a conversation. I couldn't even hear the major pick up. All I heard her say was "Taylor is here."

She just as quickly hung up, and as if she had no idea the reason or the attitude that awaited me on the other side of the door; she simply said, "The major will see you now."

I started walking past her oak desk and noticed the dented trash can in the corner. In my head all I could think of was *"Cono!"*

Chapter Five

I F YOU HAVE ever had that feeling that you've walked into a room where everyone is discussing you, yet upon your appearance the direction of the conversation immediately changes course—well then, you must have a sense of what I was feeling.

Major Brunson was pretending to be in mid-conversation. I walked in as he was saying to Gary,

"Okay Gary, you got what you need, thank you for being here."

First of all, no one ever calls someone by their name as they are sending them out—unless it's a pointed cue to exit, stage left. Secondly, Gary's quick but knowing look that he gave me as we passed at the door's threshold told me volumes about what potentially lay ahead. Besides, it was obvious that any non-sworn personnel would not be a part of the discussion going forward. Major Brunson was quick to transition Gary's exit with a half-warm welcome of, "Cade have a seat."

I wasn't feeling any allies here, but at the moment there weren't any overt hostilities either. Major Brunson and Lieutenant Poulsen sat across from each other at the far end of the table. No one sat at the head of the table. I slid into the nearest open chair which must have been Gary's seat, as it was still slightly rocking. This placed me next to a Miami Dade Police lieutenant at my left. His beige-over-dark-brown uniform was spotless, as were the single gold bars on each of his short sleeve lapels. A slightly faded U.S.M.C tattoo was partially visible on his right bicep, just under the shirt sleeve. He appeared Hispanic and was in his early fifties. He faintly smelled like cigars and a citrusy cologne. He gave me a customary nod of his head and slid his cell phone closer to himself on the table, providing more room for me to sit down. I took that more as a polite gesture than as a welcoming gesture. I in turn put the colada down on the table and opened both palms, welcoming anyone in attendance to partake. Across from us were two other law enforcement types. The first was a somewhat heavy gentleman in a dark blue suit with reddish hair and the carry-over of adolescent freckles on his face. If Barney Rubble had ever worn a suit, this would have been a decent facsimile. The other individual was a moderately-tanned man in a dark brown suit with a small Miami Dade Police badge pin on his left lapel. His white dress shirt accentuated a mint colored necktie adorned with deep brown diamonds. As I sat down both men across from me as well as Lieutenant Poulsen simply looked at me rather impassively.

Upon settling into the faux brown leather chair I looked towards Major Brunson and in the background spied the hot sauce on his desk a few feet behind him.

"Ass Whooping."

Major Brunson started the conversation flowing again by politely introducing me to the men in the room.

"Cade, sitting next to you is Lieutenant Fausto Ramirez from the Special Patrol Unit and across from you is Captain Teofilio Zambrana from Homicide." Captain Zambrana was in the brown suit and both he and Ramirez once again nodded their heads.

"Sitting here next to Lieutenant Poulsen is Steve Edwards. Stevie and I go back a long way."

Edwards smiled. Oddly enough, when a person feels very familiar with someone they sometimes neglect to inform others of the nature of their relationship. I let this social gaffe slide.

I would soon enough find out who Edwards was and why he was here.

There was a momentary silence that was broken by Edwards who blurted,

"I'm the major of TNT."

TNT was an acronym for Tactical Narcotics Team(s). The TNT units were deployed in high street-crime dens across the county and did hand-to-hand-buy bust sting operations. They were used to dismantle (as best they could), the street level narcotic trade. It was my guess that Edwards spent most of his time reviewing op plans, budget requests, and managing the volumes of overtime the TNT detectives submitted. I didn't peg him for a guy doing "jump out" and chasing nineteen-year-old ex-high school track stars turned crack dealers through the grassy no man's land within Liberty City's Scott Housing Projects.

No sooner had Edwards stated his position then Brunson let out his first expletive of the morning.

"God damn it. Stevie, I should've said that. I'm sorry."

I nonchalantly glanced around my side of the table to see if I could find the waste basket.

"For fucks sake Taylor, why weren't you here on time?"

I started to answer him when he cut me off before the first word was uttered.

"I don't want to hear no excuses." Segueing rapidly to Poulsen, " Kenny, how long were we paging him?"

"Most of the morning, sir," replied Poulsen.

"I see you aren't wearing your pager. The city pays for that pager. The city also pays you to wear it."

At this point I was curiously wondering if the waste basket was on the other side of the table. Ramirez shifted uncomfortably.

Trying to explain why my pager was left behind, that I had my cell phone, or that I was awakened at 2:11am was irrelevant. Besides, Brunson had also been awakened even earlier last night and any reasonable excuse would be met with more condemnation. The best thing I could do was to endure what lies ahead and just take my *"ass whooping."*

It was Captain Zambrana who spoke next, his Spanish syntax showing.

"Detective, we are here today because of the murder victim found last night at Matheson Hammock. I've asked Lieutenant Ramirez to accompany me here today because as the lieutenant of SPU he oversees our marine patrol unit. My guys inform me he was found in the water. No?"

"When I got there, he was in a few inches of water."

Ramirez quickly asserted, "It's still water. We should have been called."

Obviously, this was a small bone of contention that dipped and dived between the parameters of domain, statistics, call for service and most importantly, necessary overtime. It was also a Trentlocke concern. One arrow out of the quill not intended for me.

Falling back on his Spanish syntax Zambrana said, "Irregardless," the Cuban created word for dismissiveness.

"Due to the circumstances of what the homicide presents us, we want to know what you can tell us about the deceased."

"Circumstances?" I asked.

"Yes. Matheson Hammock Park is closed at sundown. A park employee is tasked with making sure the marina and park are secure. With budget cuts he's also been forced to make the rounds to Dante Fascell Park, D.B. Barnes Park, Snapper Creek Marina, and going as far south as Black Point Marina. Unfortunately, he cannot be just at one place and we aren't budgeted for more than one guy east of the Palmetto Expressway and South of Coral Way. Whoever killed him last night either knew the employee's schedule or just got lucky."

"Or maybe he was killed on a boat and dumped in the bay," interjected Ramirez.

With strained diplomacy Zambrana pointed out that as of now

it appears it was a land-side homicide but that more information would be available pending the autopsy and toxicology reports from the Medical Examiner's office.

I was following along and understanding, but failing to see what odd circumstances necessitated so much police brass to be present.

Major Edwards broke his silence and asked me to elaborate on just how it was that Gustavo Peralta had become an informant for the VIN task force.

Measuring my words carefully in my head while trying to appear nonchalant, I realized that it was not in my best interest to hold too much back, but it *definitely* wasn't in my best interest to say too much. Although the room was filled with seasoned law enforcement personnel, the cocaine-trafficking, anti-money laundering nature of the VIN task force was something that many didn't understand, and trying to educate without coming across as condescending would not be easy.

So I started.

"Well his name was Gustavo Peralta—"

Poulsen cut me off. "What was his street name?"

Pausing, but holding my immediate gaze on Poulsen I continued...

"His name was Gustavo Peralta. He didn't really have a street name but he was known to be called Costano. I think he was from Barranquilla in Colombia. He was with the Medellin Cartel but not a Paisas. People from Medellin and surrounding valleys are called Paisas. People from Bogotá are called Rolos. The coastal regions are called Costanos."

I turned my attention to the table as a whole and continued.

"The Office of Inspector General picked him up in Hialeah doing a Medicare scam out of group of clinics on Palm Avenue and West 49th Street. He was in a group of ten or twelve who were shuttling the elderly in vans to all these clinics and over-billing the government. He and three other guys had just gotten out of jail and were just starting in the scam and OIG wanted bigger fish—so they flipped him and the three guys. In the process of scaring these guys and having a come-to-Jesus moment, one of them told OIG they knew some guys looking to move some dope and work the money pipeline back to Colombia. OIG was going to turn them loose for the information they got but saw it as a twofer, and called us to see if we wanted them. I met with OIG and we ended up documenting them as C.I.s and putting them to work."

"Who are the other three?" asked Zambrana.

"Well I would have to go to the offsite and look up the C.I. files and—"

"No need." said Lieutenant Poulsen.

"I asked Gary for a list of payments to C.I.s and then ran them through NCIC and FCIC. I have their information here." He smugly waved a file folder and put it on the table.

NCIC stood for the National Crime Information Center and FCIC was the Florida Crime Information Center. Poulsen had just opened a whole can of worms. The information pertaining to C.I.s is to be exactly what it implies: *Confidential* Informant. Although it may or may not be relevant to the homicide of Peralta it was incredibly reckless of him to just put that information out there when autopsy and toxicology reports were not completed. Besides, I had a sort of familiar relationship with Trentlocke and he and I could have hashed out what exactly was needed just between us. This was a grandstand of an unsolicited gift that was not a good thing to do.

Major Edwards reached for the file and opened it. He retrieved some small half-lens readers from his jacket pocket and with a newly adapted scholarly look, read the first name from the first page.

"Roldan Osorio-Vidal." Perusing the papers, he continued. "Let's see...armed robbery, conspiracy to commit armed robbery, home invasion, armed burglary, kidnapping..."

Turning to the middle part of the file he read the name, "Don Julio Restrepo."

"Looks like the same here...armed robbery, conspiracy to commit armed robbery, home invasion, armed burglary, kidnapping, auto theft...he must have been the driver on that one."

Working his way to the back, he read, "Hector Gomez-Macias. Armed robbery, conspiracy to commit armed robbery, home invasion, armed burglary, kidnapping, trespassing, loitering and prowling, resisting without violence..."

"Taylor you actually deal with these assholes?" Major Brunson said.

I said the first thing that came to mind, all the while concealing my seething agitation with Poulsen.

"Well they weren't a fun bunch to be with but if you're playing on a muddy field you're going to get some dirt on your football. The nature of what we do in these U.C. operations causes us to have to get eye level with the devil. They're part of a stable of C.I.s that we use, deeply connected to the cartel. It's necessary for us to have a working relationship."

"Well I'm looking now at this Peralta fellow," said Edwards, "and he looks to be the worst of the bunch. Looks like he was arrested for homicide by Palm Beach Gardens but beat it when the witness was 'not able to be located' at trial."

Turning to Major Brunson and bypassing Lieutenant Poulsen, Captain Zambrana requested a copy of the file.

"Charlene!"

Charlene dutifully appeared in seconds and upon being told of the request took the file to be copied.

Wonderful. More people involved. Ramirez was really not necessary to be here, and now a civilian was involved.

I wanted this to move along but Captain Zambrana had now opened the colada and was pouring thimble shots of the aromatic Cuban rocket fuel for everyone. With practiced precision he crimped the Styrofoam cup and the dark sludgy elixir poured into each thimble. It was a ritual of sorts. One person pours and then we each take a shot or pass them to those out of reach. I handed Lieutenant Poulsen his, which he took with nary a nod of appreciation. Caffeinated to the gills, the meeting continued.

"Captain, you mentioned *circumstances*. What circumstances make Gustavo's death any different than any other normal homicide?"

Captain Zambrano looked at Major Edwards who had just finished tossing back his cafecito. Major Edwards nodded in approval and Captain Zambrano began to speak.

"TNT was aware of Peralta. He'd been seen by their surveillance units picking up cash from the drug holes in Coconut Grove and frequenting a potential stash house in the grove. TNT got a court order to put up a wire on the Coconut Grove location and a person identified as Costano was heard on the wire. It seems that this Costano was getting ready to move some heavy product and didn't want a separation from cocaine and money. He said he 'couldn't trust no one,' and that there was a cop who needed to be 'taken care of' are the words he used. This cop either through aggravation or partnership, was causing him to charge more to front kilos of cocaine to the dealers. He said "red kilos" were next. At first we didn't know what that meant and we still aren't too sure. We didn't know if this cop or as he calls him *"Los Tombo"* was to be taken care of as in a bribe, or maybe it meant he needed to be taken care of as in being killed. Our linguistic expert as well as our people think it means killed. Red kilos meaning blood, as in the blood of whoever is in his way. Lo and behold, days later our TNT units saw him meeting with suspected traffickers and money launderers. They lost him a few times on surveillance and now he's dead.

This was not good.

"So when you said last night that the deceased had a nickname of Costano, the on-scene detectives put it into the Miami Dade Field Intelligence Database—"

"And I was called. So I called Major Brunson and Captain Zambrana and requested this meeting," said Major Edwards who had chimed in, cutting off Captain Zambrana.

"TNT has been sitting on this information for a while, trying to figure out who it could be he was talking about but as far as we can tell it really leads to a few conjectures. Only one cop we know of had contact with him. That's why you're here now. After all it was your business card found in his pocket."

The atmosphere in the room took on an air of suspicion. The eyes of everyone were now looking at me. Were they looking at me as a suspect in Peralta's death or were they looking at me as the person who Peralta wanted dead?

All I knew was that the guy who was awakened this morning by a clinking Heineken bottle was about to have one crappy day.

Chapter Six

FUCKING DUMPY.

But I had to hand it to him, it was good work putting the nickname "Costano" through the Miami Dade Field Intelligence Database. It saved Miami Dade days of tracking Peralta through the NCIC/FCIC files and provided a direct link to an ongoing separate Miami Dade investigation. Good work.

Fucking Dumpy.

I was sitting there trying to decipher which side of the dial I was supposed to be tuned into. Was this conversation about a crooked cop with Peralta, or a crooked cop who was on the verge of being killed by Peralta? The ever-so-faint aroma of cigar and citrus now tinged with cafecito clarified it. Lieutenant Ramirez, aside from asserting his domain for SPU overtime and notification in the future, was actually here for me. Major Brunson was old school. If something involving me merited an arrest he wanted Miami Dade to lead me out of my own agency in handcuffs and not have one of our own people do it. If they decided to arrest me or have me leave with them for questioning Major Edwards, aka "Stevie," would more than likely lag behind with Major Brunson when he called the Mayor or City Manager. Their long-standing friendship and cooperation would be a buffer for the embarrassing news. Our Chief of Police, Robert McIntyre was convalescing from a near-fatal stroke he suffered in

September. It was highly improbable he'd be coming back. Until a determination could be made which appears the city was in no hurry to do, Major Brunson was serving also in the capacity of acting Chief of Police.

I was looking at judge, jury, transporter, and executioner all in the same room.

There weren't any union people in attendance. No attorneys or anyone from legal either. Nor were there any visible audio or video recording devices. These were good signs. My mind was rapid fire spinning the wheel of fortune and calculating my current odds.

What did they have?

One of the Horsemen was dead with my business card in his pocket and a telephone wiretap intercept of him talking about a cop.

That's it.

Besides, Peralta was dead. Threat over.

My momentary trance was over and I looked back at Major Edwards.

"I don't know what to say about my business card."

Mostly out of obligation I looked at Lieutenant Poulsen and then focusing on Major Brunson I asked if they were requesting me to assist Miami Dade with Peralta's homicide outside of anything I have already provided.

Captain Zambrana was quick to answer before Major Brunson could say anything. This caused both me and Lieutenant Poulsen to slide our eyes over to the Captain.

"This is a Miami Dade homicide and although we have, as I said earlier, 'circumstances,' we will continue this investigation as we always do and will let you, Major Brunson, and the Gables know if and when we need anything further. Thank you for your offer—or actually your inquiry—but no. We have this covered."

"Well I'm available as well," said Lieutenant Poulsen.

"Thank you. Well, if Major Edwards is fine with it, both me and Fausto will be heading out. Thank you everyone."

As Captain Zambrano and Lieutenant Ramirez got up to leave, Lieutenant Poulsen had learned long ago that lingering in post-meeting chit chat was a great way to have extra duties designated upon him. He offered to escort them out and jumped quickly out of his seat and started for the door.

I rose from my seat as the three headed out the door. Major Brunson motioned for me to stay a little longer.

Ugh.

With the three of them gone and the door still open he again called out, "Charlene...call Ortanique and get a table for me and Stevie, say around 11:45."He turned to Edwards and said,

"They got a gal over there that does something to a grouper filet with a rum curry spice thing that I swear I'd knock over old ladies and small children to get to."

He then steadied his gaze on me and in a quiet, church-reserved voice said to me.

"You got a cell phone, ain't ya?"

"Yes sir. A Nokia 3210."

"I thought so. Okay. Goodbye, Detective."

I started out the door and heard Major Edwards call out as I left, "Oh, and thanks for the coffee."

Walking down the hallway back towards the VIN office, I debated whether to stop back inside or just stay to my normal daily routine which consisted of two objectives: working my cases and staying out of the VIN office.

I rounded the corner, intending to get out of there, when coming in the opposite direction fresh from the parking apron was Lieutenant Poulsen. His hair was slightly out of place and he was combing it down with one of those old plastic flexible hair combs that your fingers slip into and the bristles lie within your palm. I hadn't seen one in years.

"Cade, before you go I want to remind you the Kiwanis Jamboree is in two months. Last year you were in for twenty bucks. I can count on you again this year, can't I?"

I basically just had a murder accusation put against me a scant few minutes ago and now this guy is asking for twenty dollars as if the morning's events hadn't even occurred. I just looked at him, perplexed for a second and he continued with his train of thought.

"Good. I like a team player. I'll have Ileana call to remind you but can you get it in by Friday and check only. Just like last year, check only. No cash. Just make it out to 'Kiwanis of Coral Gables.'"

"You'll have her call me? Why didn't you have her call me today instead of paging me?"

"I made a lieutenant's decision."

"What?"

"I made a lieutenant's decision. I am the Lieutenant. I make the decisions. That's all you need to know."

"Practically no one uses pagers anymore. It's a back-up to a back-up."

My argument was met with a bored detached look.

"Try not to make Ileana have to call you too much."

There was nothing really to say. I just headed out to the Explorer. He had always been an ass. Very few if any in the department liked him. He'd been a security guard at a Burdines Department Store when then Major McIntyre met him and took a liking to him. He started helping him and 'breastfed him' through the hiring process till he got hired by us. McIntyre went onto become Chief and Poulsen stayed in his slipstream all the way. Poulsen was smarmy and cloaked himself in unsubstantiated confidence. He'd never really done anything in the agency. He had gone through the patrol division, spending barely any time there, when he was taken off the road to work on the implementation of our great 486DX computer system. By the time he had done all of the vetting, measuring, remeasuring, researching and reconfiguring, three things occurred:

The computer age had accelerated and everything he had done

was obsolete. He was paid a truckload of overtime making us obsolete, and he used his comfy inside position to study for the sergeant's exam and passed it easily. As a sergeant he never supervised anyone and was quickly put in charge of special events—including the Kiwanis Club Junior Orange Bowl Parade. There he got to know all the politically-charged residents in the city. Protected and coddled, he became even more intolerable and egotistical. His appetite for social interaction was often brokered on using his position in the agency to extract things and praise from his subordinates, of which this latest one was going to cost me twenty dollars.

For the time being I was relieved that one of the most glaring issues mentioned in that little meeting went unnoticed: the fact that I had not properly controlled my informant. Whatever Gustavo was involved in, he was involved in it without my knowledge. So my biggest concern was just how long would it be until one of those police commanders realized that one of our informants—and most importantly one of *my* informants—had gone in the wind. Just how long had he been off the chain and how far did he roam? Was he really looking to take care of a cop giving him heartburn, and was that cop me? Were the other three Horsemen involved and how should I approach them? If they killed Gustavo, was I possibly next? If they had nothing to do with Gustavo's death, were they next?

I jumped in the Ford and put the key in the ignition. The chiming of the open door was drowned out by the sound of Poulsen's voice in my head.

"I made a lieutenant's decision."

Chapter Seven

THE REST OF the day was a bit of a blur. I couldn't tell if it was the cortisol easing slowly out of my system or the monkey chatter in my brain. I started cataloging in my head what the upcoming day's events would be like. There would probably be at the earliest, forty-eight hours before anything from Peralta's autopsy results were available. In the meantime, I needed to track down the other three Horsemen. Divide and conquer was the best strategy I could come up with. Isolate them as best I could and see if any of the three had anything to say about Peralta. I needed to also reach out to them before Miami Dade Homicide got too deep into the files that Poulsen handed them. I also had to be careful not to get in the way of even be perceived as interfering with the homicide investigation of Peralta. Any encounter with the Horsemen would be even more cautiously undertaken as the possibility of them aligning themselves with Peralta to possibly have me killed was still weighing heavy on my mind. This was not going to be easy. The Horsemen routinely operated rather autonomously of each other and then came together for the common cause of making money, often cutting each other in and out of deals at will. They struck continual alliances and just as continuously broke or changed the alliances.

The world of an informant by its very nature orbits around distrust and betrayal. They betray those close to them who have bought them into a closed relationship or business arrangement. Infidelity not just to one's spouse but to the truth and to the common good is a mainstay with them. Their views are only in line with your views as long as the common view has a favorable outcome for themselves. This is not an environment for the faint of heart or for those who like to daily decry, "not fair" or "but you promised" in their daily conversations. There is no fairness, and promises are just adjectives in their language. Dealing with Confidential Informants is a fluctuating exercise of pretending to have your views in line with theirs as you keep the actions and words directed at fulfilling your own true actual objectives. You commiserate over the U.S. immigration policy on spousal entry while discussing the next dope or money deal. You act as though you have interest in the Millonaris soccer match with Atletico Nacional as you gather intelligence about the drug cartels. You promise to look into a reason why a C.I.'s brother-in-law's frozen shrimp shipments keep getting stalled by U.S. Customs at Miami International Airport; even though you fully know there isn't much you can do. It is an unscripted ballet of trust and mistrust that you try to keep from becoming irrevocable distrust.

Credibility is everything. Both yours and theirs. Aside from the superficial aspects of conversation and personal concerns when it comes to buying or selling cocaine, or moving and laundering money, the information provided and the action taken better all be in synch. Nothing cuts a C.I. loose faster than wrong information or misleading information. Nothing will cause a C.I. to want to break free from his handler more than inept or compromising actions by a cop.

Peralta was dead. Poulsen just handed over C.I. files to an outside agency. This put me in the possible 'inept and compromising' category.

I needed to get my hands on the reins and bring it all back in control. I was flummoxed as to how less than twenty-four hours ago all appeared to be running smoothly and now it was becoming an incredibly problematic mess.

I saw the day getting away from me and decided to head home

and shower and change clothes. Once again reminding myself to start carrying a change of clothes and a toothbrush in a "go bag." The reason it's called a "go bag" is because when it all falls apart you just grab the bag and go. It wouldn't hurt to have additional toiletries and cash in the bag as well. It seemed prudent, especially living the lifestyle I'd been living being in VIN.

The drive home was uneventful and the passing palm trees juxtaposed against the blue February sky were a welcoming sight. The house was comfortable inside, the CB block walls retaining the night cool air from hours earlier. I headed straight to the shower. I looked in the cabinet vanity under the sink for any spare toiletries I could put in the go bag. Gina's curling iron was still under the sink. I unceremoniously dumped it into the bathroom waste basket. It was a futile effort—I'd have to just empty the receptacle to the garbage can outside. Nonetheless, it was a small notch in the marital exorcism.

The shower was hot and sorely needed. Upon dressing and gathering an unused athletic bag from the guest bedroom closet I began to assemble my go bag by throwing jeans and T-shirts plus a medium weigh jacket inside. Hairbrush, spare toothbrush, hotel travel-size shampoos and soaps that I found from the bathroom, as well as another Hartford Whaler baseball hat, all went into the go bag.

Feeling refreshed from the shower I decided to get things under way.

The first Horseman I attempted to reach was Hector Gomez-Macias. I dialed the pager that the task force had provided him. I put in my cell phone number and waited to hear from him.

Ten minutes later my pager, still partially submerged in the pennies, started to vibrate. I picked it up and saw seven separate displayed pages: six were from the VIN office which must have been the morning pages sent by Ileana. The seventh page was a coded message and it had just come in.

6263*81215352

Doper code.

Gomez Macias was sending me doper code to my pager rather than call me on my cell phone.

The standard keypad of a telephone has four rows of numbers. The first three rows comprise numbers 1-9. The fourth row has * 0 #. The number 1 on the keypad has no alpha numerical lettering.

The number 2 has A, B, C.

The number 3 has D, E, F

The number 4 has G, H, I

The number 5 has J, K, L

The number 6 has M, N, O

The number 7 has P, Q, R,S

The number 8 has T, U,V

The number 9 has W, X, Y, Z

Using the keypad of my cell phone as a guide I translated the message.

6263 meant Number 6 second letter (N), and Number 6 third letter (O).

The asterisk is space from one word to another word.

81215352 meant Number 8 first letter (T), Number 2 first letter (A), Number 5 third letter (L), Number 5 second letter (K).

NO * TALK

What could "No Talk" mean? Does Gomez-Macias mean he cannot talk due to duress, or does it mean he cannot talk for another reason? Was he aware of Peralta's murder and even more so did he have a hand in it? Was he stalling because it was me, and there were plans to try and kill me as well?

I needed to get a read on him and soon. I dialed his pager again and this time put in the same 911 code for urgency that the agency used to get me to call the night before.

Thirty minutes went by before my cell phone rang.

The digital display said, "Out of Area."

I picked up on the third ring.

"Hello."

No proper salutation or greeting on the other end.

"Damn. What's so important that you got to be calling me and causing all this shit?"

"What shit?"

"This shit. This shit! I got everyone looking at me. I had to go to the *gasolinera* to use a pay phone. By the way, you're paying for this call. I'm keeping track of the pesos."

"Pesos? Where the hell are you?

"I'm in Colombia!"

"Colombia? When the hell did you decide to go to Colombia?"

"I didn't *decide* to go to Colombia. The Green Bay Packers decided *for* me by losing to the Broncos in the Super Bowl. *Pendejos!* They cost me thirty-two large to that *iguazo* Ricky at the Molino Rojo Bar. Besides my cousin is getting married, so I'm going to be here for a while 'til I decide what I want to do."

"So when did you go down?"

"Like Avianca says 'it's for you,' well, I made it all about me and jumped on the morning flight."

The sound of a jitney bus and its disembarking clattering clientele could now be heard in Gomez -Macias' background.

"You mean Monday right after the game?"

"Hell yeah Monday after the game. I would've left then and there if there was a flight to get on. I had to deport myself. Ricky had guys coming to my house as soon as that bucktooth Elway started waving that football when they carried him off the field. I needed to get out. I checked into a hotel by the airport. Jumped on the morning flight."

"Anybody else part of that action that might of got lit up betting?"

With this bit of information I was beginning to wonder if Peralta was also in debt but not fortunate enough to get out of town.

"He takes bets from all over. I don't know about anyone else. I just needed to be gone. I'll be back. Shit, all my stuff is still there."

"What hotel by the airport did you check into?"

"What? Why are you so into my shit?"

"Because you are still working for me; that little fiasco in Hialeah with OIG, remember? You even remotely think of coming back I will put you on a Customs watch order and keep you in INS at Krome for weeks 'til they find me to get the paperwork straightened out. That's why. Now quit screwing around and tell me where."

Threatening him with the Immigration and Naturalization Services and sticking him at the Krome Detention Center in Southwest Miami Dade County was the quickest way to leverage my advantage.

"Okay...okay don't be getting all bad cop on me. I stayed at the Travelers on NW 36th street."

"So if I go over there they'll remember you and verify you were there."

I couldn't tell him that I was trying to eliminate him as a possible suspect in Peralta's murder.

"Yeah, but why you want to do that kind of shit?"

"I don't. But you need to remember you work for me and you can't just be up and leaving the country because you owe Ritchie—"

"Ricky."

"Whatever. You can't just leave without notifying."

"Okay. I paid cash. I used the name *Alfromba Gastada.*"

"What? Who is that?"

"It's nobody. The night clerk was some kid who couldn't speak Spanish so I saw the lobby carpet was dirty and worn so I told him *Alfombra Gastada* was my name. Worn carpet," he said.

"Clever. Do not just surprise visit back here. Call me before you think of making your way back here. Don't just reappear in Miami," I told him.

"Okay."

"I don't care how many pesos you have to spend, you call and check in every other day until you come back. You hear me?"

"Okay."

"And you're paying for the calls," I said as I hung up.

He never asked about Peralta and I never said anything either. Whether or not he was in the crosshairs was not as important to me as determining if *I* was in the crosshairs. Well, if what Gomez-Macias said was true, that he was in fact in Colombia and that he hightailed it the morning after the Super Bowl, then he couldn't be responsible for Peralta's murder. At least not physically responsible. The other positive sign was if Hector was down in Colombia as he said and if he was inconvenienced making calls he may not be in contact with the other Horsemen.

The afternoon shadows were starting to play against the walls. While the rest of the U.S. got dark very early in February, we in South Florida still managed to squeeze a little more daylight in our winter days until about 6pm. I ordered a meatball parmigiana sub for pick-up from Papa Rico's, relieved that I still could get one before they transitioned to their nighttime dinner menu. Regardless of what you order or where you order in Miami it's always "twenty minutes."

Forty minutes later I was back home eating the sub and thinking about what I'd need to do later on in the evening. I devised a checklist. With Gomez-Macias in Colombia I should verify what I could of his story. I still was going to put a U.S. Customs watch order on him. If he left the country without informing me, he sure as hell regardless of my insistence was going to come back without informing me, too. Besides, it would be good for his safety as well as mine. If Customs stops him at the airport and then INS takes him to Krome I'll know where he is, I can go talk with him face to face. It will be an aggravation and sore spot with him, but he'll get over it. It would only be for a day or two. If he was involved with Peralta's murder than I'd be doing both Lloyd Trentlocke and Captain Zambrana a big favor. If he wasn't involved then I'd still be doing them a favor by having him centrally located so they can interview him. If there's a chance that I am on the murder hit list, I'll be doing myself a favor by getting him put down.

Satiated from the sub and knowing my day was still not fully over, I set an alarm on my cell phone for 9pm. I settled into the large tropical-print couch and turned on the local news.

Body bag journalism.

If it bleeds it leads.

Miami local news is a fast-swirling, graphic-infused loud display of murder and misery. Tourists must be terrified to leave their hotel rooms, seeing the daily carnage of inhumanity splayed across their hotel television screens. For me it's just sensationalized background noise, and I soon was asleep on the couch, the TV volume turned down to a low murmur of mayhem, lulling me to sleep.

I woke up with an inconsistent fluttering of my eyes. The house was pitch black except for the TV, the bluish-green light from the picture tube helping to quickly remind me of where I was. The remnants of the meatball sub not nearly as appealing now as it had been earlier in the evening. I looked at my cell phone.

No calls.

It was 8:57pm.

It never ceases to amaze me the biorhythms of the human body and how we can manage or own internal clock. I was up.

Literally.

Sitting up.

I turned the alarm off on the cell phone, feeling stealthy that I'd gotten to it before it chimed. I padded through the house in the dark to the back bedroom. Turning on the bedroom light, I removed my pager from its coppery nest and checked it as well.

No pages.

Within twenty minutes, about the same time it takes to pick up a to go food order in Miami, the go bag, the pager, and I were in the Ford, heading north. My first stop was to the VIN office.

I card-swiped my way into the VIN office and turned on the light.

I never understood the whole conglomeration of family pictures on a work desk but here I sat at Ileana's desk, surrounded by her own personal Kodak moments. I pulled my checkbook from my back pocket, hurriedly scratched out a twenty dollar check to the Kiwanis Club of Coral Gables, and stuck it to Ileana's computer with a post-it that said, 'Lt. Poulsen.' I then spun around in her office chair and logged onto the secondary computer on the credenza behind her desk. I went to the U.S. Customs Blue Lightning Task Force website. I opened the domain with my task force password and username and scrolled through the left side of menu options to "Watch Orders and Interdictions."

I got up briefly and retrieved Gomez-Macias' C.I. folder from the locked C.I. filing cabinet. Using my left knee to hold the folder, I transposed the vital information necessary to put a U.S. Customs watch order on Gomez-Macias. For the reason for the watch order I wrote "Questioning in an open Miami Dade Homicide Investigation."

A big yellow pop-up window appeared on the screen asking me to be sure of my request and telling me a representative from U.S. Customs would be calling to confirm. I clicked yes.

No sooner than a minute had passed when my cell phone rang. It was U.S. Customs officer and upon verifying it was indeed me and getting a small rudimentary back story he issued me a long digital code to use for tracking and for further information.

U.S-98-10552198-621P

I jotted down the code and hung up the phone. Next I logged into my email and emailed the code to myself as a back-up. Closing my email and any other open windows I then from the desktop clicked the NINJAS icon.

NINJAS was an acronym for Narcotic Information Network Joint Agency System. It was created just a year or so earlier and was a valuable tool for us in the VIN world. It was designed to avoid having undercover cops conduct cases with an adversary who in fact might be an undercover cop himself. It was a secretive clearinghouse for the undercover operations in Miami. This basically kept cops from doing cops. An example would be if a C.I. and a bad guy were to come to me looking to sell ten kilograms of cocaine but the bad guy was actually a Miami Beach undercover cop. Then he would put in the date and location and the nature of the deal; in this case a ten kilogram deal. I in turn would also log into NINJAS and show myself as a buyer of ten kilograms of cocaine. NINJAS would work in the background and see the location, date, and nature of the deal and recognize a conflict. It would then warn both agencies of a potential conflict.

It was simplistic, but had it been in effect early in my VIN career it would have averted so many trepidatious approaches to surveillance cars and strangers all over Miami.

Using NINJAS I showed myself at the west Miami Dade bar "La Covacha" tomorrow at 7pm, meeting with an individual about a possible money laundering contract. It was prudent of me to create this NINJAS event prior to setting the actual meeting because it locked La Covacha as my location, and kept other agencies away. It also gave me a documented location in case Miami Dade Homicide starts snooping into where I am and how I spend my time. They won't know I was there but if I needed to explain my whereabouts, I could do so.

After logging off the computer I headed out to NW 36th Street to pay a visit to the Traveler's Hotel.

Moving north on Lejeune Road I passed a Gulf gas station probably one of the last ones in Miami. This heavily-trafficked corridor was a straight line to Miami International Airport and aside from the Gulf station, there were many long forgotten iconic places like the Miami Playboy Club and the Aquarius Lounge, all of which were now long gone. Their buildings were now serving as a muffler shop, and a rental car agency. I chose to come out to the hotel at this late hour because it was most likely near the time that Hector had checked into the hotel. I was hoping to have an opportunity to talk to the same front desk clerk or if not him, perhaps the one he'd be relieving for the midnight shift. I was trying to maximize my success opportunities.

Miami International Airport at night was a greatly reduced yet still viable cacophony of airplanes and ground personnel. From Lejeune Road you could see the movements and busyness of the airport.

The Traveler's Hotel was on the north side of the airport. Its front door looking out across NW 36th Street onto a scattered assemblage of neglected and derelict airplanes being scrapped and cannibalized for parts, their glory airborne years all but faded from memory.

The hotel itself was in dire need of some aesthetic assistance, its front door very nearly opening directly into the bustling traffic of the street. A small alley separated the hotel lobby from the pool area and from some of the rooms. An odd configuration, obviously a hold-over from its original inception in the 1950s.

Stepping into the lobby the aroma of moisture and dueling dehumidifiers were omnipresent. Behind the front desk was a young man in a blue blazer conspicuously missing two nickel-plated buttons on its sleeve. The blazer was slightly too big for his frame and clashed with his stone washed jeans. He had a small name tag that said "Stuart."

It appeared that Stuart was a college student working his way through college as was attested by the three Florida International University textbooks behind him on a table. The table was enhanced with more than just a few noticeable water rings.

"Hello Stuart. Are you the manager?"

"No. I'm the night clerk."

On a thin chain I wore around my neck I carried my Detective badge which I kept tucked in under my shirt. I pulled out my Detective badge and introduced myself.

"You don't look like a cop," he said.

"You don't look like manager material," I said.

"Stuart, I need to see your registry from January 25th."

"I don't know if I can do that?" he slightly stammered.

"You don't know if you can do that or you do not know if you *will* do that? Because you *can* do it. But if you're telling me you won't do it, then I'll tell you what I am going to do. I'm willing to bet the water lines to your ice machines haven't been purged in years. Can you imagine the backlogged bacteria harboring in there? I mean the Health Department would have a field day. Speaking of field days, have you ever seen a truly intensive fire inspection? The one where they check for asbestos and other carcinogens? It's usually not a concern unless a building was built before the 1970s. How about that swimming pool? You guys have an anti-vortex drain cover?"

Stuart was young but wise enough to see that he didn't want to go in the direction I was alluding to and he held up his hands in mock surrender. He took a brief step back and reached under the desk for a worn black vinyl binder.

He thumbed the pages briefly and turned the book towards me on the counter. There were just a few names on the 25th of January, but one stood out in the small group.

Alfombra Gastada.

To try and cover my tracks I turned the page to the 24th and admonished Stuart for giving me the wrong date as I pretended to look at the names on the 24th with interest.

"You said the 25th" he protested.

"I did not. I said the 24th. It's okay, I'm on the right page now. Do you remember this guy who checked in on the 24th? Archie Geiger?" I said with mocking interest as I pushed the book back across the counter to Stuart.

"No. Sorry I don't."

"Well, thanks anyway Stuart and if this guy Geiger ever asks...I wasn't here."

"Yes sir."

I walked out the front door feeling the whoosh of cars driving by and looked out at the decaying fuselages across the street. My only thought was:

Four Horsemen. One in Colombia and another more than likely heading to Colombia in a casket.

Chapter Eight

I COULDN'T BE SURE if it was the morning sunlight filtering through the plantation shutters or if it was the sound of my neighbor starting up his lawn mower but whichever came first or abetted the other it made no difference. I was most certainly awake now.

7:46 am.

I love my neighbor like the last piece of Entenmann's but just because *he* has no agenda since his retirement doesn't mean the rest of us have to be up this early listening to him pull the starter six times, curse three times, and then get the lawn mower underway. I opened the French doors that led out to the screen-enclosed swimming pool. The morning light danced on the flat aqua blue water and the noise of the lawn mower was now much louder. I had stopped off at Bryson's Bar after leaving Stuart and his textbooks. A few shots of Jameson and the build-up of courage to enable me to come home to an empty house, and I was back home pulling into the driveway by 1am. I knew the water in the pool would be cold, but I probably needed the heart resuscitating surge. I stepped through the French doors and did a rather ungraceful easing but more like shuffle, into the bracing chlorinated water. The water wasn't refreshing as one might think, but more of an eye-opening assault that jolted me skeletally and neurologically. Feeling proud to have done it while simultaneously thinking it was one of the stupidest things I have done in a while I lasted in the water about forty seconds. It was enough to completely immerse myself and then I rushed up the steps in the shallow end and out. The morning air although just warming from the sunrise, was not warm enough to keep me from chattering my teeth. Reaching for a towel that was kept poolside I started to dry off, that's when I heard the pennies vibrating in the ashtray.

It was the VIN office. I just wouldn't feel right talking to Ileana with nothing but a towel draped around me, so I got dressed in a pair of jeans and T-shirt and using the same towel to continue drying my hair I then called the VIN office.

The telephone rang twice before her accented voice answered.

"*Veen.*"

"Good morning Ileana. I answered my pager. That's good, right?"

"Yes, *ju* should have been an astronaut instead of a cop."

I had no idea what that meant and wasn't even inclined to ask.

"Did you get the check I left for Poulsen?"

"I already put it in his box. He wanted me to tell *ju* that Miami S.I.S. wants *ju* to call them before 10am. Do *ju* have their number?"

"Yes, I have the number."

"Good then *ju* are set. Bye."

I didn't even have a chance to say bye properly. I held off on getting dressed any further until I knew what Miami S.I.S. wanted. S.I S. was an abbreviation for "Special Investigations Section," our counterparts and it was just a different terminology. Being a much larger agency than we were, they felt a more generic terminology would encompass more of the things they had to do. We worked with Miami S.I.S. and select members of their unit were directly assigned to the task force via a mutual aid agreement we had written between us. I called Miami S.I.S. and spoke with one of their sergeants who I had done some work with. He wouldn't be there later, but he asked that I come by their offsite office at 1pm. He explained that they were short that day due to a visiting dignitary from Ecuador. That necessitated S.I.S. augmenting their dignitary protection unit at the Chopin Plaza downtown off of Biscayne Boulevard.

Miami was intending to flash two kilos to two Dominicans from New York City. The deal was set to be fifteen kilograms of cocaine but in good faith for this preliminary meeting, only two of the supposed fifteen kilos would be shown. If all parties agree, then the next meeting will entail the full fifteen kilos being exchanged for the determined price set by Miami. The going rate was around $23,000 to $28,000 a kilogram. Miami S.I.S. were very good and I'm sure they would not try to sell for anything less than $24,000. They have to keep credibility. Offer it too low and you will, as the dopers say, "smell federal." As in being a cop. The Dominicans would be getting a bargain. Them buying direct in Miami enables them to cut out two to three mid-level transporters and save on the current going rate in New York City which is about $29,000 to $35,000. A sizable savings.

This entire deal had been set up through intermediaries over the phone and neither party had met in person yet. The Dominicans were extremely wary of dealing only with Cubans. They called Cuban drug traffickers "rip off artists." The Miami undercover, although Cuban himself, said he would be bringing his gringo brother in law to assuage their concerns. Unfortunately, due to inept police management, the gringo undercover they had in mind was now wearing a suit, tie and earpiece, watching a dumpster behind Chopin Plaza for the day. As it was explained to me, they just needed me to act like a typical brother-in-law who doesn't know a lot about the drug business but is standing by with his wife's brother while he talks to these Dominicans.

1pm at the offsite.

3pm for the meet.

7pm at La Covacha.

My day was filling up. I didn't get further dressed and actually retooled my attire to be a bit more "gringo-fied." I opted for the suburban uniform of a striped polo shirt adorned with the crest of the Doral Country Club. The shirt, a long-forgotten, back-of-the-closet gift from my brother, the golfer. I went out to grab a quick breakfast at Reuben's Cafe. I made a point to call first and make sure they were open since the owner had a tendency to close up when the swells were ideal for dolphin fishing. A heavy-accented Cuban woman answered and I hung up and continued to the cafe. On the way, I decided to reach out to one of the two unaccounted for Four Horsemen. I placed a call to Don Julio Restrepo.

Everyone called him "Donito," which was a homage to his father Don Julio Restrepo Sr. Aside from the nickname, there wasn't anything really little about Donito. He wasn't gargantuan, nor did he have a very commanding presence, but I just assumed that wherever he came from his father had some measure of prominence and therefore he just became "Little Don."

I didn't expect him to answer his cell phone this early in the morning and true to form my expectations were not disappointed. After the fifth ring, it went to his voicemail. There was no greeting. It just stopped ringing and then there was a simple singular beep. It was common in the drug-trafficking-money-laundering world to not have voice greetings on your cell phone. The assumption was that if you dialed ten random numbers and reached a telephone, then you must know who you are calling.

Breakfast at Reuben's Cuban Cafe was delicious and it provided me an opportunity to sit at the counter and just compose my thoughts while reading the *Miami Herald* over the scrambled eggs, crispy bacon, Cuban toast and steaming *cafe con leche*. The din of plates being dispersed and collected mixed with the conflicting and sometimes argumentative Cuban conversations would have unsettled some, but to me it was the urban sound of my youth. In the corner of the cafe was a framed poster circa 1940s promoting Varadero Cuba. It depicted a rendering of a very attractive Cuban woman, her dark tresses cascading down past her shoulders spilling onto her midriff yellow blouse. The fabric strained to contain her heaving bosom. A Cuban man in a multi-colored striped shirt danced under the swaying palms alongside her. Another Cuban gentleman in a white fedora and white panatela suit looked on. I wondered, as many often did, if Cuba really was as exotic and passion-filled as it was depicted in art. The lifestyle at least pictured in this pre-Castro era poster seemed so carefree and enticing.

Now carefree and enticing was the furthest from my mind.

I looked at the bill and left cash and tip on the counter.

Walking out, the matronly Cuban waitress reminded me I had left my newspaper behind. Not wanting to overburden her by making her come around the horseshoe counter to clean I just grabbed the newspaper, crumbled napkins and bill and walking out. I threw them in the sidewalk trash can.

I got back into the Ford and tried to call Donito again.

He picked up on the second ring.

"Allo."

"Donito. It's Cade, what are you doing?"

"Oh Cade, hey what, Cade hey."

Those of us who are native English speakers sometimes take for granted how hard it is for people who speak English as a second language to flow with the cadence.

"Donito, I need to see you tonight. We need to talk. Understand? We need to talk about your rate? *Comprender?*"

"We need to talk? Talk now."

I couldn't have this conversation get away from me and be answering under his direction.

"No. It's about the new rules. Meet me at El Torito on Northwest 107th Avenue by the mall at 7pm.

Make sure you bring a blue ink pen. *Pluma Azul!*"

"What rules? Why a blue pen?"

"I can't get into it right now, I got lots of calls to make. Be there. El Torito at 7pm."

With that I hung up. I didn't need him to bring a blue pen and there were no rules to go over or a change in his commission. I just said those things to keep him off balance. One of the best ways to get your C.I.s to drop what they're doing and meet with you is to make them think they're either getting paid or that their pay is being altered. If he was going to be a no show, it was now incumbent on him to call me back. I intended to make it as difficult as I could for him to do that in the next eight hours. I'd told him to meet me at a Mexican restaurant adjacent to the Miami International Mall. I had no intention of meeting him there. I would change the location to La Covacha at the last minute. La Covacha was about a mile away, just west of Northwest 107th Avenue on Northwest 25th Street. Setting my meeting with him at one location and then changing it at the last minute should give me the upper hand. He won't be able to set me up if I am on the hit list, and I can negate any counter-surveillance or *amigos* he might intend to bring with him.

I casually started making my way to the Miami S.I.S. offsite across town on the fringe of Little Havana. It wasn't exactly Little Havana, nor was it considered "the roads' section of Miami. Traffic was moderately heavy and I tried as many surface street shortcuts as I could, but between construction, and congestion it was slow going as I was essentially driving diagonally across the county.

The offsite is called an offsite for the exact reason you would think it is. It's an office maintained from the site of the Miami Police Department. It's clandestine and cloistered and there are strict rules concerning it. Firstly, you are never to talk about it or acknowledge its existence. Secondly, you never ever go to it with a police radio in your hand, badge exposed, or a blue light on your dashboard. No police markings or anything that even denotes you're in law enforcement. So suffice to say, the offsite was near Coral Way, close to downtown Miami. There was enough parking in the rear to hold the widely diversified rented and leased cars and trucks that the Miami detectives drove.

I parked next to a maroon sedan that had a guy sitting in it. The engine was running and he was on his cellphone. Cars make great places for privacy moments to talk to wives, girlfriends, or for some, both. I was briefly transported back to a not-so-distant past when

I would be that guy, talking to Gina. The normalcy of life drifting through the phone's earpiece with each soothing word. With a definitive reality check, I knew that there was no normalcy; at least for me anymore.

I walked to the gray industrial door and noticed the keypad next to the door. I had been here before but didn't know the code. There was no way anyone in the upstairs offsite could hear me knocking on the door, so I didn't even try. I turned back towards the guy in the maroon sedan. Looking at me through the windshield, while still on his cellphone, he held up the universal finger, conveying via sign language to me to wait a minute.

Within a minute he'd hung up and was exiting the sedan. He was a little younger than me and obviously Cuban with dark hair and eyes. He was thin, but strong in a wiry sense. His face was a little pock-marked from a teenage bout of acne and he had a silver bracelet around his left wrist. He asked who I was and I told him and he then readily introduced himself as Javier Solis. He was Miami S.I.S. and had been in the unit just short of one year.

The stairs up to the office were functionally industrial with gray paint upon both the staircase and the metal bannister. The S.I.S. door was unmarked and wooden except with a small number 325 in black plastic numbers above the doorframe. It was odd as we were only on the second floor, but like a lot of things that didn't always make sense, I just did not feel compelled to ask. Javier pushed open the door and inside were an assembly of mostly men. Seven to be exact and one lone female. She, like the majority of the men, appeared to be Latin except for the one African American.

Detective Johnny Morris.

Morris and I had gone to DEA Clandestine Lab School together in Pointe Verde Florida a few years back and had run into each other often since then. With the exception of Solis and the female detective who they referred to as *"Chispa,"* I knew everyone in the room at some level or another. *Chispa* in Spanish means "spark," as in a combustable explosion or ignitable substance. Just like the number

325 above the door, I chose to abstain from asking about her name figuring I'd hear about it sooner or later.

Sooner came barely later when Johnny sidled over and said hello almost immediately as I crossed the threshold. After a brief catching up he motioned with his eyes and a slight, quick upturn of his mouth towards "Chispa."

"That one over there is Araceli Serrano. She's only been here about six months, came in from the youth resources unit," he said.

"A kiddie cop?"

"Yeah, but she's pretty ballsy. Blends well, plays the girlfriend a lot."

"Really?" I asked. "Most Colombians don't want to deal with women. They think they're bad luck."

"Yeah but they like to look at them," was his response as he himself looked in her direction.

"We call her Chispa because when we were doing a prostitution sting on the Boulevard up by Buena Vista she was the decoy, looking fine. Some A.C. repair guy looking to pay for some extra got all handsy, tried to pull her into his work truck. She gave the take-down signal—they missed it. So she's fighting with this guy half in, half out of the truck on the boulevard? She pushed in the cigarette lighter, stuck him twice in the throat with it. Guy had one full moon and a half moon-looking burns on his neck. She sparked him up, so to say."

Johnny Morris called for everyone to settle down and listen up. Just off to his right was Ignacio Quintero. Ignacio was a good guy. I had worked in various capacities with him before and he was always a real solid U.C. Everyone called him Iggy. He, like Detective Solis who I just met, was also Cuban American. Just like myself, I suspect everyone else in the room was raised in Miami. Iggy had a very sunny disposition and a mega-watt smile. He was in excellent shape. He didn't dress overly fashionable but his taste in clothes exuded independent financial stability and he chose to often wear tight dark T-shirts and jeans with casual but stylish footwear. No one in the office was wearing tennis shoes, or the cop-requisite black Casio watch. Both are dead giveaways that you're law enforcement. Shoes are the key. Dopers are notorious shoe aficionados. But if you're trying to look the part of an uninformed gringo brother-in-law who's just along to keep family harmony, well then you wear a nice striped polo shirt and tennis shoes.

To their credit, the roomful of detectives ceased their jostling around and settled in to hear Morris.

"Sergeant Brookings is at the Chopin Plaza with the Ecuadorian security team. I will be the A-Slash today."

"A-slash" meant acting supervisor. He'd be in charge in this case. Morris had the most seniority of anyone in S.I.S. so it fell upon him to take on the supervisory role.

"Iggy will lead the briefing and will be the U.C. today with Cade here, from the Gables. Everyone here know Cade? If you don't know Cade then take a long look at him and know he is one of us. We don't need anybody getting hurt because they don't know who's who. Cade, come stand up here by Iggy please."

The redundancy of saying my name was meant to reinforce me to the group as an ally. I got up and was immediately ribbed by the assembled group of detectives about my attire. I expected that and it was all in good fun. Once the group settled down again Iggy began his briefing of the Operations Plan which he started to talk about as he handed the ops plan to the detectives.

"We got two unknown players," he said with an almost comically raised eyebrow. "They *say* they're from Queens, New York. We've been going around and around on the phone since late December. Now? They're in town, looking to score a minimum fifteen kilos. Which is good because we don't need to do more than five to upset their lives, if you know what I mean. We told them we have fifteen kilos that I pulled out of a larger shipment we're holding for a group out of Orlando. They *think* I intend to sell them the fifteen and will restock the fifteen kilos I'm borrowing. They know I plan to buy from someone else at a rate lower than I'm selling to them before the big load goes to Orlando. *They* want to buy low here and sell high in New

York, I'm looking to sell high from this sale and restock with a good profit on the side. This has frosted them a little because they want to buy from us for the lower price that I'm getting the restock for. So be on your toes for any type of hostility or rip-off mentality. This is only a meet and greet. Any questions so far?"

He stopped speaking for a beat to allow for any questions of which there were none. He then continued:

"Okay, these guys are already hinky about Miami and Miami Cubans so *that* is why 'my brother-in-law Cade' is here—to put them at ease, that this is a 'family thing,'" he said, gesturing with his hands making air quotes.

"Dude, your sister's a moron," was uttered somewhere amongst the group causing a hearty and necessary moment of levity.

After the brief respite, Iggy said, "So, this is set for 3pm at Casablanca's on the River."

Casablanca's was a family-owned seafood restaurant and market. It has a decent size footprint on the north side of the Miami River. It has outdoor seating on the river and a sizable bar.

"Cade and I will be inside waiting for them at a table. We'll have a red Macy's shopping bag with one kilogram of coke, and one sham kilogram, representing two of the fifteen kilos we're trying to sell them."

Ignacio was an experienced U.C. The red shopping bag would be easy to see if there was any type of rip-off planned by the Dominicans. It was necessary to have at least one kilogram of real cocaine in the deal to warrant at the minimum a conspiracy to traffic charge. If you tried to sell only phony kilograms or what we called "shams," than there is no actual conspiracy to buy or sell anything illegal.

"So here's the OP's. Like I said, Cade and I will be inside. We'll both be wearing Kel pagers."

Johnny spoke up and interrupted Iggy while he pulled the Kel pagers out of a bag. He didn't want Iggy to go further until he tested them. Kels were listening devices disguised as pagers or cellphones so our back-up could hear everything. They were named after the ultra-secretive Kel Corporation. A company so secretive they wouldn't even acknowledge their Massachusetts headquarters to Wall Street Investors. The interruption was partially unnecessary, but Johnny's attention to detail was welcomed, at least by me. Once both Kels were tested and deemed operable Johnny asked Iggy to continue.

"As I was saying, we'll be inside. Chispa, you'll be at the bar. Make sure you're not directly facing us but use the mirror behind the bar to keep your eye on things. Ivan, I know we usually use you on the inside—but looking like that we can't."

A young detective with a thick streak of pink in his hair mimicked consternation, but knew Iggy was correct.

"Bro, it was my daughter's third birthday. I had to be My Little Pony. I've washed this shit like six times. The fuckers need to say something on the can" he said in resigned protest, once again causing the room to erupt in laughter. I picked up on his name right away.

Ivan.

Very characteristic of his age and lineage as many Cuban women commingled with Russian military advisors who were staged in Cuba in the 1970s during the Angola War.

"Well, My Little Pony will be across the river as an eyeball, just in case any of these *locos* try to jump in the river," continued Iggy

"I hope they have their tetanus shots. Because that shit is nasty," said Alex Ramos, referring to the notorious filth of the long-neglected Miami River. Ramos was easily the tallest one in the group and had been a decent high school basketball player at Miami's Christopher Columbus High School. Looking at the ops plan, I saw Iggy had him just around the corner from us, staged at the famed Scottish Rite Temple.

"Speaking of nasty... Alex, you'll be at the Scottish Rite Temple on 3rd. Javier, you and Silvio will take the avenue for takeaways west-bound. Claudio, *you'll* be closer to Alex—but be ready for east takeaways, Alex, you'll help him if they go that way. Ivan, once they're on the move, *you* join in as soon as you can. A-slash Morris will be two blocks in, across from Casablanca, and be first arriving for tactical if we need him. He'll have a long weapon in his car. When this is over, Chispa, you and I will take the kilos back here and meet up with A-slash Morris to secure the kilos. Cade, you can bug out. "

The Ops Plan paper had each make and model of the detectives' cars, cell phone numbers for each detective, the radio frequency they would be on, and the nearest hospital. In this case, Jackson Memorial Hospital, simply written as JMH. Due to the commercialization along the river there was no landing zone for a medical air rescue helicopter. The proximity of JMH negated that as well as the lack of safe sites to land a helicopter. There was no vehicle or physical description of the two Dominicans. Everyone was to be in their assigned places by 2:30pm.

Morris requested that Claudio Fuentes go with him to the S.I.S. safe in an adjoining room and witness as he signed for the removal of an actual kilogram of cocaine and a sham. Fuentes, as well as Silvio Pena were excellent tactical narcotic trained officers and usually filled a role as back-up and takedown officers. I'd worked with them on other situations and they were always more than capable of handling whatever came their way.

Morris with Claudio standing by, put the cocaine and the sham in a moderate-sized red Macy's shopping bag.

Everyone had a copy of the ops plan and wordlessly filed out to get in position for the 3pm deadline. The last two to leave were me and Iggy.

I parked a few blocks away from Casablanca's and waited for Iggy to pick me up. Being that I was supposed to be a novice rube, it was just a better appearance if I rode in with my "brother-in-law, Ignacio Fernandez." You never know—there could be counter-surveillance.

Quintero, like many of the U.C.s in Miami, always went by their real first name in case someone they knew outside of work should see them in public and inadvertently out them by calling them by their first name. So just as Ignacio "Iggy" Quintero was Ignacio

Fernandez, I was Cade Daniels and I had the driver's license and credit cards to prove it.

My wait was momentary as Iggy tooled up in the black U.C Audi A8.

We spoke in generalities and he quickly told me of the relentless phone tag he had over the last forty days with this guy known only as *"Lobo."* When I heard that moniker I did an eye roll that could have sunk the Seventh Fleet. I had a lot of other things going on with Peralta getting whacked. I didn't need to be a bit player in some out of town Dominican's inflated version of himself as a sly wolf.

We drove right past Ramos who was in position, covertly tucked aside an eighteen-wheeler flatbed trailer. The temple is in the process of being revamped and the trailers and trucks gave Ramos good cover. His undercover white pickup truck blended in completely.

The architecture of the Scottish Rite building is majestic with Greek columns supporting the entryway. Enigmatic eagle statues topped the temple with the number 32 on each of them. I had no idea what that meant. It just seemed that numbers over doors was becoming today's top trend. Across the street is Lumus Park. Low income apartments dot the street, although by their design I would venture to say they use to be hotels from the turn of the 20th Century. In direct view through the rusty chain link fencing and seeping corroded barrels was the Miami River where you can see a lot of freight coming and going.

Today Iggy and I were going to try and move a different type of freight.

We pulled up to the front of Casablanca's which is appropriately painted white. Loose papers and cigarette butts were blowing about the parking lot—easily identifiable remnants of lunch trucks or as they're more aptly known "roach coaches," that feed the riverside longshore-men and scrap metal dealers.

In the restaurant we both settled into one of the riverside white marble tables. It was primarily empty during this after lunch and pre-dinner timeframe. Chispa was at the bar engaged in flirtatious banter with the young bartender. She didn't in the slightest measure even seem to notice us walk in. It was odd with both of us sitting on the same side of the table rather than across from each other. I got up and walked to the westside of the restaurant and waited a few minutes, busying myself. Right on time, two Dominicans briskly walked in and sizing Iggy as more than likely the voice they had been talking to on the phone, they approached the table. I reached the table just a few beats before they did and simply said to Iggy,

"...Forget it they can't get Sportscenter on the TV."

As I finished the sentence, both Dominicans', now assured they were at the right table, ambled quickly to the two seats across from us.

The first one who sat down was about 5'9 and very thin. He had a deep mustard-colored shirt rolled at the sleeves, black slacks and shoes. His hair was slicked back, moderate in length, just touching his collar. His thin-set but wide eyes and faint mustache immediately had me think of a squirrel. A thin, inch-long vertical scar slashed across his chin. To the uninitiated it may have seemed menacing, but I figured it to be the result of a childhood swing set accident.

The Dominican sitting across from Iggy was heavier and more jowly in the face, with a thick shock of wiry black hair that he looked to have made multiple attempts in his life to part in the middle. Now he just let it grow as if a wild bush was overtaking a well-worn foot trail. He had a noticeable chip in his front tooth. He was wearing black Vuarnet sunglasses that he immediately pulled up and then rested on the wild nap on his head. He wore a white short-sleeved shirt with a blue geometric print splashed across it in all directions. His dark slacks and grey Fero Aldo slip-ons completed his attire.

No handshakes were exchanged.

It was the one across from Iggy who spoke first just as his butt was hitting the seat.

"Ignacio?"

"Lobo?"

"Yeah. This is Concho."

"This is Cade."

Being the perceived novice gringo in the group and not knowing drug underworld culture, I extended my hand and by doing so created a round of quick, reluctant, perfunctory handshakes amongst the four of us.

Iggy then started the conversation by turning to Concho.

"Concho? Why do they call you 'Taxi' ?"

"I pick things up." was the straight-faced, blasé answer.

Asking for elaboration would have been a futile act, so it just died there where he said it.

"After all those calls I didn't know if you'd get here. I started lining up with some guys from Baltimore but its good you're here. I'd rather get this done with you,'

Iggy said to them both.

"That could be all well and as you say here in Miami 'sunny,' but I will not get into a bidding war with some Baltimore phantom you just pulled out of your ass. We're here in good faith. Good faith to meet you, here, inside at a place you chose. If this goes—and I do mean if—then the next time we meet, we choose the location, and it won't be indoors. Indoor is for ice skating rinks and movie theaters and shit like that. I like open. Out in the open. No wondering who or what is lurking about," said Lobo as his eyes wandered over the restaurant, to the bar, then up and down Chispa's very attractive body.

Iggy reminded them we were on a deck overlooking the outdoor river. Both men just looked at him.

"And you? What do you do, Cade? Don't tell me no office because you're here at 3 o'clock and your hair is too long to be some white-collar fuck."

"I own a pool liner company. We do liners for pools. Most lately though it's been fish farms for Talapia," I said.

"That's a shit fish and if it was on the menu here I'd walk out. Dolphin Frito or Dolphin Coco, now that's a meal," said Lobo with complete believability. He waved off an approaching waiter. "We won't be here long," he said brusquely.

Once the waiter was gone and out of ear-shot Lobo leaned in closer, while Concho just continued to stare at me with his wide eyes.

"Ignacio. I don't care what you do with that Orlando package. But you're gouging me on my fifteen. I want the same price you're buying for."

Iggy kept to his business stance. "I'm not taking fifteen shirts out of the closet just so I can go buy fifteen new clean shirts to put back in the closet," he said in cryptic doper code.

The wheels were spinning in Lobo's mind. He was more than likely calculating the effort and time put into this venture and decided to listen.

"Very well. And what do you plan to sell these fifteen shirts for?" asked Lobo

"Twenty-five each. But since you've come in here acting like your balls are the size of New York, there's an aggravation cost. You're aggravating me with this meet-only-outside-and-on-your terms, plus I had to drive Cade here just to appease your bullshit prejudices. And that's what they are—prejudices. You want to meet outside? You want to set the meet? You want to dictate all this crap in my backyard? Then this, to me, is an aggravation deal. I need to be compensated for my aggravation. Twenty-five each plus $500 each for the nonsense. Twenty-five-five."

As he finished, Iggy looked Concho straight in the eye and said, "Consider it taxi fare."

Lobo put both hands on the table and leaned back in his chair.

"You're not going to be getting any repeat business with this shit. How do I know for sure you can deliver?"

Iggy then reached under the table which caused Concho to start to stand up.

"Relax," he said as he brought the Macy's shopping bag near to table height. He looked around, as did all three of us, and made sure we were alone except for the hot Latina talking smack at the bar. He opened the shopping bag. Inside were the real kilo and the sham kilo. Morris had been smart enough to mark each one with a Sharpie adding authenticity, denoting that they were part of an Orlando shipment. Each one said "Pluto" on the tightly tape-bound kilos.

Whether they were satisfied or not was a hard read to decipher.

"We'll be in touch," said Lobo as he and Concho started to rise.

"What about you? How do I know you got the suits that go with these shirts?" said Iggy, now fully standing.

Lobo looked at Concho and nodded almost imperceptibly to him.

Concho pulled from his front pocket a Polaroid photo. He briefly held the Polaroid up to Iggy's face. It showed clearly a hotel bed with today's *Miami Herald* newspaper lying atop, of at least $100,000 in cash.

As they started to leave the restaurant Concho drew close to Iggy and said,

"Is that enough fare to cover the ride? Asshole."

Chapter Nine

IT WAS ABOUT ten minutes before Chispa's cell phone rang. She notified me and Iggy that Javier said the two Dominicans had left westbound in a white four-door Mitsubishi Diamante. They didn't appear to have any confederates with them, and it was determined by Morris to have the staged S.I.S. units keep a loose--moving surveillance on them. Chispa sweetly asked for and received from the bartender some to-go bags and take out containers. Discreetly the two kilos as well as my Kel pager were transferred to the to-go bags. This was a precautionary measure in case someone affiliated with the Dominicans that we'd missed was waiting outside, intending to pull a rip on me and Iggy. Chispa walked out with the kilos covertly in the bags and quickly got into Morris' car. They headed back to the S.I.S. office.

In the Audi, Iggy thanked me for assisting them and we discussed the probability of the actual deal being conducted in the future. He dropped me off and reminded me that "Cade the pool liner guy" might be needed if the deal does go. He also asked me where I came up with that boring occupation.

I just shrugged. I really had no idea other than that I was hoping to be in something that wasn't very exciting, and most people wouldn't care to ask about.

"Well, it worked. I'll keep you posted," he said as I exited his car and got into my own. I needed to go west myself but didn't have any idea what the status of the moving surveillance was and didn't want to by chance, all of a sudden find myself at a stop light next to Lobo and Concho. I decided to head east and get up on I-95, south towards U.S. 1 and then angle my way westerly.

Within an hour of leaving the river and navigating through a horde of traffic my cell phone rang.

It was Poulsen.

Before I answered I looked at my pager I'd clipped to the passenger visor of the Explorer. No pages. I picked up on the third ring.

"Hello."

"Status update?" was how he greeted me.

Mentally sidestepping his rudeness, I provided a bare-bones recap of the meet at Casablanca's. It's Miami's case and besides, I'm sure he already got a run down from Sergeant Brookings who had probably cleared the Ecuadorian detail, or at the very least from Morris. I didn't want to get too detailed and end up incurring more inquiries especially if he already knew the answers to what he would be asking me.

"Does Miami think they'll need you again for this?"

"Maybe."

"Well, in the future I would appreciate more communication from you, and in a timely manner."

Timely manner. That got me thinking.

"Did Ileana get you the check?"

"Yes. It should be a big help. Keep communication open. Bye."

The conversation was over.

Not a word of thanks. As for keeping communication open, I just thought to myself, *I made a Detective's decision.*

In many ways I wish I hadn't told Donito to meet at El Torito. Driving by the place I could've used a few beers and some tacos. I continued north to NW 25th Street and in a few minutes was pulling into La Covacha's gravel parking lot. Parking next to a dumpster, I opened the passenger and rear passenger doors of the Ford. Using the space between the doors and the dumpster as a personal outdoor changing room, I changed my shirt from the ubiquitous polo shirt to a more stylish, unstructured dark green T-shirt from my go bag. The whole area that La Covacha sat upon had once been part of a mile-long illegal dumping ground where old refrigerators and duct-taped couches were discarded from the back of barely moving pickup trucks. They were cast to the side of the road to be someone else's problem or new-found treasure. I guess which one was based on perspective.

I never could quite understand how the ownership of the place had by passed Miami Dade's strict hurricane building codes. La Covacha was basically a series of thatch-roofed huts with some CB block walls interspersed underneath the eaves. The Seminole and Miccosukee tribes of Indians were incredibly adept at building the open-air structures known as "Chickee Huts." These huts are constructed by tribal builders upon which cypress log pilings and trusses are then topped with multi-intersected layers of palm fronds that are fastened together, comprising the roofs.

La Covacha must have contracted a slew of the builders to build this multi-roofed Colombian drinking establishment. There was food served here as well. A herd of young men frequented the place, many whom vie for the attention of the scantily-clad female clientele who bump and grind to Colombian music well into the night. The front exterior was a stucco facade that had smooth curls, almost as if ocean waves topped the roofline. The green neon lit "La Covacha" above the opening was welcoming but upon stepping through the palm tree shaded facade on into a tiled courtyard it was obvious the place was just a mix of chickee huts lashed together.

It was early and the *thump thump* of the music hadn't started yet, which was good because the *thump thump* in my head was starting to rise from not eating. I sat down at one of the many bars and ordered the meat intensive Colombian soup *sancocho,* as well as a two small *chorizopan* sausage and bread sandwiches. The food came rather quickly and the *choriopanes* dipped in the *sancocho* was delicious. Midway through eating my cell phone rang.

7:16pm.

I didn't even bother answering it. It was Donito's number on the caller I.D. I'm sure he was calling to say he was running late. With the exception of today's Dominicans, dopers are notoriously late.

My cellphone rang again.

7:28pm.

This time I answered.

"Hello."

"Cade, where you now?"

"Donito. Oh, hey man, change of plans. Meet me at La Covacha."

"You said Mexico." His accent making it sound like 'Mehdiko.'

Although I'm sure he meant the restaurant, the juxtaposition of El Torito and Mexican cuisine were clearly understood by me.

"Yeah, yeah I know but I didn't like the atmosphere. Plus, it is right in the flight path of the airport. Ever since that DC-8 cargo plane crashed on Milam Dairy Road last year I don't want to be in the flight path. So just come to La Covacha. I should be pulling in myself in a minute or so," I lied.

Donito simply said, *"Puta,"* and hung up.

Being called a bitch regardless of your gender is fairly common and the insult or expression of exasperation Donito uttered really meant nothing to me. I couldn't have cared less. It was a minor verbal transgression lobbed at me. I was comfortable with it especially since it afforded me the advantage of being in place to gauge if Donito had any setup or ambush intentions. With Peralta quasi-swimming with the fishes as they say in every Italian Mafia movie, I wasn't taking any chances with any of the Horsemen. I thought about stepping outside to wait for him to arrive but a slow salsa love song with a steady beat had kicked in. Two very attractive Colombian women began to dance, the first to start dancing tonight but surely not the last to be on the dance floor by night's end. The raven-haired beauties were drawing the eyes of most of the men in the place, each man watching the hypnotic sway of their round asses. My approaching headache was stymied by the hearty meal, so I decided to order a Colombian Aquila beer. I was studying the blue and yellow label and couldn't help but notice the condensation on the bottle's dark glass. Gina always wrapped my beer in a paper napkin to avoid the wetness on my palm. I used to always rebel. I am very brand conscious and like the color and affinity of a brand to be shown.

Funny how your mind wanders into innocuous corners of your memory. I mean the simplest little thing can take you either whimsically or agonizingly down memory lane. Whimsical, I guess, is for the Hallmark moments of life, whereas agonizingly is its own version of PTSD.

I quickly realized that the two very pretty Colombian women were dancing seductively just feet away from me and I'm thinking about my ex-wife and her handling of my beer.

Something's gotta give.

I looked at the Corona beer clock behind the bar.

8:07pm.

I started to wonder just what was taking Donito so long to get here. My beer was nearly empty, and I contemplated ordering another, and perhaps one for Donito as some sort of Colombian amulet that would bring him here.

My decision process was interrupted by a young woman dressed in a white linen dress with wild, frizzy blonde hair topped by dark roots. She had a panicked look on her face and she was standing half in and half out of the establishment's double front doors shrieking,

"Alguien llama al 911, un tipo aquí está enfermo o algo"

I didn't get it all but I did pick up "Call 911, somebody's sick."

People who aren't accustomed to emergencies often just stop what they're doing and immediately fall into a voyeuristic trance as the world unravels in front of them. I've never known if it was a defense mechanism or just a whole lot of lack of life experience that causes people to gape and watch. We've all heard countless stories of a diner in a restaurant, choking. No one does anything until some busboy taking a cigarette break in the alley comes rushing in, dashing past the entire dining room, administers the Heimlich Maneuver and saves the patron who is seconds from death. It was very similar here. Most people either stopped and stared at her or actually ignored her and continued drinking and talking.

Being undercover is a bit of a dilemma because if you act in the capacity of a law enforcement officer then you'll possibly blow your cover. If you turn a blind eye to what's going on, then you're essentially turning a blind eye to an oath you took to serve and protect.

I kept my eyes trained on her as she implored again for someone to call 911. I had my phone lying flat on the bar and dialed 911. Miami Dade dispatch answered on the second ring. My phone wasn't on speaker but I could faintly hear the operator.

"Miami Dade Police and Fire, do you have an emergency?"

Rather than go into a big dissertation which would be time-consuming and possibly reveal me to the bar as a cop, I leaned way down and spoke very rapidly in code to the dispatcher.

"3-41 at La Covacha Nortwest 25th Street and Northwest 107th Avenue. Start fifteens."

Code is a second language that she fluently understood. She knew I said someone was injured and sick and it was an emergency and to send police units as well as rescue.

Her equally quick response was "QSL en route, QSK unit?"

In that short sequence of words she informed me that fire rescue and police were on the way and she was now asking me who I was.

As I disconnected the call, I noticed the bartender also hanging up the bar phone. Thankfully he called it in just prior to me calling. More calls meant more urgency.

A woman in black spandex pants and yellow and black zebra print blouse went over to the hysterical blonde in the doorway. Both a bouncer and a male patron hurried past the blonde and out to the parking lot. This was my cue to act like a curious patron and I steadily walked past the two embracing women. The zebra-shirted woman was trying to console the blonde.

I stepped into the parking lot which, although darkened with the twilight, still has a decent amount of visibility due to the high-crime vapor streetlights. The vapor lights cast everything in a surreal orange sepia light. Without the frizzy blonde to direct them the bouncer and patron were standing in the parking lot, trying to get a bearing on exactly what she was traumatized by. The parking lot had filled considerably with cars since my arrival, and I too was a bit perplexed—but for a moment.

It was then that I saw Donito's car parked about thirty yards from the front door and near the end of a row of cars and trucks.

But no Donito, which concerned me.

If he was here why didn't he come into the restaurant?

I kept walking towards his car. As I drew closer, that's when I saw Donito leaning over to his right side in the driver seat of his gray BMW 320i. He was slumped over towards the passenger seat and the passenger door was partially open a few inches. I called him a few times through his open driver side window.

No response.

I then reached in and shook him a little, and then shook him more vigorously. There still was no response.

Keeping my left hand on his left shoulder I looked over the roof of his car and scanned the parking lot. It was quiet, with the exception of the faint sounds of music wafting out from the restaurant.

The bouncer and the patron had realized that I'd discovered what the woman was shrieking about and stood a few cars away, looking at me. In the background I could see approaching red and blue lights. I asked the bouncer to direct the arriving police units to come to where I was.

Surprisingly, he turned on his heels and obediently did so, never asking me who I was.

The bar patron simply said, "*Boracho*" then turned and headed back into the restaurant to possibly become a drunk himself.

I was now alone with Donito. I put my three fingers on his carotid artery. There was no pulse.

Donito was dead.

Not only was Donito dead but he was dead in a parking lot that I'd summoned him to.

The bouncer walked briskly, keeping up with the first arriving Miami Dade police officer. The officer slowed, and started walking towards me very wary, keeping his hand on his holstered service weapon as he approached me.

I still had my hand on Donito's shoulder which was probably not the best thing to have been doing with a nervous police officer approaching me in a dark parking lot.

"Sir, step away from the vehicle and remove your arm slowly!" the officer commanded of me.

I slowly withdrew my arm from the window and bent both my arms at the elbow in a hands-up gesture. In doing so, I spread my fingers wide and my right thumb hooked the chain around my neck, sliding the chain up as I raised my arms, causing my badge under my shirt to rise up. Simultaneously as my badge was being exposed, I told the officer, "QRU he's 45."

Within the same amount of time to get a take-out order of food in Miami the parking lot was filled with police, fire rescue, and enough yellow crime scene tape to make Tony Orlando and his old oak tree extremely happy. I had already bound the bouncer to secrecy about my identity, and the first arriving officer and I had bonded since my declaration that I was a cop and that Donito was dead. I mentioned that they needed to sequester the blonde in the white linen dress. I had also told the officer that aside from notifying Miami Dade Homicide, he should specifically request Trentlocke as there was a good chance Donito's death is related in some way to Peralta's death.

I then went to one of the first few pick-up trucks that were in the parking lot, yet outside of the crime scene. I tried the tailgate and it was unlocked. Sitting on the tailgate of the pick-up truck under the pumpkin orange glow of the vapor lights, I waited for the inevitable shit show to start.

Chapter Ten

THE TEDIOUS TASK of interviewing anybody who may have seen anything, as well as the scouring of the surrounding areas for any potential security cameras fell upon the uniformed officers. It was now nearly 10pm, and although Homicide was processing the scene, Trentlocke still had not arrived. I waited until 10pm purposely before calling Poulsen. I wanted to nullify his inclination to come out to the scene. I was thankful the owner of the pick-up truck hadn't left yet and still used the tail gate as my sitting perch when I called Poulsen.

He picked up on the second ring.

"Yes, Cade?"

"Lieutenant, I wanted to bring you up to speed. I'm out here in West Dade and it looks like one of our informants got murdered in a restaurant parking lot."

"What? Who?"

"It's Don Julio Restrepo. "

"Wasn't he one of the cowboys?"

Correcting him slightly I replied, "He's one of the Horsemen. He was connected to Peralta from Matheson Hammock."

"How did this happen and how did you get called?" he asked.

"I was here at the restaurant, La Covacha on Northwest 25th street. I was supposed to meet him here and they found him in the parking lot in his car. Not sure yet how he died."

"Let me get this straight. One guy shows up dead with your business card and now you mean to tell me that days later another one that you're meeting is dead, too?" he asked incredulously.

"I don't know what to say other than yeah, at this point that's about right. Now I'm just here and they're processing the scene."

"Look Cade, two dead informants in nearly as many days, I don't need to tell you that Brunson will go ballistic. Has Zambrana shown up?

"No, its just the on-call homicide detectives so far."

"Alright, sit tight. Don't answer anything they ask that isn't absolutely pertinent. I'll call and have an FOP rep at least come by and be there if you need it."

Arguing about why or why not I would need legal representation was not going to get me anywhere.

"Okay," was all I said.

"I'll call Brunson and break the news. Be in the office at 9am. I'm sure he will want to see you. Look, try not to let this rattle you. Keep your cool. Don't paint yourself into a corner over this."

"Okay."

With that, he hung up.

There was no need to make any more calls for the evening. Besides, I could clearly see where this might be heading.

I walked over to my car which thankfully was out of the crime scene. I'd parked next to the dumpster in the far reaches of the parking lot. I opened the cargo area of the Explorer and in the side cargo area was a flush, but accessible compartment for the tire jack. I turned off my phone and put it in the compartment. I closed the lift gate and locked the Ford via the remote. I walked back and reclaimed my seat on the tailgate.

Under the vapor lights the fingerprint dust being applied on

Donito's car gave the gray BMW an Impressionistic-looking paint design of black inky swirls set against the metallic gray paint. A midnight-black sedan pulled up on the periphery of this decently populated scene. It was Zambrana looking not nearly as dapper tonight as he did in Brunson's office. He was wearing jeans and a navy banlon that said, "Coral Park Rams Booster Parent."

Seeing as it is mid-February, I suspect he got pulled from one of his kid's high school basketball games.

As he walked towards the scene, he noticed me sitting on the tailgate of the pick-up truck and momentarily glared at me with no hint of recognition. He kept walking and awkwardly bending at the waist, went under the crime scene tape. The knot in my stomach tightened just a little more and the headache I had chased away with the sancocho was making a reappearance.

The usual steps of a homicide investigation fascinates the curiosity in most people and kept a milling crowd of people entertained on the other side of the yellow tape. Every time a tape measure or flash bulb was employed a voice in the crowd would either give a narrative of what was happening or make an announcement of what the actual action was. The police had closed La Covacha for the night, and any possible witnesses were still being interviewed. A thick female officer with a yellowish ponytail and maybe one too many barrettes in her hair began herding the crowd with her open arms, saying to those who were not already being interviewed that "They don't have to go home but they can't stay here." Her technique, although done with a smile, was all business and quickly the crowd dispersed. Those whose cars were in the crime scene were told to come back in the morning and retrieve their cars but for now either get a ride home or call a taxi for themselves. There were some groans and disagreements to that idea, but she was very firm and her smile started to fade, which caused even the most vocal in the crowd to fade as well.

By 11:15pm the only people still in the parking lot were the M.E. personnel, the uniformed officers, homicide investigators, the bouncer, the now somewhat composed blonde in the white linen dress, and one bored tow truck driver summoned to tow Donito's car to the Medical Examiner's office.

The Miami Dade Medical Examiner's Office had a deep-bay enclosed garage. In an effort to preserve as much of the crime scene as possible they would be towing Donito's car with him still in it straight there to continue the investigation. I was able to hear a little of what the blonde was stating to investigators. She said that as she was parking her car she noticed Donito trying to open the passenger door from the driver's side. He was leaning to his right but was having trouble getting across the center console. She said he had a terrible look on his face and his eyes "looked big."

Zambrano came out of the scene and walked to me.

"Anyone talked to you yet?"

I was waiting for the lecture and hoping for the stall.

"No."

"We are going to continue this at the M.E.'s office."

"Okay."

"Which car is yours?"

"The dark blue Explorer over there by the dumpster."

I knew what was coming before he even said it.

Turning to the tow truck driver Zambrano said, "Take the Explorer to the M.E.'s office and get someone else out here to take the Beamer. Make sure they have a flatbed too." He then said to me, "Give me your keys."

I dutifully fished the keys out of my pocket and handed them to him. He in turn gave them to a nearby detective and told him to assist the tow truck driver by backing my car onto the lowered flatbed of the tow truck. He also admonished the detective to "wear gloves."

My vehicle, and in effect myself, were part of the investigation.

I asked Donito to meet me here. Donito was dead. The police showed up and saw me with my arm inside Donito's car. I could clearly see where this was going.

First came the lecture.

"Detective Taylor, perhaps you haven't noticed, but my county keeps finding dead guys that are connected you. I mean it's uncanny, no?

There was his Spanish syntax again.

"So, what is it about you? We hardly never hear anything about Coral Gables and now in the past couple of days I've had my morning and one of the best J.V. games my son has played this year, all interrupted by you. I don't know exactly what it is that causes death to follow you. I'd prefer you did it in Miami or Miami Beach because I'm not enjoying this little Mad Hatter tea party you seem to be a part of."

I was relieved he'd abstained from using profanity as I knew I'd hear enough of it from Brunson in the morning.

The tow truck driver had driven to my car. I could see the detective behind Zambrano maneuvering my car to be aligned for the cable of the tow truck.

The lecture continued, helping the stall.

"Seriously, I've been with the county nineteen years. Nineteen years! I can count on one hand how many times I've had to deal with your city and here I am twice in the same week. Twice!"

Zambrano felt that repeating tenure gave emphasis.

"The only common denominator is you. I've never met you before and now you're all over my desk. I asked about you. Not a lot of people know you. Those that do say you're a straight-up guy but that you're involved in dope and counterfeiting—"

"Money laundering. It's money laundering," I interjected.

"I don't care if it's Monopoly money! Can't you just do it somewhere else? Do me and my team have to keep sweeping up your mess?" His exasperation getting the better of him.

He recognized that people had taken notice of our conversation, so he adopted a softer tone and acting more like a chastising father than a police captain, he held out his hand and said,

"I need your phone."

Here comes the stall.

"Am I under arrest?" I asked.

Silence accompanied by another Zambrano glare.

"Am I?" I asked again, our eyes locking.

Since he wanted my phone, he was concerned with me calling someone.

I knew that putting it in the back cargo area of the Explorer it would become part and parcel to the Explorer. They were going to have to get a warrant to search my car.

This protected my phone for a few hours.

"I'm going to say this again. I need your phone."

Stall completed.

My car was on the apex of the tow truck, hooked, and being put onto the tow truck. I hesitated briefly to make sure the Explorer was off the ground and being loaded.

"It's in the Explorer."

The detective was now standing aside the tow truck my Explorer fully on the lift.

Zambrana spun towards the Explorer and said "Stop that driver—"

"You used one of *your* guys to put my car on *your* tow truck. *You* ordered him to do it. My car and the contents of my car are in your care and custody. You need a warrant to open the car and you'll need a separate warrant for my phone." I quickly said

By placing my phone in the tire jack compartment, I nixed any plain-view probable cause assertion they might try and create to expedite their investigation.

This time with the glare came a tightly-lipped hiss of profanity à la Brunson.

"You fucking asshole."

Chapter Eleven

T HE EXPLORER WAS loaded and red evidence tape was placed across the doors and the door frames. I infuriated Zambrano even more by using a pen to sign my name across the tapes in an attempt to secure an even greater lack of tampering along the way to the M.E.'s office. While I was signing the last one, I wondered if there had indeed been a blue pen in Donito's car.

A tarp was placed over Donito's car with him still in it, slumped over the center console. His car was put on a second flatbed and towed to the M.E.'s office. Zambrano played the emerging douche card well, not offering me a ride to the M.E.'s office and instead asking the female officer who earlier had dispersed the crowd to drive me. She feigned remorse that she couldn't clear away the contents of her passenger seat which was overloaded with her police gear, reports, and forms. I was put in the back of her patrol car.

It was definitely intentional.

The passive aggressive disrespect exhibited by Miami Dade by offering me a ride yet making me sit in the back was just gamesmanship.

That's all.

Gamesmanship.

In the back of the car I sat on the hard plastic seat. The seats are designed like that so that any blood, urine, vomit, or sweat can just be wiped down, or in worst case scenarios hosed out and released under the car via an insertable plug. I wasn't really interested in knowing much about her. She told me her name was Jenny. Her uniform nameplate said Irving.

Jennifer Irving.

It made no difference; she could've been Washington Irving for all I cared.

Ford makes two types of Crown Victoria vehicles. There's the taxi edition used to make the majority of taxis in the United States, including the swarms of yellow cabs in New York City. The other version is the Police Interceptor edition, of which most police departments in the United States choose for their fleet. Like Elwood Blues said in the Blues Brothers movie, "It's got cop tires, cop suspensions, cop shocks." At this very moment it was a Police Interceptor acting as a taxi.

That is what I was in.

Pulling out of the parking lot we passed a white Ford Contour pulling into the parking lot. The driver looked a little bewildered and had a lit cigarette dangling from the corner of his mouth. Ten-to-one odds he was my FOP union representative.

The cross-county drive was a blur. From Peralta to Donito I was trying to connect the proverbial dots in my head and was looking at it from Miami Dade's perspective. I just stared out the window at the passing cityscape. Zambrano was right. *"The only common denominator is you."* I was in the center of this. I had focused primarily on keeping myself safe and may have exposed Donito. Maybe I should have told him about Peralta and then he may have taken better precautions. I had always been very good at protecting my informants and now two of the Horsemen were dead. This was becoming too much to comprehend.

"I don't know exactly what it is that causes death to follow you."

That was a serious verbal judo chop. It certainly felt like death was following me. Taunting me. Circling around me. Now there were two Horsemen dead and one either luckily—or for all I knew, conveniently—out of the country.

Gustavo Peralta dead.

Don Julio-Restrepo dead.

Hector Gomez-Macias in Colombia.

The remaining Horseman I hadn't been in contact with yet was Roldan Osorio-Vidal. He was still out in the wind. I thought to myself that once I was through with Miami Dade, or actually when they were through with me, I'd need to smooth the choppy waters that Brunson would stir and then locate Roldan.

Now I was wondering if Roldan was responsible for both Peralta and Donito. It made sense that if Roldan was looking to cut two, if not three, of the other Horsemen out of the profits he could do quite nicely for himself. Maybe Donito told Roldan of our meeting.

It gave me reason to think maybe Roldan intended to smoke both me and Donito.

I remembered what Major Edwards said about TNT having a wire on a house in Coconut Grove. I made a mental note to learn what I could about the house, the wire, and just how Peralta got mixed up with all of that. Of course it would be much more difficult now that Peralta would be wearing a pine overcoat for eternity. Edwards specifically said that Peralta was heard on the wire saying said he couldn't *"trust no one"* and that there was a cop that needed to be *"taken care of."* There was no doubt in my mind that I was being targeted; it was just still very confusing to me as to why.

From my vantage point I could see the looping exit for 17th Avenue and the famed Orange Bowl in the near distance. I knew we were crossing over the Miami River by the vibration and whirr of the tires over the metal draw bridge. Downtown Miami off to my right was lit and shining in the night sky.

Jenny knew the way mostly until she got close to the Dade County Jail. No doubt prisoners who had sat in the same seat I was in had been transported to DCJ by Jenny plenty of times, but her knowledge of the M.E.'s office was sparse to say the least. As we neared the M.E.'s office which is very near to DCJ, her hesitancy started to show. She drove slowly past DCJ looking for a sign that might direct her. From the back seat and talking to her through the glass partition, I helped guide her to Northwest 9th avenue also known as Bob Hope Drive. Which made no sense because if your destination is the morgue at the Medical Examiner's Office there is a good chance you have seriously run out of hope. Bob's or anyone else's.

The M.E.'s office had the same odd taupe brick facade as the Coral Gables Police Department. This led me to wonder about the appeal of sheer lunacy and inept architectural design that had once been in South Florida.

We turned in off of 9th Avenue and were admitted through a manned gate. She parked on the side of the building adjacent to an empty but idling ambulance.

"End of the line," she said, not intending to be funny or ironic.

She opened the back door and as I stepped out she and I were both met by Trentlocke, who silhouetted by the buildings lights, cast a startling figure.

"Irving, just walk in with us 'til we get settled inside," is all he said.

Wonderful.

My old academy buddy wanted a back-up officer to walk with me until we were in a fully secured portion of the building.

Doors opened, doors closed, and through a short stretch of hallway. We ended up in a small office that must have been where young interns ply their trade. Boxes were on the floor with numerous pathology books and a few medical diplomas were on the wall. A few were on a chair. Neither had matching names. Obviously, an office in transition.

Irving stayed for the briefest of time and upon getting easy directions from there to the Dolphin Expressway, she was gone.

Trentlocke closed the door and he swept the representation of someone's medical school loans off the chair and into a pile near the chair's legs. We sat across from each other.

"You're not under arrest," he said.

"I know that. I'm only here because I left a Starbucks mug in my car that I'm really fond of."

"You got a real attitude," he snarled.

"Fuck you, I got an attitude. You and Zambrana have been intimating I'm involved in this from the start. He says his desk is full of me. You put me in the back of patrol car with an officer who can't find the M.E.'s office but likes to slowly drive by DCJ so I can get a good eyeful of our wonderful jail system. I might have been born at night but I wasn't born last night. That kind of stuff might work with first-time offender weenie whackers and high school kids toilet papering a house but I think you know me, Lloyd. Hell, you cheated off me in constitutional law in the academy. I've been out here as long, if not longer, than her or anyone else you want to throw at me so cut the bullshit and let's figure out who's killing these guys."

The memory of cheating on a test in the academy broke through the veneer and actually made Trentlocke smile.

"Okay let's back up some here. This guy you were with tonight, Restrepo. What can you tell me?"

"Lloyd, don't start that with me. You had to be clued in. I was not with him. I repeat: I was not with him. I was supposed to *meet* him. He showed up, obviously, but I was inside and didn't know he was there."

"Responding officers saw you exiting his car," he flatly said back.

"Exiting his car? Look, some girl came into the place saying someone was sick outside. I went out and saw his car. I saw him. He was unresponsive. Now, unless I was sitting on his lap how was I supposed to be exiting his car? When the units arrived, I'd just done a shake and shout and was checking his pulse from outside, through his window," I said.

"Fair enough. Still…it needs looking into, wouldn't you agree?" he retorted.

I was getting heated.

"I *don't* agree. I don't agree to anything. I'm *complying*. See? I'm sitting here, gratis. I don't have to be here. This is not agreeing. This is complying. This is me, trying to help *you* but also help *me*, because whatever's going on has a *me* component to it—as in me here, me there, me next, me possibly dead. Get it? Right now, I'm all about me. We have a shared objective. Your objective and my objective are in line. You want these murders solved. I want them solved. So I can stop worrying about me."

"You know he's still here," said Trentlocke.

"Who? Peralta?"

"Yup. No one has claimed him yet. Autopsy done, report finished."

"Okay, so how'd he die?"

"I'm willing to bet this BMW guy was probably killed the same way."

"Quit screwing with me. How'd he die?"

"Better yet, why don't you and I walk over to the cold storage section and we'll get one of the attendees? Or if we're lucky, one of the pathologists will be here so you can see for yourself."

Trentlocke rose from his seat with those words, opened the office door and stepped out. I waited a beat, mulling over how this was all of a sudden becoming such a production, then decided to just stride out behind him.

We walked through a series of fluorescent-lit hallways, past offices and bulletin boards. Some of the doors had charts in plastic sleeves outside; others had a birthday greeting or a note reminding people not to use the vending machines because they aren't giving back change. This was a building of death. Live people come here to spend their living days working until they themselves die. That was all that I could think of as we traversed through the labyrinth of hallways. It was a longer walk than expected and I realized we were traversing the length of the building. We turned a corner that had a large bank of glass windows, providing a view of the brightly-lit garage. Donito's BMW was there and they'd removed the tarp. Two Miami Dade Homicide detectives and three M.E. employees were there, all garbed up in TyVek suits. I could just see Donito's left shoulder. He was still slumped over to his right. I stopped to look for a second. Trentlocke kept walking before noticing I'd stopped. He came back and looked through the window at the milieu on the other side of the glass with me.

"It will be a while, but if my assumption is correct, I still think they both went the same way," he said.

He quietly turned towards our original direction and with one last glance at Donito—or more aptly his shoulder—I followed along. We finally got to a secure section and Trentlocke picked up a telephone mounted outside a set of double doors. The bottom eighteen inches of the doors had thin sheet metal plates screwed into the doors. I thought we must be near to where we are going because those plates are meant to keep the doors from being damaged by gurneys. My thought was interrupted by a loud clicking sound as the doors were unlocked remotely and Trentlocke pulled the handle. We stepped into a large reception-type area that smelled faintly like formaldehyde, and Simple Green cleaning solution. A young man who Trentlocke introduced to me as Arum was inside. Trentlocke asked to see Peralta and assisted Arum by pointing out to him he was in #18.

Arum was proud to show off the new directory system they had and punched up a series of codes and numbers on a laptop computer.

"You want to go in with a copy?" Arum asked hopefully.

"Yes," said Trentlocke.

Almost giddy with pride Arum punched a few more keys and remotely a printer started printing a thirteen-page document.

"They call it S2S, stands for Source 2 Source. We got a grant and MCI installed it. No more walking to the printer and lifting the lid," Arum said with pride.

The thirteen pages printed very quickly. Arum, who failed to see the irony that he still had to walk to the printer, got up and crossed the room to retrieve the pages, and handed them to Trentlocke.

After Arum punched a numerical code into a keypad, we stepped into a much colder room than the one that Arum worked out of. It was eerily quiet but for the slight hum of the air conditioner chillers. Large stainless steel drawers were recessed into the walls, arranged in columns of two and two rows deep twenty aside. Eighty potential drawers for cadavers. The facility had come a long way since the early 1980s when the building's namesake, Dr. Joe Davis, had to rent a refrigeration truck for the overflow of corpses from all of the drug killings and rip-offs..

With a practiced ease Arum tugged on the handle of drawer 18. The drawer rolled on smooth casters and as he pulled it to its full length it revealed Gustavo Peralta.

He was lying on his back a white sheet with a small yellow stitched tag at the bottom liner of the sheet. The sheet tag had a 98-029 written on it in marker. Gustavo had a yellow plastic band affixed to his left wrist—it too had the number 98-029.

He had definitely looked better.

The pallor of his skin under the fluorescent lights was a jaundiced yellow and the sutures of the autopsy were professionally haphazard. They were binding enough to be passable but designed to be reopened if the medical examiner needed to go back inside his corpse for additional inquiry. That left a zig-zag pattern of staples and thread that were most unbecoming. The lifeless form on the stainless slab was devoid of any essence and for a brief moment my mind reflected on the religious ideology of souls and spirits.

Trentlocke stood across from me, Gustavo between us. He looked over at Arum, and with a slight head shake communicated that he wanted some privacy. Arum excused himself dutifully and asked that we come get him when we were finished.

Trentlocke started perusing the documents. Although far from a medical doctor his homicide experience was far superior to my own and he started looking for the exact paragraph that he wanted to share with me.

I continued to survey Gustavo with intent, much the same as the guy broken down on the side of I-95 with a raised hood looks at his car engine, pretending he knows what he's looking at. I didn't exactly know what I was looking for but it was a good use of time faking it until Trentlocke finally spoke.

"You see the slight bruising in the thorax area and blotchy pin red dots on his cheeks and orbital areas?"

I wasn't entirely seeing the red blotches but the differential in yellowing with some darkened areas around his neck was evident. I just nodded, pursing my lips.

"M.E. says Atlanto-Occipital Dislocation," said Trentlocke

"Atlantic what?"

He repeated, "Atlanto. Atlanto-Occipital Dislocation. The report abbreviates it as A.O.D."

"What does that mean?"

"Basically, he died of a broken neck. According to the M.E. report... 'Noted rupture of spinal meninges and anterior Atlanto-Occipital ligamentous structures discovered via roentgenographic comparisons in conjunction with Vinke tong stabilization. The deceased had surface facial petechial hemorrhages, type III posterior dislocation, unsurvivable force injury to the ligaments between the occiput and upper cervical spine. Connective ligaments joining the axis and atlas to the clivus, occipital bone and occipital condyle were trauma-frayed and sheared. Bruising or post-mortem tissue degradation to the Sternocleidomastoid, Scalenus Posterior and Serratus Posterior Superior as well as most areas of the Capitis and Medius show mild to semi-tensile loss."

"All that to say a broken neck?" I asked him.

"It goes a little beyond that. You see all this bruising, especially on the right side of his neck? The neck was broken in such a way that the head no longer had the rotating function it normally does on your shoulders. Airway was compromised most likely as well."

"Well your Lieutenant Ramirez was making an issue of it possible being a floater from the bay."

"Yeah, I know. I had to go through the whole thing with Ramirez to get it clearly understood—it wasn't a marine patrol issue, not an overtime opportunity for them to sea-grid search the bay for others. Your boy died right where we found him."

Now looking even more closely at Gustavo's neck I asked Trentlocke what he did think.

"I think the pictures in this report show that someone pressed deeply on his lower back and mid to lower ribs. Our deceased here was face-down in the water and the back of his pant legs were dry. He was never fully in the water. Someone kneeled or stood on his back and killed him, face-down at the water's edge. Torso and chest pushed into the rocky water line, he lifted his legs to try and kick or buck our killer off his back. Based on an A.O.D. cause of death there's a good chance the killer stood on him, maybe straddled him, and pulled his chin and neck up from his prone position. Connective neck ligaments were sheared, head started to flop, untethered, and more pressure was applied, breaking the neck. That, in addition to neck trachea swelling and being face-down in water, he died. But realistically, by themselves or in combo he was dead."

I took in everything he was saying and tried to visualize just how it was that Gustavo was murdered. He didn't walk into Matheson Hammock Park at that late hour. The county worker who checks the parks at night never saw him or his killer enter or leave . He must've been driven in by the killer. The killer must've had something to say or show him at the water's edge.

What brought them to the water's edge?

"You still here?" Trentlocke asked.

"I was just thinking back to that night. Does it say anything about his bladder?"

Thumbing through the pages Trentlocke settled on page five.

"Deceased combined lung weight was 675 grams. Right lung was 334 grams, left lung was 341. Lack of plural effusion or any fluids from the environment, air-infused sputum or blood in trachea as well as lack of other liquid in lungs. See, so that's why it's a broken neck and not drowning. No fluid in the lungs," he said.

"Okay, but what about the bladder?"

"I'm getting there...let's see...stomach contained only twenty-four milliliters of a congealed brownish-auburn liquid that had a finely chewed and undetermined food source intermingled within. The bladder was empty."

"How much is twenty-four milliliters?" I asked him.

"Just under an ounce. Very little emptying of the stomach and digestive system starts in the first half hour. Food leaves the stomach after four to six hours, and it's varied by amount and density. What's up with the bladder?"

"Well, I'm trying to figure out why he was at the water's edge. I remember his zipper on his pants was partly down. I'm just thinking, if he was taking a leak and he got jumped from behind. His right arm was under his body...maybe the killer jumped him while he was pissing and that's how he died."

Trentlocke was giving me an A for effort but quickly shot holes in the theory although he didn't deviate from it entirely.

"There was a decent struggle, I'm sure. No one usually goes through a death like that without a struggle. That's why I think he was kicking and bucking. One of his shoes came off in the struggle. I see what you're saying and I agree, he might've have been looking at the city lights or even peeing. But upon death, all those muscles you learned as a kid to contract your bladder, they release when you die. Him being in salt water he could've just peed his pants in the surf there, post mortem. The marks on his back lead me to think that the killer straddled him and then did a classic wrestling lariat. As a kid if you ever watched 'Wrestling from Florida with Gordon Solei,' there was a guy called The Great Malenko. He did a signature move, the 'Russian Sickle,' where you get your opponent on his stomach then you sit on him or straddle him, and you interlock your fingers under his chin and you pull up 'til he submits. But in this case, our killer pulled up 'til he killed him with an A.O.D."

"You're serious?" Looking down at Gustavo and then back across at me, he dryly said, "I'm dead serious."

Chapter Twelve

TRENTLOCKE SUMMONED ARUM. He came in and pushed Gustavo back into the recesses of drawer 18.

Trentlocke and I started walking back within the maze of hallways to the section of the building that he and Officer Irving had initially brought me to. I wanted to ask him just how he thought that Donito was murdered in the same fashion as Gustavo. It made no sense to me. There wasn't enough room in Donito's BMW for someone to get behind him and wrench his neck until he died. I thought that Trentlocke had made an absurd hypothesis and I needed to challenge him and see why he thought that.

"So you think that Donito was killed the same way as Gustavo?"

"Not exactly. But there is a similarity, if my guess is right," he replied.

We were drawing closer to the garage where we'd seen Donito inside his car when it was being preliminarily examined.

Trentlocke knew the M.E.'s labyrinth of hallways better than I did. I could sense he was thinking something. I assumed we were getting closer because the semi-darkened corner ahead had an incandescence of light just beyond it. The light got stronger as we neared.

"I saw something out on the scene in the parking lot. It was in the car. I still think he went out similar to the last guy," said Trentlocke.

"I'm still curious. Why are you hanging out in those types of bars?" he asked me.

"Why are you hanging out in morgues?" I asked in return.

"Good point."

We rounded the corner and the formidable bright lights of the garage were shining through the large plate glass windows into our hallway vantage point. The two Miami Dade Homicide detectives were not there. Only one M.E. technician, off to the side, sitting on a barstool by a red Milwaukee mobile work station. He was wearing magnifying loupes on his glasses, and was studying something in his gloved hands.

Standing by the driver side door of the BMW was a woman. I had not seen her before. She was slender and wearing lavender surgical scrubs. Her medium-dark skin, almond-brown eyes and coal-black hair in a loose bun were a striking contrast to the over-lit brightness in the room. Three hair nets were on the floor near her feet. From the hairnets I assumed she'd been in and out of Donito's car a lot and was concerned about cross-contamination of the crime scene. Whatever it was she'd been doing, it seemed as if she was taking a break. She was holding Titanium EMS Shears in her left hand and a small black 35mm camera in her right hand. Every so often when she moved her left wrist, the intense overhead lights caught glimpses of her stainless steel Movado bracelet watch. The flitting light was both distracting and entertaining from the hallway windows. She noticed me looking at her through the window. Our eyes met. She then turned back towards the outside driver's side door of Donito's car. He was still inside.

Trentlocke opened a flimsy metal cabinet in the hallway and pulled out two vacuum-packaged Ty-Vek suits and tossed one to me. He ripped the packaging off of his suit and with well-practiced ease, stepped into the garment.

"Coming in?" was all he said.

I followed his lead and emulated his dressing technique. With a little assistance from him I too was fully garbed in the suit. From the mounted basket near the door he retrieved three sets of surgical latex gloves. He tucked two inside the suit near his chest and donned the third pair. I did the same.

We walked into the garage from the hallway door and the suits made a paper rustling swish sound with each step. Trentlocke called out to the woman in the lavender scrubs. "Dr. Bashir, I see we got you in here at this late hour." As we closed the gap between us, he introduced the doctor to me.

"Dr. Bashir, this is Cade Taylor from the Gables. Cade, this is Dr. Sabah Bashir, the Assistant Medical Examiner."

Small talk ensued for a few minutes as Trentlocke explained why I was here, my connection to Gustavo, my connection to Donito, and I in turn learned that she was here only for another six months since she would be moving on after five years of being in Miami. She'd be going back to her home city of Toronto to be the M.E. there. It was odd, talking casually as if we were all at some sushi restaurant, except for dead Donito and the two of us dressed as though we were doing haz-mat detail in Chernobyl.

Trentlocke also explained that Dr. Bashir did the autopsy on Gustavo. I could feel my eyebrow arch. Infused with a bit of doubt and desirous of going straight to the source, I asked her how Gustavo was killed.

She slipped the camera into a hip pocket of her scrubs as she answered me.

"Lateral displacement of the spinous and dispersal of the axis center from occipital protuberance was the largest factor to cause Atlanto-Occipital Dislocation and inherently damage the Medulla oblongata."

I looked at her and was thankful for what Trentlocke had told me as we stood over drawer 18, but coming from her it started to sound all foreign to me again. She could sense I was processing her comment and to ease my lack of complete medical jargon she just said, "His neck was broken."

I could see Trentlocke reflected in the BMW windshield as he looked up at the ceiling and just shook his head in a "Hey dummy, I told you so" fashion.

I then asked her how much strength would one need to be able to kill someone the way Gustavo was killed. This time she spoke in plain speak so I could understand her.

"Not much at all. It's a leverage act. You've seen some people twist a bottle top off a bottle by holding the bottle in one hand and twisting the top with the other hand, while others pop it off with a thumb, holding it in the same hand? Same principal. The ability is more in leverage and technique than strength. The head is attached by the spinal column, held by ligaments, the throat cavity, and muscles. If you twist and pull it against its normal resting position, or further than its permissible axis, it dislodges from the spinal column causing paralysis, but most often death."

Looking past her I spied Donito still slumped over to his right in his car. I asked Trentlocke what happened to the two homicide detectives. He explained that one of them was Homicide and was probably around the building somewhere using his cell phone. We were now near 2:30am and the feasibility of someone making a phone call at that late hour was a stretch.

He's off processing my own car, I thought.

The other detective we'd seen in the Ty-Vek suit wasn't Homicide but was from the Accident Investigation Unit, according to Trentlocke.

"Why did you need AIU?"

"I saw something on the scene that I needed to rule out and I think by having him here it will help Dr. Bashir do her job easier."

Dr. Bashir informed me and Trentlocke that the AIU detective had gone through the whole front end of the car and had gone under the undercarriage. He left Dr. Bashir with his notes, which the technician handed to Trentlocke.

Trentlocke read the notes out loud.

"Undercarriage shows no discernible ripples or crash impact marks. Slight remnants of long-standing fur, most likely from striking a cat or possum weeks, if not months ago. Paint samples consistent with rear and all four doors. No discernible effects or evidence of any prior damage or collision present."

Trentlocke looked at Dr. Bashir. She notified him that Homicide had taken their pictures and she was done taking her own pictures of Donito in the car. Trentlocke motioned to me to draw closer to Donito's driver side door.

"What do you see?" he asked as I peered into the BMW. I kept looking at Donito. Trentlocke saw the direction my eyes were focused and corrected me to look at the dashboard and instrumentation of the BMW. Since AIU had been called in and gave a summary of whether the BMW had ever been in an accident I steadied my gaze upon the dials and gauges of the car.

"You see those small drops of blood and what looks like spit or saliva on the odometer and gas gauge?

Now that I'd been prompted to look, I did in fact see the drops. They were small but had little tails on them.

"The little elongations at the end of the drops are directional indicators," Dr. Bashir added. "When they look like little comets it can tell us how close the secretor, or in this case the victim was from origin to droplet deposit. Each of these droplets has an elongation going in the same direction. So, if our victim here had cut his finger and was driving, as he turned the steering wheel, the droplets would give either a round, left, or right pattern. Here we see that the droplets are all going in the same direction."

I was peering into the car with my hands on my knees slightly bent over. Trentlocke had moved over to the passenger side of the BMW and was looking in from the open passenger window. Our eyes met over the dead body of Donito. Oddly enough it was the second time we had looked at each other over a dead body, although not the same dead body, in the last hour. This had to be a new personal record.

"Like Dr. Bashir said, they are all going in the same direction and relatively the same in pattern, density, and diameter. This looks like a forced strike and hard impact spray," said Trentlocke, who appeared to see nothing peculiar that we were once again talking face to face over a dead body.

"Look at the steering wheel," he prompted.

The steering wheel had some type of smear marks and a very slight bend near the top right. Pretty clearly, some serious blunt force trauma had occurred.

Dr. Bashir, also looking at the steering wheel, said to Trentlocke, "I definitely see what you were talking about when you called."

Now that I was much closer I looked at the entire interior of the car, including Donito. I noticed something was odd about his hair. The usually well-coiffed Colombian's hair at the back of his head was noticeably out of place and entangled. It reminded me of a certain drum majorette from college who was more than just a bit promiscuous. My roommate always commented on her "fuck knots" at the back of her head.

"I don't know if this means anything but Donito was always impeccably groomed and his hair here looks like a Kansas tornado went through the back of his hair here," I said to anyone out loud.

Trentlocke and Dr. Bashir just looked at each other knowingly.

"Detective Taylor, if you don't mind, can you step aside and let me in here? I want to look at the body even closer," Dr Bashir asked.

"Yeah come over here and see it from this side," Trentlocke said.

The view was indeed different from Trentlocke's side. The right side of Donito's face was smooshed into the passenger seat, his right eye winced and shut. His left eye was just an opaque milky-white orb, the pupil pushed up to the top of his orbital socket. His bottom lip was caked with dried blood and between the tight grooves of his bottom teeth were small ribbons of darkened red blood, making each tooth to appear as though they'd been outlined haphazardly by a child with a crayon. His tongue, although not fully protruding out of his mouth, was slightly visible, and it appeared to be twice its normal size. The swollen tongue made his cheeks seem full. His entire throat was a yellowish-purple color and it looked like maybe his left collarbone was broken or bruised because a lump jutted against the fabric inside his collar. Rigor mortis, especially on his right side, had started and the pooling of blood on his right arm and side were becoming evident. His right hand and fingertips had equally swollen larger than their normal size and were engorged with his now useless body fluids. Dr. Bashir cut away the left side of Donito's expensive Franco Musso designer shirt. Her shears effortlessly cut a straight line from the bottom hem line all the way to the arm pit. She cut across his chest, then across his left trapezius towards the very back of the shirt's collar.

She peered at Donito's exposed skin, stepped back a foot or two and said, "Guys you might want to come see this."

Chapter Thirteen

I WASN'T TOO SURE what to make of her request. Usually when someone says, "you need to see this," it does not bode well for the object of the request or the person being asked to partake in the observation. Trentlocke and I both walked around to her side of the BMW and stood adjacent to Dr. Bashir.

Donito with his shirt cut away was a dull, sickening white color but clearly visible under his left armpit and along his side were four small red welts, slightly raised and close together. They looked a little like a wasp sting or an allergy reaction.

Trentlocke looked over Dr. Bashir's shoulder and matter-of-factly said, "Yup just as I figured." Dr. Bashir nodded in agreement. I was obviously not involved in this post-mortem discussion and was waiting for more clarification so I could at least make some comment rather than just stare dumbly at Donito's skin rash.

"Skin rash?" I asked.

Dr. Bashir looked squarely at Trentlocke and jutted her head my way with raised eyebrows.

"Cade, when you saw Peralta in the water at Matheson Hammock he was face down. Do you remember this 'skin rash?"

In my mind I replayed being led by Trentlocke to Peralta's body in the water. He was face down. One shoe was off. Right arm tucked under his body. He had a contusion or small scrape on...and then it hit me.

"Actually now that I think of it I do."

Dr. Bashir smiled. It was her time to say something.

"He actually had four others, all in the upper shoulder blades and one near his spine at the belt line. They aren't skin rashes. They're thermal burns. Each thermal burn caused pre-deceased ischemia to the localized area of contact. Very slight vasoconstriction which caused the visible erythema. Had it been more serious we would be seeing coagulative necrosis but since these are minor thermal burns and they were post-mortem they retained in the epidural. Since they are on both of the deceased we can preliminarily say that the same killer or killers killed both men in similar fashion."

Thankfully without prodding or making me feel stupid she repeated herself without the medical terms.

"Both men were probably killed by the same killer or killers with the same technique. Part of that technique involved a very potent electrical charge that did minimal damage but enough damage to cause a reddening and swelling at the point of contact. It's a slight burn and the recuperative value of the marks were basically forgotten as the body was too busy trying to save itself rather than tend to a minor burn, so when they died the marks stayed on the skin for a little longer."

Trentlocke punctuated her explanation with one word.

"Stun gun."

I had never heard of a stun gun being lethal and needed to know more.

"You mean a stun gun? Like a taser?"

"My guess is more of a stun gun. Five years ago, Taser introduced the 'Anti-Felon Identification System,' where when it's deployed it releases confetti pieces of paper that have a model number registered to the exact unit. We would have found some of them out at Matheson Hammock, had it been a taser."

"Unless it was a drive stun," I countered.

"A drive stun?" asked Dr. Bashir.

I explained that a drive stun is when you remove the taser cartridge and use the taser itself as a spearing weapon. The copper leads and charged prongs are in the cartridge. If you remove the cartridge you can pull the taser trigger as you directly place or drive stun the taser against someone. It will effectively render someone incapacitated as long as you keep the gun's electronic charges against their body.

According to Trentlocke's theory Gustavo Peralta was at the water's edge in Matheson Hammock. The killer, using a stun gun jolted Peralta in the lower back near his belt line. This caused Peralta to drop to his knees and convulse from the electronic charge. The killer, using his left hand, subsequently pushed Peralta onto his stomach with Peralta now falling nearly completely into the water. The killer straddled Peralta from behind and moved the taser from his lower back to his upper back near his shoulder blades. The second charge caused Peralta to flail and in between charges he fought by kicking and trying to buck the killer off his back, thus losing one shoe in the process. With the taser in one hand and the other tightly around Peralta's neck the killer used both hands to pull up and stretch Peralta's neck while straddling him. Each time Peralta showed formidable resistance or was close to breaking free he got stunned again. The killer, with stun gun in hand, then went back to using his hands to wrench up and back on Peralta's neck, the force of which coupled with the stun gun in one hand caused the tracheal bruising on Peralta. He zapped him enough times and pulled up enough times to create the A.O.D.

It all made total logical sense.

It all made total sense pertaining to Gustavo Peralta—but I wasn't following the connection to Donito.

"So if what you're saying is true about Peralta, how do you figure it's the same with Donito?" I asked.

"Detective Taylor, both Detective Trentlocke and I are in

agreement about the manner of death that occurred with the deceased, Peralta. But what we're about to tell you is not an official determination but one that in my telephone discussion with Detective Trentlocke merits a directional path to be taken in our approach to a conclusion. So I will turn the floor over to Detective Trentlocke but I think at this preliminary junction his theory and our findings are running parallel."

Although I was wearing something akin to a moon suit after her little dissertation, I felt that I was at some parliamentary meeting at a Rotary Club.

Trentlocke began where she left off.

"Okay, so let's see what we have here in the BMW. You noted that the hair on the back of his head was ruffled and unkept. Dr. Bashir has shown us the same type of thermal burns we saw on the body of Peralta. I pointed out the smudgy and slightly bent steering wheel and blood droplets on the instrumentation of the BMW. So, let's walk through the process of all three observations. Our killer is predominantly right-handed. Donito here knew him and opened the car door to him. Our killer steps in and with his right hand, grabs Donito by the hair at the back of his skull. With his left hand he jabs the first stun charge into Donito's left side. Donito is now incapable of moving or fighting and is in full electrical surge. Still holding him by the back of the scalp, the killer slams Donito's chin into the steering wheel an undetermined number of times. Spit and blood spew onto the instrument board and steering column. He keeps drawing Donito's head back and then forward into the steering wheel. We can see that by the trajectory of the droplets." At this point Trentlocke has stepped into the open door adjacent Donito's body and was pointing at the dashboard of the BMW.

"So now more drive stuns and now Donito is injured and being shocked. More slams into the steering wheel but now it's his neck that is being rammed into the steering wheel repeatedly. Crushed windpipe and possible neck fractures, Donito's aspirating blood, windpipe is potentially crushed. He's struggling, tries to crawl out the passenger side, and this is as far as he made it." Trentlocke motioned at Donito sprawled across the center console.

"Minutes later our witness Maritza Delano, walking into the restaurant, sees his last gasps and runs in and screams for someone to call 911."

"You mean the frizzy blonde, right?" I asked.

"I'm going off of the road unit report. I wasn't there. You were. You were there and you were standing here in the car doorway when road units arrived. You also knew both deceased individuals. I'm giving wide berth here but you can see how we view this."

I took note of the plural use of him saying how 'we' view this, although I wasn't sure if he meant himself and Dr. Bashir or the Miami Dade Police Department as a whole.

I could feel my face redden and was acutely aware of Dr. Bashir potentially witnessing an outburst by me so I kept my tact as civil as I could when I asked him, "I'm sure there are security cameras in La Covacha. Why don't you, or someone else review the cameras and see me? Better yet, scan the parking lot footage and see if you can spot our killer on tape."

Our warm, fuzzy, late-night talk under the bright lights of the morgue was nearing its expiration point. Through the side door entered the other Miami Dade Homicide detective. He looked tired. He'd pulled his Ty-Vek suit down to his waist, wrapping the arms around his waist and knotting it like a sorority girl at his midriff.

The detective had two clear zip lock bags in his hands. One had my car keys in it. The other was bigger and looked to have multiple items in it.

Dr. Bashir shot him a look of displeasure. He immediately picked up on her look and before she could say anything he announced that he was only dropping the bags off and would be out of the garage right away. The bags were put upon the Milwaukee mobile work station. He left as quickly as he entered.

After he left, Dr. Bashir spoke first.

"We've done what we can here with measuring and photography. I'll have two of our guys remove him and we'll prep him and store him for autopsy. I won't be doing it now. I'm too tired. I need a few key people and things here as well. I have gone into the scheduling coordinator's office and penciled him in for 11am. You both are welcome to come back at that time. It should take about three hours. If not, Detective Trentlocke you can stop by or call my office after 4pm. Detective Taylor, have a good night."

She then met with the technician at the Milwaukee mobile work station and walked out of the garage.

"You piss me off," said Trentlocke.

"You piss me off too," I said.

I followed him over to the Milwaukee station. He grabbed the two plastic bags and then we went back into the hallway to disrobe and discard the Ty-Vek suits. Once in the hallway and free of the suits he opened the zip lock bag and handed my keys to me. "Usually they put it on the south side when they're done. Near where that ambulance was when you came in." I looked at the keys and since my cell phone wasn't in the bag I assumed they either didn't find it, or opted out of securing a warrant.

The bigger bag he opened, splayed the contents on a table in the hallway. It took a second, but I soon gathered it was the relevant contents of Donito's car. There was a prescription pill bottle from Navarro Pharmacy for Cimetidine, a known heart burn medication usually prescribed under the generic name of Tagament; a BMW key chain with keys and a small miniature woven jai alai cesta all on the same key ring; three business cards, one from a realtor, a window installer, and a flooring company; two receipts from Jiffy Lube oil changes, both spanning 9 months.

And there were three blue pens in the bag.

There also was a restaurant check written in Spanish and dated less than twenty-four hours ago.

In crudely scripted Spanish it said, *"Huevos revueltos, tocino crujiente, tostadas cubanas y café con leche"* Scrambled eggs, crispy bacon, Cuban toast and cafe con leche.

It was from Reuben's Cuban Cafe.

Chapter Fourteen

I SAW THE RESTAURANT check from Reuben's and almost jumped out of my skin—which if you're going to do such a life threatening thing, I guess the morgue is as good a place as any to do it. I was shook to my core and needed to hide my aghast state from Trentlocke. I immediately dropped to one knee and started untying and tying my shoe to buy some time to compose myself. I needed to get away from Trentlocke soon, and I needed some fresh air too.

I gave a grunted affirmative response when Trentlocke asked me if I remembered the way out. We shook hands very quickly and I averted my eyes as best as I could as I turned and began to seek my way out of the Medical Examiner's office. With only one fleeting wrong turn I did, in fact, find my way to the south side exit where the Explorer was parked in a marked loading zone. There was some remnants of fingerprint dust on the doors. It was obvious that Miami Dade had tried to clean up there processing mess, but like every good plumber will tell you, they leave the pipes leaking a little so that you know they were there. So did Miami Dade. They left enough of a mess to let me or anyone else know they'd been there. There was a latex glove on the seat and the driver's floor mat was crooked and creased from where they'd closed the door on it.

I stood outside the open driver's door and just took in the night air. I needed an oxygen-infused brain sweep. I always operated very well on very little sleep but the pace of the past days was catching up, even to me. I opened the lift gate and retrieved my cell phone from the back compartment. It was untouched.

I started up the Ford and unlike Officer Irving, I knew exactly where I was going when I drove out of the parking lot. I took the 12th Avenue bridge south over the Miami River and continued south on 12th Avenue to the odd triangular intersection at Coral Way. Turning west on Coral Way I stopped at the first twenty-four hour gas station I saw that had a car wash. I took the opportunity to top off my tank using a U.C. credit card, and I opted for the deluxe car wash too. The water from the automatic car wash was loud on the roof of the Explorer but the beading and cascading water droplets on the windshield were hypnotically soothing. A bright red light was shining in front of me and made the car wash water seem like red beads of glass sliding down the windshield. It was in the car wash that I started to actually think about what was happening around me.

It was too coincidental. How could Donito have gotten my restaurant check? How did he know? How could he have known? None of it made any sense to me at all.

The car wash had ended and the red light had turned green. It was 4:17am and Poulsen had said to be in Brunson's office by 9am. I needed to sleep, although I wasn't sure if I could. I drove further west into Coral Gables. I didn't want to revisit the options of two nights ago in the VIN office or even onboard *The Ruthless*.

I drove past the retail shops and restaurants where Coral Way becomes known as Miracle Mile. I continued into the ficus tree-darkened parking lot of the Coral Gables Library on Segovia Street. It was quiet and empty. I climbed into the back seat and used the go bag as a pillow. Just before drifting off to sleep I heard the soothing rhythm of rain drops on the Explorer. Early spring night rains. My last thought before falling asleep was had I known it would rain I could've saved $4.50 on a car wash.

That and Gina.

I hadn't set an alarm and was counting on warm February Miami sunshine streaming through the Explorer windows to wake me up. Instead of waking to bathing sunlight I got the ear screeching sound of a leaf blower from a yard crew cutting the library grass and trimming the croton rushfoil bushes.

It was 8:05am.

Fifty-five minutes 'til I had to be in Major Brunson's office. The avoidance of sleeping in my own home was starting to weigh on my mind. I knew it was my own thing going on in my head but I was feeling it more and more. I needed to come to terms with the finality of Gina and I being done.

I also had to figure out how Donito had gotten my breakfast receipt and what was he doing holding it in his car?

I replayed the conversation with Donito on the telephone. I should've asked him where he was. Like with Hector Gomez-Macias, I just assumed he was in Miami until he let it be known he was actually in Colombia. That reminded me that a follow-up phone conversation just to keep him steady should be placed soon. I couldn't assume anything when it came to the Horsemen. Had I asked where Donito was I might have been able to keep my control of him. Now I was playing catch-up.

The leaf blowers were becoming intolerable. I didn't want to go to the station looking a mess, especially if I had to see Major Brunson. I drove north to the Granada Golf Course where there was a little cafe adjacent to the golf pro shop. It was serious old guard clientele there and the entire place still had a retro 1960s, 1970s feel. Jalousie windows and thread-thin green carpet in the pro shop. Behind the old Formica counter was "Swifty," the golf teaching pro. The ceiling-mounted television was tuned to the "Today Show." I don't think he ever left the operable range of the TV remote control, let alone gave a golf lesson. I walked into the terrazzo floor, red vinyl bar stool cafe and was met sweetly by the nearly octogenarian waitress. She had a lot of pleasant talk and nearly as much Jean Nate body splash. I ordered a three egg special with coffee. She told me it would be about ten minutes. I used that time to breeze past Swifty into the men's locker room. There was a stack of towels, some complimentary mouthwash and plastic combs on the sinks. I found an open locker. I stripped quickly and took a rejuvenating eight minute shower in the men's locker room. Dressed and refreshed, I exited to see Swifty none the wiser or perhaps just not caring, his head buried in the *Miami Herald* newspaper. I sat down just as the delicious breakfast plate was put on the table and I relished every bite. The clock on the wall said 8:45am when I finished. I was soon out the door and heading to the station. I had no idea what the next sixty minutes would be like, but I certainly wasn't looking forward to it.

I parked in my normal fashion and decided to just bypass the VIN office and the pronunciation-challenged Ileana. I went straight down to Major Brunson's office. Charlene looked up at me from her desk and by way of directional advice just motioned with her head towards Brunson's door. I mouthed the words "Everything cool?"

Her response was quick and on point as she whispered back, "Is it ever?"

I knocked on the door, light enough to not appear brash, but authoritative enough to pretend to be holding my ground.

"Come in," Major Brunson gruffly called through the door.

I again felt the swoosh of the carpet from under the door as I opened it. Inside was Major Brunson at his desk and Lieutenant Poulsen across from him. I was secretly relieved to not have to deal with anyone from Miami Dade this early in the morning.

The three of us settled into our chairs around the conference table. "Detective, both Lieutenant Poulsen and I have been discussing not only the direction of the VIN unit but quite frankly, your role in the unit going forward from this day. Now, I'm not so far down the line in years that I can't recognize good work and hard effort when I see it—but all the good work and hard effort isn't going to help anyone if people keep turning up dead."

My initial surprise was not so much the angle of conversation that I was being removed but more so the fact he was talking without cursing.

"These fucking past few days with you have been a God damn nightmare," he said.

I immediately went back to the angle of conversation that I was being removed; the cursing part had been negated.

"Lieutenant Poulsen has been pointedly telling me you're an integral part of VIN, that you understand the nature of the VIN investigative process better than anyone. But from where I sit you seem like a tornado of turmoil. You're not controlling your informants, who knows how many you have left now that aren't being embalmed as I sit right fucking here and look at you. You're not managing your cases or yourself very well."

At that moment Charlene rang his phone and informed him Gary was outside the office door.

"Send 'em in," he said more to the closed door than the phone receiver he was already putting back in the cradle.

Gary walked in with about twenty pages of single line documents. I don't think he was expecting me to be in the office. He looked at me and immediately I could tell whatever he was holding was directly related to me. He handed the packet of papers to Major Brunson and left. Major Brunson, without even looking at them, handed them to Lieutenant Poulsen.

"Make sure Miami Dade get these and tell them to stay the fuck out of my hair 'til at least lunch."

Lieutenant Poulsen just put them on the conference table and used them to prop his forearm like a broken-armed snow skier.

"Those are your phone records from the past ninety days. I understand you got testy with Miami Dade last night and wouldn't give them your phone. Oh, I'm sorry, did I say *your* phone? I meant to say *our* phone. The very same one *we* pay for and loan to you to use as you act like a detective. Now, I say 'act' because if you really were a detective you wouldn't have all these fucking people dying!"

This was not going well for me on many fronts. The realization that informants under my control were turning up dead was beginning to be understood by people who normally don't understand what it is we actually do in VIN. Secondly, confidential numbers of other informants and other illegal narcotic contacts were now being handed over to an outside police agency. My cell phone would have very little bearing on Donito's murder investigation, but since Zambrana had a wild hair up his butt over my interrupting his tranquil life, all this was now in motion.

"Major with all due respect," Lieutenant Poulsen said, "Miami Dade did not subpoena Detective Taylor's cell phone. They requested ninety days. *Requested*. I suggest we give them the past ten days with a promise of the other 80 days if needed. We'll tell them we're still working on it. There may be some sensitive numbers in these records, and us just handing them over could really jeopardize ongoing investigations. Why don't I separate the past ten days and send those over and wait and see if that satisfies them?"

For a moment Major Brunson thought about it, more so out of the appearance of giving it weight than out of actually caring about the confidentiality of the phone records or Miami Dade.

"Okay. That's fine, but I also want transfer papers drawn up for Taylor and in the hopper, ready to go."

Lieutenant Poulsen again surprised me with his next verbal declaration.

"Major, what we do in VIN is multi-faceted. Detective Taylor is one of the best at it. Not only for us but county-wide. Yes, two informants have died but this is a nasty business as it is. Until we know more about what's going on here, I'd like to suggest we continue status quo. He's a good man and he knows what he's doing."

"Detective," Brunson started saying by way of looking at me. "Transfer papers to Uniform Patrol will be drawn up and ready. If more headaches like I'm having continue, and if *you* are the cause of my headaches, I don't want any delay or union interference. You're done. You hear me?"

I just nodded because I was a little stunned by Lieutenant Poulsen actually going to bat for me and I did not want to exacerbate the situation.

"Okay, Major. I'll send over the last ten days of cell phone records and have papers at the ready." With that Poulsen got up and went out the door.

Major Brunson just looked at me, studying me.

"So bring me up to speed, what is the major aspect of VIN you're involved in?"

I cleared my throat and leaned forward resting my forearms on my thighs, my hands clasped between my knees.

"It can be a little complicated but in a nutshell, I pose as a money launderer and work with informants who are money launderers for the Colombian drug cartels. Based on reputation I bid to move drug money in Miami, New York City, sometimes L.A through the system into Colombia."

"The system?"

"Yeah the banking system, capital good trade based products, currency exchanges, precious metals..."

"It is complicated. So why are these guys dying?"

"Good question. I wish I knew. It's money and cocaine. Its volatile and without rules or trust."

"So just how does all this money movement benefit us?" he asked.

"We try and identify the source of the drug money and seize the money before it gets laundered to the cartels."

"You still doing dope deals?" he asked.

"Yes. The most current one is helping Miami S.I.S."

I didn't want to go into further details than just that I was helping Miami.

Now it was Major Brunson who was leaning forward and drawing closer to me.

"I may seem like I'm just a guy waiting for Chief McIntyre to die or retire. I can assure you I know more about the comings and goings of this place than you realize. So carry on, but don't ever think for a second I'm not aware of all that's going on here, as well as with my people. There's a reason why I sit in the biggest office in this place."

He held his stare and then finally broke from it and announced that we were through. As I was leaving he asked, "Will there be any calls to any attorneys on those cell phone records?"

"No, not that I know of. Why?"

Already moving behind his desk and picking up papers without even looking at me he just said,

"Nothing. Say hi to Gina for us."

Chapter Fifteen

I STEPPED OUT OF his office and slipped into the building's stairwell. I took a few steps and then sat down in mid-staircase.

Gina.

Just what was that supposed to mean? Why did he mention saying hi for *us* instead of saying hi for himself? I took it to mean that he knew more about my personal life than I thought he did. It was his way of notifying me that he has a conduit of information coming to him, possibly from multiple sources. The comment about me not managing my cases or myself very well also had strong implications. Not managing myself, any attorney calls on my cell phone? To me it all meant that he knew I was on the road to a finalized divorce and maybe the hardened exterior I was trying to show was starting to crack. Just where was he getting his information from? How much did he know?

I sat there on the stairs. The cool, institutional, flat-gray painted steps and banisters could've been any staircase in any city in America. There was respite in the industrialized staircase. I was confident I wouldn't be disturbed as I tried to reason with everything. No one ever took the stairs. No matter how health conscious or heart conscientious they said they were. It was like those people at those trendy fitness clubs who wait for the elevator to go up to the fitness club so they can get on the stairmaster.

The state of my relationship with Gina came flooding into my mind. Such a feeling of loss and betrayal. What had started as a great courtship and marriage that now at least for me, had deteriorated to a point of destructive psychosis. My sleep patterns were whacked, and I was drinking more than I should to help me sleep. I was avoiding my own home as often as I could, and I was doing it all through a potent sense of denial.

I'd supported Gina in her desire to be a successful artist. I just had no idea that she would strike up a sexual affair with her art studio owner.

When I found out about their affair whereas most men would exact revenge, conduct a scorch earth campaign, and smear reputations I simply retrieved two suitcases from the storage closet. One for me and one for her. I packed one suitcase. The second suitcase was put before her at her feet. Holding my own, with one hand on the door I told her I'd be back in a week. I also told her to start with her own suitcase and add from there but be gone when I come back. I took a five day sabbatical to Islamorada Key. I spent the five days drinking in the warm sun, puking in the cool shade, and then doing it all over again.

I returned fifteen pounds lighter from being unable to eat, and palm-frond-striped from passing out on the beach. She was indeed gone. For weeks I had no idea where she was until the first round of communiques from her attorney.

Last I knew she was in Palm Beach, her married lover having decided to leave his own marriage of seventeen years to move into a duplex with her near Manatee Lagoon just outside of Riviera Beach.

So for the past few weeks I'd been trying to hold it together and keep the facade of a normal life. Now sitting here on these steps, I could hear the occasional gurgle of water running through plumbing piping in the stairwell. In my head the intermittent rivulet of the water was acting like a chime, marking time for a new thought to pop in my increasingly tortured mind. I just couldn't understand exactly what Major Brunson meant by that concluding remark. Was it an ill-timed innocent or polite comment?

There was no way it was an innocent or a polite comment. You don't ascend to a level of police administration like he has by being innocent or polite. The man swears like a drunk sailor and kicks small metal garbage cans. There was a definite meaning behind what he said. But what was it?

I kept hearing his voice in my head.

"You're not managing your cases or yourself very well."

I was beginning to think he was right. I was coming apart in such a way that I hadn't fully recognized just how outside of the lines I was coloring. In the past few days I had slept on couches, boats, and in cars. I showered in a locker room I don't belong to. I used my swimming pool as a deep-plunge to sober up from a night of Jameson in an Irish Bar. I was drinking to keep the memory of Gina suppressed and the reality of dead Colombians away from my twilight dreams. I needed to get it together or I might be not only pushing a uniformed patrol car in a zone but maybe even be out of a job.

"These fucking past few days with you have been a God damn nightmare."

I was pissing off nearly everyone I knew with a Miami Dade badge, and was now holding back intelligence related to not one, but two homicides. I'd met with Peralta just days prior to him turning up looking like a beached loggerhead turtle. He was also *my* informant—not a task force informant. I was directly responsible for him. Donito was also my direct responsibility. How did all of this go so sour so quickly?

My deep thoughts were interrupted by the ringing of my cell phone. In the stairwell it was an echoing shrill. In my haste to silence it I answered it without looking at the caller I.D.

It was Gary calling from the VIN office.

"Hey, you still here?"

"Yeah. What's up?" I asked.

"Where you at?"

"Right now?" I said looking up at the stairs above me which was purely reflexive, as I knew exactly where I was. "I'm in the west stairwell near the third floor."

"Stay there. I'm on my way." He hung up.

Two minutes later I heard the door above the landing swing open. I decided to get up and appear to be standing rather than sitting when Gary came down around the bannister. It would look better. I'd look more in control—not deflated, the way I was feeling.

"Dude what are you doing here?" he asked.

Although nearly the same age as me, he liked to call everyone 'dude,' an obvious holdover from his days growing up in Hobe Sound, the mecca for surfing in Florida. He had a very short buzz cut and the straightest, whitest teeth of anyone in the department. He also had a bar code tattoo at the base of the back of his neck and a small "F" tattooed on his right middle finger. He once told me that when he waves his hand sometimes in greeting or when accepting a volley of directions from someone he doesn't care for, the tattoo signified inwardly to him that he could give "a flying fuck."

"I went to the second-floor vending machines by the Professional Standards Division and wanted an RC Cola but all they have was Coke and Pepsi. Doesn't anyone sell RC anymore? You said 'stay here' and this is where I was when you called. So I stayed here," was my reply.

"Dude you're getting peculiar."

"... *you seem like a tornado of turmoil*," I heard Brunson's words in my head.

"So what's going on, Big G?" I asked by way of deflection.

"I just wanted you to know I'm not handing you up, it's just that when they ask for stuff I have to give it to them."

"Gary, I know that. We're cool. There's nothing to worry about between us."

"Well I don't suggest anything to anybody, I just fulfill requests…

but they're asking for things that they seem to already have the answers to."

"Who is they? Poulsen and Brunson?"

"No, not Poulsen. He's actually sticking up for you. It's Major Brunson and Miami Dade. They're angling at something. Whatever it is, you're in the center of it."

"Really? Like what?"

"I don't know, dude. They had Ileana go to Human Resources and pull your file, and they wanted your cell phone records."

Once again, I heard Major Brunson's voice in my head:

"You got a cell phone ain't ya?"

"Now they're asking for your gasoline purchases. I told them I had to go to the bathroom before I do it. That's when I called you," he said.

"My *gas* purchases?"

"Yeah, all the places you've bought gas outside of the motor pool using your U.C. Chevron card."

"Did they pull my U.C. credit cards?"

"No, not yet but I wouldn't be surprised if that was next."

"Any idea what this could all be about?" I asked.

"Dude, I don't know but my job is becoming a full-out mess between them and the audit-crazy City Manager."

"What audits?"

"The City Manager is looking to cut the budget. The task force has been so successful seizing money that the Law Enforcement Trust Fund is bulging, so he wants to tap into that money. The problem is he can't. It can only be used for non-budgeted items. It has to go to law enforcement projects and needs, so he wants to cut *our* budget and supplant it from the seizures the task force makes. What we once were getting from the city in the budget is now being paid for by narco dollar seizures. So city hall is all over each division, questioning everything, even seeking restitution for things they think aren't agency-specific, but personal. Like the motor unit is getting dinged for sunglasses. Can you believe it? The sunglasses from the budget are now considered a personal item!"

This was an eye-opening revelation from Gary. It also meant that if I had any leverage in my potential transfer it was that as long as seizures made by the VIN task force were coming in they might need me to stay where I was headaches none withstanding.

"So, what do you think, Big G?"

"What do I think? I think that I didn't get a Masters in Finance from F.I.U. to be copying phone records and gas receipts. Crazy. I just wanted to let you know that me, and Ileana are in your corner. We hear things, but until the papers get generated, I'd let it slide."

"And Poulsen?" I asked.

"Like I said, surprisingly he seems to be not only looking out for you but keeping the Major and Miami Dade held back. I heard him this morning on the phone, chewing out some union rep for not meeting with you. I don't know what that was about and I don't want to know. When I heard 'union rep' and then them asking for phone records, I just wanted to check on you dude."

"Thanks amigo, but it's all okay. No worries."

"Well dude, I'll keep my ear out for you. I better get back before they wonder where I am. You need anything?"

"No I'm good. Thanks."

Gary shook my hand and then darted back up the stairs.

The stairwell door closing behind Gary jarred me back to my previous thoughts—only now I had a few more things to think about.

By pulling my gas records from the U.C. Chevron card, they'd get a better idea of where I was on certain days and times. It would help them figure out my activity and measure it against my activity reports.

If Miami Dade were to pull my U.C. credit card records they may just in fact see that I had actually met with Gus Peralta at Casa Juancho two days before he turned up dead.

There would be no record of Peralta on my credit card statement.

If Miami Dade was worth their salt as an investigative agency and they took Peralta's picture out to Casa Juancho, they may actually find a busboy, waiter, or car valet who might remember him. Not hard, since Peralta had such a caustic personality and was habitually irritating people around him, especially with his anti-Cuban rhetoric. No, it wouldn't be hard at all to find someone who'd remember him. Anyway, even without finding an actual eye witness who could place Peralta at Casa Juancho with me, any number of in-house or neighboring security cameras would show us at Casa Juancho together.

I needed to get it together. I was starting to freak myself out.

I climbed the few stairs to the landing and exited out to the detective parking section. The sun was cooking the cars on the concrete apron. Any car in the adjoining impound lot not moved by July would be a soldered mess of plastic, rubber, and steel. I could feel the heat of the sun bearing down and reflecting back up at me. I walked to the Explorer and although freshly washed, it was in a bit of a disarray as far as the back seat was concerned. My go bag and loose clothing were scattered. I opened the rear door and then went around and opened the other side as well to try and cross ventilate my impromptu sleeping berth of last night.

Still freaking out, I started pushing clothes back into the go bag and then realized the ineffectiveness of that. I took a deep breath, carefully pulled out and then repositioned the items so that when needed, it would truly be a go bag and not an oh no bag. The orderliness of repacking the go bag helped transition my brain to a calm, collected state as well. I regained my composure and started thinking through the situation more clearly.

They had not asked for my credit card records. Either they were not going to ask for them or it was an oversight that might get lost as time goes on.

Each passing hour would give any restaurant employee more faces and events to confuse when or if Miami Dade came asking about Peralta. The same for security cameras. Each hour that passed would be another hour eating up the storage capabilities of the camera's memory. Most cameras can't hold more than four or five days of footage.

I was beginning to feel better about my time with Peralta at Casa Juancho more so than just a few minutes ago in the stairwell. I found it odd, yet refreshing that a little physical organizing of some clothes in a bag would help me to steady myself and think more clearly about what Gary had said. Rationalized thoughts started to percolate.

Major Brunson was probably aware of my marriage disintegrating because Gina's attorney must've called the agency or Human Resources seeking information about my pay rate and tax information. That made more sense to me. Maybe that's why they had Ileana pull my file. I could feel myself starting to feel more at ease. I had reasonably thought of what might have been the reason for all the things happening. If the City Manager was indeed nit-picking over every little thing, then maybe a few personal phone calls to a divorce attorney on my cell phone would be enough to torque up Major Brunson. I was also fairly relived and equally surprised to hear that Lieutenant Poulsen was actually an advocate for me and looking out for me.

I don't know if I was rationalizing these things to appease my own trepidations, but it did make sense. At least to me it did.

But then there was Donito.

How did the receipt from Reuben's Cuban Cafe end up in his possession? Was he going to use it in some sort of blackmail attempt or something else? If he and Peralta were killed by the same killer or killers, then it makes no sense. Peralta had my business card. Donito had my cafe bill. How did this all tie into me and why?

Then, like an aftershock earthquake tremor, I was unnerved a second time without warning.

The revelation that I called Donito *after* I'd eaten at Reuben's set in.

How could he have *possibly* known I was at Reuben's? There was no way he could have.

Someone had been following me. Did that same person follow Donito to La Covacha?

Why?

I instinctively looked all around the parking apron and up at the neighboring office buildings wondering if I was being watched. In a Yogi Berra sense I literally had the paranoid feeling I was becoming paranoid.

To compound my anxiety, I then realized that I'd actually called Reuben's Cuban Cafe from my cell phone. Miami Dade was now getting those phone records faxed to them. It wouldn't take much effort to cross reference the numbers from my cell phone. If they showed my picture to any of those chattering middle-aged Cuban waitresses, how difficult would it be to remember the gringo who orders eggs with crispy bacon? Plus my fingerprints were all over that restaurant bill.

I was no longer feeling a tremor. This was an all-out earthquake inside me and I was literally shaking. I just sat down in the back seat, my go bag the only thing neat about me.

Chapter Sixteen

ENHANCED BY THE sun glinting off my side view mirror, I glimpsed myself in the rearview mirror from the back seat. I looked weary and my eyes were squinting partially due to the sun and partially due to fatigue.

There was no time to rest.

I had to start unraveling the secretive parts of these situations on my own. My easy breezy use of contacts and resources was not going to be available to me. I had no idea what part of my intelligence network was working with me or against me.

There were certain things that were out of my control. There were other things I could try and minimize the effects of. From the back seat I reached between the two front seats and inserted the key into the ignition. The blast of air conditioning from the car vents was a welcomed relief. I was able to see how much fuel the Explorer had; full tank, thanks in part to my nocturnal filling of it when I got the car wash.

Good.

A full tank of gas meant no issues with the rental agency when I took this one and swapped it for a different car. If someone was following me I'd make it harder for them to continue to do so. That would mean more trips to city motor pool and less usage of the

U.C. Chevron gas card. Whoever it was they may have a Teletrac on the Explorer. I moved into the passenger seat and searched the glove compartment for a Teletrac monitoring device. It's easy to place a tracker behind the cardboard interior at the back of the glove compartment. It isn't the stealthiest place to put it, but never underestimate the laziness of a government or municipal employee.

I hesitated to pull back the cardboard. If I found a tracking device, what should I do? I could leave it and pretend I wasn't aware of it, and possibly use it to lure my follower or followers to a position where I could confront them. Conversely, if I found one and then just left it in the Explorer and turned this rental back in whoever was tracking me would have to try and retrieve the device. There still was no way of keeping them from putting another tracker onto the next rental I took out of the rental agency. I decided to pull back the cardboard and see for myself anyway. As neatly as I could I pulled back the plastic insert and then the small pressed cardboard firewall.

Nothing in there.

I then opened the engine hood and checked there as well. I found nothing there either.

My mind made up, and my paranoia raging, I headed to the rental agency to turn in this Explorer and get something else.

The drive north towards the airport was uneventful so long as you didn't count the divergent yammering thoughts my mind was going through. The task force had a choice of three different smaller independent rental car agencies that were all owned by the same conglomerate. Rather than do a car shuffle and to ease the transition, I took the Explorer to the same agency I got it from.

There happened to be a black Infiniti Q45 that had just been delivered and was new to the rental agency. Without hesitation I switched over to the Q45 and within fifteen minutes had my go bag and other possessions transferred over. I also held onto the rental agreement. Normally we just had the rental agency fax all copies to Ileana. This time I told them I'd bring it to her myself. Due to our continual business and cordial relationship the manager was fine with it. The agreement was just a record keeping thing with us. The rental agency charged a flat rate regardless of the vehicle and the actual paperwork always stayed with them. My hanging onto the agreement a few days would not affect the billing. It only hampered the ability for anyone in VIN to know what car I was in. It would just be for a few days. I felt it would be the few days I needed to get in front of the Miami Dade cops and others who might actually think I had something to do with two of the four horsemen being dead.

It took a few minutes and a few miles to get used to the Q45. My mind which had been flip-flopping from angst to revelation had started to clarify an action plan. I knew what I needed to do.

I needed to make contact with Roldan Osorio-Vidal, the last unaccounted-for Horseman. I was reluctant to use my cell phone and searched the strip shopping centers for any of the remaining pay telephones still left in Miami. The technology and ease of cell phones was killing the landline telephone business model and the biggest casualty in that field were pay phones.

I managed to find an upright unsheltered bank of three of them near a tire store on Flagler Street. Only one worked, the other two perhaps rendered inoperable by tire customers slamming the receivers upon hearing their car insurance doesn't cover new tires. I didn't expect Roldan to pick up from a number he didn't recognize, and like the other Horsemen his cell phone just had a singular beep for leaving a message. No greeting or instructions.

I left a message asking him to call me on my cell phone, but to make the call from a pay phone. My next call from the pay phone was to Johnny Morris. I wasn't sure if he would pick up from a number he didn't recognize, but I needed to try. I was pleasantly surprised when he picked up on the second ring.

"Hello."

"Johnny, its Cade from the Gables."

"Oh, hey man, we were just talking about you earlier. Iggy is still burning up the lines going back and forth with those two jokers from New York."

"Yeah, yeah, that's cool. Yeah, whatever you guys need," I said.

"So what's up?" he asked.

"I need you to do me a little favor, and keep it between us."

"Um...well okay, I guess...I mean, what is it first?"

"Keep your radar out, maybe somebody in S.I.S or street narcotics...can you ask around discreetly and see if anybody has noticed any U.C.s or Feds in the Grove?"

I could feel the reluctance in his voice, but it was momentary as he rationalized that anyone working a case in his city without notifying Miami P.D. was fair game.

"Well, if they ain't checked themselves in I guess we need to check them out," he said.

"Thanks Johnny, I appreciate it."

"What number are you calling me from? It didn't show up on my caller I.D." "I'm at Cellular One getting my phone upgraded. The only technician they got stepped out while working on my phone. The thing's in pieces in the back room. I can see it through the window. I mean how do you let some guy just go to lunch or something with my phone all taken apart? I pitched a fit. This is a loaner they gave me while I sit here looking at display cell phones waiting for him to come back. I'll have my phone back hopefully in about an hour."

I lied. I didn't want to get into the minutia of how things have been and why I felt the need to make certain outbound calls from a pay phone.

"Alright well good luck with that. If anybody knows anything I'll call you on your cell later."

We exchanged goodbyes and as I hung up the pay phone, I noticed the mungy black ring around the receiver earpiece and pictured all the ear wax, hair gels, and sweaty faces that must've been pressed up against it. I raised my right shoulder and ground my right ear into the cottony fabric of my shirt in an infantile and equally ineffective way to stem an invasion of staphylococcus.

Within a few minutes I was driving south on Douglas Road. I had decided to see what I could find in Coconut Grove myself. Johnny Morris may not call back for a while, or even at all for that matter.

Coconut Grove is a neighborhood community that is primarily in the City of Miami, although the western section of Coconut Grove was in Coral Gables. It was officially annexed by the City of Miami in 1925. The western section had been primarily established by black Bahamians who started arriving in America in the late 19th century, many of them working as day laborers and wreckers. The original clapboard and ship debris constructed homes were made by the new settlers. Those homes were nearly gone now replaced by developers with a keen eye for modern glass and construction materials. This new construction gave the Grove a revitalized and expensive look. The quiet tree shaded streets and leafy narrow lanes now a sundry of architectural style and design. The main heart of the Grove was ground zero for Miami's counter-culture movement in the 1960s. Now towering condominiums and high-density vertical storage boat yards were there. It still had its charm with cafes and shops near the intersection of Main Highway and Bayshore Drive but the encroachment of development was looming.

The streets of the Grove are densely vegetative and can be very confusing to those who are geographically challenged. Every roadway designation is employed in the free-flow mapping of the neighborhood without regard to direction or section. Every street type name was in the Grove.

Marler Avenue.

Anchorage Way.

Kiaora Street.

Munroe Drive.

Tequesta Lane.

Lime Court.

The street names have no rhyme or reason and navigating is clearly best done through familiarity and repetitiveness. It was that navigation challenge that I was counting on. I made an assumption that the Miami Dade TNT units were comprised of detectives county-wide and many of them may be unfamiliar with the Grove.

Being unfamiliar lends itself to uncertainty.

Uncertainty seeks familiarity.

Using that axiom I drove towards the Burger King on Southwest 27th Avenue and staked out the fast food parking lot. I was hoping to see some late model sedans or SUVs crowded under a shade tree like lions at a watering hole on the Serengeti. They wouldn't be hard to spot. Each vehicle singularly occupied, engines running for the air-conditioned comfort, and more than likely a small, but somewhat noticeable, diverse gender and ethnic mix.

As I neared the intersection of U.S. 1 and Southwest 27th Avenue, I spied a young Hispanic male exiting a gold four-door Chevrolet Malibu. He was walking into a marine supply store. The car had a built-in spoiler on the rear. The window tints were inordinately too dark—hideously too dark, especially for that type of car. With the exception of the spoiler, this was a car usually driven by a pharmaceutical rep, not a young man with a fashionable fringe mane haircut. He wore blue jeans and a tight, horizontal cream and white striped shirt. Thin gold necklaces and a gold bracelet on his left wrist. The carefully chosen jewelry clashed mightily with the black Casio wristwatch and clean white tennis shoes.

Like I said, they wouldn't be hard to spot.

Rather than hunt and seek the others I parked across at a Shell gas station and watched and waited for him to come out of the marine supply store, hoping he could lead me to his *compadres*.

True to form, he came out of the business with a small bag in his hand, got in his car and backed out rather quickly. I was very fortunate to catch a seam in traffic and slipped in a few car-lengths behind him. We drove south on 27th Avenue and right past the Burger King which was absent of any noticeable congregating TNT-type cars or people. When he turned west on Bird Avenue I held back and idled in front of the Big Daddy's Liquor Store. When I did make my turn he was easily three blocks in front of me. I stayed a safe distance behind and then saw him turn into the K-Mart parking lot just off of U.S. 1 and Southwest 32nd Avenue.

Either he was still shopping or this is where he and maybe others in the TNT unit are staging as they rotate taking turns being the direct "eye" on the surveillance of the house. I was hoping it was the same house Major Edwards had mentioned.

I turned into the K-Mart parking lot. The Q45 was unnoticed to "Mr. Malibu" or the three similar sedans he met with. They were in the far corner of the parking lot under some gumbo limbo trees. I continued straight through the parking lot out to U.S. 1 and drove around the block, and found my own shady spot under a ficus tree on West Trade Avenue just across from the K-Mart parking lot.

The ring of my cell phone in the silence jolted me for a second. It was Johnny Morris.

"Johnny. Talk to me, man."

"I see you got your phone back. Hey, listen, I asked around for that thing you mentioned and no one knows anything," he said

"You didn't ask too hard, did you?"

"No, I played it cool. I said someone thought they saw some U.C.s in the Grove at the Hungry Sailor arguing with someone and I wanted to see if it was any of us."

The Hungry Sailor was a raucous bar that straddled the business district between Grand Avenue and Main Highway, where the inter-secting roads come to a blunt point. It was literally a wedge-shaped triangle between the corner and the rest of the stores and cafes.

"Anyone say anything?" I asked.

"No. I was hoping someone might've known if another agency was in our city and might've suggested them, but no one said anything."

"Cool. I appreciate it."

"You care to tell me what you know?" he probed.

"You know, I really don't know. The guy at the Steak-N-Egg in the Gables said he heard some landscapers talking about I.N.S. being in the Grove, doing a round-up of illegal immigrants, so I was just curious if that was what it was, or something else."

"Oh okay. Well, while I have you on the phone, our friends from Casablanca want the whole fifteen. Iggy has been non-stop back and forth with them on the phone. They decided to meet, two o'clock tomorrow. They keep calling Iggy on his Cuban heritage. Typical Dominican 'our island is better than your island' stuff. They said no Cade, no deal. The one guy, Lobo, said he wants to see your gringo face when they hand over the money. Whatever that means."

"That makes no sense to me," was my only perplexed response.

"Me neither. He must think you're an actual pool liner guy with a station wagon, house with a picket fence, and 2.5 kids."

"You guys ever figure out where they went after Casablanca?" I asked him.

"We had a good surveillance on them for a while. Alex thought they were doing a heat run on the side streets by Grapeland Park. He laid back and Silvio and Javier took over but lost them for a while too. Claudio found the car twenty minutes later at the Embassy Suites Hotel on South River Drive. Alex went in this morning and asked to see a room, said he was from a tour group, scouting properties for a volleyball tournament on South Beach. They let him in a room and he snapped some quick pictures. Iggy says the bedspreads in the pictures match what he saw in that Polaroid they flashed. We got units watching the car in the parking lot. If they don't move we'll have DEA with us in the morning, as well on the car. If we can get them on the road tomorrow before they get to the meet we'll just take them down on conspiracy."

"Sounds good. So, we might not even have to go through with it. What time tomorrow?" I asked.

"Sergeant Brookings wants everyone at the offsite by 10:30 tomorrow morning. Iggy was told to call at 11am and they would tell him where you guys are supposed to be at 2pm. It'll be seventy-five degrees tomorrow and they like outside, so keep that in mind."

"Yeah will do, I'll have sunscreen," I said.

"I don't have that problem," he deadpanned.

After we said our goodbyes, I directed my full attention to the TNT units across the street. One of the guys was now standing outside his car brushing the crumbs off his lap from his recent in car meal.

My ability to fabricate plausible instances was becoming my own version of fact versus fiction. Johnny never questioned my Cellular One story or the INS round-up in the Grove. The rogue factor was creeping into my mind and inhabiting my persona. I'd been omitting information from two homicides in an effort to keep from being implicated as the main suspect in those murders. Now I was staking out the Miami Dade cops who were staking out a suspected stash house. For all I knew they could all have my picture on the front seats of their cars mixed in with their issues of the *Miami Herald, USA Today, Men's Fitness Magazine,* and the assorted snack foods and empty Gatorade bottles they pee in when on long surveillances. I was technically interfering with another agency's investigation. I was becoming the smudgy side of correctness, the part that's neither black nor white but more of a pewter gray.

The events of the past days had illuminated the seediness of the narcotic trade. It wasn't just kilos of cocaine and duffle bags of money. It was sublime subterfuge, decadent deception, incessant interference, and damning death. I was mixed in with a fistful of festering false innuendoes that were poised to not only end my career, but potentially my life. The TNT units picked up Gustavo on a tapped phone line saying he could trust no one.

Well, now I was fully aware that I could trust no one.

Chapter Seventeen

A FTER ABOUT FORTY-FIVE minutes I saw three of the TNT guys standing outside of their cars. They were discussing something. One of them walked away and got in a car but the other two played a game of rock, paper, scissors. After three quick flashes of hands and arm movements one of the TNT guys clearly lost. He then walked over to a red Dodge Avenger. Red has never been a suitable color for a detective car. I assume this guy either didn't care or actually chose to look like a rolling strawberry. I kept my eye on him, waiting for when he started to move out of the parking lot. The others stayed behind. I figured he was the relief for whoever was watching the house.

I pulled out onto Southwest 32nd Avenue. I started to move parallel to him as he drove south through the K-Mart parking lot. It was my intention to follow him. He surprised me by turning east on Bird Ave.

He was now heading towards me.

I didn't want to miss this potential opportunity and have to wait another hour or so for a change in the surveillance of the eye. I also didn't want to burn myself right out of the gate especially if they were tipped as to who I was and what I looked like. It was fortunate that I'd changed out my car at the rental agency. I slowed up as I got to the intersection of Bird Avenue and Southwest 32nd. The light was turning red for me and I coasted through it as it changed.

The red Avenger turned south and was now about six car lengths behind me. I continued driving at a leisurely pace, watching him in my rearview mirror as I continued south across Shipping Avenue.

He closed the gap and was only about three car lengths behind me.

As I crossed Day Avenue I continued monitoring him in my rearview mirror. He then turned west on Day Ave. He was out of my sight. I needed to catch up to him or risk losing him.

The next street was Percival Avenue. I cut quickly west on Percival and then made a hard north-bound turn onto Margaret Street. My quick circuitous route around the block brought me back to Day Ave.

That's when I saw a blue Toyota Avalon pulling out of a driveway and the red Avenger pulled into the same driveway, taking its place.

I pulled in front of a house that had conch shells on their mailbox post. I parked on the grass adjacent to the conch shell-adorned mailbox.

I had found the suspected stash house.

It was one of the small houses just behind the red Avenger. By the way he was parked he was obviously surveilling it from his rearview mirror. Slouched down low in the seat, he was seemingly unaware of the dripping condensation from his air conditioning. The water would soon pool under his vehicle. Normally a dead giveaway to savvy street narcotic sellers that the parked car is actually occupied, but in this case I don't think TNT was concerned about the street smarts of the house's occupants. Major Edwards had said in that morning brouhaha that Peralta had been heard on a wire talking. He also said that TNT had seen Peralta by their surveillance units picking up cash from the drug holes in Coconut Grove and frequenting a potential stash house in the Grove.

I kept my eye on the Avenger making sure that I was seeing exactly which house he was looking at while I processed what I'd heard from Major Edwards. Peralta was not the type to be doing errand work, picking up cash from drug holes. He wasn't on the bottom of the food chain. The Four Horsemen had learned the intricacies of the Miami drug business rapidly and their ascension in the drug trade was just as rapid, but they still weren't averse to moving product. Anyone in the drug trade will touch both *"blanco y verde."* White and green, both words denoting either cocaine or cash. The Horsemen had gravitated from importing multi kilos of cocaine to vulgar amounts of cash movement. The cash was a tsunami and these guys surfed it right into the shores of Miami.

So why was he dirtying himself with low-level street dealers and running over here to a simple house hidden from the road by fencing and shrubs?

It didn't make sense. Major Edwards also said that upon TNT getting a court order to tap the phones of the house they heard a person who identified himself as Costano on the tap.

"Costano was getting ready to move some heavy product and didn't want a separation from cocaine and money. He said he 'couldn't trust no one' and that there was a cop who needed to be 'taken care of' are the words he used. This cop either through aggravation or partnership, was causing him to charge more to front kilos of cocaine to the dealers. He said 'red kilos' were next.

Even if Peralta was back in the cocaine side of the equation he was too smart to keep money and cocaine in the same location. It still didn't make sense.

Who is this cop he was heard talking about?

He referred to him as *"los tombo."* He used the Colombian slang for cops. He must've been talking to another Colombian. Was he talking to any of the Horsemen or was he talking to someone else?

The Avenger brake lights came on.

I thought he might be moving but he must've just hit the brakes accidentally while adjusting himself in the cramped car.

I went back to my thinking about Peralta and what Major Edwards had said. If what he said was true, that Peralta didn't want to separate money from cocaine, then why didn't TNT use that information and just serve a warrant on the house?

Because they're waiting to see just who this cop is.

What if that cop in their eyes is me?

I'd identified the house; there was no need to push my luck here any longer. I'd be in a serious mess if they discovered me here. Even by explaining how I followed the TNT detective in the Malibu it would seem improbable to Majors Brunson and Edwards. I was well past my expiration stamp here. It was time for me to leave.

I threw the car in drive and tried not to rush out of my parking spot but almost hit a guy who was wheeling his garbage can to the curb in my haste. Luckily a slight hand wave and a mouthed apology was all it took to placate the guy. It could've been bad for me. I could just imagine explaining how I side swiped a pedestrian near a stash house I wasn't supposed to know about.

Not unless I was *Los Tomba*.

Tomorrow was going to be a full day with Miami S.I.S. and I still hadn't gotten a call back from my last Horseman, Roldan. Traffic was building on U.S. 1 and I decided to head south by cutting through the leafy streets of Coconut Grove. I was able to avert the frenzied and frustrated traffic snarls attributed to decades in the making of ill-advised and equally ill-planned growth in Miami. I soon was turning off of Main Highway and heading south on Old Cutler Road. I figured I must be only about twenty minutes ahead of the rush hour commuters, each of them preoccupied with office politics, dinner plans, youth soccer practices, and karate lessons for their kids. My mind was also drifting from the attention of the road. I guess I was no different. One person's fixation on getting to youth soccer practice is another man's dead Horseman. Continuing south I drove past Matheson Hammock and looked over at the entrance as I passed. My thoughts went back to Gus Peralta bobbing, ghastly silent, face-down in the briny bay.

My phone rang, bringing me back to real time.

It was Trentlocke.

"You're not going to believe the terminology Dr. Bashir used for Restrepo."

"Was it still a broken neck?" I asked.

"Yeah, that and a few other things. She determined his cause of death as 'cervical fracture and thoracic aortic transection caused by steering wheel intrusion resulting in spinal shock.'"

"Huh?"

"He died of a broken neck so to say. It's more a situation of certain bones in the neck being broken and others trying to hold it all together. His neurons were probably all misfiring with the brain saying one thing and the body responding differently. But the trauma of the broken bones he did have caused a sudden loss of nerve supply to the body. That would include his heart, capillaries, and blood vessels. Nothing is pumping. His BP probably tanked in about twenty seconds. He was dead within two to four minutes."

"Damn. Can you even imagine?" I said.

"She also detected pneumothorax."

"What is that?"

"It's when you have a puncture in the space between the ribs and your lungs and you get air between the lungs and the rib cage. Your chest will expand but your lungs are having no part of it. Scary as hell to be breathing air in and have it go nowhere. It's probably what he was experiencing at the very end as he was scampering over the console. If it was indeed a scamper. He may have just keeled onto his right side."

I was just silent with this official interpretation of Donito's murder. It was brutally savage, and I couldn't help but feel some responsibility. I'd asked him to meet me under false pretenses and now he was heinously murdered because of it.

"You still there?"

"Yeah, I guess you called it pretty accurate last night," was all I could muster to say in a soft, subdued voice.

"You want a copy of the report?"

I knew that having a copy of the report at this moment would serve no purpose, plus having something like that faxed to the VIN office would not be ideal for me.

"No, I'm okay. If I need one I'll just ask the M.E.'s office or get with you."

"I think I've had enough of you getting with me the past few days if you know what I mean," he said in such a way that I did not know if he was joking or not.

When we'd finished our call I realized that I had been driving on auto pilot and had actually missed my turn. I needed to eat something and to try and separate myself from all of the varied and intense activity of the past few days. I just decided to keep driving south on Old Cutler Road. I was getting used to the responsiveness of the Q45, despite my mind drifting. While checking my rearview mirror I took notice that I would not be comfortable sleeping in its back seat.

My thoughts went to the Old Cutler Oyster Company. The locals called it the O.C.O.C. Although local myself, I preferred to call it by its formal name.

It was where I had first met Gina.

She was at the bar, celebrating with her co-workers from the salon. One clear life lesson is that when a bunch of hair stylists gather in one place, don't focus on the one with the most fashionable or greatest hair style. Try and focus on the one who gave her that hairstyle for she may be cutting your hair one day. The night I met Gina there was a brown-haired beauty with frosty highlights that complemented her sun-tanned features, waiting for the ladies' room. I asked her who cut her hair and she pointed me in the direction of Gina at the other end of the bar. I took one look at Gina and it was magnetic. She was resplendent in her custom-cut, chic dark blazer and black pants, a hint of décolletage peeking through her lapels. Her laugh was infectious, and her brown eyes shined like newly-minted pennies. When I first saw her the sun was setting and the sunlight invading the bar from the lead paned windows cast all of us in a sepia bronze light.

The beers were flowing and the oysters were fresh and succulent. It was a good night.

That first night.

Not like the last night when I handed her a suitcase and then walked out the door. Both nights I don't think I will ever forget.

I turned just east off Old Cutler Road on Southwest 168th Street. I parked in front of the vacant weed-choked large lot that once was the Old Cutler Oyster Company. Hurricane Andrew had come through here just a little less than six years ago and demolished the place. The storm surge that swept up from the neighboring Deering Estate carried momentous sea water. The relentless howling wind carrying fractured tree limbs and downed telephone poles tore the place into a pile of wood and glass. The logic-defying strength of the hurricane buried what was left of it under a morass of sea water, mud, and churned debris. Now a few months from the storm's anniversary the sun was setting. It was setting just the same as I recall that first night. The gray catbirds and palm warblers were darting in and out of the saw palmetto and high grass that was once the parking lot. It was in that exact parking lot that I walked Gina to her car and got her phone number with a promise to call the next day. I did call the next day. I called the day after that too. Soon the calls led to us moving in together and then getting married in her uncle's backyard. It was a small civil ceremony in front of a backdrop of palm trees. Now with the red hued sunset casting a glowing light on what was once here and is no longer I also thought about what was once mine and is to me no longer. I must've just stared at the parking lot for easily twenty minutes. The retreating sun my only sense of time.

I eventually composed my thoughts and looked for a way to arrest the feelings inside of me. They were raw feelings, framed with remorse. I got back on Old Cutler Road and drove further south a few miles, eventually turning into the asphalt parking lot of Rodbenders Raw Bar and Grill. I ambled into the small, cozy raw bar and bypassed the dining tables and sat at the bar. The overly-dyed blonde bartender in her black tank top emblazoned with *Reel Girls Like Big Rods* across her ample bust tossed down a paper napkin in front of me. With a well-rehearsed, yet somewhat genuine smile she asked me what my drink order would be.

"Double Jameson, neat, soda back," I said.

One of the drawbacks in speaking the language of bartenders is they either peg you as a knowledgeable drinker or as a drinker who spends way too much time drinking in bars. Since Gina left I wasn't sure which category I'd fallen into.

Upon closer inspection, the bartender had that too-much-time-in-the-sun and too-much-fun-in-her-youth look to her. Depending on your outlook in life, her eyes had laugh lines or worry lines around them. Her hands betrayed her age, regardless of her bosom and hair. She did have a heavy hand on the pour and the Jameson came quickly. I ordered a grouper sandwich with fries and sat amongst the predominantly male clientele. They could've been construction workers, real estate salesmen, middle school teachers, it made no difference. They were belly-up to the bar and in no hurry or desire to go home to the lives they had. Lives that were vastly different then what they probably had envisioned. That was a driving force for men like the Horsemen. The freewheeling world of cocaine and money. No alarm clocks, no United Way contributions, no jockeying for assigned parking, or holding weeks of receipts to hand in to an anal-retentive comptroller. You took the risk, you reaped the reward. No taxes to pay. They reasoned, why should they pay taxes anyway? So the government can fund a drug reduction program that's counter to how they prosper in the world? The drug-trafficking, money-laundering world is a pleasure ground fraught with pitfalls, but also inundated with pleasures. This was not a world for construction helmets, property prospectus, or graded papers. It was a world of guns, money, sex and acquirement. Acquiring in a finite life all that you infinitely want.

The sandwich was delicious, and the bartender poured me another double. She resembled an older version of Ellie Mae Clampett—or maybe it was the Jameson influencing my memory of the Beverly Hillbillies ingenue.

A Hispanic worker came into the bar through the kitchen door. He asked for the key to the gate so he could take out the garbage.

That's when it hit me.

I looked at the tab in front of me. I threw down enough cash to cover the bill and leave a sizable tip.

Then I got out of there as fast as I could.

Chapter Eighteen

THE Q45 INSTRUMENTATION when lit was a subtle tangerine color. It was the first time I had seen it in the dark. I liked the warm color but was more focused on getting home as soon as I could. The Jameson's had started to take effect but the kitchen worker had spurred an idea in me. I had to get some sleep and soon. I needed to be ready and at Miami S.I.S at 10:30 am.

Pulling down my street I also realized that Roldan had not called. I started to get concerned but had a more pressing issue to address first; most notably, sleep. I pulled up to my darkened house and hurried towards the front door. There was a note on the front door.

I thought in my Jameson haze it might be from Gina.

It was from my neighbor, the retiree with the lawn mower. He was kindly reminding me that the fence line on my side had "expanding kudzo" and would I kindly remove it before it overtakes the aesthetics of the fence. Like I said I had more pressing issues but the appearance of the note and my reaction to it possibly being from Gina was heart-sickening.

I went inside and didn't bother to turn on a light. I sought the couch more as an avoidance to my former matrimonial bed than for its preferred comfort.

It was 7:08pm. I set the alarm on my cell phone for 2am, then remembering I got called out to Peralta's murder scene at 2:11am, I changed the alarm setting to 3am.

I didn't fall asleep. I quasi-passed out from exhaustion and the Irish whiskey. Drifting off to sleep, I realized I hadn't slept in my own bed in days, and that was all by my own choice.

The cell phone alarm was a steady chirp that also vibrated. I knew fully the reason I was getting up I just didn't know if the reason was going to be worth it all. I was beginning to wonder if maybe I needed some time on the couch—and it wasn't the large tropical print type I was sprawled upon that I was referring to. The department had a psychological counseling service that was completely confidential. It was a team of outside counselors and psychologists who understood the mental health aspects of law enforcement. Completely confidential, they said. Who were they kidding? As soon as the health trust got the bills everyone in the agency would soon know I was seeing a shrink. This was 1998, not 1978. The advances in computer data would've linked me as being a liability, and then where would I be?

I tried to banish the thought from my mind and started stripping off my clothes as I headed to the master bedroom shower. In my marriage to Gina I was highly accomplished at entering and leaving the bedroom in the dark so as not to disturb her sleep. These were the same skills I employed as I trudged through the lifeless bedroom and into the master bathroom. I thought about just submersing myself in the pool for a quick dunking but the brushing of my teeth had a direct correlation to just stepping into the shower.

By 3:20am I was dressed and backing out of my driveway, back on my way to Old Cutler Road. The drive back to Matheson Hammock was no different than the night of Peralta's murder. The shadows and the moonlight both played navigator and obscurer as they filtered through the road's tree canopy. I pulled up to the locked gate at Matheson Hammock and exited the Q45. I walked to the gate to see if the county worker that Captain Zambrano had mentioned was there. Peering into the darkness, the Q45's high beam headlights my only source of light, I saw no sign of him or a county vehicle.

With a sigh I got back into the Q45 and continued north, eventually winding my way through the maze of darkened quiet streets. I drove down Margaret Street and midway within the block I turned off the car lights and coasted easily and quietly right to the same position I was at twelve hours before. I minimized as much sound as I could and gently exited the car, not closing the car door all the way to thwart sound. I stood there for a second adjusting to the street sights and the street sounds. My car was between me and the conch shell mailbox post. I thought about cutting across the lawn but opted to stay on the street. My shoes would make less sound on the gray gravel asphalt mix that comprised the street. I lifted the garbage lid from the garbage can that I saw the man wheel out earlier. I counted the bags. There were four hefty bags in the can. Continuing towards the stash house, I stopped at the next garbage can and lifted the lid. It was horrendous. It smelled like someone had cooked pungent Indian food in a baby's soiled diaper. There were five bags visible; thankfully I didn't have to rummage through the bags but could see the white bags in the dark. I closed the lid as quietly and quickly as I could, repressing the sickening Jameson burp that was brought on by that olfactory assault and moved onto a third garbage can. There were four bags in this one, too. I used the three cans as a measuring gauge of the weekly garbage each household disposes of. I silently moved across Day Avenue towards Indiana Street.

I kept to the shadows, but not in such a way that I would arise suspicion, passing the stash house. I was almost certain that Miami Dade wouldn't be paying around-the-clock overtime for a team of people to be out here. They had a wire on the telephone, and if anything, they might have someone back at their offsite listening for a call to come across the line. The idea of them paying for four to six people to be out here was not likely. Every car I saw was unoccupied.

I back-tracked up the street and then stepped closer to the stash house. It was an older Miami home that had fallen into a noticeable margin of disrepair. Its mailbox was crooked and supported on one side at the base with a pile of loosely stacked coral rocks. The circular gravel driveway was burglar's nightmare because of the crunching sound under each footstep. There was an assortment of ceramic pots with plants in them but only two were upright, the others lying on their sides, the plants it seemed not knowing if they were plants or vines. Even in the moonlight the paint was visibly splotchy and had hard water rust stains at the foundation from a long ago, but now inoperable sprinkler system.

The garbage can was in homeowner's No Man's Land. It wasn't fully at the curb as mandated for trash pick-up and it wasn't completely tucked away either. I wanted to pull the garbage and see if there was anything in the refuse that would help me know more about the house, Peralta, or anything related to this derelict carnival my life had become.

I ventured onto the property and very deftly lifted the lid. There was only one small bag in the can. It had been in there a long time. I reached in for it but its contents and the heat had permeated a sticky substance in the bag that had leaked out, causing it to partially adhere to the bottom of the can.

I immediately realized that this garbage run and looking for the county employee at the gates of Matheson Hammock may have been a good plan in theory but were actually both a colossal waste of time. I could've been home catching much needed shuteye. Instead I was out here living like a vampire dependent on shadows and darkness to operate. I was still leaning into the can and just pulling away and closing the lid when I heard him:

"What do you think you're doing?" came a voice from behind me.

This was not good. I know good things and this was not going to be a good thing. I had to think fast. I'd been holding the large hinged plastic lid in my left hand with my arm fully extended while I reached into the can with my right hand. The lid was blocking the only source of decent light being cast by a neighbor's porch light three houses down. Still leaning more over the can than actually into the can, I looked back over my right shoulder dipping my face as far against my right shoulder as I possibly could. I was hoping the Hartford Whaler baseball cap was concealing my face as much as it was telling the world I was a fan of an unsuccessful NHL hockey team. I didn't need to see him, I just needed to know if he was a cop or not.

He was about thirty feet behind me, partially in the street. It was ten yards. A first down in NFL football. With the lid still fully raised and held in place by my left arm, I peered just barely over my right shoulder and saw black sensible shoes, dark brown BDU cargo pants, thick lower legs and wide thighs.

Miami Dade police badge on his belt.

I stopped right there. I didn't need to go any further. I didn't care if he was black, white, Hispanic, young, or old.

I slammed the lid and simultaneously turned away from him. The noise of the lid slamming down scared me I think as much as it did him.

I started running right towards the side of the house, flinging the garbage can on its side behind me, hoping to slow him down if gave chase. My heart was in my throat, adrenaline, fear and stupidity intersecting within me at the same time. I ran past the front porch and right through a large spider web. I reasoned whatever arachnid had spun the web was as surprised to have me run through it and was left dangling by a broken strand. Overgrown bushes that had encroached over the side yard path rubbed my head and neck as I tore through them. I couldn't hear anything behind me more mostly due to my own hyper breathing as I ran blind through an unfamiliar dark back yard. By the rear door of the house I teetered precariously on the lip of a fetid, algae-scummed koi pond, just regaining my balance before I stepped in.

A heavily-damaged chain link fence stood between the stash house and its rear neighbor, the top post gone, luckily for me. I attempted to jump the fence like an Olympic hurdler. My right foot caught the top of the linkage, my momentum and weight causing the fencing to fall into itself with an imploding rattling sound. I was able to hop free of the tangling mess and distinctively heard him say from somewhere behind me, "Fuck!"

The loud jangling of the chain link fence coupled with his rather loud expletive caused the first dog somewhere in the vicinity to start barking. That rapidly became a crescendo of dogs interspersed in the neighborhood, barking at various pitches and intensity. It seemed as if each one was a town crier, announcing my loping run through the yards.

I just kept running.

My fear of being garroted by an unseen clothesline was as strong as my fear of being brought down by him. The house to the rear had a shadow box six-foot wooden fence separating its front yard from its back yard. Aesthetically it made no sense to have wood in the front and chain link in the back, but now was not a time to judge residential decisions. I knew that if I could scale it quickly I might have a decent chance of getting away.

If I didn't make it on my first attempt and fell backwards…my odds of getting away would drop dramatically.

I'd barely been able to scale a four-foot section of chain link and my confidence was not very strong, but my fear was stronger. Historically fear has been a good challenger to confidence.

History proved correct.

I planted one foot hard against the shadow box fence, careful not to wedge my foot in between the slats. Using that momentary boost of redirected inertia, I flung my arms and chest up as high as I could, and the top of the fence met my upper abdomen. It scraped and hurt but that was barely registering, my need to escape was that great. I bent at the waist and flipped over and down onto the other side of the fence. I was hoping that based on the girth I saw of the cop's legs he might be just as thick above the waist as well. I landed mostly on my feet in a low crouch and staggered forward using my hand to push from the ground and put me back upright to continue my sprint. I dashed past a boat with a torn tarp over it and turned north on Southwest 32nd Avenue. I just kept focusing on running north and not looking back. If he was behind me I didn't want him to see my face, and if he wasn't behind me I needed to outrun any police assistance he might call in on his radio.

I only slowed down when I approached the next cross street which was Shipping Avenue. I was now half walking and half running due to my Jameson fitness regime catching up to me. I put my hand to my face to obscure it as much as I could, did a quick turn around, and walked backward, looking back down the street. My breath was coming in deep gasps and I was trying to breathe normally and stay quiet at the same time. I don't think I was doing either of them successfully. I could see no one behind me. That gave me no comfort since I had not seen anyone when I was at the stash house either.

He seemed to have materialized out of thin air. Either that, or I got careless and just missed him in one of the parked cars. I was also now acutely aware I was directly standing on the major avenue his fellow officers would be driving down to back him up. It would take a few minutes for City of Miami to be notified to assist as well. This could be a big police search perimeter of K-9 dogs and both agencies within minutes. My mouth was dry and I felt like throwing up but I knew it would just be Irish whiskey dry heaves. I stifled that urge and got out of the middle of the road, walking forward intently, looking for headlights and listening for revving engines or sirens. My plan was to get my wind and start running again.

At the corner I heard a car engine idling. I ducked behind a hibiscus bush and thought of my options. I really didn't have many. I moved along the bush, peering out between its colorful flowers at the street.

On the corner I saw a vision that could only be classified as serendipity: a taxi idling in the south swale of the road. Its interior light was on and its Haitian driver appeared to be writing something on a clip board. I scurried over to him. He still had not seen me. I rapped on his hood lightly with my knuckles and proffered the best Crest whitening strips-smile and friendly wave I could. He looked at me with a combination of surprise and suspicion as he lowered the window partially and I strode up abreast his car door.

"Hey good evening. My dog broke from his leash and I've been all over looking for him, can I get a ride back to my place so I can get my car and go looking for him?" I pleaded.

He shrugged and said nothing but I interpreted the thunking sound of the automatic door locks opening as a yes. I quickly ducked into the back seat.

"I need to go to Tigertail Avenue and Lucaya Street."

I said it as fast as I could, hoping he would get under way and turn off his interior light. He tossed the clipboard across his passenger seat and put the taxi in drive. The light stayed on a few seconds longer than I was comfortable with, but by the time all four wheels were rolling east he reached up and flicked it off.

I just needed to get away and out of eyesight of approaching police cars as quickly as possible. I sat low in the seat and for a while pretended to be looking for the dog I'd conjured up to keep the ruse going.

"You're sweaty for the night, man." he finally said breaking the silence between us.

"Yeah. I know. That damn dog was fast. Something spooked him. My wife is all into natural stuff and wanted us to have a fiber husk leash. Freaking thing just shredded when he pulled and he was off and running."

He didn't reply.

I used the quiet time to think about what had just happened. I never saw the Miami Dade TNT detective. I *looked* but I never saw him. I let my preconceived notion of how much importance Miami Dade was giving the stash house to cloud my own judgment. It was a stupid mistake on my part. I continued to pretend to be looking for the dog, when in fact I was checking every cross street for any signs of Miami police cars heading west. I didn't see any. I hadn't seen any TNT units either. From a police perspective I probably just came across as a guy down on his luck rummaging through garbage cans looking for a late night meal. There is a very good chance that he gave a nominal if any chase and wasn't going to reveal to his co-workers that he let someone walk-up to the stash house unchallenged. He may have been asleep, slouched down dozing in one of those cars and awoke to see me leaning into the garbage can. He may have never even got on the radio and called it in. Maybe his expletive was for his own spider web entanglement and not related to my failed Edwin Mosses leap of the chain link fence.

When we got to the corner of Tigertail and Lucaya the taxi driver slowed and waited for me to tell him exactly where to let me out.

"You're not going to believe this but I left my keys back at my brother's place on Margaret Street. I'm going to need to go back."

He sighed and his shoulders rose and fell with an obvious shrug. He swung the car around in the intersection and headed back east.

"Can you take South Bayshore back towards Cocowalk? That's where we walk him in the morning and he may be over there."

He cast a quick glance at me in his rearview mirror, most undoubtedly thinking about income disparity with him driving a taxi at 4:20am and me buying overpriced dog leashes.

Having him take us south helped to ensure a northbound return rather than driving straight back into what I just ran from. It was a circuitous route but I needed to ascertain if the area where the Q45 was parked would be crawling with cops. We neared Grand Avenue and Southwest 32nd Avenue by the veritable Grove Cinema.

Still no sign of police.

Hoping he wouldn't notice, I sadly wedged the Hartford Whalers hat into the space where the back of the seat meets the bench seat. As I'd hoped, he turned up Margaret Street from the south and I had him stop five houses from the Q45. The fare was $15.45. I gave him a twenty and prayed he wouldn't stay parked with his interior light on, looking at his clipboard like when I discovered him. To my great pleasure not only did he wordlessly let me out but he drove relatively slow north towards the corner near the stash house. I walked directly behind him, using the taxi and its headlights to help conceal me. When I got to the Q45 I opened the passenger door near the conch shell mailbox, climbed over the console and started the engine. I reversed the car into a driveway and conducted a quick turn and was now southbound away from the stash house, driving cautiously with one eye in my rearview mirror.

That was clearly way too much risk for very little reward, I thought as I lit out of there with urgency once I was away from Margaret Street. On any other occasion I'd have been able to articulate myself out of the situation. Just not this time. It would've been incredibly ruinous to me to have been seen or even worse identified at the stash house by anyone from TNT. I was engaged in a game that I did not know the rules to, nor what cards the other side was holding.

The night was getting away from me. This of all nights I should've been in a deep sleep to be rested for the full day that laid ahead. My harebrained notion to seek the county worker and to do a garbage run was predicated on my disregard for rational thinking, my penchant to overindulge in Jameson, and my avoidance of thinking about Gina. It was reckless to be out here, to have gotten that close to a house that was known specifically by me to be under the watchful eye of TNT. I was slipping. I was missing turns to go home and thick wide cops sitting in cars.

Now, for the sake of what professionalism I could eek out of myself, I needed to plop into a bed, couch, futon, or settee soon. The tight turns of Main Highway in the Grove negated the full experience of making quick time, but once on the somewhat straight stretches of Old Cutler Road north of Kendall Drive. I gunned the Q45 and its yawning engine perked up and went into beast mode. Passing Kendall Drive, and approaching Matheson Hammock I slowed enough to discern if the county employee was at Matheson Hammock.

As I neared I could see parking lights of a truck through the brush and plantings of the entrance. Against better judgement that was simultaneously fraught with defiant intention, I pulled up to the gate, and my lights illuminated the white Miami Dade County pickup truck. As a courtesy I killed my lights and then switched on only the parking lights. We were like two unannounced adversaries with our parking lights dueling through the locked gate. I stepped out and caught a flash of the green and blue Miami Dade logo on the driver's door as he did the same.

I called out in the dark to the unseen figure approaching me and identified myself, holding the chain around my neck up, presenting my badge for him to see.

A weather-aged black man emerged from the darkness. He was thin and looked as though he had seen a lot of life that many would've preferred to not have seen. Experience and exposure to the world were the only things I could think of to justify the way the skin on his face was wrinkled and creased. His eyes were heavily-lidded and he exuded an indifferent affect. He had on a long-sleeve white shirt, dark green pants, and some sort of work boot. My low-emitting parking lights revealed us both from the shins down and I noticed paint droplets on his boots. We stood with the gate between us momentarily and then he only said two words.

"Hold on."

He walked back to the truck and retrieved a white golf-sized towel and came back to the fence. He held his keys in one hand and the towel in the other hand. Somewhere between leaving the gate and coming back to it, he'd been able to light a Salem cigarette. He clenched it in the corner of his mouth, the cool menthol aroma betraying its brand. He did something I had never seen done before. The gate was slightly off plumb, most likely due to an errant weekend boater's inability to maneuver his boat trailer through the gate. The gate needed to be lifted and swung at the same time to open it. He draped the orange-brown streaked towel over the rusty gate, unlocking it, then looped his arm over the gate with his armpit on top of the towel. He lifted and swung the gate back as he shuffled with it. I started to help him but he rebuked me telling me I'd get my hands all dirty.

He had the gate swung back and pulled the towel off of the gate.

"My wife will kill me if I come home with anymore rust stains on these shirts. She just can't get them out. She even washed my clothes in CLR."

CLR was a commercial calcium, lime, and rust remover that I'm sure was just as detrimental to the fabric as well.

"You ever forget the towel?" I asked.

"Once," he said looking up and slightly shaking his head in remembrance.

"She was like a cat on a curtain. I swear. I think her wrath was biblical." His voice trailed into a nicotine cough.

I was actually wondering if the wrinkles and creases had come from life or maybe more so from his marriage.

I tried to steer the conversation away from rust stains and marital discord.

"I wanted to talk to you about the other night. You are aware that there was a body found in the park late at night, just a few ago?"

"Yeah I spoke with that young man for about thirty minutes."

"Young man?"

"About your age, from Homicide, Lonnie something," he said.

"Trentlocke. Lloyd Trentlocke?" I said, refreshing his memory.

"Yeah, that's him. I like that he came out to the plant to see me. I didn't have to waste time in traffic. Good guy."

Someone keeping you out of traffic was becoming an instant personality plus in Miami.

"I was hoping that you might be inclined to tell *me* anything you might know as well," I asked.

"There isn't much to it. County's got me zimming and zamming all over the south end and I'm never able to be in any spot too long. I don't go too far past the entrances because I need to be here if a fire truck needs to come in. Like even here, you know how many boaters try and get in early by jimmying the locks? Mini lobster season; you might as well just have an army here. They have no home training or courtesy. There's nothing common about common courtesy. Not in today's world there ain't," he lamented.

"I can understand that, but on the night that the man was discovered in the park, do you recall that particular night?"

"Oh yes. Like I told that detective, I was doing my nightly check-ins and got held up at the maintenance center because the check engine light came on. It was because the gas fellow hadn't put the gas cap on tight. Took us about an hour to get it figured out. He called his cousin in Utah who had some computer thing called Prodigy and he read what it might be to him and we fixed it by tightening the gas cap. You imagine? Calling some guy across the country with a computer who can tell you what's wrong with your truck?"

"Yes, it is very futuristic. But what exactly do you recall about that night? Anything else stand out?" I inquired again.

"The thing I remember most is when I got here, there were police everywhere. I thought maybe a crocodile had bit someone or something. They told me some man was found dead by the tidal pool parking lot near the Red Fish Grill. All I know is that the gate was locked when I left and it was open when the cops were here."

"Anyone else have a key?"

"Now, how would I know? It's government. I took this job when my position at Recreation was eliminated two years ago. They gave me some keys and that was it. But you got dock masters, restaurant people, maintenance crews all kind of people who were all here before me. There's just no way of knowing who has keys."

"I never got your name."

"You also never asked. I'm Godfrey Pinder."

"Pinder. You Bahamian?"

"My dad was from Eleuthera, my mom from Maryland. We lived in the Grove on Franklin Street since I was five."

"You've seen a lot of changes."

"I seen a lot of things," he said back with a serious look.

I transitioned the conversation back to the subject at hand.

"So basically nothing out of the ordinary," I said, getting ready to finish our gate chat.

"Not unless you consider that some man was killed," he said, stubbing his cigarette into the ground and then picking it up and holding it.

In the military field, stripping a cigarette or retaining the filter to be discarded later is a known habit, used to make it harder for your enemy to know you were there.

"You ex-military?" I asked.

He flung the towel back over the top of the gate and closed and locked it from his side.

"Like I said. I seen a lot."

Chapter Nineteen

I T WOULD HAVE been a short, two-minute drive, but sleeping on the *Ruthless* was just not an option. It would throw Octavio into a tizzy and of course be a great starting point for any rumors about my marriage—even if they are true rumors. It wouldn't be courteous to show up twice in one week. Like Mr. Pinder had said,

"There's nothing common about common courtesy. Not in today's world there ain't."

I definitely was not going to go to the VIN office. My little Jameson 1k run through the Grove caused me to perspire justly and a shower was in order. I put the Q45 through its paces and got back to my house as soon as I could. The clock on the oven said 5:36am. Sunrise would be in less than two hours. I had to be at Miami S.I.S. at 10:30am.

I didn't think we would be doing the fifteen kilo deal anyway. More often than not, the Miami tactical narcotic unit and DEA would just get Lobo and Concho when they leave the Embassy Suites Hotel to drive to the meet. I still needed to be prepared if it does in fact go, but I went to sleep not expecting it to.

I went into the master bedroom and thoughts of Gina flooded my mind. I refused to ever sleep on her side of the bed and the only reason I was even in the bed the night Peralta died was because I had clothes in the dryer. I fell asleep waiting for them.

That's what I told myself.

The reality was there was still a faint trace of her perfume on the bed and it brought me comfort. Painful comfort. My rational mind said it was unhealthy to sleep on sheets that hadn't been washed in months. So to appease my rational mind, rather than wash the sheets I just abstained from sleeping on them. It made sense to me in my heartsick way. It was once said that a divorce is like a death, except the other person doesn't have the decency to die. That's what I remember thinking as I drifted off to sleep, curled in a ball at the foot of the bed, an afghan blanket my only source of warmth. I was either afraid or reluctant to muss up the sheets and opted for a compromise that made sense in my fatigued mind.

I don't know if I dreamt during the night but I do know I was deep asleep when my phone started chirping and vibrating. My side hurt and the scrape from scaling the fence left angry red striations on my torso. I had ninety minutes to get to Miami S.I.S.

I put on the local TV news. While waiting for the traffic report the morning weather woman came on. I had no idea what she was saying. In Miami, most men, and I suspect a few women, have to watch the weather report in the morning at least twice. The gorgeous, buxom, short-skirt women they hire to report the weather are such a distraction that rarely is what they're saying ever initially heard.

Women hadn't been a part of my life since Gina. I was like a parachutist whose parachute fails to open. I couldn't be latching onto someone and hoping their steady full parachute can support themselves plus my tumbling out of control life.

My head wasn't screwed on right and the recent days were a testament to that. I stopped taking count of the flagrant lies I told, my intentional omissions, the copious drinks I consumed, the unnecessary rules I broke, and the necessary rules I bent. My life had become a presage for unimaginable chaotic situations. It was as if each new twenty-four cycle had a divergent set of problems and actions.

The local weather ended and now the news said it was a "first look at traffic," which was probably the twelfth look at traffic since they went live on the air at 5:30am.

The roads were exceptionally clear and I was beyond pleasantly surprised. The traffic reporter mentioned a teacher's workday for Miami Dade County. That clarified the reason for such light traffic. Days without school were astoundingly different when it came to road congestion. I took advantage of the ease in traffic and availed myself to a longer than normal shower. The water stung my side and chest at first and I just gritted through it. After that nocturnal garbage run I really spent some time scrubbing and cleaning especially around my fingernails. In the shower I conducted a mental checklist of what I had in my go bag. I was satisfied that everything was passable, but I did want to add just a few more clothes to offset what I'd pulled out the past few days. Tactically I didn't want to start adding extra handcuffs, flex cuffs, raid jackets, back-up batteries, portable battery chargers and the like. All that cop gear just negates being undercover. Coming right out of the police academy my training officer carried only a gun, a spare magazine, and a singular pair of handcuffs. He carried the portable radio in his hand and used it as a radio, a less than effective truncheon, and an even less effective throwing spear. I learned from him that minimalism has its advantages.

The shower snapped life back into me. I exited feeling refreshed and clear-minded. I needed to get going and put out some white sneakers, shorts, and two shirts for the go bag.

I decided to wear a pair of jeans and a Jamaica Jaxx shirt. It was black onyx and had subdued black iris and palm prints. I chose dark slate gray casual Klein Wager shoes. I went to the top of my closet and located an all-black Florida Marlins baseball hat. I did still have a spare Hartford Whalers hat in my go bag but it would be a while until I felt comfortable wearing such a distinctive hat.

Satisfied, and with time to spare, I left the house and was soon driving up U.S. 1 towards Southwest 27th Avenue on my way to Coral Way and the Miami offsite.

Traffic was light and the drive was pleasurable. The buildings, billboards, and assorted storefronts went by in a blur. The offsite parking lot for Miami S.I.S. was crammed to the edges with cars and trucks. I parked on the side street by an old decommissioned U.S. mailbox. It had been welded shut. I reasoned that the postal service found it more advantageous to weld it inoperable rather than remove it. They should call it "Government Art in Public Spaces" and just keep leaving and dumping things across the landscape of America's biggest cities.

When I approached the parking lot my cell phone rang.

It was Lieutenant Poulsen.

"Hello."

"Did you intend to tell me you were with Miami today?" he started with another impolite greeting.

"Of course I did. But I don't think this is going to go, so I held off until I knew for sure," I answered.

"Let us try this again, shall we? I'll say it again—I want more communication and in a timely manner. That means you check with me and keep me appraised. I need to be in the loop. The loop circles around me. You see? That's how it goes. Now the Major has expressed a desire to take you out of the loop. I have put my neck *in* the loop to defend you. So I think it's woefully incumbent upon you to keep me in the loop, or I might just side with the Major. Understood?"

"Understood," I said.

"Understood?" he repeated for emphasis.

"Understood." I affirmed again.

"Call me when you know, so I will know," he said as he hung up.

The parking lot door was wedged ajar with the *Miami and the Beaches Real Yellow Pages A-K* book. I wondered how many cities in America were so big that they had to have an A-K and an L-Z phone book. We had enough people to warrant two volumes of phone books but not enough to justify standalone U.S. mailboxes.

Obviously some law enforcement genius who was tired of coming down to open the door for the assembled-and-still-arriving outside agencies decided to put personal safety and operational confidentiality secondary to his lazy ass. Using my foot, I swept the book aside making sure the door closed behind me. What compromised security they had prior to my arrival was not of my concern, but now that I was going to be inside with them, I did have a concern.

I went to the second floor and into the same room with the black numbers 325 above the door. Inside were everyone from last time plus a few people I hadn't met. Sergeant Brookings was back from his Ecuadorian detail and that freed up Johnny Morris from the acting supervisory role. I learned that two of the other three people I didn't know were from the DEA,, the other one from U.S Border Patrol. The final two to arrive after me were from the state attorney's office. One was an investigator named Carl Klenner and the other was Harvey Binchel, an attorney we all knew. They both came in complaining about the door and wondering where the phone book went. Obviously that breach of security was a well-used practice. I stayed quiet.

Iggy was off to the side jotting down notes on a pad and looking at his cell phone. Ivan had finally gotten a lot of the pink out of his hair and was laughing and joking with Alex and Javier. Claudio sat in a swiveling office chair, one leg splayed across a desk, the other rooted to the ground. He was leaning back and pressing a tennis ball in his right hand with bored detachment. Chispa was sitting on a desk, cross-legged, swinging her legs. She gave me a slight smile when she saw me looking at her. The sun from a transom window above her highlighted her beauty. I pondered for a second how she felt being called "Chispa" rather than her given name, Araceli. Johnny was walking amongst each group, speaking softly to each individual either in pep-talk mode or assessing their needs or preparedness. The DEA guys stayed to themselves each one a carbon copy of the other with their thin beards and New York accents.

Iggy got up and said that he needed to "make the call."

Upon hearing that, Johnny made a very loud announcement for everyone to silence their cell phones and pagers.

Claudio got up from the desk and joined Iggy. They went into the telephone room. The telephone room was a small adjacent cubby that had been outfitted with thick insulation on its interior walls and a thicker than normal door. Inside was a small desk, two chairs, telephone, and recording equipment. It was designed to maximize quiet so that when making undercover telephone calls the other party couldn't hear any background noise that may reveal your identity or location. Car alarms, overhead airplane jet engines, train whistles, and even barking dogs can throw off the negotiations of a drug deal. Nothing brings the bad vibes more so than a passing fire truck or police car with its siren blaring. It also served a purpose to allow for optimum clarity when recording calls. That was paramount if needed for courtroom evidence. Once they closed the door, a blue police light above the room came on, its rotating blue strobe wall-washing the office. In the dark it would probably have been very disconcerting but in full daylight and with the office lights on it was benign. The light was intended to inform the rest of us a call was in progress and to minimize all unnecessary noise and conversation.

Quietly, sections of the *Miami Herald* were passed amongst a few people and even the opening of a Diet Coke can by one of the DEA guys was stifled as best possible. They were in the phone room for a while. Finally, the blue light stopped roving and in a minute or two both Iggy and Claudio exited the phone room.

All eyes looked to them to hear what was going to be. The news was delayed as they went straight into Sergeant Brookings office to meet with him and Johnny. Ten minutes later Johnny came out and notified everyone that it was set to go but that they were drawing up the operational plan. He asked that no one leave and then he asked Harvey, the attorney, to join him. Five minutes later they all emerged. Johnny went back into the telephone room but kept the door open and did not activate the blue light.

Sergeant Brookings called the room to order.

"For those of you who weren't here two days ago, myself included, this is where we're at. We have two Dominicans down here from New York looking to buy fifteen kilos. They met with Iggy and Cade on the river at Casablanca's. One of them identified himself as "Lobo," the other was introduced as "Concho." They expressed some mild agitation over pricing and location. They've agreed to the pricing but are setting the location. I know we don't usually do it this way but all of us here are in agreement."

With that he motioned in a sweeping manner to Harvey, Claudio, and Iggy. He then continued.

"We feel it's a doable locale. We're also only bringing five real kilos—the rest will be shams. We've spoken with Harvey here from the state attorney's office, and the five kilos will seriously ruin their day."

Harvey then spoke up.

"Five kilograms of cocaine, and the conspiracy to possess with the intent to distribute under 21 U.S.C., Statute 846, will be statutory maximum life. There's no need to haul fifteen legitimate kilos out there when five will suffice."

When he said "haul kilos out there" I knew this was going to be outdoors and in a place we didn't normally conduct business. Iggy was checking and fine-tuning the operational plan. He was writing with one of those little bowling alley pencils that doesn't have an affixed eraser. Without an eraser he frustratingly kept crossing over things.

"We think we got them locked in," Sergeant Brookings said. "Iggy heard an airplane in the background; we think they're still at the Embassy Suites near the airport. Hopefully when they come out, our in-place surveillance team will take them down. We can all get credit for the victory without having to suit up for the game." He finished by turning the floor over to Iggy.

Iggy looked up from his notes and with a slight exhale, addressed the room.

"Claudio listened in on the call, and based on what he heard he agrees with what we're planning."

He momentarily paused as Johnny came out of the phone room and gave him a thumbs-up.

"The meet will be at two o'clock on South Bayshore Drive and Southeast 15th Road. For those of you unfamiliar, it's where Southeast 15th Road ends. It becomes South Bayshore Drive and curves along the bay by Brickell."

"Like near Porcao and the Four Ambassadors?" interrupted Alex.

"Yeah, but further south. They want to meet on the paved bay walk by the sea wall. They want the 15 kilos in a red igloo cooler and they'll have the money in their own red igloo cooler. They don't want anything out of place and they want me and Cade to just be fishing off the sea wall. They'll act like they're fishing too and then do a cooler switch."

"Yo bro, when this is over can me and Alex do some fishing for real and maybe stock one of those coolers with some *cervezas*?" joked Ivan.

"When this is over we can all have some *cervezas*," replied Iggy.

"So to bring everyone up to speed, SWAT is training with Monroe County down in Ramrod Key and they're out of play. We have no SWAT on this one. If this goes, we'll have units set up along Southeast 15th Road from Brickell to the Bay. Cade and I will be positioned just inside the curve on the bay walk. When they come down 15th and after we meet with them, we'll quietly start bringing in units closer. The audible take-down signal will be either 'For God's Sake' or 'Aye por Dios.' The physical take-down signal will be hands up."

Iggy said the take-down phrases again and even demonstrated the hands up signal by raising his hands above his head in a classic surrender pose.

"Ramos, you still have a white pick-up truck, right?" asked Iggy.

Alex nodded.

"When the take down signal is given, you'll block 15th. Take your white pick-up truck and block the westbound lane. There's a high median there and usually a lot of parked cars. That should hold them in so that they can't leave. Just in case we have a runner or they break free."

Alex nodded again.

"Johnny will be on foot and staged at the corner of 15th and Brickell. There's a Catholic church there." Iggy fumbled for the exact name and scanned his notes.

"Saint Jude Melkite," blurted Chispa.

"*Cono,* we got a nun! Its Sister Mary Elizabeth Chispa," joked Ivan.

Everyone in the room had a quick laugh.

"You wish, you fantasy-driven pervert. My sister had her baby christening there. The only nun you're going to see is spelt n-o-n-e." She gave it right back to him garnering an even bigger laugh.

Sergeant. Brookings brought the room back to order and Iggy continued.

"So here's where everyone will be: On the corner of Southeast 15th Road and Brickell, Johnny will be solo on foot at Saint Jude Catholic Church. He'll be the first eye looking for them driving in. Silvio, you'll have both DEA agents with you and be staged midway down Southeast 15th Road. There's a condominium parking garage entrance midway down that will be a good place to get an eye on the street."

One of the DEA agents suggested that three to a car might be unnecessary, to go with two instead. Sergeant Brookings agreed and made sure that the DEA agents were provided a Miami S.I.S. radio. He instructed Iggy to reposition Silvio. Iggy used that tiny pencil to scribble a new position for Silvio on his ops plan.

"Silvio, you will now be with Claudio on the raised ramp at the front door of the condominium where 15th bends into South Bayshore Drive. You should have a good view of both of us from there. Border Patrol and Harvey will be with Sergeant Brookings in a floater position but mostly along Southeast 15th. Ivan will also be a floater, primarily on South Bayshore Drive, further north from where we'll be standing. Chispa, you'll be with Investigator Carl Klenner and also staged further north on South Bayshore. Ivan will be mobile down on Bayshore

Johnny then handed Iggy and I our Kel pagers as he informed the room he placed a call to the Miami Police Marine Unit. He was able to secure an unmarked boat and two marine officers who would be in plain clothes. The two marine patrol officers were in case any of the Dominicans tried to evade arrest and jumped into Biscayne Bay. The briefing continued with the information of what radio frequency will be used, what hospital was designated as the primary medical center of choice, the color and make of the marine boat, Lobo's car, what tow truck agency will be used if needed and the other small details that comprise an effective working operational plan. The room was asked to stay intact and not leave until the ops plan was printed, then sent into NINJAS and checked for any conflicts.

Sergeant Brookings addressed the group one final time before dismissing everyone.

"Just a happy reminder, everyone: we have their car under surveillance. Harvey says the conviction can still go even if we intercept them on the way to the meet. Let's hope it goes that way and we can wrap this up early. If not, do not be complacent. Johnny and I will be drug security and will load up Iggy's car. When this is over we'll take the kilo cooler with us back here. Claudio and Silvio, you will load the money cooler into Carl and Chispa's trunk and follow them straight back here. The four of you are money security. Got it? Now everyone needs to be in place no later than 12:30pm. The sooner the better. This is set for 2pm and they could be mobile even before that. Cade and Iggy, we'll meet you in the parking lot of David Kennedy Park in thirty minutes." The room dispersed and that left me and Iggy as the last ones to leave "How you feeling?" I asked Iggy.

"I feel good. They seemed cool and less of a pain on the phone. I think they'll get popped before they even leave the hotel parking lot. If it does go, I'm okay. You just be the gringo brother-in-law. I'll do the talking, get them to commit. If any of us says something like 'For God's sake, you got your line tangled,' we'll know it's take-down time. It should go smooth."

"Alright, then I'm going to go get some fishing stuff for us and change real quick. I'll meet you guys at David Kennedy Park," I said.

I shook his hand firmly and pulled him in for a support hug, then I headed out the door and down the stairs. I saw the Yellow Page book at the foot of the stairs and back-tracked up to return it to the office.

Iggy was one of the best in the business. He'd done countless hand-to-hand drug deals and was as sharp and as knowledgeable as anyone I'd ever worked with. He knew the business intimately. He had swagger and confidence and a good mix of charisma.

That's why when I opened the door to throw the book on a desk I wasn't surprised when I heard him in the bathroom puking his guts out.

Chapter Twenty

I DON'T THINK IGGY was aware I'd come back to the office. I eased out and down the stairs. This was classic doper time and it was predicated on the theory of "hurry up and wait." I never, ever saw any of these deals go on time. I had no reason to think this would be any different. Granted, Lobo and Concho had been on time at Casablanca's. Still the historical precedent was that they never go on time. My own clock was ticking and I had to get my own mind focused. When I got to my car the first thing I did was call Lieutenant Poulsen. I cradled the phone in my ear while I retrieved a beige pair of flat front shorts, a dark blue polo shirt, and the white sneakers from the go bag. He answered after the second ring.

"Yes, Cade?"

"Hey, I wanted to let you know that Miami thinks this is a go and it will—"

"Yes, Brookings called and told me. Make sure you represent."

With that he hung up. It was arguably one of the shortest telephone calls I'd ever had and rather than be peeved about it I was inwardly happy for the brevity. I needed to get things done. The side street was quiet and I opened the passenger back door. I sat down on the seat and quickly took off my shoes and jeans. I put on the shorts and then the white sneakers. I shed myself of the Jamaica Jaxx shirt and then trying to be as unnoticeable as I could wrestled myself into the polo. If changing my clothes half in and half out of the car was an Olympic sport, I would be a medal finalist.

I headed straight west to Southwest 32nd Avenue, and without delay to a McDonald's. The drive-thru line was long but I didn't care. I pulled the car right up against a garbage can with a large mouth opening, leaned out the car window and pulled a relatively clean McDonald's bag out of the garbage. I shook the cheeseburger wrappers and napkins out of the bag and put it in the back seat. It seemed that my life in the past twenty-four hours had reduced itself to pulling things out of garbage cans. I back-tracked east on Coral Way and then south on Southwest 27th Avenue. I went to the same marine supply store that I saw the TNT detective walking into yesterday.

For good measure I put on the black Florida Marlins baseball hat. Given the geography, it couldn't hurt to be inconspicuous, especially after last night. I wondered about the irony of being in a marine supply store and displaying a leaping baseball fish on my hat, albeit one that had won the World Series only two years earlier. The sports writers predicted the Marlins barely winning fifty-five games this upcoming season. What a fall from grace.

I used the U.C. credit card and bought a fairly inexpensive medium-quality fishing rod, mainly because they offered a free five foot cane fishing pole with the sale. Both came outfitted with fishing line, cheap synthetic purple worms, and bobbers. I also bought a white five-gallon bucket. I scurried to the exit, clumsily left through the narrow automatic doors lined with point of purchase displays, nearly tripping over the awkwardly-balanced poles in my arms. I got creative and opened the sun roof and stuck the poles in the car through the opening. I drove south to Bayshore Avenue crossing the same roads the taxi had taken me upon just last night. I made very good time getting to David Kennedy Park. I turned into the park going through its wrought iron gates and alabaster columns. Straight in front of me I could see the rigid masts of sailboats bobbing in the bay, their sails a pageant of color peeking above the tree line. I also saw Sergeant Brookings and Johnny to my left, holding a red cooler. I pulled in next to them and rather than get into a discussion of what car to drive to the meet, I popped the trunk; an obvious indication to put the cooler in my car. Johnny hefted the cooler into my trunk. We waited a few minutes and Iggy pulled in and parked the A4. We said a few words amongst us and then decided to start the drive to the meet. Johnny and Sergeant Brookings followed behind us as I drove.

Iggy was quiet, but not in a bad way. Like an athlete who immerses himself in game mode, I could tell he was visualizing what was potentially going to transpire, choreographing in his mind how it should go. The reflective calm before the storm.

Driving through the eastern section of the grove we passed the Viscaya Estate and the old Planetarium. Iggy's only comment was, "Just looking at this street and trees you could think you were in Argentina."

I let that comment go without a word as to not disturb his reverie.

We were driving now north on Brickell Avenue which was basked in two layers of darkened contours. That time of year the Royal Poinciana trees aren't in bloom, but their distorted trunks and limbs frame the avenue. The opulent trees front the avenue in a mix of shadows intertwined with the shifting shade from the towering bayside condominiums. Each condominium's ornate landscaped entrance harkened a regal and inviting name like Atlantis, Santa Maria, and Villa Regina.

We slowed down as we got closer to Southeast 15th Street so that Sergeant Brookings could drop off Johnny. Johnny got out very quickly and then Brookings' remaining drug security team stayed with us as we turned east.

The Catholic church was a solid quilt of flat smooth stones topped by a Spanish tile roof. The church had hard-angled corners and very few windows in the front. He'd told us at the park he planned to act being destitute and sit on the steps. The steps were indeed a great place for Johnny to set up and watch the street. The street from Brickell east was lined with parked cars on either side and just a few open spaces. As I passed the condominium entrance on my right, I looked for the DEA agents, and although I didn't see them I was confident they were there. I also looked for Claudio and Silvio on the white raised condominium carport. Once again, I didn't see them, which oddly enough bolstered my confidence even more so that they were there.

The expansive azure waters of Biscayne Bay were before us in an intoxicating vista. The road curved north in a bend, and it seemed as though the blueness of the bay waters fought with the temperate blue sky for my rapt attention. Ivan was crafty and had been in a parking spot along the bay, idling in his car. As we approached, he pulled out, leaving the vacant space for us. It was a perfect parking space for what we needed. Flush against the curb just north of the curve in the road. It would provide Claudio and Silvio a direct line of sight to our trunk when we pulled out the red cooler packed with the kilos. I pulled into the space and Sergeant Brookings whizzed by my door and he and Ivan were now moving down Bayshore and away from us. It was at that moment that a brief, but palpable quietness settled over Iggy and I. I would equate it to how a child feels on his first day of school, watching his parents drive out of the school yard.

Both Iggy and I knew it was all on us now.

We sat there for a second with the sun beaming down through the open sun roof and it was Iggy who spoke first.

"I think we should drop some lines in the water and set up a little territory so that no innocents wander into our party."

"Agreed," I said as I continued to take in my surroundings. I put the Q45 keys in Iggy's hand.

"They'll be expecting you to be in charge of the precious cargo."

The vantage point that Claudio and Silvio had was from behind us. Across the street was an equally bland condominium painted in an uninspiring beige paint, its grounds surrounded by a wrought iron fence and thorny overgrown fuchsia colored bougainvillea. It was quiet, the waves lapping against the sea wall the only sound. Although there were cars in nearly available parking space along the bay side of the road there were very few people out walking along the bay walk. We seemed to be in that ideal time between the runners and baby strollers of the morning and the joggers and strolling lovers of the evenings. The cycle of life as seen in a purely recreational context.

We both got out of the car, the soft, breezy salt air wafted about me without invitation or refusal. A sensory affirmation of why we all lived in Miami. Neither of us were ideally suited to effectively conceal any handguns. There were some U.C.s in Miami who did conduct deals and meetings unarmed.

I was not one of them.

I was counting on something to make it possible for me to have accessibility to my gun. I assumed that every municipal government would try to entice its residents and visitors to clean up after themselves; especially at places people photograph and like to take in the views. It's less costly than having city workers go out daily and clean the grounds. As I expected there was a stand-up garbage can very near to the front of the car, on the grassy parcel between the concrete walkway and the sea wall. It was an industrial grade can made of mesh metal that had been inserted into what can only be described as a concealing wooden barrel with neatly-spaced lacquered furring strips. Fortunately for me it was nearly filled to the top with garbage.

I reached into the car and retrieved the McDonald's bag from the back seat. Using my body as a shield from any prying eyes, I put my .40 Glock 22 and a spare magazine into the McDonald's bag. I crumbled the bag as best as I could and laid the bagged hidden arsenal atop of the garbage in the can. I suggested Iggy do the same and that he take the white bucket and turn it upside down. He put his weapon under the upturned bucket along the sea wall. We retrieved the fishing poles from the car and I sat on the bucket securing Iggy's gun. I dropped my line into the water. The cane pole wasn't exactly ideal for casting. Looking out across the peacock-blue water I saw two guys moored about 500 yards offshore on a thirty-four foot Baja Sport, outfitted with dual 250hp Mercury engines.

"Those your guys?" I asked Iggy.

"Yeah, that's them," he replied with a tinge of disappointment.

"I don't know what their draft is but we should've thought about the tides before we asked for marine support. This looks like a decent low tide and if we need them I don't know how soon they get in."

"We still got time on this one. If they move your guys should get them in the parking lot and we can all go home," I said.

Iggy just shrugged as he laid his rod and reel down by a decorative four-foot piling on the sea wall. We were careful to put ourselves in a position where Claudio and Silvio could see us and the car. We also left enough room between us so that Lobo and Concho would have to be a little spaced apart when talking to us.

We were in a section of the bay called Point View. Biscayne Bay is normally only about three to five feet deep nearest to the sea wall there. The low tide now was visible by the brown-green barnacles and marine adherences to the sea wall about six inches above the water line. We both stayed quiet. I just focused on a vanishing point in the horizon somewhere near Virginia Key and Key Biscayne in the far distance. Although feeling a little edgy, there was a serene quality to the bay. Minutes went by and then we both heard a voice say in a quick, three-burst repeat,

"Nothing yet. Nothing yet. Nothing yet."

It was Ivan. He was shirtless, riding by on a rusty beach cruiser bicycle. He peddled holding the handlebars with his right hand. In his left hand he held a Budweiser beer bottle down low by his thigh. An obvious and equally hopeful prop for his undercover status. His white T-shirt was bundled in a big knot along the top tube of the frame of the bike. In the sunlight the pink remnants in his hair made it seem as though his scalp had a sunburn. He never stopped as he curled around the median in the curve of the road and then continued leisurely northward on Bayshore.

I just started laughing. So did Iggy.

"Your boy is all kind of ate up," I managed through my chuckles.

Seeing him on the bike and wondering how he acquired the bike as well as the beer bottle became a lively conversation between Iggy and I. Ivan was the source of levity that we both were in need of.

It was now 2:30 pm and there was no sign of Lobo or Concho. According to Ivan nothing had happened at the hotel. It was looking like this was going to be an empty day. Sometimes these deals can be negated by some very small things. One partner might get cold feet. The full financial backer might decide to pull out. Someone might have undercut our price. Someone loses their nerve. It's really no different than the so-called legitimate business of the world. Both Iggy and I were discussing how long we'd extend our wait before we literally pulled our lines out of the water and went home. Unbeknownst to us at the time, one of the DEA agents was transmitting on the radio.

"We got two in a car parked here on the road."

Chapter Twenty-One

A DARK BLUE HONDA Prelude had pulled into one of the parking space along Southeast 15th Road, midway between where Johnny was sitting on the church steps and where the DEA agents had positioned themselves in the Condo parking garage. Johnny had his radio wrapped in a thin towel by his side. He was able to listen and transmit through the towel. There was some discussion between him and the DEA agents about whether or not they were seeing the same thing. Johnny hadn't seen the car come down the road.

Johnny got up from his position at the church and walked out towards the sidewalk. Scanning the parked cars and looking towards the bay he finally saw the Prelude. It was idling in the parking space on the same side of the street as he was on, about six car lengths from him. He could distinctly see two people in the car. He stepped back away from the sidewalk and sat on the grass using a low hedge by the church as a means of concealment. He and Sergeant Brookings began having some radio discussion about whether to just approach the car and take them down on conspiracy or wait to see if they got out to approach me and Iggy. Sergeant Brookings in turn was having not only an ongoing conversation with Johnny but also an instructional debate with Harvey in his car about legality and criminal case integrity. The DEA agents were getting antsy and were all in favor of using Chispa's car to pin the Prelude to the curb and use the fender wells to block the driver's doors from opening. The DEA agents and Johnny could approach the car from the sidewalk on the passenger's side. Alex suggested that he do it with the truck and leave Chispa where she was on the north side of Bayshore.

Iggy called Claudio to tell him we were only going to wait another ten minutes then we were going to pack up and leave. Claudio informed Iggy of what was happening just down the street from us. Iggy hung up and told me about the Prelude "occupied two times." We continued to act as though we were two fishermen although we both couldn't help but keep sneaking peeks over our shoulders west towards the heightened attention everyone else had taken. We couldn't see or hear anything; we just knew there was high interest behind us somewhere on Southeast 15th Road. Sergeant Brookings was going to do a drive by to determine what would be the best approach.

It was at that moment that the brake lights of the Prelude flicked.

The driver's door opened.

Johnny was now on the sidewalk walking towards the car. The passenger door also began to open and the dark sock and shoe of a man emerged right in front of Johnny. The DEA agents had left their position and were now walking rapidly in the street along the parked cars, covertly hiding their handguns behind their thighs as they approached the Prelude. Alex had whipped the pick-up truck around the center island under the Brickell traffic light and was barreling down Southeast 15th Road. Johnny was almost at the back of the Prelude as the passenger was now nearly fully out of the car. He was distinctly Latin and with a narrow build.

He never saw Johnny.

Johnny pushed him hard into the gap between the car's body and the opening door. He bent him at the waist and shoved his Glock hard up against the back of his head.

"Miami Police! Don't you fucking move!" he shouted.

Simultaneously both DEA agents helped extract the driver from the car with a fair amount of force.

Both Saint Jude parishioners were as surprised as Johnny and the DEA agents to be in this unexpected and completely mistaken situation.

Alex was the first to get on the radio and tell everyone to stand down. We never heard or saw any of this. It was just as well because I looked north on Bayshore Drive and could clearly see both Lobo and Concho walking on the bay walk towards us. My pulse quickened and my mouth went dry.

There was no red cooler with them. That was not a good sign.

I had no idea where they'd come from. It was unsettling, their ability to just *appear,* as if they'd materialized out of thin air. Iggy still had not seen them. Keeping my lips pursed and rather tight I said in a low voice audible only to Iggy,

"We got company."

I was sitting on the bucket, my line in the water. I opened my legs and turned my left foot towards the garbage can, teetering on the bucket, very awkward. If need be, I'd make a try for my gun and leave Iggy's gun available to him under the bucket. Iggy looked over my head and saw Lobo and Concho approaching us . He wanted to make sure they knew he saw them.

"We're running out of ice, so don't ask us to open our cooler unless you got something we can put in it."

Concho showed brief hesitation at being called out to so openly. He stutter-stepped for a second, but Lobo continued walking towards us with a confident stride.

"Oh, we got plenty to add to your cooler. You should let us see just how much is in your cooler so we can know how much to put in."

By now they were almost to us. I didn't want to take my eyes off of them, but I did give a quick look towards where Claudio and Silvio were—no signs of them. This time my confidence was no bolstered. I was at a physical disadvantage sitting on the bucket and knew I needed to meet Lobo and Concho on equal ground. I didn't want to completely relinquish physical contact with the bucket so I struck what can only be described as a Captain Morgan pose; one foot on the bucket the other on the ground.

By way of greeting, Lobo asked me, "What you planning to catch? A mermaid?"

"Talapia," I answered.

Lobo let out a very throaty guffaw and then spit a clotted wad of phlegm in the grass.

"Damn, you make me laugh."

Concho was less than agreeable. His squirrel-like brown eyes were now more interested in Iggy than in me. My threat potential to them must not have been as high as Iggy's was.

I was careful not to move too much on the bucket so as not to alarm them. I took mental note of what they were wearing. Concho was wearing a pair of dark black designer jeans and white long-sleeved shirt embroidered with gold thread stitching on the right wrist. The stitching said "Jordache." Lobo had more of an unmade bed look to him in his sloppy hunter-green polo shirt. The shirt was easily a size too big and was untucked over a pair of baggy jeans and grey Rockport shoes. I looked for signs of guns in their waistbands or ankle holster bulges but was unable to see any.

They had no red cooler. This was not getting off to a good start at all.

I knew where our red cooler was but had no idea if they even *had* a red cooler anywhere nearby. More specifically, how long had they been on the street, and did they watch us arrive?

My mind raced through everything from the moment we arrived and from I what I could recall, we were okay. I was hoping the Kel was working and that Miami S.I.S. was listening. Iggy went into deal mode and started bluntly steering the conversation directly at Lobo.

"You got a cooler?"

"Yeah. We do, but ours is full. Maybe if you're done with yours we can have yours."

"Where is your cooler?"

"Where's yours?"

"Nearby. But I'm about to take *mi cunado*," [my brother in law], "and these size tens I'm wearing and walk out of here. I'm not here to play I got/you got. Where is your cooler?"

Lobo looked over at Concho and motioned with a sideways glance back towards the road. Concho slowly and ever so slightly lifted his shirt and a car remote was hanging on his belt, tethered by six inches of old shoelace. He pressed the trunk release button.

Further north of the curve a cream-colored Lincoln Navigator's rear cargo gate audibly popped and the gate rose very slowly, like the wing of a large metal gull, until it opened fully. I could clearly see a red cooler in its cargo area.

Lobo smugly stared at Iggy.

Iggy's bluff was called and he needed to pony up his portion of the deal. He kept his eyes fixed on Lobo and pointed behind him with the remote for the Q45, causing the car trunk to open just as the Navigator's did, but with less of a dramatic rise. Iggy walked to the Q45 and lifted the trunk to its full opened height. The red cooler with the kilos inside gleamed its newness in the bright sunlight. Lobo started to walk towards the Q45. Iggy slammed the trunk down and laid out the parameters in a firm tone.

"Not until your cooler is here. I'm not going to your car. Concho you said you pick up things. Why don't you take you a trip by the sea and go pick up the cooler and we do the exchange here, one for one."

Concho was not happy being told what to do and his animosity for us began to show.

"I think you're an asshole, and—"

Iggy cut him off and took the stance of high school quarterback in a classic Statue of Liberty play. He held the keys in his throwing arm and loudly said, "If I want any shit out of you I'll squeeze your head. One more word out of you and these keys go in the bay."

I was just watching it all, darting my eyes between Lobo and Concho, keeping my foot on the bucket. Worried they'd notice, I removed my foot from the top of the bucket and stood adjacent to it, clutching the cane fishing pole. Oddly enough it was Lobo who broke the tension.

"Hola amigos, amigos, sin preocupaciones. Está todo bien. Concho, sé un deporte y ve a traer a este hombre su cooler de presidentes de papel."

[Hey friends, friends, no worries. It's all good. Concho, be a sport and go bring this man his cooler of paper presidents.]

Concho scuffed his foot at the grassy swale in agitation and stomped off to the rear of the Navigator. He retrieved the red cooler from the Navigator but rather than walk back along the grassy strip he chose to walk in the street along the parked cars.

He put the cooler on the grass between the Q45 and the sea wall.

Iggy once again opened the trunk of the Q45.

"Put it in here and we'll do the exchange from my trunk."

"Fuck no we won't!" bellowed Lobo.

"You just threatened to throw the keys in the sea and I said to you we do it in the open no bending over a trunk or back seat bullshit. You bring it here side by side. We open at the same time."

Then would've been a good time to say, "Oh for God's sake you're acting like a baby, Lobo." but for some reason Iggy didn't choose to give the take-down signal. Perhaps out of Latin machismo or some other perception of sleight, he pulled our cooler out and pushed it down next to theirs, the force of which made both coolers bump against each other.

I very slowly inched my way further from the bucket, giving Iggy access to his gun under the bucket. Iggy had already flashed two kilos at the restaurant when we first met them. Although he'd been indignant with the process and location of the meet, he had no compunction about flippantly lifting the lid to our cooler.

The whiteness of the cooler's interior illuminated the off-white taping and muslin-wrapped kilograms of real and fake cocaine. Both Concho and Lobo glanced down into the cooler. Concho's eyes squinted as he muttered the word, "Pluto." He was obviously reading the markings on the kilos. Lobo had a very broad smile spread across his face. The chip in his front tooth stood out like a rip in a circus tent.

I continued holding the cane pole but had sufficiently maneuvered myself closer to the garbage can. Concho was in front of me and off to my right. Iggy had his back to the bay and Lobo across from him. Iggy started to move towards their cooler to open it.

That's when I saw it.

Chapter Twenty-Two

I T WAS A Miami Dade Transit bus. Caked with dust and greasy grime, it was hurtling from the north on Bayshore at an incredibly high speed. It looked as though it hadn't been washed in weeks. The grungy, smeared dirt swatches coated the exterior and windows, with the exception of where newly placed handprints were all over the doors. "Out of Service" was digitally displayed on its front sign board. It looked totally out of place on the street.

The street was not a known transit route. The bus hugged the center yellow line of the two-lane street. Overhead, tree limbs and palm fronds were being ripped away by the roof of the bus, the torn branches falling upon parked cars and in the road.

The bus lurched and swayed due to the high rate of speed, making a hostile rumbling sound that made me wince. I couldn't see the driver completely, but I did observe that he was wearing aviator sunglasses and a maroon T-shirt—not a licensed transit driver. His acceleration of the bus seemed to grow with each revolution of the wheels.

Iggy must've been looking at the bus as well because I don't remember the cooler ever being opened. The bus side-swiped a parked "Mirror and Glass" work truck, causing a plate of glass roped to the side of the truck to pull back like a cheap vinyl countertop. The glass shattered between the truck and the roaring bus, creating a cloud of glass shards that spun up behind the bus like pixie dust. The bus had become an atrociously loud ground-comet of metal, rubber, and Cummins Diesel.

It was coming right at us.

The tires were gripping into the asphalt, trying to maintain contact and avert air from getting under the chassis and lifting the behemoth frame. The bus was nearly astride us when the loudest swoosh of air I have ever heard gave me such a scare that I actually flinched. The air brakes were being applied as if the driver were standing on them; which might've been exactly what he was doing. The smell of searing rubber and noxious white smoke engulfed all of us. The bus heaved to one side as it approached the curve in the road. It tilted and rose and then resettled as the driver turned the wheel hard to the left causing the back heavy bus to equally pitch to the right. The engine groaned and black diesel smoke poured out of the back. The bolt pin to the rear engine hatch snapped from the torque, flipping the engine hatch up and down like a damaged, unhinged metal grate. It had the fury of a metallic hurricane and was yawing with swaying recklessness.

The driver leaned to his left and curled around the steering wheel, the centrifugal force being the only thing keeping him from being thrown into the dirt-encrusted bus doors. It was like watching an industrial savage beast swerve by. As the bus bounced once, then twice over the concrete curbing I saw another male figure standing in the middle of the bus, his arms wrapped tightly around a safety pole inside the screeching machine. He had a look about him that was nothing short of terrified confusion.

The braking of the bus had slowed it to what can only be described as a manageable crash. It hit the curbing that separates oncoming traffic in the curve. It rose over the median and slammed back down on it, denting the left front rim. The front tires still turned fully to the left directed the bus towards the bay as the bus came to rest, broken and smoking, completely across both lanes of traffic right in the middle of the curve, becoming a literal transit dam across the road.

Car alarms blared from the ear-splitting noise, lending a general air of chaos.

The bus had been stolen from the Miami Dade Transit yard. It was exactly the diversion Lobo and Concho had wanted, created by them. It was coming together just as they had planned.

When Concho opened the Navigator's lift gate it was a signal to the bus driver to get ready. He walked in the street so the bus driver could see him and would know it was time to create a literal hell on wheels. Certainly, Lobo and Concho did not know we were cops. What they did know was that all traffic from Brickell would be halted, and if we had any back-up players of our own that would be the direction they would be coming from.

It wasn't the smell of burned rubber, the iridescent smoke from the tires and brakes, or the deafening car alarms that snapped me back to the present; it was the sound of Iggy's voice yelling the take down signal "For God's sake!"

I turned my attention back to the deal and saw Lobo lifting his shirt, reaching deep into his waistband.

It happened so fast I don't think Iggy had a chance to react.

Lobo's hand came out with a Smith & Wesson Model 669 9mm handgun. Chrome with black grips. It looked huge, but I think that was the fear in me. It was maybe just a second or two, but to me it was as if I saw everything in kinetic slow motion. The chrome barrel glinted a bluish hue in the white smoke swirling about us. From nine feet away he aimed it at Iggy and pulled the trigger.

My ears went momentarily deaf from the gunshot. A tinnitus-like ringing in my ears made even my own voice sound distant and foreign. I was yelling 'For God's sakes" over and over but it sounded to me like it was faintly coming from someone else blocks away.

The bullet struck Iggy in the left shoulder and spun him back. The powder burn was visible and a brief plume of whitish spray rose out of the burn as the bullet burrowed into the ligaments and fascia of his shoulder. An aerated splotch of blood spurt out in a crimson surge like a volcanic eruption once, and then just oozed rapidly saturating his shirt from his shoulder to his chest area. His right heel crammed against the raised concrete of the bay walk and he fell on his back, straining with his right arm, trying to reach the bucket. He only succeeded in tipping the bucket over, exposing his gun laying inert on the white concrete.

Lobo saw Iggy splayed upon his back reaching for the gun.

Lobo chose to shoot again.

I could hear the sound of boat motors in full throttle and screaming and yelling, but Lobo's next round came out of his gun so fast it silenced all other noises to me. Iggy was grasping and extending his fingers as far as he could, his eyes wide with fear and pain. Tears were in the corner of his eyes and sandy grit was caked on his face.

Rather than shoot Iggy center mass, Lobo shot at his hand as Iggy futilely scampered on his back towards his gun. Lobo's choice of target was obviously honed from watching countless television shows and not from actual combat gun training. He missed, and the bullet caromed off the concrete and I assume went somewhere out into the bay.

I stepped towards Lobo with my right foot planted hard. I pulled the cane fishing pole from my left side and mimicked a classic two-hand tennis racquet smash stroke. I struck Lobo across the face with the cane pole as hard as I could. The raised nubs of the cane pole opened a gash along his right cheek. The follow-through on my swing traveled up his face and split his eyebrow as wide as the Panama Canal. My hands tingled from the crack of striking his head with the pole. Blood poured from both wounds. He was blinded with pain, blinded with anger, and blinded by the blood pouring down over his eye.

Momentarily stunned, he bent down at the waist, still holding the gun out in his outstretched arm. Iggy squirmed on his back and kicked, propelling himself from a prone position right off of the sea wall and into the bay. I felt the salt water from his splash hit the back of my neck.

Concho had also pulled a gun from his waistband. I saw his

white shirt rustle out of the corner of my eye. I'd started to take a Samurai stance and was raising the cane pole above my head with the full intention of splitting Lobo's head like a coconut. Lobo was white hot with anger screaming obscenities in Spanish and vowing to kill me. He was bleeding profusely. His face was a maroon mask of O-positive. His vision still obscured by the blood pouring down upon him, he aimed his gun.

Holding that cane fishing pole and staring down his gun was one of the most disadvantaged feelings I've ever had. Concho was now running between me and Lobo fully intending to shoot Iggy as he lay in the bay. Lobo fired blindly where he thought I was. The round was explosive, and it caught Concho straight into his side.

The look of surprise and anguish was a facial combination I could never replicate. His squirrelly eyes briefly widened, and then just suddenly closed. I think he was dead before he hit the ground. He folded like a cheap suitcase and he most certainly was dead. He fell right between us, his gun still in his hand.

I once again was aware of voices and now gunshots near me. The arid smoke from the bus was now being dispersed by the bay breeze. My first instinct was to get away but I had to get to Iggy. It took a moment for Lobo to realize that I did not have a gun and I did not shoot Concho. He must've had that odd, sickening realization that if I didn't have a gun…then he must've killed his friend.

I wanted to make myself as small as I could. So like a baseball runner on first base diving back to the bag to avoid a pickoff, I lunged towards the garbage can and got into a low crouch behind it, only stopping my momentum with one hand or I'd have sailed right past it. Using his right hand like an awning over his eye to keep the thick roiling blood from blinding him, Lobo was now shooting with his left hand—badly. The first round he fired at me hit the left side of the can near my hand and it splintered one of the furring strips. A piece of the jagged wood hit my forehead. I reached above my head and grabbed the bag. I was worried about Iggy but relieved he was not in my backstop behind Lobo. I needed to get a few rounds at him to allow me a better shot.

The Glock was still in the bag and I found the trigger guard by touch through the paper. I got off two rounds. One round cleared the can. I felt the percussion and loud twang of metal from the other one as it splintered on the can's rim.

A riderless bicycle come bounding into my line of sight and the bike crazily bounced and tumbled, landing right near Lobo. The McDonald's bag was scorched and tattered and I pulled my Glock completely free of it.

There was more urgent yelling to my right.

I peeked over the can and saw Lobo now pointing his gun off to my right in the direction of the voices. I fired one round at Lobo—but I heard three shots.

Lobo was hit three times in center mass.

Quivering and shaking, he staggered backwards. He convulsed a few times more, his eyes fighting to focus with a noticeable release of urine instantly spreading across his pants. He then dropped with a quick and resounding thud. He was dead.

I looked to my right and I saw Ivan, wide-eyed, pink hair, and shirtless, still holding his Glock in a ready position, pointing at Lobo.

Ivan had rushed in on the bike and jumped off of the bike, leaving it to crash at Lobo. It was enough of a surprise that it allowed me the opportunity to get my shot off at Lobo and hit him center mass. Ivan had concealed a small Glock 22 in the knotted t-shirt on the bike—and that was the gun he had used to shoot Lobo twice. Center torso hits.

While all of that had been going on the driver of the bus had pushed the filthy bus doors open. He was armed, and expecting to come and join up with Lobo and Concho. He did *not* expect to see Claudio and Silvio running towards him yelling "police." He took a shooter's stance and fired two rounds at Claudio and Silvio. He missed with both of them and they were the last two things he ever did before dying. From a full-on run, Claudio squeezed off two rounds. One hit the side of the bus; the other caught the accomplice in his clavicle. The bullet shattered the clavicle then traveled downward and severed his aorta. The blood flow was sickening and deep enough to drown in had the bullet not killed him.

The passenger on the bus was a more formidable foe. He was a few steps behind the driver and when he came out the side door, he knew already there were cops outside. He came out firing, his bullets haphazardly peppering the street, most of which found final trajectory in parked cars.

Silvio had taken a tactical position behind a burgundy Dodge Durango and shot back at the passenger while Claudio was bravely at the front of the bus to help us or to outflank the passenger. The passenger was now near the rear of the bus, his back up against the dusty exterior, returning fire at Silvio.

Alex had driven the pickup truck east in the westbound lane of Southeast 15th Road. The shooter transfixed on Silvio never saw Alex, and Alex drove the pick-up truck right into the rear of the bus, pinning the shooting passenger between the truck and the bus. He died laid across the truck's hood, looking vastly different from the waist down than he did from the waist up.

The marine unit was coming in hot. The wake behind the boat was a rooster tail of displaced Biscayne Bay water. The driver cut the engine and into reverse, slowing the boat down.

Ivan jumped into the bay and sunk into about a foot of muddy silt.

Iggy had stayed flat in the water on his back, much like a limbo dancer leaning back in the buoyant swells, his feet and calves touching the bottom.

More of the Miami S.I.S. units were arriving on our side of the bus.

Chispa arrived and she and I also jumped into the bay. The boat driver turned the boat sideways. Ivan was the first to be with Iggy. Chispa and I helped to keep the now drifting boat from crunching into the sea wall or hitting Iggy as we hoisted him up towards the boat. Both Marine officers pulled him in. I told Chispa to go as well and without anytime to question me I was pushing her up to the boat and she was also helped aboard. I knew Ivan and I would have to be here on the scene for a shooting team inquest.

The operation plan had designated Jackson Memorial Hospital for emergencies. Mercy Hospital was on the bay and had an Emergency Room in the back near a helipad. There was a dock to bring the boat right up to. From where we were it was a five-minute, balls to the wall full-throttle run.

"Take him to Mercy. For God's sake take him to Mercy."

Chapter Twenty-Three

THE BOAT WAS optimum planing as it rocketed south towards the Powell Bridge. I could only see the driver as both Chispa and the other marine officer were down low attending to Iggy.

Hands. Lots of hands.

I remember lots of hands pulling Ivan and myself out of the bay. I'd scraped myself on the sea wall and felt lucky that was all that had occurred to me. I also saw the irony in scraping myself the night before jumping a fence, and now getting scraped again from being raked up over a sea wall.

If this continues I'll need a skin graft.

The next forty minutes were the most surreal moments of my life.

Waves and waves of people and equipment swarmed the area. They seemed to come in synchronized occupational segments, as though there was a calculated orderliness to the post-action arrival of everyone with a siren or a blue light. The amount of Miami Police cars, Florida Highway Patrol cars and Miami detectives was staggering.

It was over.

Yet they still streamed in, each jockeying for a place to park and a piece of the street to walk upon. Since the bus was an immovable part of the crime scene, the north strand of Bayshore was now equally land-locked with police and fire rescue vehicles. Miami police cars comprised the bulk of the assemblage, each one of them parked differently from the other to render the eventual removal of all of them to be a fiasco unto itself. Three separate Miami Fire Rescue trucks and one large Miami Fire pumper truck also found their way into the mix. A very large police perimeter from Brickell and Southeast 15th Road was set up and that annoyed residents and delivery drivers alike. The yellow crime scene tape fluttered in the breezes of the bay and it was as if every forty seconds a different detective was ducking under the tape, many of them mustachioed carbon copies of each other. This was to be expected.

What I had not expected were the four news helicopters jockeying for prime air space hovering above us. Sometimes their aircraft came low enough to rotor wash a small chop on the bay. They were like multi-colored dragonflies, each emblazoned with colorful striping and a bold-painted numerical graphic of their channel designation. On the ground the multitude of uplink satellite trucks with their raised antennas were like an Orwellian nightmare. The flimsy yellow crime scene tape was the only thing keeping them from bearing down directly on top of us. A cadre of officers started erecting large tarps at the outer perimeter scene to keep the long lenses of the trucks from zooming in on many of the undercover officers present.

A command post was eventually established further south on Brickell Avenue at the Immanuel Lutheran Church's parking lot. That helped to push back the media and residential voyeurs. Countless police officials milled about each with some sort of star, bar, fruit, nut, or leafy designation on their uniforms. The gold badges severely outnumbered the silver badges. It was just a brief spate of time before the BDU-wearing crime scene technicians descended upon us, each of them adorned with measuring tapes, thirty-five millimeter cameras, and enough latex gloves to stock a veterinary clinic.

Ivan and I found ourselves in a constant huddling vortex of shuffling cops each asking if we were okay. Each of them also wanting to shake our hand, which I knew would wreak havoc on the crime scene technicians who'd want to scour our hands for gunshot residue, also known as GSR. We'd already been in the bay; the briny water more than likely would of already affected the GSR test anyway. It was hot outside but it was still February in Miami and the bay was a chilling experience that did not recede once I was out of the water. The sun would be setting soon and the coldness I was feeling was not abating.

This was going to be a Miami scene and the person at the front of any firing line would be Sergeant Brookings. I was sitting in the back of a Miami Fire Rescue truck more so to avoid the media's probing cameras than for any other reason. Sergeant Brookings came by. He and I had a quiet talk about it all. Every car driven by any of the detectives that discharged their weapon would be processed by a crime scene technician. The processing was for any prescribed or non-prescribed medications and any possibility of alcohol being a contributing factor. Once again, my phone was secured in a crime scene and unreachable. The redundancy of my life was becoming comically tragic. I asked him to call Lieutenant Poulsen since my phone was in the Q45.

I also asked him to have Ivan come into the truck with me. He left and I was alone in the Fire Rescue truck with the exception of a male paramedic who seemed to have the good sense to not venture out of the truck and get entangled in the confluence of agencies and people. From my limited vantage point I watched it all swirl as it crossed within the opening of the truck doors. I did see Dr. Bashir and a small contingency from the Medical Examiner's office. With four new arrivals soon destined for her facility, I'm sure she wanted to get as much information as she could to assist her with autopsies. Her hair was a black sheen of unmanageable tendrils caused by the blowing soft bay breezes. She looked over at me and saw me looking back at her. She tried to brush the tousled hair from her face and gave me a tight-lipped smile.

Two minutes later Ivan sauntered over and climbed into the truck. I spent a measurable amount of time thanking him for his bravery. It was his first in the line of duty shooting. Ivan joined me in camping out in the back of the Fire Rescue truck. We sat together, both of us swaddled in aluminum heat-retention blankets. A female paramedic stepped into the truck and proffered forms of consent for blood to be drawn from us both. She drew two vials of blood from each of us and capped the vials. She then had us endorse our signature over the secure tape on the vials. She secured them into a red biohazard bag and left the truck.

Ivan wanted to talk, the adrenaline coursing through him like a runaway train. I cautioned him to suppress the urge to talk or elaborate about what just happened. There were too many people around us and too many of them wanting to be the first to have an inside scoop on what was easily the biggest news story of the day.

There are three types of communication: telephone, telegraph, and tell a cop.

Ivan was a little younger than me and his need for affirmation and confirmation was showing.

"This a first for you?" he asked me.

"There aren't many things about me that are a first," I said, looking out at the gathering amount of people and resources.

The male paramedic in the truck with us was trying to busy himself; although he was obviously listening to our conversation.

From the open doors of the Fire Rescue truck I saw a cadre of investigators walking through the crime scene, not processing or evaluating much of the carnage that was everywhere. They wore their Miami badges displayed on lucite placards stuck into their breast pockets. They seemed to have the same taste in mundane haircuts as they did in uninspiring suits. The paramedic continued to pretend to write on a clipboard, but his eavesdropping was still evident. It was clearly obvious that Ivan and I were being regarded with an odd, if not morbid, curiosity. I turned towards the paramedic.

"Hey buddy I know you guys took my vitals but I'm feeling a little shaky. I don't know if it's the cold or the adrenal dump but it's making me a little queasy. Do you have anything you can give me, please?' I asked the paramedic.

The paramedic reached into a sturdy orange plastic case and pulled out a pill vial with Alprazolam, or what's more commonly known as Xanax. He gave me a one millimeter dosage to help with any anxiety, or panic disorder. I swallowed it greedily as I watched the group of police officials coming nearer to the truck.

"Ivan, how you feeling?" I asked.

"I'm good, bro. I'm good."

"I don't know man, I've been through these before. Why don't you take one of these from the paramedic? It will be easier on your system. You've been through a lot," I implored.

"No really, I'm okay," he said.

I kept a watchful eye on the group of investigators. They were now talking with a young Miami officer who was pointing towards the rescue truck we were in.

"Seriously, Ivan. Take one," I said.

I stared intently at Ivan and he deduced that there must be a method to my madness. Besides, we'd just killed a guy together and I think the bond of trust was clearly forged.

The paramedic was happy to be a part of the inner circle and dispensed a millimeter tablet to Ivan. Under my intense gaze, Ivan swallowed the pill.

Within a minute the open back doors of the truck were filled with the group of investigators looking up at us. They were aligned in a bit of a wedge and reminded me of first graders queuing up to an ice cream truck.

The one in the front identified himself as Commander Tom Dolan, head of the Internal Affairs Division at Miami. He looked expectantly at each of us, expecting a reaction or acknowledgment of his professional status.

Since I didn't work for Miami my reaction wasn't as obvious as Ivan's. Dolan picked up on that immediately and motioned at Ivan with a raised eyebrow look.

"You're one of ours, right?"

"Yes sir" said Ivan.

"Then you must be the one from the Gables," said Dolan, now directing his attention to me.

"Guys from what we've heard, this was quite an event here today. Looks like a good shoot to all of us." The minions with Dolan in the tight little wedge against the bumper all nodded their heads.

"We would love to leap-frog over all the forensics and reports and get a clearer understanding of how this all happened. Detective Contreras, why don't you tell me what happened. Help me to piece this all together."

Ivan started to speak and I put my arm out across his chest.

"Commander, I don't know if that's a good idea right now." I said.

My penchant for angering police personnel was becoming flagrantly obvious to me.

"Excuse me, but I'm talking to one of my personnel and I will kindly ask you to not interfere with Miami Police official business."

"Well, I just know that both he and I have been medicated for anxiety and nausea and he might be under the influence of the narcotic and anything he says at this moment may not be admissible in court, or in your own internal investigation. Especially if it's *official* Miami business."

Dolan fumed. I wasn't sure if he was irritated at my audacity or at the paramedic who was now trying to quietly clamber over some oxygen tanks and access the truck's cabin through a narrow passage. I called out to the paramedic and told him we were ready to go to JMH for observation. To his credit he picked up on the cue and retraced his steps back into the transport area of the truck and closed the rear doors, shutting Dolan and his crew outside.

"I remember that jerk from labor relations meetings. That felt good," said the paramedic.

He got on his radio and requested an escort to JMH. It took about ten minutes for our police escort to carve a path through the police cars and whisk us away from the crime scene. As we left the scene two of the uplink trucks hastily lowered their antennas and tried to follow us but an enterprising Miami police car blocked their passage, slowing them going through the Brickell intersection and provided us the opportunity to get to JMH without a news truck filming us exit the truck.

On the way to the hospital, I spoke to Ivan.

"Don't say anything to anybody unless you have an attorney with you or a good union representative. They have enough eyewitnesses and forensics that your statement can wait."

The truck lumbered west on the Dolphin Expressway ramp from I-95. We would be at JMH soon. The siren was not nearly as loud inside as it was outside.

"Did you really need to take something for your nerves?" Ivan asked me.

"No."

"That was pretty slick, having us take a Xanax to keep them from questioning us. Especially for me. How did you know that?"

"Like I said, there aren't many firsts in my life."

Chapter Twenty-Four

THE JURY IS still out on who has brighter lights boring down on their clientele; Dunkin' Donuts or hospitals. The atmosphere about hospitals is strangely interchangeable from one to another. The sound of carts wheeling through hallways, chimes over the intercoms, and the ability of nursing staff members to avoid eye contact and pretend not to hear the questions posed to them from visitors and family members is incredibly universal. It's been said that the walls of hospitals have heard far more prayers than the walls of churches. This I believe.

And for Iggy's sake, I hoped that was true.

The clean, but blandly painted walls of the hospital were not where I'd wanted to spend my early evening. I was there partially by choice and primarily by protocol necessity. I wondered about Iggy who was at Mercy Hospital and had no say in the matter.

There were two Coral Gables patrol officers outside my hospital door. Their need was more ceremonious than security. They were awaiting me as I was wheeled from the E.R. to a quieter part of the hospital. I didn't need to be wheeled anywhere, and especially to or from the E.R., but there was as I said, a certain necessity of protocol. I sat up as soon as the orderly was done pushing the gurney.

I was on the third floor in a room larger than most hospital rooms. Awaiting me there were Lieutenant Poulsen and the police chaplain, Bob "I Just Bless 'Em" Messon. Reverend Messon was from the Saint George Antiochian Orthodox Cathedral, which was about a seventy-five step walk from the police department. Being the police chaplain, he'd actually had been provided a uniform, although this time he was in obvious golf attire, as was the Vice Mayor of Coral Gables, Ted Langer. Langer won more votes than any other city commissioner. He had a whopping 1,298 votes in the last election from a city with a population of 49,800. Whoever said democracy favors the majority never accounted for low voter turnout. Reverend Messon and Vice Mayor Langer had been on the back nine at the Riviera golf course when my shooting Lobo disrupted their game. Poulsen was fidgeting with the remote for the adjacent empty bed when I came in. He seemed intrigued by the pneumatics. The Reverend set a soothing tone by having us all bow our heads while he said a prayer for Iggy, myself, and for the police department as a whole.

The Vice Mayor had never met me and remarked that I didn't look like any cop he had ever seen before. It was a show-and-tell. It allowed Poulsen to highlight some of the operational situations the VIN unit was involved in, an obvious ploy to keep it all together especially with an audit-crazed city manager in our midst. Not many people know what to say when the small talk ends, and the fact that people died today, one of them directly because of me, made the silence all the more awkward. The Vice Mayor spoke first and suggested that maybe he and Reverend Bob should "mosey on out."

Poulsen was on his cell phone a lot and when he hung up he said Miami had found my car keys in the grass where Iggy must of dropped them. They were finished with my car and he'd have one of their officers or public service aides drive it to JMH. He started to ask me for specifics about the shooting. The questioning may have seemed normal, nonchalant, but anything said can be admissible. As a qualifying condition I let him know the Xanax I was given was still making me a little woozy. He was smart enough to see that any questions about the shooting would have to wait.

He turned the questions to how I felt about Donito's murder and what did I think was behind it instead.

I briefed him on how Miami S.I.S. and I had met Lobo and Concho at Casablanca's. I also informed him of my inability as of yet to reach Roldan, the only unaccounted for Horseman. He got a chuckle hearing about Macias' betting debt causing him to flee to Colombia.

"Cade, all this back and forth with your life. It's got to be unsettling and bit unnerving just in its own sense of action. You need to try and structure your life. Control the things you can. A little regimentation would be good for you. Take me, for example. I try and go to bed at the same time every night. Every morning before I even go into the office, I get a newspaper at the Circle K on Ponce de Leon, I stop by the motor pool at Fire Station 2 and fill up the car, and I start my day, each day, the same way. It keeps the crazies from being part of my entire existence. You should try it. Build in some structure and the craziness will seem less overwhelming."

Three crime scene technicians from Miami arrived and entered the hospital room. Poulsen took yet another telephone call and upon hanging up said my car was downstairs in the E.R. parking lot. He sent one of the posted officers outside to get my keys for me.

He also said that after conferring with Major Brunson he had put me on administrative leave for the next two days. I was to report back to the station then.

I wanted to change from the hospital gown, so I asked that he have the officer bring my go bag up since my soaked clothes were nowhere to be seen. He left shortly after that, just missing the arriving Miami Crime Scene technicians.

The crime scene technicians dutifully swabbed my hand for GSR, and two of the three exhibited consternation that my hands had very minimal traces of it. The salinity from the bay and the sweat and oils of all the handshakes from cops on the scene had contaminated me. They asked where my clothes were and I assumed they were down in the E.R. I signed a consent waiver allowing them to take possession of my clothes. They also asked for consent to take a vial of blood to which I agreed as long as a JMH nurse took one as well to allow for independent refute or validation. They summoned the nurse and we waited again in odd silence for the nurse to arrive. One of the technicians did tell me that Iggy had spent three hours in surgery and would be looking at more surgery in the coming days. They said he was resting comfortably and the bullet hadn't severed any major arteries or caused significant damage to any nerves. He had a long road of therapy and recovery ahead of him. He may not be able to throw a ball or raise his arm above his head, but physical therapy would be the final answer on that.

For a brief spate of time the only sound was that of the machinery in the room as the silence became even more awkward. The nurse finally came in and it seemed as though everyone in the room wanted a vial of my blood. From the paramedics on the scene to the gaggle of three, now I was feeling like a human pin cushion. When they were finished the crime scene technicians and the nurse all left the room and for the first time since early this morning, I was alone.

That's when the release of the nerves hit me.

I began to shake.

The events of the day and the smell of cordite and diesel filled my olfactory senses. My nostrils flared, seeking a relief from the pungent memory, and seeing Iggy tumble into the bay caused my eyes to well with tears. So many thoughts broke through the floodgates of my mind.

I thought about Gina and about the things that were never said and done in my life.

The emotions inside me crested and fell like a toy boat bobbing on a turbulent sea. I gripped the ends of the gurney and locked my arms rigid, scrunching the paper sheet.

I stared at the floor, transfixed by the grout lines of the tile.

I forced myself to stay in the moment and not let it all invade my mind. I assumed that mental calisthenics would hold back the flood of thoughts from brimming over. I stared at the floor tile and pretended the grout lines were a highway for ants and I was plotting the best routes to travel across the room.

I must've looked catatonic to the uniformed officer when he came in with my go bag and car keys. Once he left, I knew I just needed to get going and be on my way. I wasn't even sure if I was officially checked into the hospital but if there was anything wrong with me it was not something medically. I hopped off the gurney and quickly put on the jeans and T-shirt from the go bag. I was dressed very quickly and just looking to make my highly impromptu exit when Dr. Bashir walked in.

"What do you think you're doing?"

I'd heard those exact words less than twenty-four hours ago, and it had resulted in me running madly though the darkened streets of Coconut Grove. I clearly needed to work on my powers of observation and quit having people just walk up on me.

I was very surprised to see her. I didn't say anything; I guess my surprise was evident.

"Leaving on me? Well, I guess you're like every other man I've met in my life."

The casualness and flirty response was very unexpected and compounded my surprise even more so. She had the residual look of a woman who pulled her hair back all day and now just let it fall loosely at her shoulders. The hospital lights are harsh but not nearly as harsh as the lights in the medical examiner's garage bay. In this light, her features were softened, and her silver double earring hoops sparkled. She was less rigid and more approachable than she had first appeared to me when I saw her in her lavender surgical scrubs. Her deep dark blue cotton blouse was cinched at the waist by an equally deep dark blue belt. She was wearing beige slacks and open-toed sandals that accentuated her well-manicured toes.

"I hope you don't mind that I came by to check on you. I saw you in the rescue truck, didn't know if you were hurt or not. When I left the scene I went home and called Trentlocke but he didn't even know you'd been involved in today's craziness. So, here I am."

Although touched by her kindness I could only mutter a subdued thank you to her.

She looked around the room and took in the standard hospital-styled environment and remarked that it reminded her of doing her residency at Michael Garron Hospital in Toronto.

"Do you miss the cold?" I asked her.

"Sometimes. I actually like the cold."

"Then going back to Toronto suits you ? Is the head M.E. job any more active than the Assistant M.E. in Miami?"

"I can be a teaching fellow at the University of Toronto—my alma mater as well as guide-specific research grants and endowments. I can't do that here and rumor is the University of Miami is looking to be a bigger partner here at JMH which is counter to where I want to see my career go."

"So you're giving up the tropics for the frozen tundra?"

"Well, Toronto is not such a barren outpost you know. We have electricity, and even running water. We have the Argonauts in football, the Blue Jays have Roger Clemens and we just picked up your Miami son, Jose Canseco."

"I'm a homer for the Marlins and the Dolphins, but I'm more of a hockey guy myself."

"Me too, except the Maple Leafs haven't won the cup since 1967 and the Hall of Fame is right in our city. You know how it sucks to see that cup displayed in your home city, but your team hasn't won it since 1967?"

My thoughts went to my dismal Hartford Whalers, but rather than get into an I-can-top-that conversation I just let her stew in her Toronto Maple Leafs agony.

"So you follow sports?"

"My father was a pretty decent cricket player and he instilled in me and my sisters not only a love of sports, but also of the arts and the obligatory culinary skills."

In a deep voice she did what I perceived as a mocking tone of her father: "Sabah, you must know about the world and how to be a good wife or you will be alone in the world."

Following upon her sarcastic comment about all the men who have left her I asked if she was indeed alone in the world.

"You mean am I married? No."

"You have sisters?"

"An older sister, Olivia. She's a chemical engineer for Dow Canada in Calgary. My other sister is two years younger. Naseem. She's an accountant for KPMG in Toronto.

"Are your parents still alive?" I asked.

"Yes, my father is originally from Odisha India and my mother is from Tehran. They met when they were both studying at the University of Liverpool in England. My father emigrated to Canada to work for the Toronto Stock Exchange as an arbitrage specialist, my mother followed and began working at The Toronto Waldorf School where she's now vice chancellor. Academics and holistic societal integration were very big in the Bashir household."

"Well, as you can see, I'm okay. Although I'm sure we caused a lot of work for you today."

"Oh, most certainly. It will still be some time until we examine the bodies. The scene's rather convoluted. They're in our facility but not released officially to my office yet. It's a formality but since they're coming to us we might as well store them until we start the autopsies. I'm sure by the looks of it that it was quite an ordeal. You okay?"

"I'm okay."

"You sure? I mean it can be a heck of jolt to your parasympathetic nervous system."

"Yeah, really. I'm fine."

"So where are you going Cade?"

I think it was the first time that she actually addressed me by my first name. Her sincerity caught me off guard and before answering with a patented response I honestly said, "I'm not sure."

"When is the last time you actually ate a decent home cooked meal?" Before I could answer she said, "Because before all of today's commotion I started a white bean and turkey chili in the crock pot. Why don't you come to my place, have something to eat?"

I hesitated thinking that she was feeling sorry for me but then realized she knew very little about me.

"I live in El Portal. Traffic should be light on I-95, why don't you come with me?"

I looked into her deep dark brown eyes and knew that it would be pointless to try and create a reason why such an endearing invitation should be allowed to pass so I relented.

"Thank you, that sounds real nice. Real nice."

I walked with her in the parking lot and she got into a dark blue Jeep Grand Cherokee.

"The dealer said it was Patriot Blue. I like to think of it as Maple Leafs Blue."

"I hope you have more success with this than they do on the power play."

She laughed and closed the door.

It was easier if I just followed her. Her directions were confusing and my mind was just not firing on all cylinders. I got in my car and saw the cell phone on my passenger seat. My phone battery was nearly dead. I followed her out of JMH and then north onto I-95. We exited east on 95th Street and then a few short turns to her place on Northeast 2nd Avenue, a former two-story duplex that had been converted recently to a single home. It was on the corner, directly across from a large Methodist church with a big parking lot in the back of it. She parked on the grassy swale just adjacent to the house.

Her house was designed in an art deco style with east-facing windows to catch the bay breezes. It had a small portico in the front with a door that had a "Miami Slide" window in the center. The large house numbers were set vertically left of the door which was framed by double hung porch lights. The most interesting feature was the long semi-exposed staircase that led up to the top floor. Narrow, with a swooped concrete arch and long, square pillars. There was a lone coconut palm tree in the front yard that was easily fifteen feet higher than the top of the roof line. I pulled in next to her car and saw her standing at the foot of the stairs.

"I always go in from the top since that's my primary living space," she said as I was closing my car door.

The moon was arching over the east horizon and the breeze brought in a fleeting whiff of night-blooming jasmine. The street was very quiet and the church across the street loomed over the neighborhood like a watchful centurion. As we reached the top of the stairs I could see in the moonlight the expansive rear yard with a nicely appointed patio festooned with ceramic pottery, a wrought iron patio set, and a wood framed hot tub.

When we entered the house it had a welcoming smell of concocted herbs and simmering food wafting from the white bean turkey chili she had in the crockpot.

"I hope you're hungry because I am famished."

"It smells delicious."

Her place was decorated very nicely with a matching set of supple deep brown leather couches that faced a large TV in the corner. There were afghan throw blankets on the arms of the couches and Persian carpets on the floors. The indoor plants were healthy and thriving and there were candles in jars. I also saw medical journals as well as some Fodor's travel books about Ottawa and Vancouver on the end tables. She lit a few candles for ambience and put on some Pat Metheny jazz on her stereo before retreating to the kitchen and coming out with a bottle of J. Bouchon Malbec Gran Reserve from Chile.

"Do the honors?" she asked, and upon providing me with a corkscrew I began to open the wine. I followed her back into the kitchen. There were two crystal goblets on the counter which I poured the wine into as she ladled steaming portions of the chili into bowls. We also had some delicious crusty bread to go with it.

The food was nourishing but so was the conversation. We talked about her growing up in Canada and what it was like to now be in

South Florida. She was interested in knowing the changes that Miami has gone through over the past few decades. The wine flowed and so did the positive calming manner that she exuded. Time seemed to slide away. My only gauge of it was the waning candles burning steadily down to a hot liquified pool. I did notice that neither of our cell phones had rung and the lack of interruption made it seem as though the world was outside and we were sheltered inside from the ravages of life that creep into our day-to-day existence.

Even at this late hour, as we cleared dishes, the moon shone brightly onto her back patio and yard. From the upstairs window I could see much of the patio lit from the lunar casting. She noticed me looking out the window and suggested we go outside.

Once outside she stood very close to me. Maybe too close. We began to kiss and I felt sheepish, having not been involved with anyone since Gina. She sensed my uneasiness and suggested we relax in her hot tub. She pulled back the cover and turned on the soft gurgling jets. I mentioned that I didn't have a bathing suit.

She informed me that neither did she. Ever.

She told me to get in and get comfortable while she went back inside to "tidy things up and get the wine."

I stripped off my clothes and slipped into the inviting warmth of the hot tub. She emerged from the house carrying the same two goblets and a different bottle of wine. Her naked body silhouetted by the soft lights of the house and the moon was exquisite.

It was 11pm and all was well.

Chapter Twenty-Five

T HE CLOCK RADIO on Roldan Osorio-Vidal's dashboard said 11pm as well. He was right on time. The text message he received said:

"A los once. Ir a tío's y obtener su equipaje para el crucero mañana."

At 11pm go to Uncle's and get his luggage for the cruise tomorrow.

The luggage mentioned were indeed suitcases set up at the stash house by Gustavo. It was an easy chore. Gustavo had never steered him wrong before. It was all coming together. When he last saw Gustavo he'd told him the cops were taken care of to await his next text or phone call. Here it was. The call had come in, albeit a text, but nonetheless the time was now. Gustavo said that once they had been given the following instructions, that then and finally then, they would be charting their own financial density. No more profit sharing.

Roldan pulled up to the darkened stash house in Coconut Grove. A Miami Dade TNT detective watching the house from a vantage point two doors down notified his team that he had movement at the house. The fellow TNT units started to converge on the house, this time covering the rear avenues in case they had another runner. Roldan was completely oblivious to all of that. Although he had not spoken to Gustavo in over a week, when he got the instructions to pick up three stuffed suitcases from the back bedroom closet he already knew he was to go and get them. He had been anxiously awaiting his instructions.

Now the pay-off was near. Finally, big commissions and big cash movements without police interference.

He was confused by the number on his phone but not surprised. It was Miami after all, and everyone has a face that isn't the same as the one they show the world. He thought about keeping the engine running but he had no idea the full weight of each suitcase and if he had to make a few trips ferrying the bags to his trunk it could get time-consuming.

The gravel crunched under his shoes, but he wasn't concerned. Most everyone in Miami slept with the air conditioning on and neighbors wouldn't likely hear him. Besides this was going to be a very short stop on the road to financial prosperity.

The moon was out, but the trees cast spotty shadows that concealed most of his movements. He dipped along the side yard brushing past the crocus bushes and went to the last window on the side of the house. He reached up and located the hidden spare key tucked up under the rusty hurricane shutter. It was exactly where Gustavo said it would be.

The pathway along the back of the house led to three small concrete steps at the back door porch. There was an aged wrought iron rail astride the steps. The rail's paint was flaking off in big chunks that were abrasive to his hand so he stopped using the rail and casually stepped up to the rear door. The door was a mess with weather-affected frayed strips of wood peeling from the bottom. The wooden door was more than likely rotting from within and it had a slight musty odor to it. A mesh grid covered the screen under the jalousie windows, an obvious holdover from when a rambunctious dog once lived there. The hinges of the door were rusty and had a metallic orange dust along their slots and grooves. The rusty mechanisms left small streaks of orange stains down the door just like aircraft contrails.

Roldan must of thought to himself the only thing holding the door upright might just be the rust. The key fit into the lock without any difficulty but he fumbled with which way to turn the lock. He thought he had it opened but the door only opened at the most, a centimeter. There was a moldy, water-logged door mat wedged up against the door. Holding the doorknob in his right hand, he bent down and pulled the mat away with his other hand, freeing the door to open.

The door, wired for explosives, blew out.

It was fortuitous that Roldan was bent at the waist when the bomb went off. The panes of glass in the door shattered with such ferocious force that in the aftermath Miami crime scene technicians found multiple two-inch shards embedded in a palm tree forty-six feet away. A forgotten pile of landscaping soil spewed a black pattern of splattered sand granules, reminiscent of a violent volcanic eruption, across a dilapidated shed at the rear of the property. Miami bomb technicians later theorized the bomb had been rigged to blow up and out with the intention to obliterate whomever was standing at the door from the waist up. When the bomb went off the wooden door bowed out and almost simultaneously sucked back into the frame, due to the rush of oxygen pushing in at a percentage per square inch and then forcefully being thrusted out a percentage equally 100 times greater per square inch.

Roldan never had a chance to even consciously know these things.

An ungodly hot white phosphorous burst shot out from the door and split its trajectory, shooting past Roldan with whistling streaks of hot illumination as a tendril of it curled over and then under his bent form. The heat was searing but brief as the blast pushed the comet like flames further out into the yard. An avocado sapling in the center of the yard got the brunt of the damage as its brown-ish-green leaves became easy tinder for the flames. The paint above the porch blistered instantly and then became full of sooty black bubbles trapped in the scorched latex.

It was probably lights-out for Roldan the very second he started pulling the mat away. The door hinges were rusty and corroded from years of salt air, neglect, and hard rains being driven against the unprotected door. The hinges burst at the frame and the door became a human projectile. I say 'human' because when the door blew off its frame, it carried Roldan with it. It's the only reason he lived. The door splintered nearly in half vertically, the glass primarily flew over Roldan, but plenty of fragments of all sizes embedded themselves in the top of his head and across his shoulders and back. His shirt was shorn away, what remained of it tattered and held barely along his waistline from being tightly tucked into his belt. The door separated and flew about eight feet, carrying Roldan on the underside of it. The door came to rest on top of Roldan who in turn had landed in the mucky algae slimed decorative pond. The same pond I almost stepped into the night before.

Where his luck ran out was that the same door that blew out and propelled him into the pond now was atop him in the water. He'd been concussed from the blast and both his eardrums had ruptured. His right hand had been holding the door and the twisting torque of the explosion had wrenched his arm in such a way that he had a compound fracture of his clavicle and four broken ribs on the right side, not to mention a lacerated kidney and a large piece of the door wedged into his thigh. When he hit the water, it is believed he was fully unconscious.

When the blast went off, the TNT officers said from the street it looked like a monstrous barbecue fire had shot up into the air over the roofline. Front windows cracked and a brief very hot breeze swept out from the front of the house. Three TNT officers went to the rear of the house and reported that all the windows back there were damaged significantly. A fire had started in the rear of the house by the blasted door. One TNT officer tried to go in and search for Roldan but only was able to get near the doorway before the choking toxic smoke of burning plastics, synthetics, and solvents caused him to gag and dry heave. His two buddies pulled him away and they went back to the front of the house where the neighborhood had come alive with shrieking car alarms and frightened neighbors. A wide assortment of bathrobes, gym shorts, T-shirts, and sweatpants converged in the street as each neighbor kept asking each other the same question;

"What the hell happened?"

The Miami Fire Department arrived about ten minutes later and within forty-five minutes had extinguished the fire by shooting their hoses straight through the front windows. From talking to the TNT officers the fire department wasn't concerned about casualties or survivors and had no intention of entering the house until the Miami Bomb Squad technicians cleared it.

It would be nearly two hours until arson and fire inspectors were cleared to go into the house. There were no duffel bags of cash or any sign that there ever had been.

And another two hours until Roldan's body was found in the pond.

Chapter Twenty Six

I WOKE UP AND at first had no recollection of where I was. I was in Sabah's bed and it took me a few moments to gather my wits. She wasn't in bed and for that matter, wasn't in the house either. There was a note taped to the bathroom mirror. Thankfully she didn't have the affliction of doctor handwriting and I was able to read it:

Hello sleepyhead. Stay as long as you want or better yet stay as long as I want which is to be here tonight when I get home!
- S

Smiling, I ambled off to her shower. It's always odd how when in a new shower I never can seem to master the hot and cold faucet handles. The shower felt wonderful and the sundry of her shampoos and hair conditioners would rival a hair care aisle in any CVS. I chose a Moroccan oil shampoo that appealed to me solely on being Moroccan and its flashy bottle and label. Whether or not it was appropriate for my hair I don't know, but if it did anything for me like it did for her thick, raven locks, then I'd be happy. After the shower I padded around wrapped in a towel, taking in the feminine aspects of her cozy place. I purposely avoided turning on her TV and hearing via the local morning news how Iggy and I may have inadvertently derailed the local tourism projections. Unknowingly had I turned on the TV news and seen the second biggest story about a house explosion in Coconut Grove, my day's intended activities would've seriously changed direction.

I got dressed and decided to drive down to my own place, replenish the go bag and tend to my own domestic chores. All the while, blissfully ignorant that Roldan had been killed hours earlier in the backyard of the stash house.

I left from the upstairs door. There was no way to lock the door, so I just closed it tightly.

The drive south was uneventful, but as I turned down my street I noticed a deep brown-colored sedan with two men in it on the corner.

There was a puddle just under the driver's door. I was willing to bet that puddle was from dumped urine.

They'd been there a while.

I didn't know who they were. They *looked* like they could be cops. Outside of the officer who brought up my keys to me at the hospital, no one knew I was now driving the Infiniti. I intentionally drove right past my house and around the corner. I parked at my retired neighbor's house which is directly behind me and shares the rear wooden fence between our yards. He was in his open garage working on a decorative bird house. I told him they were sealing my driveway and asked if I could cut through his yard to get to my own backyard. Always the agreeable neighbor, he cheerfully allowed me to do so.

As we parted ways I slipped the battery out of my cell phone. If those guys in the brown sedan were who I thought they might be, I didn't need them pinging my phone for a location. Ideally I'd have done it blocks away but I had no idea I might have a welcoming committee.

I traipsed across my backyard and went to the back door by the pool.

I entered my house. The majority of the window shades were drawn and it was cool and relatively dark inside. I kept it that way just in case the car I saw on my street was actually looking for me or watching my house. I felt I was bordering on being paranoia, but my instincts in light of recent events would not be ignored.

A pile of mail was just inside the front door accumulating haphazardly under the mail slot. I started to gather the mail up but couldn't stop myself any longer. I dropped the mail back down on the floor and turned on the TV midday news to see exactly what was being said of our shooting yesterday. The mail could wait.

I had turned the television on as the news about the shooting was wrapping up. I must've missed a heck of a story as the screen was sectionalized with three reporters, all holding microphones and looking back out at me. One reporter had Mercy Hospital under name, another had Bayshore Drive, and the last one had Miami Police Headquarters under her name. Three separate female reporters all doing stand-ups, being moderated by a news anchor back in the studio. The only part I caught was the news anchor thanking his reporters, Sharon, Marisol, and Yvonne for "their coverage."

I was now wondering if I really wanted to see it later in the day on the 6pm news.

The anchor started to introduce the next story which was about a house explosion in Coconut Grove. I heard it but wasn't exactly sure I had heard correctly. I stopped dead in my tracks, turned my attention back to the TV and immediately recognized the street the reporter was standing on. In a hurried but informative manner, the reporter stated that a house just a few doors down from where he was standing, outside a cordoned-off police scene, had blown up in the night. Fire investigators were still investigating but sources told the reporter that the Miami Bomb Squad had been on the scene prior to the reporter and his crew arriving. The newscast cut away to a taped interview of a neighbor identified as Magda Cottoro, who with curlers in her hair and wearing a pink bathrobe told the reporter that she had, "been in bed watching the news waiting for Jay Leno to come on when I heard a loud explosion and looked out to see the house across the way blowed up. I got dressed and went outside but Miami Dade cops told me to get back in my house. I don't think that's right 'cuz I live here, you know?"

Shit.

I knew immediately that while I was having my oil changed at Sabah's house all kinds of shit had happened. She said Miami *Dade* cops. She didn't say Miami cops. This was not good. It was definitely our stash house and TNT must still have been on surveillance of it when this happened. The reporter who finished up by saying an unidentified male was found deceased by police and arson investigators on the scene.

"Unidentified male was found deceased by police..."

Double shit.

Who could that be? Who could've been in the stash house, especially if it was under constant police surveillance? My mind began to spin.

So how did someone manage to be inside the house when it went sky high?

Menial tasks helped me to focus, so I gathered more clothing to supplement the go bag, thinking the whole time. Whoever was killed in the stash house must've been a regular coming and going person or TNT might have tried to intercept him as they did me two nights previously. What caused this dilapidated, uninhabited house to blow up with such ferocity? If it was gas leak why didn't TNT or anyone else, including the deceased, smell it before it erupted?

It wasn't adding up.

What also didn't add up was how I was supposed to play this all out. Major Steve "Stevie" Edwards of Miami Dade's TNT unit said that that Gustavo had come up on a wire at a stash house in Coconut Grove. He never revealed the location. I had to figure that one on my own. As far as I knew, no one was aware that I was privy to the location.

Or do they?

Maybe that's why there were two guys outside in a parked, car peeing in Gatorade bottles. *Is the unidentified person in the explosion connected to* me? My mind reeled through a ticker tape of facts, head spinning to put them together:

Major Edwards referred to Gustavo by his nickname, "Costano."

He said Costano was getting ready to "move some heavy product."

That he'd been heard on the wire saying that he "couldn't trust no one."

That there was a cop who needed "to be taken care of."

Gustavo had called this unknown cop, "*Los Tombo.*"

The Miami Dade linguistic expert deduced it meant that an unknown cop needed to be killed.

I doubted the two guys outside were on a protection detail for me.

Like a kid who breaks a lamp and can't decide whether to try gluing it back together or sweeping it under the couch, I needed to decide how I was to comport myself when they inevitably present me with this latest literal explosion in my life. I had to break it down in simple Cobol language-type steps.

A house blew up in the night.

TNT has been watching this house. My informant was heard in a surveillance wiretap talking to someone in the house.

That informant was now dead.

Dead with my business card in his pocket.

I was never told of the location of the house. I *deduced* the location.

I visited the location.

I ran from TNT at the location.

That location was now on the news as the house that exploded.

There's a dead guy there.

I needed to look at it in its barest sense to understand what may or may not actually be going on here.

My first course of action I decided was to feign ignorance about the location of the house. I'd let Miami Dade or someone else tell me about it, if they do at all. In a day or so whoever was killed at the house will be identified, if it hadn't been already identified the body at the M.E.'s office.

I'll be seeing Sabah tonight. Maybe she'll say something which would be of help.

My go bag was packed and by force of habit I started for the front door but then remembered the brown sedan was outside and positioned to see my house clearly. I stopped just short of absent-mindedly opening the door. I was actually standing on my mail. I once again stooped down and picked it up. Gina's *Victoria Secret* and *Nine West* catalogs went straight into the trash, as did most if not all of the advertising fliers, and junk mail. There were assorted bills—and then there was a light blue legal-size envelope with an embossed return address written in a boldly powerful designed font that screamed solid legal competency. It was from Gintel, Nicolosi, Stanis, and Gilot P.A. Attorneys at Law.

The law firm that Gina had chosen to represent her in our divorce.

I sat down and opened the letter. There were no niceties or cordial salutations. It was a quick and harshly-worded, terse message that accused me of being untruthful in the financial disclosures pertaining to our divorce. Gina, who was being referred to in the letter as the "aforementioned client," and her attorney Philip Gilot were demanding explanation and a percentage of "an undisclosed $48,000.00 in discretionary income that a cursory examination of my bank account discovered."

$48,000.00?

I never thought of myself as a great mathematician and my checkbook has probably not been fully balanced ever in existence, but my error ratio usually hovered in the twenty to sixty cents variety, not in a $48,000 swing; especially a $48,000 swing in my favor. I re-read the letter and made sure that I was actually seeing that they were claiming I not only had a $48,000 surplus, but that I had not reported this minor windfall in the court-mandated financial disclosures of our divorce.

This was all becoming very Alfred Hitchcock to me.

People associated with me were dying either very close to my vicinity or, as in Lobo's case, directly by my hand.

I couldn't tell if I was being paranoid or just crazy. I was imagining men sitting in cars watching my house, I could feel the eyes of my peers upon me, their whispers reverberating in my head. Suspicion and doubt hung over me and now I was suddenly and without explanation wealthier than I knew. I was destined for a soon-to-be adjourned fatal police shooting inquiry, and all of these divergent and odd things were swirling around me. Whatever this was, it most definitely centered around me. And here in the house, I was in a potential hotspot.

I made my way out and back across the lawns to my car.

My neighbor wasn't in his garage when I got in my car. I casually drove away as to not generate suspicion from him or any other occupied parked cars I might have overlooked.

I drove a leisurely route for the first mile or so, constantly checking my mirrors for a fast-approaching marked Miami Dade police unit summoned to pull me over; or at the very least a tail but there was none. I drove for a few miles, then went to a branch of my bank. I parked on Sunset Drive right under the large green Barnett Bank sign. The lobby of the bank was cool, the stark walls and polished tile helping to keep the temperature low. I was ushered into a faux office of thin glass walls that was more like a financial fishbowl than an office. Behind the dark wooden desk was a cheery assistant branch manager. I asked her to research my bank account and she efficiently punched in my information into her computer. She left to retrieve a print-out of my account and sat with me to review it.

The balance of $51,239.81 jumped off of the pages right at me.

Eight days earlier a deposit of $48,000 was made. I asked her what the coding message was attached to the deposit and she said it was from a wire transfer. She went back to her computer and looked up the message number sequence, then explained that the American Bankers Association had a national numeric system for designating wire transfer sources of origin. They called them ABA numbers. It's a unique nine-digit number for each bank. She kept punching in the coded message but was unable to locate the origin of the wire transfer. She tried three times and still had no success.

"Hmmm. I can't locate the origin of the wire transfer." She said.

She then picked up the phone and dialed a co-worker. It was evident from their conversation that this co-worker had the ability to see my account on a computer screen as well. After some back-and-forth discussion they soon determined that I did not have a wire transfer from an ABA bank, but actually from an International Bank Account Number or what is known as an IBAN account.

The number sequence was twenty-three digits long and it had thrown this young assistant branch manager into a spate of confusion.

"I'm sorry Mr. Taylor, this will only take a few minutes," she said as she excused herself to confer with someone outside of the glass fishbowl.

I quickly went to her side of the desk and spying my account on her computer screen, I jotted down the string of numerical digits and anything else that seemed pertinent.

She returned a few minutes later with a look of satisfaction on her face.

"Okay, I think we got it all sorted out," she said.

"The Bank Identifier Code, or what we refer to as a SWIFT code was imbedded up against the country code and that was what was causing some confusion."

"So let me explain." She sat next to me again with papers in her hands.

"The SWIFT code is here. It is BTAMBSNS. The bank is the first four numbers in front of this string of numbers just in front of the country code; the last two numbers are the location within the country. So the first four numbers are 'BTAM' and the next two numbers are the country code, BS, followed by the location code which in this case is NS. So this wire transfer is from the bank whose code is BTAM and the country is the Bahamas and the location is Nassau.

"So you're saying this wire transfer came from a bank in Nassau, Bahama?"

"Yes, the bank code BTAM is for Fidelity Bank, 51 Frederick Street, P.O Box N 7502, Nassau, Bahama. They also have another branch in the Cayman Islands. Most wire transfers get held by the sending bank as long as they can to bolster their international lending portfolio, but it seems that this went out pretty quick."

"So, what does that mean?"

"It means that more than likely the account holder who sent this transfer is well-regarded at the local branch or has a substantial enough portfolio to be excluded from any holds or delays."

She provided me with a copy of the wire transfer, negating my hastily-scribbled notes from her computer.

I stepped outside the bank and this time found myself scanning the avenue looking for anybody who might be surveilling me. When I got in the car I picked up my cell phone and reinserted the battery. I called the VIN office.

"Veen."

"Hey Ileana, it's Cade. Is Gary around?"

"Cade! Aye preciosito! Are ju alright?"

"Yes, thank you Ileana, I'm fine."

"Aye por Dios, the place is like crazy gone over this. Are ju sure ju okay, because everyone is talking about jesterday."

"Yes, I'm fine. Is Gary there?"

"Hold on, *precito.*"

Precious was not how I felt. Her endearing words were obviously due to the shooting yesterday.

A few seconds went by and then Gary's cool, detached voice got on the line.

"Bro you sure know how to sell newspapers."

"Yeah well, it's a gift I guess."

"Well thanks to you I got to stand next to that hot news anchor chick from Channel 6 in the elevator. I mean the place is *crawling* with media. One of those jack balls had me blocked in and I almost missed my daily wheat grass smoothie at lunch."

"Yeah, I feel for you. Sorry my almost getting whacked yesterday nearly cost you a pancreatic cleanse."

"That's funny. So what's up?"

"Hey you remember us talking in the stairwell. Well I want to put that Masters in Finance you got to good use."

"Yeah bro, what do you need?"

I told him I was tracking a wire transfer from the midpoint of the transaction. I wanted to see if he could discover who the owner of the Fidelity Bank account in Nassau was. I needed him to see if there had been deposits or transfers into the Fidelity account and determine if Fidelity was just a pass-through and not the account of origin. I provided him with all of the numerical sequences the Barnett Bank manager had given me.

"In theory, it's real easy," he said, "but in reality, with bank secrecy laws and stuff, it's not so easy, but I know a few people from my analyst classes who know some dudes in the islands. I'll see what I can do."

Thanks. And Big G? Just for me, okay? Let's not mention this to anyone."

Chapter Twenty-Seven

I DROVE THE INFINITI to the local Cellular One distributor and strode in. I was relieved to see the place was devoid of the normal long lines of customers. I explained to the rep that the cell phone was dropping calls and I wanted to keep my same number but switch out the actual cell phone for another one. Our contract was pretty large with Cellular One and just as I assumed, they had no issues about switching the phone for me. Capitalism 101: Keep your biggest clients happy.

I kept the paperwork for the old cell phone so that if I needed it, I would still have my old ESN number. With a new cell phone and subsequently a new ESN number, I left confident that my cell phone location would not be easy to trace... at least for a while.

The day was ebbing away and the notion of retreating to the haven of Sabah's was not only ideal, but smart. It was a fair assumption that no one knew of our previous night's interlude and her place would be a safe refuge from the surveillance that I was either imagining or that was actually real. Aside from that, the inquiring media might still be seeking a story to what they were now calling the "Bayshore Shootout." Whether those guys were media, cops, or something else was immaterial; obviously my home was now on someone's radar. Whoever they were, it wasn't boding very well for me.

I traipsed up towards the northeast quadrant of the city and after getting turned around a few times, I found my way back to Sabah's house. I figured it would be a while until she got home and I chose to park in the rear parking lot of the church across the street. The parking lot was empty, and stepping out of my car and walking across the gray, sun-bleached asphalt, I smiled at all the markings where children had used chalk to draw hopscotch and box ball grids.

I kept to the sidewalk alongside the church. The trees along the sidewalk afforded me a little bit of concealment in case any neighbors might be inclined to call the El Portal Police Department about an unknown man wandering around. A major thoroughfare like Northeast 2nd Avenue and a small municipal police department that has very little to do could easily put a patrol officer very near to me rather quickly.

I took notice that the side street was Northeast 88th Street, also called East Blue Jay Street. Small municipalities looking to distance themselves from the grid-mapping benevolence of Miami Dade County often attach their own naming of a street to an already established numerical street. It wreaks havoc with tourists and locals alike. Ask anyone who has ever driven in the municipalities of Hialeah or Opa Locka. Many of the streets are named for people and places most have never heard of. Politicians quick to maximize voter appeal or hefty campaign contributions will often name a street with very little research of whom the street is named for. The embarrassment of facing the inquiries of a *Miami Herald* reporter when the aforementioned honoree is a war criminal or drug dealer has fallen upon many a Miami Dade politician.

Second Avenue was devoid of traffic and I quickly crossed and ascended the stairs to Sabah's. The same door was still unlocked. The air-conditioned coolness of her place was inviting and I sat in a burgundy papasan chair and familiarized myself with the new cell phone. The model was just a slight upgrade and learning the new aspects of it only took a few minutes. The battery needed to be charged and until it was at least partially charged, the phone was useless. I plugged it in then sat in the chair and dozed off for a few minutes. I was awakened by the chirping of the phone as it was now at 20% power. I opened the phone and saw that during the day there was a backlog of voice and text messages. One was from that dipshit attorney Philip Gilot, asking me if I had received their letter about the $48,000 discrepancy.

Delete.

Another from Miami Commander Tom Dolan's office, asking if I'd be available to speak with Commander Dolan tomorrow at 1pm.

Delete.

Cellular One calling to welcome me to the "Cellular One family, where the emphasis is on you being the one." Talk about aggressive suggestive sell.

Delete.

Lieutenant Poulsen advising me of an after-action meeting at Major Brunson's office at 2pm, but to be at the station at 1:30 for a pre-meeting before the meeting. I entered it into the calendar function of the phone.

Delete.

Sabah called and hung up without a message, and then called again to say she was thinking of me and asking what my plans were.

Delete.

But I called her back.

"Hello."

"Hey, it's me, Cade."

"I think I recognize your voice, Cade. Plus I have your number in my phone. I called you earlier, remember?" she said chuckling.

"Yup, that's me a little flustered sometimes. So how's your day going?"

"I am slammed with stuff here. Did you hear about the house explosion in Coconut Grove?'

"Yeah, I saw it mentioned on the news, some guy died, right?"

"Yes, and I'm just waiting for a confirmation on his identity, his prints were hard to retrieve but we got it done."

My eyebrow shot up and I subconsciously looked around the room as if someone might be listening to our conversation.

"Well that's good, I guess. What are your plans tonight?"

"I was hoping you were my plans tonight," she said.

"I think we can make that happen. When do you think you'll be done and what did you have in mind?"

With a noticeable weariness she said, "I could use a little down and away time. Want to meet me at Mike Gordon's at 6:30?"

"Sounds like a plan. I'll see you there."

When I hung up the telephone I once again looked around the room and was secretly relieved she didn't ask where I was. It might seem creepy that I was in her house leaving a deep body impression in her papasan chair. Or it might signal a strong acceleration in a very quick relationship.

One thing I was sure of was that it didn't reveal a need to secret myself away from either real or imagined adversaries.

The daylight was giving way to shadows that were starting to play and flit across her walls. It would be dark soon and I needed to make an exit from her place only to meet with her for dinner and hopefully be invited to come right back to where I was standing by late evening.

Mike Gordon's seafood restaurant was a veritable institution in Miami. It was right at the mainland base of the 79th Street causeway that spanned Biscayne Bay. It was touted as "a touch of Cape Cod on the Bay." It had started out as a bait shack in the 1940s, eventually morphing into a waterside restaurant that endured hurricanes and fires only to be rebuilt each time from each cataclysmic event by the owner and namesake. It was rustic, authentic, and definitely old Florida with big windows affording the patrons great waterside views.

I set out across Second Avenue, my phone now with a 41% battery charge. I needed to stay in the northeast corridor of Miami. My rendezvous with Sabah was still at least ninety minutes away and I needed to find a place that I could spend time at until our dinner date.

I headed south on Biscayne Boulevard and then east past Mike Gordon's on the 79th Street Causeway. The sun was blinding in my rearview mirror and I turned it downward, nullifying the approaching sunset in an hour. With hypnotic blue water on either side of the causeway, I continued into North Bay Village past one of the local television stations. I pulled a U-turn near the infamous Top Draw Club and pulled into the parking lot of Happy's Stork Lounge. The bland beige rectangular shopping center that housed the lounge was drab and very uninspiring. Happy's Stork lounge was a long-established, no-nonsense, very local-patronized bar that many—including the management—liked to refer to as a serious dive bar.

Inside it was narrow, dark, and dank. The sturdy, serpentine-curved wooden bar was adorned with baseball cards and playing cards shellacked into the bar top with clear varnish. The walls were a deep wood paneling circa 1960s that had all the appeal of drinking in your grandmother's basement or in a Wisconsin Moose Lodge. A well-worn pool table was in the back which was either in full time use as a pool table or a sitting bench for the overhead television. Above the pool table large swatches of the ceiling's paint were missing, a testament to pool cues being handled incorrectly in the low-ceilinged room. The rest of the decor was early American VFW hall with a few adorned beer posters and enough exposed wiring to make you seriously question the competency of the town's electrical inspector. There were more ash trays on the bar than coasters. I searched for a seat at the bar and chose one of the high-top stools that had the most vinyl seating intact.

The bartender neither cared that I wasn't a regular, nor cared to be very welcoming to an outsider either. I ordered a Saint Pauli Girl beer and it came cold, with his calloused wet hand wrapped around it. I noticed a painting of a woman lounging back with a lit cigarette and copiously big diamond earrings. She had a mixed resemblance of Faye Dunaway and Madonna. She also had a bullet hole right through her cheek. The bullet was said to have been a long-ago accidental discharge from a drunk cop.

By my second beer the surroundings were increasingly filling with regular customers who all seemed to know each other; some begrudgingly. The music was getting louder and the bartender even less attentive. I figured it was time to leave before someone said or did something that would necessitate my involvement and if it was serious enough for me getting involved, it might be serious enough for the television station down the street to send over a truck. I paid my tab with a wrinkled ten dollar bill, leaving it on the beaten bar. I didn't even attempt to seek change. I made an Irish exit.

I headed west back across the causeway. Adjusting the rearview mirror back to its workable position did nothing but allow me to see the scintillating sunset leave streaking reflections behind me. I was soon pulling into the parking lot of Mike Gordon's and was punctually ten minutes early.

Sabah was there already, her punctuality surpassing my own.

She had secured a table by one of the windows overlooking the bay. She looked beautiful with the day's fading rays bouncing and glinting off the chop of the bay behind her. She was in a pair of jeans and a pink polo, her hair pulled back, exposing a yellow number two pencil tucked behind her ear.

She stood up and opened her arms invitingly. It was a welcoming embrace that I'm sure we both could've used. I pulled the pencil from behind her ear.

"Fashion accessory?"

"Oh my God, I do that all the time. I lose them so often that I either stick one behind my ear or when my hair is up in the bun. I'm so embarrassed."

"Don't be, I think it's kind of cute," I said.

"Pencils and pocket recorders—two things I can never have enough of," she said as she opened her large purse and tossed the pencil inside. When she opened it I could see a handful of pencils and at least three pocket recorders.

The waitress was very prompt and after a quick perusal of the menu Sabah ordered the Crabmeat Norfolk and I ordered the Baked

Grouper a la Louis. She opted for a Sauvignon Blanc and I stuck with another Saint Pauli Girl beer.

"I'm not a huge fan of the beer but my roommate in college had the poster and I stared at the beer poster of the fräulein daily," I said.

"I won't ask you what you were doing when you were staring. I think every guy had that poster in college. It must be a busty blonde thing with you men."

"It's not always a blonde thing," I said looking at her rather flirtatiously.

"Uh huh, right buddy."

"So, tell me about your day?" I asked.

"Today…let's see, today was one of those days where the work and the craziness of Miami just compounded. No offense but I have two garage bays, a part of a parking lot and four drawers that are related to you and what happened yesterday."

"Parking lot?"

"Got to put the bus somewhere. The guy got smooshed by the pickup truck against it. So the bus is in the parking lot, the pickup truck and the Navigator are in my bays, and the four Dominicans are in the drawers."

"Ugh…well I guess, sorry," I said sheepishly, turning my eyes to look out at the bay.

"Cade, that could have gone sixty different ways and I would take a mountain of buses and drawers to not have you in any of them."

Her sincerity and honest caring touched me inside.

"Thank you."

We talked rather in-depth about the bayshore shootout and without compromising the investigation or my culpability in it, I helped her to know the timeline of when and how things occurred. That conversation carried on through the arrival of our dinner salads and then onto the entrees. She remarked how fortuitous it was that Concho had literally taken a bullet for me from Lobo. She also said the bullet that hit Concho had fractured his rib and pushed a jagged portion of the broken rib right into his lung. The bullet caromed off the rib and went upward right through the atria of the heart and severed the brachiocephalic artery from the heart.

He had no chance and death was nearly instantaneous.

The ballistics were still not conclusive as to whether it was Ivan's bullets or my bullet or a combination of the three that killed Lobo. To her it didn't really matter; the bullets burrowed through his torso causing high velocity injuries resulting in dual lung collapse, thoracic shock, liver obliteration, bile seepage, cardiac arrest, and a hemothorax all leading to trauma-induced blood loss and cardia tamponade. His injuries were so severe that even if he had a paramedic, a priest, and a pharmacist standing next him when he was shot the only real thing he would've needed was a pallbearer.

She then asked me to tell her about my day.

There wasn't much to say, I told her.

"I went by my house and picked up some mail. I talked to my neighbor. I went to the bank. I went to the cell phone store. Pretty much just running errands," I said in a vague and dismissive way.

I kept the truth to its barest form. It was just better that way at least for the immediate moment. There was just too much uncertainty amalgamated into an increasing feeling of paranoia and confusion. What was I supposed to say? I was the major news story today, especially since I killed a guy yesterday and ruined the afternoon commute for thousands of people. There are men outside of my house watching and there was nearly $50,000 deposited into my bank account from a mysterious Bahamian bank. No, I think in the infantile stage of this relationship I should keep my complications from complicating a potentially complicated relationship.

Sabah started to tell me about the explosion and the cadaver found at the house in Coconut Grove. I saw this as an opportunity to perfect my facial expression of ignorance about the entire situation.

"I heard something about it on the news. What was that all about?" I asked

"Honestly I'm not too sure of the details. It appears that Miami Dade was watching a house in Coconut Grove."

I feigned ignorance.

"In the Grove? That's City of Miami."

"Yeah, well it seems that Miami Dade dropped the 'it's in the county' card and didn't tell anyone about it and the bickering between Miami Homicide and the county was all over the medical center today. Between your shooting and now this, Miami Homicide is pretty busy. And they are none too pleased about it."

"Sorry to interrupt. Go on." I said steering her back to the topic.

She seemed to start all of her recanting of stories with the word 'yeah'.

"Yeah, so Miami Dade is watching this house and some guy shows up and was around the back of this house in the Grove and before they can get out of their cars and approach him the house blows up. Miami Dade goes around the back of this incinerated hovel of a house and can't find the guy. The pictures are incredible, it's as though the whole back porch and roof of the house were ripped away. About two hours later they find the deceased in some scummy fish pond thing in the back yard under the back door and other stuff.

"With the paperwork they found in his car they thought they knew who he was, but it was dental and fingerprints that helped to confirm it. But I got to tell you, dental in Miami isn't always the best since so many people get dental procedures done in South American clinics and Hialeah carports by anyone who wants to call themselves a dentist."

"But you were able to make an I.D.?" I asked.

She started to speak but stopped as the waiter placed two key lime pie desserts in front of us.

"Yeah, it wasn't easy. I mean there were partials. His right hand had nearly every distal phalanges sheared away."

I looked at her, not understanding what she was saying. She immediately sensed my confusion.

"Fingers. His fingers. The proximal, intermediate, and distal phalanges articulate with one another through interphalangeal articulations. That's how your fingers move and work. Three fingers from his right hand had been ripped away. This was no routine gas explosion. The heat was lightning hot and nearly as quick. The palm of his hand had the door latch impression seared into it. Like a branded calf."

"So you made the identification from his left hand?" I asked her.

"Eventually. The water in the pond had shriveled the eccrine glands. We had to flatten the dermis by injecting the fingers with glycerin to swell them so we could flatten the tissue to get prints. The fingers on his right hand that weren't gone were burned pretty bad, although we did get a partial side palm print from his right hand."

"So based on your prints and the paperwork in his car you think you have positive identification?" I asked.

"Yeah, luckily he was in the AFIS due to some prior arrests. So between the paperwork, and the prints we think we got a positive I.D."

AFIS was an acronym for the FBI's automated fingerprint identification system which is the repository for all fingerprints on file. I gave the conversation a brief pause to see if she would tell me the identity. Finally, I just asked her.

"So who was the guy?"

"These Spanish names trip me up sometimes. But I have a copy of his confirmation fax from AFIS here in my purse."

She reached down and pulled out a single sheet of thin white paper, the ink on it slightly askew due to a misaligned fax machine. I thought to myself that maybe Arum from the Medical Examiner's office would have got that set right. I looked at the paper in the dim light of the restaurant table's candle.

It took a brief perusal of the legal and technical jargon to get to the confirmation section. Then I saw it. Obvious and legible.

"Roldan Osorio-Vidal."

Chapter Twenty-Eight

I T WAS AS if Roldan's name leapt off of the page and went straight down my throat lodging there like a stone. Sabah noticed my demeanor and asked if I too was having trouble pronouncing the Spanish name.

"No I got it, I was just wondering what he'd done to end up in AFIS," I stammered.

"I heard Miami say he had been arrested previously for armed robbery and armed burglary. That's your end of the equation. I'm the medical end of it," she said.

My mind transitioned quickly to how Miami Homicide might be interpreting this explosive death scenario. Known burglar and robber goes to a house and house blows up. Miami Dade will eventually cross paths in communication that it was a stash house and the posturing and finger pointing will begin over the lack of information sharing. Someone, most likely Captain Zambrana, is going to deduce that for the record, three of the Four Horsemen are dead. Then attention will shift back towards me. What will be my alibi when they ask where I was when Roldan had his innards splattered across Coconut Grove? Oh, I'll just say I was in a hot tub with the assistant medical examiner learning the finer aspects of Canadian lovemaking. This could easily drag Sabah right into the middle of this percolating mess.

"You still here?" she asked, snapping me from my impending panic.

"Uh huh, I was just wondering how a house blows up like that?"

"Could be natural gas but from what I saw I don't think it was natural gas," she said

"What makes you say that?"

"Natural gas is an asphyxiant gas. It's concentrated and inert. Walls and doors won't contain it, it will seep and build up, creep into crevices and cracks and under doors. If it isn't released it will keep building up. It displaces the normal breathing air of a room or house. The entire house did *not* blow up; just the back portion. So since this explosion was limited to just the back of the house and since the explosion blew outward from the back door. I think it was a *detonation* not an explosion," she explained.

I just nodded my head and took it all in. When we left the restaurant she asked if I was okay. She said I looked as though I was off in the distance of my mind somewhere. I assured her I was fine. We kissed in the parking lot by her jeep. She reminded me that she did not live far away and asked if I was interested in following her back to her place. I readily said yes and we started off to her place with me following her.

I held back a little and she eventually drove through an intersection on Biscayne Boulevard that I did not make due to a red light. I wanted the time to put some space between us just in case I was being followed. I didn't want to make Sabah or her house a new destination in someone's notes. I need to clean myself of any potential trouble. I went just a few blocks north of my turn and as I approached the Publix supermarket I veered quickly from Biscayne Boulevard to the left merging onto to Northeast 6th Avenue. Within seconds I cut right on Club Drive and briefly paralleled Northeast 6th Avenue, then right again on Northeast 92nd Street, coming back out to Biscayne Boulevard in a perfect right triangle around Publix. Two laps around the triangle and I was able to see behind me if anyone was following.

Satisfied I was not being followed I drove on to Sabah's house just a few minutes away. Being overly cautious I once again parked in the rear of the church and retraced my steps back to her place. On the way I'd received a text message on my phone from her.

Some great detective you are, can't even keep up with a Canadian driver. I'm in the hot tub...waiting!

That most certainly made me quicken my pace.

Stepping into her place I was able to see out the upstairs window down to the yard below. The Miami moon was once again bathing the tropical foliage in celestial illumination. She looked like a vision.

She was leaning partially out of the hot tub, lighting candles in little ramekins that were placed along the edges of the hot tub and nearby tables. Her nudity was inviting but not overpowering. For a moment I stayed at the window like a prepubescent voyeur taking in the whole sight. She moved across the steaming tub with ease, a folkloric siren relegated to a small ocean of her own. The casual easiness and fluid movements of her moving from side to side in the hot tub afforded a different glimpse of her beauty each time she brought flame to a wick.

Like an arthouse film with no dialogue, she told a story just by breathing and moving. She wasn't beautiful in a traditional Americanized Western culture way. There were not ringlets of chestnut tresses and emerald green eyes set against alabaster porcelain skin. No, Sabah's beauty was an amalgamation of her long lineage of Bedouin beauty, poetic Persian ethnicity, and the dark complexities of her Hindu ancestry. She had an understated beauty that was fueled in part by her apparent disregard for her own natural attractiveness. Her warm almond-shaped eyes and full lips would have been a natural for DaVinci's Golden Ratio, yet she was not one to subscribe to DaVinci's Golden Ratio for symmetrical beauty, nor was she one to try and conceal her womanly attributes. She was comfortable in her own skin. Maybe the daily interaction with bodies of all types—albeit dead bodies—had caused her to have no compunction about being nude. A lifetime of Toronto winters can be erased by a private Miami backyard. She was accustomed to her nudity. It was apparent from the night before when she came out to the hot tub in her full womanly splendor. I was partially mesmerized and momentarily absent from my own reality. Like a passenger in the back of a New York City taxi who watches the world career by through a plexiglass divider, I forgot that I was actually part of the movement and existence of the moment. The visual effect and physiological effect of her conducting routine acts in the nude had purged my current concentrated worries from my mind. I wasn't sure what this was, but it was an elixir to my chaos.

There was nothing I could do at the moment about any of the Horsemen and the swirling maelstrom my life had become. I felt momentary emotional release and mental relief as I headed down the stairs and out through the back door. Her smile upon seeing me was inviting and her eyes were replete with coruscating ardor. She feigned indignation that I was still dressed and once my shoes were off I stood aside the hot tub as her warm wet hands undid my belt and tugged my pants forcefully down to my calves and ankles.

"Let's go, mister. Get in this hot tub," she devilishly said as she pushed back from the edge to the other side of the tub.

Now fully nude standing in the moonlight and visibly excited I reminded her coyly that I didn't have "my floaties" and could drown.

"Its okay, I know CPR....and other things," she said slyly with a subtle, sexy wink.

We didn't bother tidying up the area and I didn't even gather up my clothes. We both went back into the house an hour later refreshed, satiated, and exhausted. Our skin was pruny and there was a slight aroma of bromine in our hair. We went right into the bedroom. She pushed her large purse off the bed and onto the upholstered wingback chair in her bedroom. Pulling back the duvet and sheets, she climbed into the bed and sat on it cross-legged in a lotus position. I spied her purse lying open on the chair.

The pocket recorders were visible.

"Mind if I borrow one of those recorders?" I asked.

"Not at all. Take the silver one it has new batteries."

"Thank you."

"What are you planning with it? Going to record me orgasming?"

"Well I hadn't thought of that. Do you have another one in you?" I asked, easing into the bed, the recorder in my hand.

"Just don't record me snoring later, okay?" she teased, climbing under the bed covers next to me.

The next morning was nearly a repeat of the previous, only this time I was awake when she came out of the shower, her hair wet and her body sweetly perfumed.

"Hey there, sleepy head. You look like you were rode hard and put away wet," she said.

"Uh huh…is that what we're calling it now? Many ways that's pretty accurate, cowgirl," I said.

She kissed my forehead and put both of her soft hands on my chest, pressing with a little firmness. The compression felt good; it also rooted me in rapt attention as she spoke.

"Care to do a trifecta tonight? I'm thinking of doing Kabab Barg." she asked me.

"What is that, some sort of yoga?"

"No, silly. It's a traditional Iranian dish of boneless lamb. We make a marinade of garlic, lime, and I make it with tahdig."

"What's tahdig?"

"It's like a crispy rice, the rice has a crispy top to it so it's soft and crunchy at the same time. You'll like it."

"I can't wait. What time?"

"Oh, I don't know. I mean you can stay here all day if you want but we'll eat around 7pm, how does that sound?"

"It sounds great. Thank you. I need to get going, I know I have a one o'clock at the station and who knows between or after it," I said.

"Good." She gave me a deep kiss and said she had to get on her laptop computer downstairs and would get dressed and get going.

"I'll blow dry my hair at the office, see you at seven." And she was gone and heading downstairs.

I fell back asleep for an hour but woke up around 8:30am.

I padded off to Sabah's shower and arbitrarily chose some sort of scented body wash this time, forgoing the Moroccan hair shampoo. Towel-dried, and feeling much more awake, I realized that my clothes were still downstairs and outside by the hot tub. I went downstairs and got dressed outside in the morning sunlight of her rear patio. I straightened up the place a little and then headed out the door to my car.

It was nearly 9:30 and I knew I had some calls to make.

The first call was to the VIN office and see if Ileana could coordinate a time to meet with Commander Dolan at Miami and to also make sure either a Miami or a Coral Gables FOP attorney would be there as well.

Sitting in my car behind the church I called the VIN office.

"VIN, this is Gary Fowler."

"Hey Big G, good morning. What are you doing answering the phone?"

"Ileana is on one of those three-day cruises to nowhere."

"I never figured her to be much of a cruise ship person," I said.

"Well, ship happens," he deadpanned.

"Big G, that is just horrible."

"I'll be here for three days, tip your waiters and eat the veal."

Realizing that Commander Dolan and his agenda would just have to wait I quickly transitioned the conversation back to the Bahamian bank account.

"Hey, any word on that thing we talked about yesterday?"

"Actually, I'm waiting on a call back. I should have an idea for you in an hour or so."

"Cool. Call me as soon as you know anything."

"Will do."

Traffic was light and I took side streets towards I-95, blending into the jumble of tense commuters, and moms bound for aerobics class.

Once up on I-95 and enjoined by the teeming masses I texted Hector Gomez-Macias. He hadn't checked back with me in a few days and I'd heard nothing from U.S. Customs, so I assumed he was still in Colombia. It was dicey. I had no idea if he was connected to any of the murders of his four co-conspirators and as of now, I wasn't supposed to know that Roldan was the latest one to behold a pale horse. The Four Horsemen, just like in the book of Revelation 6:8, had nothing but death and hell follow them. My concern was whether or not I was going to get sucked into their whirlpool of mayhem.

Irregularities occur in people's lives but the events of late were nearly incomprehensible. Killing Lobo, you'd think would be paramount on my mind, but truthfully I was quite comfortable with him no longer walking the earth. We make choices in life. He made the wrong choice. He shot Iggy. He tried to shoot me. Literally, more than once. I had made up my mind that when I went into my meeting with Brunson I'd make it all about Lobo and the shooting. I wouldn't breach any topics concerning the house in Coconut Grove, Roldan, or even Donito having his throat rammed into a steering wheel. Need to put some miles between me and all of that or I'd be right back in the Miami Dade crosshairs.

I texted the pager for Hector again. Colombia is in the same time zone as Miami. I was beginning to get agitated with Hector when my phone finally rang twenty minutes later.

"Hello."

"Hello to you too," said Hector

The line had a little static but I could manage to hear him fairly well.

"You still down south?"

"Fuck yeah I'm still down south and might just go further south. *El Parche es no mas,*" he said. *The crew is no more.*

"What are you saying?"

"My cousin Gloria told me Gustavo's mother has been calling him and he isn't answering. *Oÿe Chüca!*" [Hey this smells bad.] "This is screwed up. I mean shit's getting real. It ain't like Gus to just completely drop off. I mean the guy loves those Cuban *putas* and sometimes holes up with one or two of them but usually something happens and he dumps them. Like the time that one's husband showed up with those three big fuckers. Remember that? Or the time he caught that lying whore trying to take his wallet. But this is different. No way. Something ain't right with Gus. I got that asshole Ricky from the Molino Rojo Bar still asking about me. The mother-fucker went to Gloria's beauty salon and threatened to hold a blow dryer to her ear till she finally told him I was down here. Now I got to think about maybe leaving Bogota and Colombia altogether, and heading even further south like down to 'Allende-Land' or 'Peron-Ville' if you get my meaning," he barked.

The crude attempt to tell me he was heading to Chile or Argentina was a clever ruse; more than likely he'd only be going as far away as Quito, Ecuador or San Jose, Costa Rica if he went anywhere at all. One of the learned lessons of dealing with the Horsemen was to take everything they ever said and just cut it in half to separate the bullshit, then look at what's left to see where the truth lies in the omissions and admissions.

"Okay, I get it. You're leaving because some gorilla with a blow dryer is after you."

"That shit hurts! She said it fried most of her ear and she can't hear so good now. She was learning English watching *Jeopardy*. Now she's pissed because she can only watch *Wheel of Fortune* and learn English from that human moth Vanna White."

I tried to suppress a laugh but it always intrigued me how other cultures see our own media.

"This ain't good," he intoned.

"What have you heard about Gus?"

"I haven't heard from him," I said.

Technically I wasn't lying.

"Right? See what I mean? No one has heard from him. We still had some business to finish up and he still owes me my points on something."

"Points? What kind of points and what kind of business?"

"Before you and before that whole Hialeah Medicare mix-up. None of your fucking business," he railed at me.

The animosity and fractured mentality that was coming through my phone was becoming tiresome. I needed to reel him back in closer to the boat and remind him I was still the Captain of this Voyage of the Damned. Rather than waste my energy playing nicey nicey I just decided to gaff him and bring him astern.

"Well, let me tell you what *is* my business. You got busted in Hialeah and there was no mix-up. If Ricky the moron can find your cousin Gloria, so can I. I'll let her know, in her good ear, that I'm doing everything I can to get INS involved and deport everyone she's had contact with in the last six months. Family, friends, co-workers, I'll even take the toll collector on the Don Shula Expressway. *Comprende?* I'll also let every newspaper in Colombia know that you're a rat, a *chiva.*; including *El Espectador* and *El Tiempo*. I'll get the State Department in both the U.S. and Colombia to put a freeze on both of your passports and you can just sit there, waiting for Ricky to show up and pull your lungs out through your nose. Hell, I'll even buy his plane ticket down there. Don't get all indigent with me over what's *your* business. *I* am your business! Don't screw with me, Hector! I'll pull your eye out and eat it in front of the other one."

It was a gamble but I decided with the proverbial walls closing in and since Hector was in Colombia, it was worth the risk. So I asked the burning question.

"Did Gus ever mention a *tomba*, or a cop?"

"Yeah he did…and it was you, dickhead. You're the only one any of us deal with."

This little morsel of information did not sit well with me since Gus had been heard by Miami Dade on the wiretap saying he had to deal with a '*Los Tomba*'. If I was the only cop they deal with then that puts me smack in the center of that wiretap.

"Anything else?" I asked.

"You there?" he yelled.

"Yeah, I'm here."

"Good, because I want to make sure you hear me when I say this: Fuck You!"

With that the line went dead.

I regained my temperate equilibrium but not after a few chosen swear words within the confines of the car. I started searching for something that I could start to rebuild a positive spin on the day upon.

Dinner with Sabah later tonight was a good start.

Ileana being out for three days gave me three days to possibly avoid Commander Dolan and stall documenting my U.C. car change.

I had some time to kill before meeting with Poulsen and tried to think of the best way to maximize what I needed to do. That decision was partially made for me when my phone rang.

It was Gary calling from the VIN office.

He told me that his buddy was doing some back-checking and had already made some progress.

"So what do you know about electric motor greases, synthetic open gear greases, heavy duty synthetic lubricants, and high temperature lubricants?" he asked.

"Not a damn thing."

"I didn't think so, but don't feel bad, neither do I. But it seems that's where the money trail starts."

"Huh?"

"Three weeks ago a corporate check from a Colombian company called *Empresa química de petróleo dorado* deposited $100,000 into the Bahamian account. Then $52,000 of the $100,000 went immediately to a plastics company in Panama."

"That leaves $48,000 left over from the $100,000," I said.

"Your math is good, but it gets better."

"What was the name of the company again?"

"*Empresa química de Petróleo Dorado.*"

"Gold Gas?"

"Close. It translates to Golden Petroleum Chemical Company. They're in Bogota and allegedly they make all kinds of industrial solvents and greases for bearings and machinery," he said.

"Okay, so this industrial lube company deposited 100 Gs into the Bahamian account, then immediately fifty-two of the 100 went back out to Panama to a plastics company. I follow you," I said.

"So the $52,000 lands in the coffers of the plastics company named 'Global Plastics Incorporated.' They're in Panama's free trade zone. According to the Free Trade Zone Directory they're a small company that specializes in plastic injection moldings."

"Great work, Big G."

"Thanks but it was my buddy in the Bahamas who broke nearly every banking rule to get this for us."

"I owe you both."

"Well the back part of this is that just as soon as the $52,000 went back out to Panama? The Golden Petroleum Bank account got a $52,000 wire transfer from the BanColombia account belonging to Global Plastics."

"So the circle is complete," I said.

"*Ju got it mang,*" Gary said in his best Ileana impression.

"From the untrained eye it looks like $100,000 was deposited to a Bahamian bank account of which $52,000 went to a plastics injection molding company who naturally needs the solvents and greases for their equipment and so they then sent a payment of $52,000 to the Colombian chemical company. Only we know the $52,000 is part and parcel to an original $100,000 from the same chemical company."

"Christ, this makes no sense," I said.

"Well, it kind of does in some ways," he said.

"How so?"

"You sitting down?" he asked.

I always found it absurd that people asked that, as if fainting was a common reaction to being enlightened by information. Besides, I was driving. If I wasn't sitting while driving than I was one heck of a contortionist.

"Gary I'm driving, of course I'm sitting."

"Well there were no searchable corporate records for officers or board of directors. But my guy found a microfiche archive Colombian newspaper blurb about Golden Petroleum donating soccer uniforms to a kids' soccer league in Bogota."

"Yeah, and...?"

"Well think of the initials. Golden Petroleum is G.P. Global Plastics is G.P. So there was a picture of the owner of Golden Petroleum with these kids all wearing G.P. uniforms..."

My eyes narrowed and then it hit me like a lightning bolt. I answered his response before he could finish his report.

"Gustavo Peralta!"

"Ju got it, mang."

Chapter Twenty-Nine

I THANKED GARY AND although it was unnecessary, I swore him to secrecy. He informed me his buddy in the Bahamian banking world would be in Miami in the fall for the Coconut Grove Bed Race and I vowed to thank him and show my appreciation then. Hanging up the cell phone put me back into my own thought bubble.

Why would Gus move money into my banking account prior to his death?

What did he know that I didn't know?

Why me?

Am I the *tomba* that was picked up on the wiretap?

This was beyond confusing but very strong within the realm of implication. The creeping feeling of dread washed over me again and I felt a clamminess on the back of my neck as I drove. I adjusted the air conditioner to be more frigid but I still felt sweat form on my brow. This whole situation was wreaking havoc on my central nervous system and it felt that if anything could go wrong, it was going wrong. Whether it was to my advantage or disadvantage, I needed to be meeting with Poulsen in less than twenty minutes. My paranoia was surely on retrograde to the normal function of my mind. I didn't have adequate time to have a plan, so my plan going into the meeting, was to go without one. Some of the best plays in my youth football days were drawn in the sand, not in a playbook. My index finger would just have to design a play that works.

Rather than fight my paranoia I let it run amok and I listened to the little voices in my head. It was immaterial that some were in different pitches and squeals of agitation.

I parked just east of the department in the underground parking garage of an archaic and nearly shuttered twelve-story office building. The rumor was a big planned multi-city block project was coming so many of the law tenants in the building had started seeking greener pastures. When I emerged from the stuffy garage I strolled across Fred B. Hartnett Park, which was in its barest form—a large, oval, grassy median in the center of Ponce De Leon Boulevard. This little side jaunt afforded me the option to enter the building conventionally or to go up to the third floor via walking the parking ramps. I chose the ramps.

The hallway on the third floor was quiet and nearly desolate. Most of the detectives were either at lunch or a few in the department gymnasium. Even Big G was out when I walked into the VIN office.

Poulsen was in his office, nestled in the interior recesses of the VIN office. I rapped lightly on the door frame and he looked up from his papers and greeted me warmly. His reading glasses were perched low on his nose and he was wearing a dark blue—so blue it was almost black—VIN raid jacket.

"You expecting something to go down any minute?" I said as I took the seat across from his desk.

"Oh this." He looked down at his sleeve and chest. "The air conditioning in this building is the most schizo thing ever invented by man. When it's kicking, it's really kicking. We could make ice cream in this building."

Having just been outside and walking a fair distance to the building, plus battling my own internal heat index I wasn't feeling the cold. At least not yet, like he was.

"Cade, I asked you to come in a little early because the Major is a bit on the war path."

I looked at him impassively, all the while concealing my concern.

"I know. I know what you're thinking—he's always on the warpath. But this whole VIN situation doesn't sit well with him. Mainly because he doesn't understand it. Rather than understand it he'd rather just abolish it, put more people in uniform on the street. It's more of the era he comes from. I don't think it's anything personal... he just thinks that phone calls from mayors, commissioners, and city managers regardless of the origin are not what he wants to do. "

He seemed to pause for dramatic effect and then continued.

"After the shooting you just had, regardless of any aggravations, no one is going anywhere. You did right out there. I mean you did the right thing. You protected Iggy and drew attention and fire away from Ivan. I can see a medal of valor in all of this."

"Thank you," I replied.

"Listen, I'm in your corner. You're by far one of the best we got here. Just take care of yourself. I think I speak for everyone here when I say we're concerned for you. What you went through is *not* an everyday thing, regardless of what people see on TV and in movies. Are you...seeing anyone?"

"Seeing someone?" I asked.

"I mean like a counselor or clergy. Have you spoken to Chaplain Messon or anyone else?"

"No."

"Well I think it would be advantageous for you to do so. Ileana will be back in a few days. If you think you can hold off I'll have her set something up with the psychological counseling service. In fact all these papers here on my desk are other agencies' policies for aftermath crisis counseling. I'm going to craft a policy for us and send it through accreditation for acceptance. It's time we stepped into the 20th Century on our mental health protocols."

I sat there listening and when I realized he'd stopped talking and was looking for affirmation I nodded in agreement. This spurred him onto continue talking.

"If you think you might need someone before Ileana gets back, well, I'll personally make the calls for you. You can even talk to me if you'd like to."

I just looked at him and he in turn looked at me. I decided it was better if I spoke than find myself unwillingly having a Hallmark moment.

"No, I think I'm fine. It's all very new and I'm okay with it so far."

"Cade, there are people who care about you. I'm one of them. Just keep that in mind."

"I will. Thank you."

"Okay then. Let's get on down to Brunson's office and let me do as much of the talking as necessary. I got your best interest in mind here."

"I will. Thank you." I simply repeated.

Charlene was in a pleasant mood when we walked in and I could sense already the odd, quasi-celebrity status that was now being offered me. Something about being the lead story on every news station, and the front page of the *Miami Herald* will cause you to be an overnight sensation, or at least big gossip fodder. I had been everyone's inside information. The news channels the past two days had referred to me as an "unidentified Coral Gables Detective," whereas everyone in the department knew it was me, and I'm sure regaled their family and friends with the self-inflated importance of being in the know. They could all say, "I know who it was. It was *Cade* but we're not supposed to say anything." Then each person had their Cade story to help sharpen their affiliation.

"He was the one at the BBQ with the green cooler."

"He was the one that gave Mateo Viegas a ride home from the Dolphins game."

"He was the one in the orange tie at Tony's swearing in ceremony."

"His wife is Gina."

His wife is Gina. That must be the one they say most often. It's easier to make a visual association with two people rather than one.

Laurel and Hardy, Batman and Robin, Woodward and Bernstein. Yes, I was assuredly aware that Gina was mentioned a lot in the past forty-eight hours.

"Anyone check with Gina?"

"Anyone hear from Gina?"

"I wonder how Gina is. I couldn't be married to a cop."

Gina. I wondered if she even got word of the Bayshore shooting. There was a good chance that being way north in Riviera Beach she had no inclination to even peruse Miami news. Out of sight and out of mind, unless someone down here called her and inquired, and lit a curiosity flame in her. Either way I had not heard from her and that said volumes, especially if she'd gotten word.

A precipitous drop in my demeanor made me solemnly plop back into a chair in Brunson's outer office. Poulsen remained standing. Dressed in brown slacks and the raid jacket, he looked like every TV extra from every cop show I had ever seen.

Charlene asked if she could get me anything, which I do believe is the first time ever that she offered to get up from behind her desk because of me. I just shook my head no with a resigned smile and awaited my fate with Brunson. Feeling adequate in her minimal hosting ability, Charlene picked up the phone and simply said, "They're here."

They're here.

Nothing announces a foreboding meeting more than "they're here." It's fully steeped in the obvious fact that you have been discussed, all other agendas have been cleared for you, and due to the preparations for your arrival the announcement that "they're here" is that distinct declaration that the big event is about to start. Those who are the "they" in the equation know who they are and don't need to be told to go in.

As soon as she hung up the phone Poulsen started moving towards the door which, like a tow line behind a mothership, meant I needed to get up from my slouched position and join in behind him.

Brunson was behind his desk, files and papers piled in front of him. The first hot sauce I laid eyes on was "Firepower." Well, that was either going to be a good omen or a bad omen since firepower had put Lobo and Concho in the morgue and Iggy in the bay.

"Gentlemen, find seats please." He half-motioned and did a little up and down on his office chair, pushing up from the arm rests which threw both of us off as to whether he wanted to sit at the conference table or around his desk. The awkwardness was quickly broken in typical Brunson fashion.

"For Chrissakes, just sit the fuck down."

I was feeling uncomfortable already but Poulsen took it all in stride.

"Major. I've been talking to Cade and I must say, I think he performed in an exemplary fashion. This was a situation of absolute mayhem and he kept a considerable amount of—"

Brunson waved at him as if he was a flitting mosquito and cut him off.

"Ken, I have not only read our offense incident report but also the Miami offense incident reports and arrest reports of the deceased. All these years and I have never understood why they bother writing an arrest report for a deceased person. I guess the state attorney wants a case closure thing. Fucking bullshit. So I'm pretty versed in all this. I just want to know first and foremost—why were you not there, Ken?"

I hadn't expected that. The cannons from the S.S. Brunson were now pointed at Poulsen.

"Well, I was made aware of it only after Sergeant Brookings from Miami S.I.S. called me. By that time their ops plan was in play and they were on the way to the meet."

So much I for "I got your best interest in mind." Poulsen just threw me under the organic fertilizer truck.

The cannons swung back where I expected them to be. Brunson directed his gaze directly on me and looking me over from my waist to my face with displaced contempt, he snarled,

"Cade, now I know that every psychologist, sociologist, and fucking knowitallologist will say that after such a traumatic event I should be easy and gentle. But they can kiss my easy and gentle ass. The way you're operating is not how we conduct ourselves here, son. All I hear is how valuable an employee and detective you are, but from where I sit—and you may have noticed, I do sit in the biggest office in this place— I have the blessed curse of seeing you in a much different light."

He paused for emphasis, but it was really not necessary as both Poulsen and I could sense the next word would be an expletive.

"Fuck!" he bellowed.

I, for one, was not disappointed nor surprised and I don't think Poulsen was either.

"Per our last conversation I do recall saying 'no more dead bodies.' Yes, I'm almost sure that I looked you right in your bloodshot eyes and said '*no more dead bodies*.' Not only do I have more dead bodies but I actually have *four* of them. Happily, four dead criminals, but still speaking metafuckingphorically, they count as bodies."

His tongue-lashing was prematurely halted as his intercom buzzed on his desk. He answered it with a quick push of the button and made his feelings known before Charlene could say anything.

"Whoever it is. Whatever it is. Put them on hold for a minute," he snapped dismissively at the little electronic box. Turning his attention back towards me he started to speak only to be interrupted by Charlene's voice resonating from outside the office door.

"Miami Dade Major Steve Edwards on line one for you."

Brunson looked at me and Poulsen with the resigned look of a man who thinks he is in absolute control and yet knows deep down he is not. He hung his head, reached out and took the phone receiver from its cradle and pressed the lit button. He leaned back in his chair looking up at the ceiling and put the receiver to his ear.

"Stevie," he said.

Poulsen and I busied ourselves by looking around the room.

"Well actually, he's right here in front of me," Brunson said into the phone.

Two-to-one odds it wasn't Poulsen he was talking about.

"Um, well yeah, sure….okay, see you then," he said and he hung up the phone.

"Major Edwards wants to come by in an hour and have a chat. He'd like you to be there," he said, staring directly at me.

"He wants a little tête-à-tête. Do you know what that means Cade?"

"It's French for a meeting," Poulsen softly said, trying to be helpful.

"Is your name Cade? No. It's French for too many Goddamn people in my fucking office ruining my afternoon. That's what it stands for!" he shouted.

"Cade, I'm going to just table this artful display of aggravating the boss 'til after Major Edwards gets here and we'll see just what yet *another* outside agency has to say about something involving you before I go any further. Ken, make sure both you and Cade are back here in an hour. Now will you two kindly leave my office? How was that? Easy and gentle enough for you?"

Both Poulsen and I left, but before completely making it out I heard the distinct sound of a metal garbage can being kicked from inside Brunson's office.

Chapter Thirty

POULSEN DECIDED TO head out for a quick bite and although he invited me, I graciously declined. What I really could've used was a two-finger pour of Jameson. Maybe somewhere nearby where I could just mull over the flaming fiasco of what my life had become. Somewhere dark and storied. A place I could drink anonymously and without a notion of whether it was daylight or nighttime. Incognito and inebriated. I knew deep inside that a snort of Jameson would not be the best thing to do, considering the afternoon's upcoming event, but who could blame me either? I may not know what the French call a tête-à-tête, but I sure know *usquebaugh* is Gaelic for "water of life." And right now I could sure use a little of life's water.

I wandered down to the VIN office and sat in the empty office just looking around at the motif of the place and really noticing it for the very first time. All it needed was a framed picture of a clown or a painting of a vase with flowers and it might have passed as a dentist's waiting room. The place was office-institutionally ugly with no charm or panache. No wonder Ileana had no inclination to advance her English language skills.

It took me a minute to realize that with no one in the office I could look up a few things uninterrupted and without any prying eyes.

The first thing I did was pull out the U.C. vehicle log from the file icon on Ileana's computer. I scanned through the list of vehicles and the task force members assigned to them. Fifth one down on the Excel list was my own name.

Cade. Ford Explorer. Dark Blue. Florida Tag ESJ 46X. Ocean Rental Cars.

I was relieved that the Infiniti in my possession was not listed as assigned to me. This would afford me more time to move about undetected, especially if my suspicions of being followed were true. We had rental contracts with five different rental agencies. The one assigned to the detective below my name on the list was Suncoast Rental Cars. For extra measure I changed the rental agency attached to me from Ocean Rental Cars to Suncoast Rental Cars. It would buy me extra time if anyone was inclined to ask. It could be explained easier as a clerical error since the two agencies were listed adjacent to each other.

Cade. Ford Explorer. Dark Blue. Florida Tag ESJ 46X. Suncoast Rental Cars.

No sooner had I closed the Excel spreadsheet than I was now back across from Ileana's desk when Gary came walking into the office.

"Big G. What do you say?"

"Like Bob Seger says, I feel like a number," was his hip reply.

"Hey, once again thank you, and thank your buddy for the help on the Bahamian bank thing."

"Not a problem. It's what we numbers guys in the shadows like to do. Makes us feel all covert and stuff. So what's up with your Uncle Stash?"

"Uncle Stash?" I asked.

"Yeah everyone should have an Uncle Stash, that mysterious brother of one of your parents that no one knows too much about but he can always be counted upon to drop some cash on the needy family. Uncle Stash. I mean obviously you got an Uncle Stash who thinks enough to dial up your bank account."

I just kind of looked at him curiously.

"I'm joking. So what do you think about a dead guy wiring money into your account? Based on the transaction numbers and speed it takes to make it all happen he might have done it just a day or so before he died. Do you think we was trying to park it with you like he knew he was going to die?"

"If you knew how he died I don't think anyone would've willingly put themselves in such a place to meet their executioner," I said.

"How did he die?" Gary asked.

"Someone yanked his neck like saltwater taffy until he died. Tried to put the back of his head to his tail bone. They nearly put his spine in his eyes."

"Damn."

"You know Big G, if Peralta had wanted to just park money in my account you think he would've put more of it in there. Granted, $48,000 is a decent amount of money but it's not earth shattering."

"Yeah, it's like a payoff fee or something," he said.

"That's exactly what it looks like. Enough money to pay for something," I lamented.

"Well, on the bright side of things, he is dead and if it doesn't come back to bite you in the ass I guess you got a doper windfall unknowingly."

That bit of financial acumen, although logical, did nothing to alleviate my flip-flopping central nervous system screaming for a shot of Jameson to smooth out the rough edges. I may have said too much to Gary about how Gus died, but in a sense I felt I owed him a bit of insight since he and his banker buddy had done so much for me. He settled further into his desk and I sat across from him and busied myself thumbing through a Coral Gables real estate magazine which was loaded with small pictures of houses and big pictures of female realtors. Each realtor wore business attire and heavy makeup, with their arms folded across their chest. I quietly wondered if they were selling themselves or selling houses. After a few minutes the silence was broken by Gary who was reading an email on his computer.

"Ah man, more crap from the City Manager's office."

"What now?"

"Remember when I told you he's on this financial tear about what he thinks are personal expenses and city expenses?"

"You mean like the sunglasses for the motor unit?" I said.

"Yeah, even the sunscreen for the Marine Patrol Unit," he said.

"What? That's absurd. The health trust should get some skin cancer studies together and jump all over that. That's just stupid. If I was Marine Patrol, I'd tell him to go pound sand," I said.

"Well, you're going to get your chance."

"What do you mean?" I asked.

"You just made the list."

"What?"

"As of 12:30 today, his 'newest findings' as he likes to call them, as if he's some sort of money sleuth. Among the forty-six new items added, one of them is attributed to you. Invoice from Vogel Printing. $17.85. Looks like a day planner or a calendar. Did you order a day planner? A bunch of people did," he said.

"No, I didn't order a day planner."

"I'll get to it later on and let you know. I like to wait 'til the end of the day and then confirm or challenge his ever growing list. It throws off his evening if he gets the emails later in the day. More than likely it's another city hall screw-up."

With that he turned back to his computer and began to softly hum and sing the lyrics to Bob Seger's *Feel like a number*.

I couldn't help but pick up the rift and sing along to myself.

"Gonna cruise out of this city

Head down to the sea

Gonna shout out at the ocean

Hey it's me."

Poulsen came in with a crumbled white bag and the remnants

of his Arbetter's hot dog lunch. Looking gorged, he stretched and yawned and looked around the room.

"The place seems so much quieter without Ileana here."

Gary looked up with a bored expression and shrugged with feigned concern. Poulsen made a big deal of throwing the bag into the garbage can as if he were an NBA free-thrower.

"Swoosh…at the buzzer. Poulsen nails it. Grown men crying in the aisles," he said gleeful. His chipper mood was counter to the industrious attitude of Gary and the forlorn melancholy of myself. Inside I was slowly starting to seethe at Poulsen's cavalier mentality. He didn't have to deal with people like the Horsemen and he most assuredly would never be in a position like Iggy and I found ourselves a few days ago. The expression that 'rank has its privilege' was very obviously coined by someone of rank. The back generals of every organization never feel the wrath from the front skirmishes. Speaking of wrath, it was just a case of prolonging the inevitable with Brunson. Poulsen's Teflon ability to wiggle out of responsibility and account-ability made my convictional thoughts about how to perform in this job just crawl. Skin and all. Maybe it was just me. Maybe I was the odd duck here. I mean who was I kidding? I was positive that people were following me. My wife had left me, and I wasn't sleeping well in my own home. I nomadically slept in cars, boats, and other people's beds, drinking way too much and thinking even way too much about Gina. I had spent more time in the last week with people who are dying than people who are living. Maybe a guy like Poulsen had the right idea. Fake it 'til you make it. Just master the art of feigning the allegiance to the cause while you bang your own drum. I needed to snap out of this blue funk and focus on the pertinent things coming at me with the aim of a carnival knife thrower. All sharp and gleaming with the illusion of control, yet administered by a complete amateur charlatan. My life had become bald tires and soft brakes on a narrow, downhill, mountain gravel road in a state that ran out of funding for guardrails. Holding the wheel only gave the illusion of control.

My wallowing and self-flagellation was interrupted when Gary's phone rang. He informed us that Charlene said Brunson was ready to see us again. Like a prize fighter who rises from his corner stool warily and with great reluctance for yet another round of pummeling, I stood up as if on autopilot. Poulsen, who makes these trips to Brunson's office nearly daily, glided out of the door with nary a care. I, on the other hand, had found the lessons in profanity and its creative uses for description and adjective tiresome.

When I got to Brunson's office Poulsen was already filing through the doorway and seemed to be in line behind others. This was going to be a guess-a-rama of which Miami Dade County brass would also be here.

I walked in and Brunson was already at the conference table and pulling chairs up were Major Steve Edwards and Poulsen. I was relieved to see that Zambrana was not there.

"Captain Zambrana is parking the car," said Edwards.

If I could've thrown my hands up and said, "Wonderful. Just wonderful," I would have, but instead I played it cool and detached.

Edwards and Brunson engaged in small talk about of all things cheeseburgers. Two high-ranking police officials from two different agencies, and yet they seem to only talk about artery-clogging food.

Zambrana waltzed in on a cloud of his own arrogance. He appeared pleasant and agreeable but by the time he'd pulled up a chair across from me, his brown eyes set their gaze on me more so than anyone else.

Edwards started the conversation, most of it emphatically about his worry for me and the Bayside shooting. I thanked him for his concern. He then must've felt that he had his web spun and was now going to see how much he had ensured me his fly.

"Obviously Cade, it seems that there's untenable amount of things affecting our caseload that has a singular component in it, and that component is you. This is not to assert anything that you are involved in this."

"Now Cade, Captain Zambrana and myself are here because of the homicides of Gustavo Peralta and Don Julio Restrepo. It's only been a couple of days since we all were here in Major Brunson's office, and now here we are again, to see if you have any new information that you can shed upon us."

I just shook my head slowly from side to side. I didn't even want to utter a response so I chose to arch an eyebrow in a concerted effort to rack my brain and shake my head.

"You do recognize that we're investigating two homicides, both of which have an affiliation to you?" reiterated Edwards.

"An affiliation or a connection?" I asked.

"Semantics," retorted Captain Zambarana.

"I beg to differ. There is a difference, because both of the deceased were informants and there *is* an affiliation, but that's where the connection ends," I defended myself.

Zambrana looked at me inquisitively, much like the RCA Victor dog looks at the phonograph. I knew that I had to be as cagey as I could without appearing disrespectful or insubordinate. Words and inflections would be my best defense.

"What are you trying to say here? Are you saying that you're not connected to *any* of these murders? Your business card is the only twinge of identification found on the first victim and our road unit saw you with your arm inside the car of the second victim!"

"I have no idea how Peralta had my business card, and all I was doing was assessing Donito when the uniformed patrol rolled into the parking lot."

"Donito? Little Don? Sounds very cozy to me, as up until this very instant we only knew the victim as Don Julio," said Zambrana.

Brunson and Edwards had decided to sit this one out and watched the banter with rapt attention.

"Donito was how he was referred to by the other Horsemen, and if you'd ever dealt with informants you'd know you have to understand and speak their language," I said.

"Oh, I have dealt with plenty of informants. You can bet your bottom dollar Cade, I have dealt with plenty. Only my informants don't get killed."

You can't argue with facts, and the facts were clearly there. It was Edwards who sidled into the conversation like a Physical Education coach breaking up a middles school locker room fight preemptively before it even starts.

"Cade, you might recall that when I was last here I spoke about TNT having a wire on a house in Coconut Grove. Well that house blew up two nights ago. Are you aware of that?"

The house blowing up in Coconut Grove and being so close to Coral Gables and the fact it was all over the TV news made my answer elementary. I quickly transitioned my defense that I would acknowledge seeing it on the news. It was too big a story to not be known about.

"I saw it on the news. "

To say any more would seem too extraneous and open up more inquiry from Zambrana, who I knew was only temporarily muzzled by Edwards.

"Well, as the news reported, the house did blow up. We almost lost two of our TNT guys."

It was a stretchable exaggeration, but I wasn't going to call him on it.

"As it would be, a lone male arrived at the house late in the evening. Our units identified him as potentially going towards the house and TNT set a perimeter up in case he ran."

I quietly wondered what exactly would've caused them to set a perimeter first before engaging Roldan. Inadvertently, maybe my little garbage run for my life a few nights ago might have saved two of the TNT guys from being in the doorway when Roldan turned the key.

"So this guy goes to try and get in the house through the back door and the house blows up killing him. According to the Miami Bomb Squad, the back door had been set up as a killing machine. The guy never knew what hit him."

"But we have a little item of concern here," interjected Zambrana.

"You'd think this would be a Miami Homicide case, but since we had the house under surveillance, and because of other linked circumstances, we will be assisting Miami Homicide with this one."

"Linked circumstances?" asked Brunson.

"Oh! Did we forget to mention that our mystery late night visitor was Roldan Osorio-Vidal? One of Cade's Horseman informants?" he said with an icy stare solely upon me.

With that pointed declaration the entire room turned their attentive gazes directly on me.

Chapter Thirty-One

I NEEDED TO MUSTER the best perplexed facial expression I could, mixed with feigned astonishment.

"You mean to tell me that Roldan was the guy the news said was killed in the explosion?" I asked.

"What did I just say? Yes. Yes, it was Osorio-Vidal killed in the explosion. Imagine that? Another Horseman killed," Zambrana said sarcastically.

Surprisingly, it was Poulsen who came to my defense.

"I've been keeping abreast of the Horsemen situation, and I don't recall Cade mentioning any recent contact with Osorio-Vidal."

He then turned the question to me.

"Cade, have you heard from Osorio-Vidal recently?"

"No," I answered.

"Not at all? Are you sure?" asked Zambrana.

"No. I've tried to call him but he's never answered or called back."

I figured the best answer was to mention the missed phone calls in case my phone records were pulled again.

"Bullshit. I don't believe you," snarled Zambrana.

Neither Edwards nor Brunson were not expecting such a response form Zambrana, but neither of them said anything.

The room was becoming increasingly warmer, not just figuratively but literally. Brunson asked for a brief respite as he turned back in his chair to his desk and inquired on the intercom if the air conditioning was working properly. Charlene's response was heard by the whole room. In anticipation of the incoming cooler weather the city manager asked that all air conditioners be turned off. Brunson swiveled in his chair back to the conference table and mumbled a terse apology to the room.

"I'm sorry. Where were we?" asked Brunson.

"Detective Taylor was just trying to tell us that he hadn't spoken to Osorio-Vidal. And I guess he'll tell us that he hadn't been in touch with either Peralta and Restrepo before they were killed either," said Zambrana.

"Captain Zambrana, you have made some very overt insinuations about Cade but if you don't have any proof of your suspicions I would kindly ask you to refrain from this personal inquisition, especially here in our own house," Poulsen said.

I was astounded by the fortitude being exhibited by Poulsen and was most appreciative of him sticking up for me. Zambrana was momentarily taken aback.

Poulsen was junior in rank to Zambrana. Although rank was recognized and respected cross-jurisdictionally, at its barest element the Miami Dade captain rank meant very little to anyone in Coral Gables.

It was Edwards who once again waded into the fray.

"Gentlemen, let's get back to the situation at hand here. Cade, I want to ask you a few questions so that we can try and gauge where we are in all of this. Did you have any contact with victim Osorio-Vidal prior to him going to Coconut Grove?"

"I had tried since I heard that Peralta was found dead in Matheson Hammock. I never made contact. Actually, I tried to reach the other three Horsemen," I said.

"Why did you think it was necessary to reach out to the three other Horsemen?"

"Of the four, Gus was the heir apparent, baddest one of them, and defacto leader. With him murdered it was possibly a power coup from one of the other three, or maybe they'd know something."

"So you interfered with an ongoing Miami Dade Homicide investigation?" interjected Zambrana.

"No. These were my informants and I had a handle on them and—"

"And you interfered!" Zambrana said, raising his voice.

The temperature in the room was rising and so were the emotions. Brunson, I do believe, was tired of having the conversation hijacked and slammed his hand hard down on the conference table.

"Enough!" he yelled to the whole room, but most definitely directed to Zambrana. Edwards then cleared his throat and restarted his questions.

"Cade, let's get back to your trying to reach our third victim, Osorio-Valdez. When did you make contact with Roldan?"

It was a nifty approach to questioning. You start with the last name and transition to the first name and create a sense of familiarity. Then ask a leading question like, 'So, when did you make contact with Roldan?' Early in my career the opening question to a person on the street was always, "So when was the last time you were arrested?" The hesitancy, or even the truth spoke volumes.

"I never made contact," I said, using the same terminology when I answered the same question earlier.

"When was the last time you saw Peralta alive?"

"Probably a week or two before he died."

I added some time to our last meeting in a quick attempt to stall the securing of the restaurants security camera footage At this point, I was hoping that Casa Juancho's security cameras had already taped over. Parking was deep behind the restaurant in a vine-covered walled parking lot that had very little light. That would work in my favor too, as pixelated images in Miami's vapor street lights are usually poor quality.

"Where did you last see Peralta?"

"Casa Juancho in Little Havana."

Brunson and Poulsen sat quietly. Edwards looked expectantly at Zambrana.

Zambrana nodded. "I know where it is," he said "There is also a Sedanos supermarket across the street. They might have some extended camera footage at the supermarket and we can see if anyone followed him in or out of the restaurant."

This was a butt-puckering moment for me. I had forgotten about the Sedanos supermarket and possible large bank of cameras. I misled them on the time frame and now to try and correct myself on it would put me in a hole that I might not be able to get out of. My mind galloped a mile a minute. I decided to cast my fate on the Sedanos supermarket not having extended security footage or any footage at all. The odds were more in my favor. I kept to my story with the pushed timeline back further. I had seen Peralta leave the restaurant and there was no one following. This was a dead end, but I didn't need to make it my own personal dead end. I also felt the first bead of sweat trickle down the back of my neck. I didn't know if it was from nerves or the heat in the room. Zambrana wasn't finished, but he opted to steer the questioning away from Peralta.

"Have you been in contact with Hector Gomez-Macias?"

"I have spoken to him twice on the telephone and he says he is in Colombia."

"You believe that? Really?"

"From what the connection sounds like on the phone and the fact that U.S. Customs confirmed he left the U.S. on the 26th of January, yes I do. I put a Customs watch order on him."

Now it was Brunson who spoke.

"You put a Customs watch order on this Colombian fellow? Good work. Make sure you give them the number so that we don't have any duplication of action here."

"I have it saved in an email," I said.

"So, what has Gomez-Macias said in your telephone conversations?" asked Zambrana.

"Not much. A lot of agitation with being in Colombia. He doesn't appear to know that Peralta is dead. He just thinks he's dropped off the map."

"What about the second victim, Don Luis Restrepo? When did you last see him?"

"I never saw him. I was inside La Covacha, and never saw him."

"You mean you never saw him alive?" Poulsen said, nudging the conversation away from any culpability to me.

"Yes. I never saw him alive," I affirmed.

"So why exactly did you set up a meet with him out there?" asked Zambrana.

"It was about the percentage he was going to make on any cash or cocaine seizures that he was going to be a part of in the future."

"What was wrong with the percentage?"

"He wasn't producing and I felt he needed to be scaled back a point 'til he started producing again."

It was an embellishment of sorts. I did say to Donito that we need to discuss a new rate. I actually had no plans to lessen any payments to him for seizures, but I needed to actually talk to him and get a better handle on what had happened to Peralta. I knew that Trentlocke and his nutritional overachieving detectives with him were itching to finger me as Peralta's killer, and I needed to delve into this myself for no other reason than to save my own ass."

"Is it normal for you to meet with informants alone and in out-of-the-way locations late in the evening? Let me rephrase this. Was this meeting absolutely necessary or were you depriving the taxpayers of Coral Gables as you socialized, on the clock, drinking beer?"

It was obvious they had reviewed the cameras at La Covacha and saw me drinking at the bar while I waited for Donito. I looked at Zambrana with a slight furrowing of my brow and for a moment was envisioning myself telling him a few choice words. Before I could answer, once again it was Poulsen who strode in and set the record straight.

"Captain Zambrana, this is not an internal affairs investigation. If it was we would be conducting it ourselves. Not you, and most certainly not the Miami Dade Police Department. Detective Taylor is a VIN detective. His hours and time working are as varied as the operation or investigation necessitates it to be. I am his immediate supervisor and I was aware of his meeting with Restrepo."

I was beginning to seriously change my opinion of Poulsen. He actually had a pair of balls and was going to bat for his detective.

"He called you?" Zambrana asked.

"Detective Taylor reported his meeting in the NINJAS system. I check the system first thing in the morning, midday, and usually evenings," Poulsen said.

"What about your breakfast meeting?" Zambrana asked me.

"I didn't have a breakfast meeting."

"Interesting. Do you know what *tocino crujiente* means?"

I just looked at him. Brunson leaned forward in his chair and Poulsen, still wearing his VIN raid jacket, appeared to be starting to perspire.

"It means crispy bacon. It was written on a breakfast receipt in Restrepo's BMW. The receipt is from Reuben's Cafe, a little Cuban place only a mile or so from your house. The waitress described a gringo that fits your description and remembers serving the breakfast the morning that Restrepo was killed. She remembers the gringo very well. Very well, Cade. Oddly enough your phone records show calls made to Restrepo within the same twenty to thirty minute window that you were there at Reuben's Cafe. Two calls exactly."

I knew that the waitress at Reuben's Cafe would definitely be able to identify me. I saw the receipt in the bag of items recovered from Donito's car at the morgue. I also figured Trentlocke to be smart enough to follow that lead. This was not an earth-shattering revelation to me and I had anticipated it with dread, but was still not prepared for it.

Trying to explain how a receipt that I threw into the trash ended up in a dead man's car twelve hours later was not a viable option.

Brunson and Edwards were now leaning forward, most likely subconsciously wanting either an answer or a piece of my hide. Either one I was going to make it as difficult as I could to extract. I needed to defer and deflect.

"Eating breakfast is not a crime. Did she also tell you that I was alone? Did she tell you that I left my newspaper and the check on the counter and as a favor to her I threw them both in the trash can outside?"

Zambrana had gambled on an *I got you moment* and although it had strong knock-out potential I was able to absorb the blow somewhat and cast a dispersion on his moment. I needed to switch the momentum and quit hoping Poulsen or someone else would take the hits for me. I straightened up, put on my most horrified and offended face, and dove in.

"A mile or so from my house, huh? How do you know where I live? So those are your guys surveilling my house. How long have you two jerk offs been tailing me and watching my house?"

Edwards was surprised by my tone and looked at Brunson for assistance.

"Cade, I will remind you—" said Brunson before I cut him off.

"No. Let me remind you. Let me remind you that you're not living in a fishbowl. I am. I got Miami Dade following me and watching my every move, trying to figure what private business cameras they can pull to track me, reviewing my cell phone records, and for what? What?"

Looking directly at Zambrana, I said, "Are you charging me with something? Then do it. Do it! If not, then back the fuck down."

Well, that made the whole room explode. Every voice were talking at the same time. It was a symphony of shouting. I think I heard Edwards say something about them doing what they want, Zambrana said something about being patient and waiting, but it was Brunson who I had my ear tuned to.

The string of profanity was almost artistic, and it caused the room to settle down and take note either at the mastery of his vulgarity or the actual meaning of his profane vocabulary which I truly feel is unrivaled. Trying to retell it would do it no justice, but I do know that he finished by saying that he "would put his foot up my ass so far that I could floss my teeth with his shoe laces."

The heat had become oppressive and everyone was standing, shuffling. There were angry looks and lots of straightening of sport coats and loosening of neckties. Poulsen took off his VIN raid jacket.

No one noticed. No one noticed at all. But I did.

It wasn't really something that stood out, but it caught my eye. I saw it clear as gin. The hair on the back of my neck stood up. My mouth went dry.

Along the side of Poulsen's white shirt, just under the armpit, were the remnants of hard-scrubbed rust stains.

Chapter Thirty-Two

THE ROOM STILL had an unruly feel to it, as no one seemed to want to be the first one to sit down. Brunson ambled over near the window looking north towards Miracle Mile and the downtown business district. Edwards inserted and removed a pen from his shirt pocket a few times in a feeble attempt to hide his rattled state. Zambrana just seethed, which I assume was something he did often. Poulsen was the first one to get back to a normal state and pulled his chair up closer to the conference table to sit down.

Brunson spoke first although it wasn't to any of us—he yelled towards his office door.

"Charlene, can you get some Pepsis in here?"

I saw this as an impromptu break and I desperately needed to get away from there, or more aptly away from Poulsen. A rust-stained shirt is no more admissible a smoking gun as is a business card in the back of a dead guy's pants. Nonetheless, it galvanized my thought process. I had an epiphany of sorts. What had been very hazy and obscure was becoming clearer. If I said anything to Zambrana, Edwards, or Brunson they'd most assuredly trip over each other to be the first ones to put the handcuffs on me themselves.

I was certainly in on this myself.

It would look like I was casting this strong suspicion that was slung around me like a horse collar directly onto Poulsen. Although it was clear to me that maybe I wasn't *la tomba,* it was still a stretch to assert that maybe Poulsen *was.*

I moved on autopilot, trying to hide what must have been a deathly pallor on my face. The walk to the door was on one of those funhouse conveyer belt floors, I was moving but getting nowhere. When I reached the door, I said over my shoulder to the room, to no one in particular, "I'm going to help Charlene, and get that Customs watch order number." This was going to be more than a typical Irish exit. This would have some serious consequences for me and for my presumption of innocence.

This was a classic case of putting myself in a position to ask for forgiveness rather than ask for permission.

And forgiveness, I was going to need.

I stepped into the hallway and momentarily felt as though the air was rarified. I went straight into the first open unoccupied office I could find and called Sabah. I got her voicemail, which I was actually hoping for. I left a very short message saying I'd be at least ninety minutes late and then quickly hung up the phone.

I knew that I would no longer be able to use my cell phone from this point on. I quick-timed it to the east staircase and down the stairs. When I popped out on the street level the heavy tumbler and latch of the staircase door banged loudly and the door swung harsh against the building facade. Anxious to get out, I pushed a little too hard.

The humidity was negligible and the air was already cooler. Weatherman like to say that we in South Florida are going to experience an "Arctic blast," "Siberian express," or a "sweeping trough of cold air" with graphics of a little thermometer encased in blue icicles. I didn't need to be told cold weather was moving in. I could feel. It would be sweater weather or at least a light jacket evening.

I kept on moving straight east once again and made a beeline right for my car. I slipped the battery off my cellphone as I cut across Fred B. Hartnett Park. I glanced over my shoulders a few times and felt nobody was following me. I got in the car and wasted no time pulling out and getting out on the road, headed south straight to Fox's Lounge in South Miami. I think the floor is black-and-white checked tile but I could never be sure, it's always so dark inside. I got the bartender's attention and ordered a double Jameson, neat, soda back and took it to a dimly lit corner booth. I sat and just hid and drank in the enveloped darkness. Astronomers have sought answers in the lighted stars of the darkest skies, but I believed that maybe the answers were not in the light but in the dark.

The lounge was marginally occupied with a few regulars who, from my vantage point, were nothing more than silhouettes of ashen gray and dark gray in the obscure recesses of the place. The Jameson tasted good and I sat there running my index finger over the mouth of the beveled glass thinking.

Just thinking.

The county employee Godfrey Pinder had said that opening the gate at Matheson Hammock had stained one too many of his shirts with almost indelible rust stains. He also said,

"They gave me some keys and that was it. But you got dock masters, restaurant people, maintenance crews all kind of people who were all here before me. There's just no way of knowing who has keys."

Poulsen had been here before me. He had been with the police department a long time. I tried to surmise the connection. Whoever killed Peralta had driven in with him in the same vehicle. This was not a chance random meeting at a spit of land jutting into the bay. This was intentional, and I had no idea how Poulsen and Peralta may have come together. I had never had Poulsen on any of my meetings with Peralta. It made no sense. I handled all communication between Peralta and the task force. It took me just a few minutes of pondering and a deep throw back of the Jameson to recall the ease that Poulsen had in obtaining the C.I. files, *Confidential Informant* files, just like it says. and handing them over to Miami Dade Police Department.

"I asked Gary for a list of payments to C.I.s and then ran them through NCIC and FCIC. I have their information here

He'd handed them over to Miami Dade PD.

This was becoming an incredible mind twist for me. I began to bargain with myself. In the darkened corner booth I was literally holding my hands up, moving them from one side to another, like looking at my hands would help me tabulate the pros and cons of what my mind was telling me. I must have looked like a drinking mime juggler sitting in the dark. A waitress came by my dark booth and I ordered a single Jameson. I really craved another double but I knew at some time I'd be at Sabah's and I wanted to keep a lid on my potential inebriation.

I began to play devil's advocate with myself. I tried to see the commonalities. Poulsen and Peralta had the opportunity to both be geographically and chronologically at the same place and the same time. The nature of the task force and Poulsen's command position lent itself to opportunity and intersection. But the question I was stumbling on was what is the commonality? One was a brusque, offensive, crude criminal who was capable of any of a number of vile things. The other was a polished, rapidly ascending law enforcement leader.

But then my mind went back to my discussions in the morgue with Trentlocke, and seeing that the handiwork of Peralta's killer was certainly the signature of a much more evil person than even Peralta.

No matter how I looked at it there was causation and opportunity for Poulsen and Peralta to be connected.

The ambience of the lounge and the onset of the second Jameson caused my own reckoning of time to go by unnoticed. The removal of the Happy Hour chafing dishes was my only indicator of time. I needed to take my leave but I also needed to confront a few new dynamic changes in my life as of this afternoon.

Walking out of the meeting without being excused and without telling anyone would heighten Zambrana's assumptions of my guilt and put me, at the very least, in the precarious state of being terminated, the end of my VIN career, for sure. I winced thinking of the profanity-laced tirade that Brunson must've let loose once he figured out I wasn't coming back. A flurry of disbelief and anger quickly followed by a contingency plan drafted on the fly. Having a cop go rogue, especially one that with each passing hour is looking more and more like a multiple homicide offender, is *not* something that police agencies want to release immediately to the news organizations. This was a very delicate situation for them. They were most likely mulling over how many people and departments they needed to bring in on this crisis. Certainly they were calling in a few trusted detectives and officers that they felt could keep their mouth shut. They'd be reaching out to my closest contacts in the department, and were asking them for any nuances or details about me that they could analyze: where I socialized, my hobbies, any girlfriends that I may have had after or even before my divorce, people I knew outside of the police department, no stone was going to be unturned. They'd reach out to Gina when they found her.

Just the thought of them telling Gina made my stomach churn. I'm sure one of those bozos would suggest protective custody on her, as if I would even think to harm her.

This was just so wrong on so many fronts.

Edwards would redirect whatever TNT resources he had to start a county-wide search for me. Of all people, they'd probably put Poulsen in charge of acting as a traffic manager, taking in all the information and discarding the red herrings from the pertinent things. This was becoming a very messy situation for them and an extremely messy one for me.

If Poulsen was in the proverbial command post, monitoring all the information regarding any sightings of me, and if he was Peralta's killer, it could be very dangerous for me.

I hadn't even begun to try and understand the linkage between Poulsen and Donito, or even for Roldan for that matter Right then and there I was in absolute survival mode first.

This was going to be an evolving process. Amassing the officers and detectives that they thought were best suited for confidentiality and for hunting me down, the longer it dragged on, and the further the quest would drill down. Within ten to twelve hours they'd be looking for where I used my ATM or credit cards, and start pinging my cellphone. They'd search for what car I was in, figure out I was no longer in an Explorer, but now in an Infiniti. That might happen even sooner if the uniformed officer who retrieved my go bag at JMH is brought in on the search for me.

I needed to hunker down and put their efforts, as well-intended as they were, into a tailspin, to buy myself very much needed time.

I brought the empty glasses to the bar and left a twenty sticking up in one of the glasses. I made my way to the exit. The air had turned even more cooler than it was when I first went into the lounge. The traffic on U.S. 1 was heavy with evening commuters in both directions. Traffic was at a stand-still mostly and I used that as an opportunity to weave through the cars and trucks and cross the well-traveled highway north right to the patches of grass and bushes under the metro rail commuter train tracks. I stepped over a small guardrail and was now in one of the parking lots of South Miami Hospital, slipping amongst the parked cars and on towards the hospital entrance. There was guard at the front entrance. I kept walking in the chilly night air out of his sight to the Emergency Room side.

Hospital Emergency Rooms usually do not have a security person at the door. It inhibits the urgency of someone running through the door with a nail gun injury. The security personnel of an Emergency Room usually sit at unoccupied desks behind the nurse's station. But that wasn't what I was looking for. From the outside I saw exactly what I was looking for.

A cafeteria.

One thing about hospitals—there is always a cafeteria or small eating place near the Emergency Room. That meant there would be an ATM, shining and bright, just inside the hospital doors. There weren't that many people inside. Although I felt the chill in the air it was nothing compared to the chill I was feeling as I took off my shirt and pants between two hospital shuttle vans. Stripped down to my shoes, socks, and my boxer shorts I walked briskly to the automatic doors. I counted on the first security camera picking me up as I entered the portico. The doors opened and the air-conditioned air which dominates the doorway upon every opening in summer retreated from the chill blowing in on my heels. I went straight to the ATM and pulled my ATM card from my sock. It would be better for the security camera if I didn't come in with the card in my hand. I didn't want this to appear as planned as it actually was.

By now I must've been picked up now by at least three cameras, not including the pinhole facial camera on the ATM. The machine accepted my card much more easily than the people in the hospital accepted me. I withdrew $300, the maximum the ATM would allow. In the process I could hear the few people in the hospital with their assemblage of giggles, gasps, and murmurs that I must be crazy. That was quickly broken by a female voice calling out to me from somewhere behind me.

"Sir."

"Sir."

I never acknowledged the voice and gritted my teeth at the slowness of the ATM.

"Sir. Hello. Man at the ATM!"

Finally the money started spinning out of the ATM on these rolling wheels. The machine pulsed a light asking me if I wanted a receipt. I punched the key for *no,* itching for my ATM card to just come out already. The same voice was now calling for the E.R. security guard.

"Someone call security. Is Carlos back there? Someone call Carlos."

The ATM released my card and I stuck it back in my sock with the cash and left just as quickly as I'd come in. I heard keys jangling in my background but I never saw or heard anyone as I left the hospital. I stayed as far as I could from any noticeable security cameras and went to the same spot between the two shuttle vans and got redressed. Once I was dressed I slipped the battery back into my cellphone and powered the phone on. When it came to life there were fourteen missed calls.

As I'd suspected, the implications of my absence had already started the search.

I put the phone on airplane mode and the ringer to silent to stretch the battery life as much as I could. I then wedged it up into the corner of the rear bumper of one of the vans.

When they checked my bank account they'd see the ATM withdrawal. They'd review the security footage and see my near-naked state, and think I may have lost a screw somewhere. That might save me from a trigger-happy arresting officer who might see me more as a mental case than a homicide suspect. It would also make it hard for them to give a clothing description of me to the team they enlisted to search for me. The witnesses to my boxer short banking practices would also have a hard time describing me but they would most certainly remember me.

It was my intention to create false positives.

They'd ping my cell phone, which would continually bounce amongst the cell towers within a mile radius of the hospital as the hospital van did its daily shuttle rounds. Between the constant movement of the van, and the lead and thick concrete walls of the hospital, the signal should bounce and cut out, making them think I'm roaming the area. The police units watching my house will report no activity or sightings of me, reinforcing their beliefs that I'm somewhere near the hospital.

This should keep them busy here looking for me while I busy myself elsewhere looking for Poulsen.

Chapter Thirty-Three

SABAH'S PLACE HAD a warm glow in the windows from her soft lighting.

I'd parked behind the church and brought my go bag in with me just in case someone discovered the car parked there. If they did find the car I'd still be prepared to go on the run.

I wasn't sure what Kabob Barg smelled like. If it was what I was smelling when I walked into Sabah's then it smelled pretty good. Sabah was in the kitchen and putting the finishing touches on the tahdig rice. She was upbeat, lively, vivacious and a real tonic for the harried and upended life I had. She greeted me with a kiss and a strong hug. She was still holding onto me with her arms around my waist she looked up, smiled, and said, "I'm so glad you left me a message because everything is just about ready." "But are you ready?" I asked.

"Ohh, what did you have in mind?" she asked, giggling.

"You know the same ...clothes everywhere lots of sweating and heaving. That sort of thing?"

"I see... well as long as you aren't talking about doing laundry, count me in." She giggled.

Dinner and Sabah's company were incomparable. She was mentally and spiritually breathing life into my damaged areas.

Minute by minute she reminded me that the rest of the world doesn't have to live like I do. They don't deal with treacherous situations, malicious schemes, and lawless souls that only reinforce what Peralta had said and gave credence to his words 'trust no one.' There, in the comfortable confines of her house, I could breathe pleasantry. I could inhale rectitude. I could actually allow the vapors of goodness to come into me and fill me from the inside with positivity, and perhaps a little hope, too. The mango tree on the north side of the house could be seen slightly blowing in the wind and I was most certain the temperature was dropping a few degrees more. I wasn't sure if the hot tub would be in our plans tonight but it made no matter. I was just very happy to be there. There, as opposed to nearly anywhere else. There, as opposed to a Miami Dade Police interview room. There, as opposed to a drawer in Sabah's morgue. I was for the immediate moment happy and relieved to be just there. I felt secreted and ensconced away from everything and everybody. I felt hidden and comfortable and immeasurably relieved to be able to breathe and feel normal.

We agreed to settle in after dinner and watch TV, both of us under a large afghan blanket and curled close to each other on the couch. When it was time to go to bed, I'm not sure how much sweating and heaving there was, but clothes were everywhere and I do believe we met the standards we'd promised earlier in the kitchen.

I slept restlessly and I must've kept her up a few times as she seemed more tired than usual when she trudged off to the shower. When she came back to the bedroom she was nearly ready for work. She had a Toronto Argonauts sweatshirt on with a big emblazoned "A" on the chest.

"Does the A stand for awesome?" I asked her.

"I wish. I think it stand for 'amiable' as I can never seem to say no to the continual workload."

"I'm going to stick with my first assumption. Awesome. How does your day look?"

"I can't know for sure but I might be able to duck out a little earlier so long as nothing unforeseen crops up. You up for some play time?"

"Always," I replied.

What we call frost on a window in Miami is just a bit of condensation. The appearance of it doesn't always mean it is fiercely cold outside just that there is a temperate gradient between inside and outside. I took note of her sweatshirt.

"I thought you hardy Canucks could handle the cold weather?"

"Oh, I can handle the cold weather. I plan to drive to work with the top down. This is just to keep road grime from splashing up on my work clothes. Are you kidding? I love the cold weather," she said.

"That is where you and I are vastly different," I said watching her gather up her purse and keys.

I told her that rather than get into a phone tag back and forth throughout the day I'd just meet her here around 4pm. I didn't want to reveal to her that I would be without my cell phone, nor did I want her to be calling my cell phone in case the posse assembled to find me was in possession of it. She gave me a sweet kiss and a hug and she left for work.

I slept in the warm, comfortable bed a little longer. I eventually got up and showered and stepped out in the backyard and got a sense of the temperature. I dressed dutifully and made sure to put on the light jacket that was in my go bag. I tucked my Glock handgun into my pants at the small of my back and left Sabah's via her rear gate. I started to circumvent the neighborhood.

I avoided going towards my car until I was sure that no one was watching it. I started walking south on Northeast 2nd Avenue and within five minutes I crossed the bridge over the C-7 Canal. The C-7 Canal meandered like a jagged shard of glass from western Miami Dade County in Hialeah all the way to Biscayne Bay, where it merges into a brackish mixture swirling around Belle Meade Island. Just across the bridge I stopped in at the Football Sandwich Shop. The decor was inspired by the Miami Dolphins 1972 undefeated season and painted in aqua with orange trim. An eclectic array of pictures and posters depicting everything from Dan Marino to Jackie Gleason adorned the walls as well as an overwhelming amount of football pictures and pennants. I ordered scrambled eggs and toast and sat outside. The chill was burning off by the warming sun. My jacket kept me warm and I sat down with my order, perusing a *Miami Herald* that was left behind by a previous customer. There was an article that said the residents of the Brickell area were highly upset that police agencies would conduct an undercover drug sting in their neighborhood. Outcries like that always made me shake my head in wonderment, as there was very little geography in Miami Dade County that drug trafficking hadn't touched in some manner or form.

Breakfast was good and I continued reading the newspaper although my interest in news and current events had been deflated by reading the article that was pointedly all about the actions of me, Iggy, and the Miami S.I.S. I had more pressing matters on my mind. My entire night was a fitful mind that was battling the idea of Poulsen killing Peralta and Donito. I momentarily steadied myself by taking in the sunshine and the cool morning air. The sports page still had heavily opinionated articles about the Miami Heat acquiring Brent Barry from the San Antonio Spurs in a big NBA trade. Nestled in the assorted tire store and automobile advertisements in the sports page was an advertisement for Vogel Printing. I ripped the ad for Vogel Printing out of the newspaper and tucked it into my jacket pocket. I went back into the restaurant and ordered a large Italian sub to go. Then I walked back to Sabah's. I planned to try and hunker down in the safe confines of her place. I am sure that a core group of officers and detectives from Coral Gables and Miami Dade were now working in a more harmonious tandem searching for me. I could just imagine the new overtime papers being drawn up, specifically designated for the search for the notorious outlaw, Cade Taylor. Who would have known days earlier that I'd be the overtime check and impetus for a Disney vacation or a month of private school tuition for some cop's kid?

I put the sub in her refrigerator. I pulled out some frozen salmon fillets she had in her freezer and put them on the counter to thaw in time for dinner. I went into the living room and put my holstered Glock on the end table near the Fodor's Canada travel books. I saw her telephone jack and followed the gray translucent wire along the baseboard to a plastic lidded bin. Under a pile of clothes and plush throw pillows I found her telephone. It was a princess model, the ringer turned off, and it was wrapped in cellophane. I ripped the cellophane off the telephone and held it to my ear and heard a dial tone. I'm sure the Miami Dade Medical Examiner's Office required her to have a hard line, but no one said she had to answer it. That would explain the ringer being turned down and the phone encased in cellophane to avert accidentally picking it up. It was immersed in the pillows and clothes to keep it from being heard.

I sat on the floor against the bin and pulled the Vogel Printing advertisement from my jacket. I looked at the phone number for Vogel. Nearly all of Miami had an area code of 305. Vogel Printing had the area code of 786 which was the new area code instituted by AT&T just after New Year's. This must be an extremely new business if they had a 786 prefix. This might work in my favor, as they may know very few people from Coral Gables and possibly not have a large volume of accounts.

I dialed the number and on the third ring a pleasant-sounding woman who identified herself as Jocelyn answered.

"Hi Jocelyn. This is Walter Samuels from the City of Coral Gables Finance Department. I'm calling about an invoice we have from you. I was curious if you could help me."

"Sure. What is the invoice number?" she replied.

"Actually, I don't have the invoice in front of me, it's already been sent to purchasing. I do have a spread sheet and it shows the amount as $17.85. Would you be able to search your records by the amount?"

"It's more difficult, but yes. Please hold for a second."

Canned music filled the earpiece and I busied my time staring at the baseboard and floor. In about a minute she got back on.

"I found it. January 7th it was ordered, and it was delivered on the 16th."

"Do you know what the item was?" I asked.

"Our records say 'stock standard medium linen 13 point business cards.'"

I reflexively put my hand to my head and closed my eyes. I swallowed hard. "Does it say what is written on the business cards?"

"No. All it says is delivery to the police department. We have mock-ups of everything we do but my boss, the owner, has those. He isn't here right now."

I thanked her and hung up. I sat there numbly just holding the telephone. I kept the cellophane off in case I need to use the telephone later I put the phone back in the bin and piled the clothes and pillows on it. I closed the bin. I ambled across the floor and sat against a big easy chair. I started to change my thought process.

Instead of trying to figure if Poulsen did indeed kill the Horsemen I was now more concerned why he tried to implicate *me* as the killer. Why me? Why did he choose me to be the one to take the fall? They could've just been random homicides. They could've even been homicides classified as killing each other. It made no sense, all the elaborate schemes to connect me.

I sat there like a grade school recess quarterback drawing a football play in the sand. My fingers traced imaginary places and drew arching connective lines to each one. I tried visualizing the whole field of play, or in this case, the howling quandary my life had become. I was deep in this process going nowhere and hitting continual nonsensical adaptions of what was going on when I could have sworn I heard a noise outside.

I momentarily froze and and scrunched my face in an effort to listen as intently as I could. I distinctly heard someone trying very hard to not make any noise, quietly trying to open the downstairs door. Sabah had told me, *"I always go in from the top since that is my primary living space."*

There was someone trying to be undetectable, fiddling with

the lock at the downstairs door. I quietly reached up with my right hand and pulled my Glock down off of the end table. I thought I had the weapon cleared from the table but the Fodor's Vancouver book came sliding off with it. I tried to catch it with my other hand but it still tumbled awkwardly and made a noticeable noise as it hit the hardwood floor. I don't know if I was more pissed at the book or at my clumsy self, but my position in the house was now known to whoever was trying to slip unnoticed in through the front door. I could detect a sense of urgency on their part as their attempt to be quiet was not as contained.

I made a conscious decision that if it was Poulsen coming in through the door I would be ready. If it was a SWAT team or a designated set of officers, I would surrender immediately. I was innocent and they'd be simply following orders predicated on intentional misinformation.

I slid across the floor on my stomach and using my elbows, I nudged my way to the staircase. I had high ground. Rather than go downstairs I would use the staircase and the elevation to my advantage and be ready for Poulsen when he came in through the front door.

Every muscle tensed as I held the gun out in front of me, my right arm extended and pointing down the staircase. I just focused on the doorknob, waiting to see it turn. It would've been reckless to shoot through the door but the thought did cross my mind.

The doorknob started to turn ever so slightly.

It was so slight that I tried to stare even harder to see exactly if it was turning or not.

The doorknob turned again, very slowly, then it turned all the way very quickly and the whole door was pushed in and the mid-morning sunlight came streaming in, I was momentarily blinded by it.

I was vulnerable, exposed up high but not being able to see down. I could just make out the form of a person stepping in through the light.

It was Sabah.

Relief and surprise collided inside of me. "What are you doing here?"

She just looked up at me from the doorway. Or more accurately, she just looked up at my gun pointed straight at her. I made a big production of pulling the gun back and away and as I rose to my feet I bent at the knee, and made an obvious gesture of putting the gun down and leaving it at the top of the stairs. I then rose fully and descended the stairs talking calmly the whole way down about how I had no idea it was her and how I had not been expecting her. She just stood there, staring at me. I think she was appalled to have been on the other side of a gun, especially in her own home. I couldn't get down the stairs fast enough to reassure her and hug her and tell her how sorry I was.

I got to the bottom of the stairs and immediately wrapped my arms around her. She stood rigid, her hands at her sides. I hugged her tight and started to tell her close in by her ear how mistaken and sorry I was.

It was at that moment that she kneed me hard right in the balls.

Chapter Thirty-Four

I JUST WANTED TO puke. She got me straight on right in both testicles and the pain was excruciating. I dropped straight to the floor. First on my knees, still in semi-hug, my arms sliding down her body and legs, then reflexively cupping my groin. I rolled onto my right, side up against the bottom stair in a fetal position. At first it seemed like I couldn't breathe then my intake of air were only small gasps that served only two purposes: the first to keep me alive and the second to make me wish I was dead. My jaw was clenched, and my eyes tightly shut, more to withhold the tears from trickling out. The pain seemed like it would not abate at all.

Sabah immediately jumped onto my side and used her weight to pin me against the stairs, her knees were digging into my kidney.

The worst of it was the obsidian scalpel she put right to my carotid artery.

The obsidian scalpel has a blade with a cutting edge many times sharper than high-quality steel surgical scalpels. This type of scalpel means business—and Sabah, with all of her training, could make serious business of my carotid artery.

She had me in a most precarious situation.

My right arm and shoulder were against the stairs and she held the scalpel against my left internal jugular vein which overlaps the carotid artery. If she moved even a twinge or if I even attempted to move the arterial spurt would create a Jackson Pollack-like spray of my life-sustaining blood all over the entire entryway and staircase. It would take a haz-mat post-death team days to clean up my blood. I didn't want to move but my balls hurt so bad that writhing and rocking in pain was what my body wanted to do, but I had enough sense to try and suppress that and just hold still.

"Who are you?"

I could barely breathe let alone speak.

"I said who are you?" she screamed again.

"Unless you want me to perform my very first live autopsy you have three seconds to tell me who you are!" she screamed.

"One…two…"

I could barely muster a hoarse and nearly unintelligible, "Cade. I'm Cade."

Knowing that my gun was at the top of the stairs and my testicles felt like they were at the bottom of my shoes she pushed off of me and stepped back. The reprieve my kidney felt was glorious, although my balls still were making me want to retch. She made sure I saw her LED screen on her phone. She dialed 911 and had her thumb poised over the send button, and held it to my face. She held the scalpel in her other hand.

"I don't care if you burst a lung, you start talking now," she said.

I felt ridiculous, holding my groin with both hands, but the idea of her boot kicking me overrode my feeling and I sort of sat and leaned against the bottom stair, one hand protecting my balls the other propping me up.

"What?"

It was all I could say at the moment.

"Okay, well I'll talk first while you try and see if you'll ever experience a Father's Day. I went to work today. Imagine my surprise when after an hour of being there Detective Trentlocke came in."

I just looked at her.

"Are you listening?"

"Yes, I'm here listening," I said weakly.

"He was picking up the final reports and he told me a term I never heard before. Do you know what it was? Do you?"

She adjusted her weight to her front foot making wonder if a kick in the balls was next. I tightened my grip on my testicles.

"What? What term?"

"He said you were a broken arrow. I had to ask him what that meant. He said you were a good cop gone bad. A broken arrow. He used all kinds of euphemisms for you. You had gone off the reservation, that you were cooking with the microwave door open. He said that you killed both of those Colombians and possibly the one at the Coconut Grove house explosion. He said all of Miami Dade County is quietly looking for you!" she shrieked at me.

I could only look at her.

"I left work," she went on. "I came home half-hoping you were here and half-hoping you were gone. Part of me wanted to deny any of this and part of me wanted to tell him you were probably at that very moment in my shower if he wanted you."

"Which did you choose?" I asked her.

"I'm here, aren't I? What does that tell you? But I need to know and know now."

I briefly entertained the idea of asking her to retrieve the frozen salmon fillets so I could put them on my balls, but the idea and visualization of that was absurdly odd. I righted myself into a full sitting position and asked her if she could fill a zip lock bag with some ice for me. She must've seen me as not much of a threat and benevolently went and filled a bag of ice for me. She had forgotten about my gun at the top of the stairs. When she came back with the bag of ice, I thanked her.

"You know, if I really was a stone cold killer, I would've gotten my gun when you were in the kitchen."

The look on her face when she realized she'd neglected to secure my gun and how unfortunate it could have been for her had I gotten up and armed myself made tears well in her eyes.

"Sabah, I'm not what they say I am. I didn't kill the Colombians. I didn't have anything to do with the Coconut Grove house explosion. They got it all wrong, and they got me all wrong. I'm being set up."

She just bit her lower lip and and pensively looked at the floor.

"Does anyone know I'm here?"

"No."

"You're sure?"

"Yeah, I'm sure. Detective Trentlocke was only telling me about you because he knew I had just met you. I guess he thought it would be a novel thing to say. You know…proximity and all."

I applied the ice bag to my groin and then slowly stood up. We went to the living room and each of us sat on the brown couches.

I started talking to her.

I went as far back as the night that I got summoned to Matheson Hammock and stood over Peralta. I told her about the Four Horsemen. I told her about my house being under surveillance. I spoke at length about my calls with Hector and all the meetings in Brunson's office. I told her about my talk with Godfrey Pinder. I told her about my recent inquiry to Vogel Printing. The biggest point I tried to convey was how I thought Poulsen was the actual killer of the Colombians. The only thing I left out was how I discovered the stash house in Coconut Grove and my hell run from the TNT detective at the Coconut Grove house. It wasn't prudent and it would inflame her to think that I feigned ignorance at Mike Gordon's when she told me about the house explosion. Aside from that omission, I told her everything. She looked at me. I looked at her. She finally spoke.

"Business cards and a shirt with a rust stain is was what catapulted you into this mess?"

"I'm telling you, there has *got* to be more connections, I just have to get my head on straight and figure this out."

She mulled it over. She was pondering everything I told her, looking out the window, her eyes fixated on a spot somewhere outside.

"Fresh eyes," she said.

"Fresh eyes?"

"Yeah. If what you're telling me is the whole shebang, let's you and I treat this just like an autopsy. We'll explore all the causes and effects and the correlations 'til we decipher the pathway that leads us to the truth. We will look at it with fresh eyes," she said.

She retrieved a yellow legal note pad and we moved to the kitchen. We split the Italian sub. I kept talking and she kept writing. She started to write down things that were extremely similar. When those pages were filled, she then made separate lists of things that were different. We then overlaid and cross-checked the unknown aspects against the lists we'd compiled. It was exhausting, going over every detail, and it carried us into the better part of the afternoon. Every phrase or comment that I could recall was analyzed for its full meaning or a potential entendre. The table was full of strewn and crumbled yellow legal sheets. One of the biggest missing pieces was motivation. What was the motivation for Poulsen to have killed the Horsemen? Even more-so, what was the motivation for him to try and frame me for these murders?

Another big puzzle piece was the deposit of $48,000 into my stateside account from the Bahamas. She reiterated back to me what knowledge she had of banking and how the process works. Her knowledge was about as solid as most people's. I explained ABA numbers and IBAN numbers to her and that took her knowledge just a hair further. We both thumbed through the scattered yellow legal sheets tracing and retraced our notes. She asked me how I paid my bills and if I wrote a lot of checks. I told her my checkbook is usually at home and doesn't leave my house.

Then I stopped and just looked at her. I felt stupid. How could I have missed it?

"Just like last year, check only. No cash. Just make it out to 'Kiwanis of Coral Gables."

Chapter Thirty-Five

"SO POULSEN IS trying to make you the tomb?"

"Tombo. Not tomb. But in many ways, I think he is trying to put me in a tomb."

All of these intuitions and feelings of paranoia I'd been having were now starting to make sense to me.

"Poulsen is the tombo. He was the one giving Peralta heartburn. Peralta needed to get rid of his agitation. Poulsen must've got wind of it and decided to eliminate Peralta."

"This is so hard to comprehend, but it makes total sense," she said.

"I get it now. He got my routing number and bank account number from the check. The money from the Bahamian account is designed to look like some sort of payoff or commission to me from Peralta. It's designed to create a motive for me to have killed Peralta. Maybe it wasn't enough, or maybe Peralta cheated me on something—so I went and killed him. That's how it would've been portrayed in court. A jury would fall for that easily."

"What about the Horseman at La Covacha, Don Julio Restrepo?"

"He must've known we were going to meet at La Covacha from checking the NINJAS system. He must've been in the parking lot waiting for Donito to arrive."

"It was brutal, Cade. You saw it yourself, that Donito fellow really was killed in a heinous way."

"I don't know if Poulsen heard about TNT watching the house the same time I did in the meeting at Brunson's office or if he knew previously. It might be immaterial. He may have already been privy to the house and had it wired for detonation long before Roldan showed up. That explosion could've been planned for any of the Horsemen, it was just a matter of getting one of them to go there."

"Cade, I don't need to tell you that this is some spooky stuff. He's killing all of the Horsemen. Except for the one in Colombia," she said.

"Hector."

"Yeah. Hector. He is still alive as best you know, right?"

"Maybe Hector is in on it, or maybe his being in Colombia avoiding a guy he knows wants to kill him is saving him from a guy he *doesn't* know wants to kill him."

Piecing this macabre and dangerous situation had been meticulous and exhausting. The afternoon had slipped by us, and although our criminal hypothesis wasn't iron-clad, it did have merit. We debated who we could go to with this information. Different agencies that might be a good conduit were discussed. Strong contenders that we thought of were the Florida Department of Law Enforcement (FDLE) and Trentlocke. We also surmised it wasn't something to be done now. Not today. Trentlocke would notify someone he was meeting Sabah and that would set up antennas. Most of the case agents from FDLE were already gone for the day and this information had too much gravity to leave it on a junior agent or nighttime desk person. We decided to just step away from it for an hour and revisit it after a break.

The salmon didn't appeal to either her or I so we ordered a pizza to be delivered. She went to use the bathroom and being overly cautious, I ordered the pizza from her landline rather than using her cell phone. I gave her cash from the $300 I took out of the ATM at the hospital. When the pizza arrived I stayed upstairs and out of sight while she paid the delivery guy.

We decided to just settle in for the night and try and arrange a meeting with Trentlocke in the morning.

I wasn't keen on using Sabah as an intermediary. I was formulating a way to communicate to him without involving her. She was the Assistant Medical Examiner. Soon she'd be embarking on a new facet of her career as the Medical Examiner in Toronto. She didn't need this blight on her career.

I planned to walk back along Northeast 2nd Avenue 'til I found a coin laundry. I'd convert some bills to quarters there. With a large pocket of quarters, I'd start finding payphones in Little Haiti and call Harvey Binchell from the State Attorney's Office. He would remember me from when he was deployed with us on the Bayshore shooting. I would tell him what's going on. I would also call Trentlocke with information and coordinates so we could meet up. I was sure he would bring cops with him…maybe even the Farkle brothers from Matheson Hammock, but at least he'd have the story before they put handcuffs on me. I hoped that Harvey would be there when it went down to hopefully protect the integrity of the investigation.

This was such a huge mess. It was overwhelming and Sabah and I both just silently acknowledged it had been a long day and retired to the bedroom to try and get some sleep. It was still cold outside and the CB block walls of her place were starting to hold the cold inside. We snuggled under some blankets and soon we both drifted off to sleep.

I may have slept only for a few hours, but I awoke with a start, pulse racing, a feeling of dread upon me.

I also had a huge feeling of remorse.

How could I have been so stupid? After they start triangulating my cell phone they'd pull an updated record of my usage. There will be no additional outgoing calls since the last meeting in Brunson's office. They'd certainly recheck the calls made to and from my cell phone and by process of elimination they'd collate those calls.

Eventually they'd see many calls between myself and the cell phone of the Assistant Medical Examiner.

Many of those calls made after business hours. It would be a no-brainer.

They will be coming here soon looking for me.

I needed to get out and get out fast, to put some distance between myself and Sabah.

Trentlocke had told her that all of Miami Dade was quietly looking for me. She could be arrested for harboring me. I needed to leave and leave pronto. I had to protect her as best I could. I pulled slowly away from her slumbering embrace and I eased myself quietly out of bed. She continued sleeping. I gathered my clothes that were folded on a chair and slipped down the stairs, grabbing my go bag.

It was nearly 3am.

The air in the house felt cold against my skin and I shivered slightly. My balls still hurt a little and I walked gingerly through the house trying not to stub a toe or knock over something in the dark. I dressed in the kitchen. I decided to use my shoulder holster since I would be wearing my jacket. Besides, my groin was still a little sore and I didn't want the extra weight on my belt. I removed my Glock from my usual pancake holster and slid it into the brown leather shoulder holster. I also transferred my spare magazine to the shoulder holster's magazine holders, then I went back into the downstairs living room. Her purse was still where she had left it.

I reached into her purse and rummaged around, trying to locate what I was looking for by feel. Even though it was dark, I still shut my eyes tightly as I foraged inside, deluding myself into thinking it would heighten my locating capabilities. Now I was up to my mid-forearm in what seemed like an endlessly deep, one-of-a-kind, excessively overpriced designer leather cavern. I pulled out a tire gauge. I didn't have the time to think what kind of woman needs a tire gauge in their purse. I kept searching through the rest of her purse. Finally, I struck the proverbial pay dirt.

Her car keys.

I also grabbed one of her pocket recorders. I left the pencils, lip gloss, and wadded tissues behind with the other nonessentials considered essentials. I crept out of the house as quietly as I could, making sure to close the door softly behind me. The brisk night air jolted me. It was moonless outside, no visible stars. The cold front had driven in a deep blanketing cloud cover.

Using the key remote, I unlocked Sabah's jeep. I leaned inside, inserted the key in the ignition, put the transmission in neutral. I began to move the jeep back and forth by rocking it until I had a small amount of momentum to get it free from the grassy swale. I pushed it down the road so that when I started it Sabah might not hear me driving away. I got in the jeep and made some seating adjustments. Even through my jeans and my jacket I could feel how cold the vinyl seats were. I turned the key in the ignition and drove off, hoping she was still asleep.

I had just added car thief to what other growing criminal charges Miami Dade might have for me. I couldn't take the Infiniti. I was certain they had discovered by now what was my U.C. vehicle. The potential of having some exuberant, right-out-of-the-police-academy rookie checking license tags of every vehicle he saw was just too great. I needed to move stealthily. I wasn't in the mindset for a police chase or for making explanations.

Cool weather seems to make everything much more quiet and serene. The streets were nearly empty of other cars. I drove south on I-95 until it literally ended in the continental United States just south of downtown Miami. I took the slightly elevated ramp and dropped down into the resurrected stretch of U.S. 1. Final stop from here could've been Key West but I was only going as far as Coral Gables. Lots of the traffic lights were flashing red or yellow the color to keep traffic flowing in the wee hours when there weren't many people on the road. Even traffic control had decided to sit this cold night out. I hadn't ventured too far into Coral Gables when I arrived at my destination.

Just a little south on U.S. 1 was Fire Station 2. Most commuters don't pay much attention to its bland paint scheme and retro, 1960s architecture. Its most notable feature is a training tower about three stories high. The tower used for stair simulation and rappelling exercises. The footprint of the station is very linear, as it's wedged between the normally bustling U.S. 1 and the Metrorail elevated train tracks. There is plenty of concrete and asphalt and the only greenery is whatever salads the firemen might be eating with dinner.

The entire station serves as a firehouse, training center, and refueling station. It also has an ample parking lot. The refueling station was set off from the tower and fire station. There were three gas pumps and one diesel pump. They were open-aired but had a winged gull type concrete overhang that was about twenty-five feet high and shaded the pumps.

The firefighters' work schedule was like many around the country; on duty for twenty-four hours, off duty for forty-eight hours. Firefighters are a rather predictable lot. Due to their work schedule nearly every one of them has a side business that they're able to engage in. Most are in the hands-on trades like plumbing, electricity, and carpentry. Inevitably, the majority of them drive pick-up trucks. I never understood the logic of driving a red fire truck at work and a red pick-up truck off duty. The majority of the trucks were American-made and dark blue or black.

Firefighters have perfected the art of economy of movement. Their gear and boots are always set in such a way to expedite speed in getting on a fire truck. It just falls in line that they tend to always back their trucks into parking spaces. The row of neatly parked pick-ups with a smattering of SUVs looked like a used truck dealership. If you didn't know it was a fire station you'd think it *was* a truck dealership.

I drove onto the fire station property and backed Sabah's jeep in amongst the trucks. I turned off the ignition and then scanned the roof line of the fire station looking for any security cameras. Two were obviously pointing down from the eaves. I waited a while, just in case a firefighter might step outside, even at this ungodly hour, to smoke a cigarette.

Sabah's jeep blended in well and the night was so dark and the lighting so poor no one could tell I was in it.

South Miami Hospital was only a few miles down U.S. 1. That would be where the majority of any group looking for me might still be. It was very quiet, and the jeep was still warm. I fought to stay awake. I figured it would be about forty minutes till the jeep started getting too cold. I was glad I had my jacket on. I had a good view of the gasoline pumps at the refueling station.

"Every morning before I even go into the office, I get a newspaper at the Circle K on Ponce de Leon, I stop by the motor pool at Fire Station 2 and fill up the car, and I start my day, each day, the same way."

I settled in, and waited.

Chapter Thirty-Six

I STOMPED MY FEET. I got out a few times and walked around under the Metrorail tracks. I even went into the training tower, its bottom door all but useless from being battered open in numerous training exercises. Nothing could thwart the creeping cold that was chilling me to the bone. It may be Miami but when you have sunshine year-round your blood acclimates for tropical weather not cold weather. The scant few hours of alternating from freezing to moving around had made me very tired and it was still very dark outside.

I was back in the jeep. The windshield had fogged up again. I was wiping the glass with my sleeve when I saw Poulsen pulling into the first set of gas pumps in a white Toyota 4Runner. I was only twenty yards from where the two gas pumps were.

I reached into my jacket pocket and pushed the record button on the recorder.

I opened the jeep's door as quietly as I could.

I eased out of the jeep. I used the adjacent parked truck to conceal me.

Poulsen was still in the Toyota with the engine running, the tailpipe belching blue gray vapors. The engine heat was being released in the cold air. I was surprised Poulsen stayed in the Toyota.

I had to change my approach. I'd planned on confronting him from the rear but couldn't risk him seeing me through his mirrors.

Stepping back away from the line of trucks, I pushed through the bushes that delineated the city's property from the Metrorail tracks. I moved slowly along the bushes, ready to advance toward him from the front of the Toyota. When I peeked out from behind the bushes, his high beams were on. The xenon bulbs were blinding and would also foretell my arrival. I skittered back to the bushes.

Midway back from where I'd come from, I stepped through the bushes, undetectable to him by the structure's wall. I could hear the Toyota's engine and see the splay from the lights. The entire vehicle was obscured by the wall.

I crept up to the wall, ready to step out and confront him using the darkness and the element of surprise to my advantage. When I stepped out he wasn't in the driver's seat.

I had severely miscalculated.

The gas pump was cycling and he'd wedged the gas cap hard into the pump handle so that he could be free of holding the hose. Poulsen was at the back of the Toyota, retrieving his VIN jacket. He came out from under the lift gate of the SUV adorning it when I stepped out by the hose. He saw me immediately.

"Cade?"

My head swiveled around.

"Cade. You know this isn't the way."

He was behind the rear quarter panel and was partially hidden by it and the lift gate.

I'd put myself at a tactical disadvantage. He had cover and partial concealment.

I never saw it. I just never saw it. He threw a portable metal fire extinguisher and it hit me dead center in the chest, knocking the wind out of me. The top of it glanced off of my chin, gashing it open. The weight of it barreling into me knocked me backwards. I stumbled back between the Toyota and the gas pump. I might've stayed on my feet, had I not tripped on the gasoline hose, knocking it from its resting spot inside the Toyota's gas spout. The gas cap stayed firmly wedged into the handle. The gasoline kept pumping, spilling under the Toyota.

The pitch of the slab at the refueling islands led toward a storm drain twenty feet away. The gasoline followed the path of least resistance and ran towards the low spot in the concrete.

I scrambled to my feet as quickly as I could, still trying to catch my breath and holding my now-aching chest with my left hand. I instinctively went right to my right hip. It was pure muscle memory—only my gun was still tightly secured in my shoulder holster. I transitioned as quickly as I could to pull my Glock from the shoulder holster.

I never completed pulling my Glock.

Poulsen had pulled a taser from somewhere in the back of the open lift gate. I heard a resounding singular *pop* and then a continuous clicking sound.

The sound a taser makes when it's fired is very similar to the sound of baseball trading cards held in a child's bicycle spokes by a clothespin, a five-second continuous *clackety-clack*.

The metal taser darts shot out, one hitting me in the right shoulder. The other hit the thick leather of my belt. Although the taser worked as intended, the darts didn't penetrate my jacket and the belt negated the connective charge that renders the incapacitating 50,000 volts. Poulsen could see the darts had hit me. He must've been confused that I was not feeling the charge. He continued pulling the taser trigger.

Clackety-clack-clackety-clack was all I heard.

I felt a slight tingle and knew that the prongs if adjusted by my movements latched deeper I would feel the full brunt of the charge. I reached out and grabbed the electrical leads affixed to me. I turned hard to my right and tripped against gas pump island. I fell on my side and rolled.

I kept rolling.

I rolled right across the gasoline hose which dislodged the cap from the pump handle. I held the leads as I rolled and pulled them out of the spent cartridge.

Poulsen was quick. He was surprisingly quick.

He jumped on me, and drove his knees into me, right at the same spot Sabah had driven her knees into me. My kidneys were screaming.

He momentarily separated himself from me. This time I didn't hear the *clackety-clack* of the taser. I didn't hear anything. When he pulled the taser trigger and drive-stunned me with it I was incapable of hearing or seeing anything. He pressed it hard against my abdomen. Most definitely and without exception I do believe every single one of the 50,000 volts went right into me. My entire body went rigid. I had a metallic taste in my mouth. I couldn't breathe. The pain was unbearable and every muscle in my body was contracting.

It was the worst pain I had ever experienced.

I convulsed.

I shook.

It was the longest five seconds of my life.

When it ended I just flopped on my back, my body limp, and I remember actually panting.

That's when he drive-stunned me again. This time I was aware of sound, but all I really heard was me screaming from the pain. As soon as I gasped for breath, he immediately straddled me and drove his left thumb into my larynx, pressing hard on my hyoid bone and trachea.

In his right hand he pressed the taser hard against my left temple.

He gritted his teeth and hissed,

"You're just like the Horsemen. You got no fight in you. I should've killed you first and then had no complications."

I was trying to focus my eyes, just fixate on anything to get me back to some sensibility. I didn't think I'd be able to take another hit from the taser.

His grip was tightening on my neck and I knew my airway was

being compromised. He'd have me choked out in a few more seconds if I didn't regain some way of defending myself.

My throat was closing and I was able to squeak out only one word:

"Why?"

"You just don't get it, do you?"

He was right up in my face, the heat of his breath was pervasive. He was on his knees on either side of me, his forearm across my neck, choking me until I had nearly nothing left. With what last remnant of consciousness and strength I had, I raised my right knee and hit him in the top of his buttocks to momentarily get him to raise off my throat, knocking him slightly forward and freeing my hands.

He pulled the trigger of the taser again and tried to drive-stun me right in my face. I grabbed the taser with both hands, squirming as best as I could and turning my head to the right.

He fell off to the left of me. The taser was still being deployed by my grip over his finger in the trigger guard.

His momentum and the force of my grip pushed the taser down and into the concrete.

The sparking electrical charge was driven right into the spilled gasoline from the gas pump.

Whoooosh!

I remember seeing him backlit by the white flash of light from the gasoline being lit. The gasoline's flashpoint was bright and hot. The flame ran like an Indy racer under the Toyota and all across the refueling station, faster than the trickling gasoline. It rode the petroleum waterfall right into the storm drain. A loud rumble shook the area as the storm drain full of pooled gasoline caught fire. The subterranean drain exploded in a fiery burst that sent a plume of flaming gasoline straight into the air. The drain cover blew up and arched past the gull-winged overhang and bounced three or four times across U.S. 1.

The sound of the explosion was stunning and instinctively I

think he moved away from the gasoline that was still burning under the Toyota. I too was scared the Toyota was going to blow up with its open full gas tank.

Vapor locks.

Vapor seals.

Fuel recovery systems.

None of that mattered to me. I knew that I had to get away from the Toyota. Poulsen must've been thinking the same thing because he got off of me. I was able to get one punch in from my prone position right into his solar plexus. He gasped, then pressed me hard as he pushed off of me and stood up.

Rolling had worked well for me in this fight and I rolled again towards the back supporting wall.

Poulsen had pulled his firearm and shot at me. The first round hit the wall just above my head, causing a large chunk of the concrete to fall and crumble in pieces. The bullet hole exposed the rusty rebar in the wall and a majority of the dusty chunks went down my shirt collar.

Whether from reflexes or fear I couldn't know, but I got up very quickly and started running towards the line of pick-up trucks. The massive fireball was no longer shooting up and the gas trail was burning out, leaving gaps in what had been a gasoline highway across the concrete. The entire area had been lit like a Hollywood sound stage but with the gas burning off, the darkness of the early morning had returned.

I was running in the dark. I pulled my gun as I ran and fired a round behind me, racing for the cover of the pick-up trucks. It was a reckless but effective way to create some distance between us.

I didn't know where Poulsen was but as I neared the line of trucks, two rounds from his gun hit the back quarter panels of the first pick-up.

I kept running.

Passing the first truck, I rammed my left shin straight into a large trailer hitch that was jutting out from the bumper of the next truck. The sudden stop was so debilitating that it caused me to drop my gun into the cargo area of the pick-up truck.

I could've sworn that I broke my leg. My left side fell hard against the tailgate of the truck and I howled and cursed from the shock and excruciating pain. I could sense Poulsen closing in behind me.

The Glock was designed to be a tactical handgun. It has a flat black matte plastic polymer and a black anodized slide. On a very dark night and dropped into the black plastic bed liner of a pick-up truck, it is nearly impossible to see. I used my right foot to step on the bumper and flopped into the truck bed. Historically speaking, being in a box when someone is shooting at you is not tactically sound. Anwar Sadat and Abraham Lincoln are proof of that.

I landed on my side and quickly rolled to my back, and made what I can only describe as movements like a snow angel to try and feel my gun.

Down by my ankle.

I curled like a shrimp and grabbed it. I then just briefly rose and toppled out of the truck, falling between it and another pick-up. I laid on the ground between the trucks. There was little ambient light from the diminishing fire by the pumps. Looking under the vehicles, I caught a fleeting glimpse of Poulsen's feet and ankles. I fired three rounds under the truck and skipped the bullets off the concrete. At least one of the bullets found its target as I heard Poulsen yelp in pain and saw him drop to one knee.

His right ankle was shattered.

A fireman had come out of the side door of the firehouse. He was still in his sleeping attire of a T-shirt and gym shorts.

I'm not sure why. It may have been confusion. Maybe it was anger. But Poulsen cranked off a shot at the bewildered fireman.

The round hit above his head. With amazing speed, the fireman ran back inside. Within thirty seconds there was the sound of approaching sirens.

"Cade. They're coming for *you*, Cade. Not me. You!" Poulsen yelled from his hunkered-down position.

"Fuck you. You killed all of them and you tried to put it on me. Fuck you!" I yelled back.

"No, Cade. I'm going to kill you and tell them the whole story, how you and Gus were in it together. It's fool-proof. I'm going to show them your bank account where Gus paid you to kill Restrepo, and you went and killed *him* instead. You're done, Cade. You tried to kill me but instead I killed you. That's all they'll know."

I shimmied between the trucks, my shin wailing in pain. I was faintly aware of headlights getting closer. The sirens also seemed to be closing in. I was able to get around and get closer to where Poulsen was. He wouldn't be moving very fast or far with his bullet-torn ankle.

As I drew closer, he fired a round at me, hitting the side mirror of a truck and spewing glass shards on me and the ground. I kept advancing on him. He was hobbling at the front of a pick-up truck and I was at the back of it. I fired three rounds through the rear window. The rounds carried through the cab and tumbled out the windshield, their trajectory and aim sluggish and slow. But it was enough to make him limp backwards away from the fray.

He unleashed a volley of shots that hit the side rails of the truck and caused *ping*s and sparks to swirl around me. I now had a better visual on him.

I stepped from the back of the truck and positioned myself along the back quarter panel. I fired a round at him, grazing his hip. He buckled, wavered.

The next round I heard came from somewhere else.

Whoever shot it had put his bullet right through Poulsen's head.

His brains and chunks of his hair and scalp landed across the hood of the pick-up. Poulsen crumpled and fell right down.

Shock and fear had me wide-eyed, looking in every direction, panting. I had no idea where the shooter was. Then I heard Brunson's distinctive voice slowly say:

"Son of a bitch."

Chapter Thirty-Seven

THE SUN WAS up. I was once again in the back of a rescue truck, having my swollen, gashed shin wrapped and stabilized until I could get transported to a hospital. Astonished and somewhat perturbed firefighters inspected their trucks, each one checking for damages. Brunson was sitting on the padded bench across from me.

"I was on my way to join the search for you near South Miami Hospital when I saw this big fucking fireball. I said 'holy fuck, what the fuck is that?' So I dashed over. Then I saw Poulsen trying to shoot you. When he shot at the fireman, I knew he was in the wrong. I heard what you guys said to each other. I heard what he said."

Wordlessly and just staring ahead, I reached into my jacket pocket and pulled out the still-recording recorder. I clicked it off.

Ten days later I was still on administrative leave. Two shootings in almost as many days. Just for the sake of decorum any police agency will sit you out of the game for a while.

Miami bomb technicians were able to match a partial thumb print from bomb fragments at the Coconut Grove house to Poulsen. They also matched fingerprints in the Toyota 4Runner to Gus Peralta. Gus had obviously been in Poulsen's car. The two of them had been cheating the other Horsemen and were looking to go it alone— except Poulsen wanted the whole operation for himself and killed

Peralta. He hadn't counted on TNT being onto Peralta. He feigned ignorance in the meeting about the TNT wiretap but he'd already known Peralta wanted him killed. So he killed Peralta.

As for the *tomba,* he decided to make me the *tomba.* The $48,000 was just a small cost to incriminate me and get clear-sailing for himself.

The DEA pulled the NINJAS entry logs and saw that Poulsen did in fact check into the NINJAS system two hours before my meeting with Donito at La Covacha. The most telling evidence was his taser. The internal memory inside the taser recorded every deployment with or without a charge. He most likely was not aware of that. When plugged into a computer with the Taser software, all of the deployments are seen. The device was triggered on the same days and times that both Gus and Donito died.

As for the waitress at Reuben's Cafe she positively identified me as the gringo eating breakfast. She also identified Poulsen as the man she saw through the cafe's window rummaging through the garbage outside. He had been following me. A review of Roldan's phone provided a log of calls made to his phone. The text message that told him to go to the Coconut Grove house had come from a burner cell phone that was located in Poulsen's house when they searched it after his death. The burner cell phone was a clone of Peralta's phone.

Hector's cousin Gloria got word from Colombia that they found Hector dead. He had been tied to a truck tire in an abandoned warehouse in Bogota. Someone had used a blow torch to burn a very big elongated "G" on his chest. Gloria swore up and down that she thought that Gus Peralta had done it. The authorities in Colombia neither confirmed nor denied that Peralta was dead to Gloria. As for me, an elongated G sure seemed like a decent attempt at the Green Bay Packers logo. I guess Ricky from the Molino Rojo Bar must have had a passport.

The Horsemen were no more.

I was medically cleared to go back to work. It was now all administrative.

My mind was mush. I'd had enough of the desk and listening to Ileana butcher the English language.

Charlene from Brunson's office called and said he wanted to see me. I walked down and I didn't even wait, just nodded at her and went into Brunson's office. He was at his desk. He looked up at me and turned his eyes to the chair across his desk. I sat down.

"Cade, how ya doing?"

"How are you doing?" I asked back.

"Me? I'm fine. The City Manager knows that I have no fucking problem killing city employees. He stays out of my way."

"Good to know," I said.

"Cade, I wasn't really sure, but when I asked you if you had a cell phone I had a sneaking suspicion that Ken was looking to mess with you."

I just nodded.

"The way he just readily handed those files over to Miami Dade made my antennae stand up, too. What kind of fucking police administrator does something like that?"

I just nodded again.

He sensed my pensiveness.

"You know Cade, there ain't no devil—there's just God when he's drunk."

I couldn't fully agree with that, but I couldn't deny it either. Whether God was drunk or sober or just searching for the TV remote made no difference to me. There was definitely some sort of divine intervention and it came in wearing dark black western-style boots, using profanity as a primary language.

I was musing about the timing and happenstance of Brunson showing up when he did. It was so unexpected. Some would venture to say miraculous. I guess to the lobsters in the ship's kitchen, even the sinking of the Titanic must have been a miracle. I didn't have the capacity or inclination to try and understand it all. It was once said to me that Miami is where reality comes to rehearse. The reality of it all needed no more practiced attempts.

"Look, it's Friday why don't you and that pretty lady dead-people-doctor, go on out and get some sun on you. Go on, take off. We'll see you on Monday."

He yelled out across the office to the closed door.

"Charlene, give Cade that bag by the desk."

I got up and I was actually surprised he got up, too, and stood behind his desk. I noticed the hot sauce on his desk: "Smoking Gun." I smiled to myself.

As I walked out, he told me to leave the door open.

Charlene handed me a plastic supermarket bag. I opened it and pulled out a Hartford Whalers hat. It was the same one that I had wedged into the backseat of the taxi in Coconut Grove.

I looked back at Brunson.

"I told you. I sit in the biggest office in this place. Now get the fuck out."

THE END

CPSIA information can be obtained
at www.ICGtesting.com
Printed in the USA
BVHW071401240220
573160BV00002B/160